HAVEN ON TOUR

By

Howard Robinson

RB
Rossendale Books

Published by Lulu Enterprises Inc.
3101 Hillsborough Street
Suite 210
Raleigh, NC 27607-5436
United States of America

Published in paperback 2016
Category: Fiction
Copyright Howard Robinson © 2016
ISBN : 978-1-326-56406-3

This is a work of fiction. Names, characters, corporations,
institutions, organisations, events or locales in this novel are either
the product of the author's imagination or, if real, used fictitiously.
Any resemblance to actual persons (living or dead) is entirely
coincidental.

CONTENTS

Authors' Notes

This story has not turned out anything like I had intended it to. My objective was to capture some of the many unbelievable yarns involving the amazing friends that I have made through playing sport throughout my life, albeit not to any great standard.

Although I have managed to include some of the stories from squash and rugby, with the names changed to protect the innocent (and the not so innocent), the characters took over the plot and the book increasingly left my control. I eventually gave up fighting to return to my original intention and my input at times seemed to be little more than the use of my right index finger to prod a keyboard. Maybe I'll have to write a second book and learn to use another finger.

I ask you to accept this book for what it is and, hopefully enjoy it.

To Mags e Bob.

thanks for many years of motoring fun.

Best wishes

Pen pictures of players from the County Cup Final programme (as written by Chubby Trevithick):

1 James Cameron. Prop forward. Born Glasgow. Age 38. Occupation Marine engineer. Married and divorced many times, Part owns boatyard in Haven. Hobbies. Drinking.

2 "Chubby" Trevithick. Hooker. Unemployed. No more information.

3 Simon Spencer. Prop forward. Aka DR Jekyll or Mr Hyde depending on state of sobriety. Occupation Car delivery. Born Castra Juxta Mare. Hobbies Football Squash.

4 Paul Bennet. Second row. Born Haven. Age 27. Occupation primary school headmaster. Single but spoken for. Hobbies all sports. Volunteer lifeboat crew, Brother of no 5.

5 Mike Bennet. Second row. Born Haven, Age 30. Occupation RNLI coxswain, single. Hobbies, sailing, fishing, reading. Brother of no 4.

6 Norman Arkwright. Plays anywhere. Aka Northern bloke. Born Preston. Age 35. Occupation Journalist and author. Married Hobbies Holiday home in Haven. Team captain.

7 Bob Church. Flanker. Aka The Saint single. Ex navy Hobbies Bell ringing, Motor Bikes.

8 Thomas Henry Orre. Number eight Aka Thor. Born Haven, Age 26 Occupation police officer. Happily married with 2 young children. Hobbies DIY, growing vegetables, real ale.

9 John David Jones. Scrum Half. Aka Curly. Born Haven, Age 26, Occupation Lawyer. married. Hobbies. Fashion, fast cars and womanising. Gifted, misunderstood.

10 Harry Thelwall. Utility back. Aka Grandad. Born Haven Occupation Grocer Age 40 plus. Hobbies Family.

11 Rhodri Emlyn Davies. Winger/Full back. Aka Red Rod. Born North Wales Age 33. Occupation publican. Single Hobby Politics. Labour councillor. Landlord of Blue Bell pub.

12 Kieran Shallcock. Centre. Aka Nipper. Age 18 Born Castra. Occupation student. Single.

13 Jon Brown – Plays where told to. Aka Farmer or Spoddy. Age 31, occupation farmer.

14 Nick Haydn – Smythe. Winger. Student. Single, boyfriend of Jenny Cameron, Blue Bell barmaid. Hobby music.

15 Father Seamus Devlin. Utility back. Occupation priest. Aka Vicar. Born Liverpool, Age 31. Hobbies Rugby, Boxing.

16 Eddie Khan. Sits on bench. Aka Teflon. Student Born Castra Juxta Mare Age 19 Hobbies sailing, cooking.

Chapter 1 – Cup Final

Curly hit the ground so hard that all his breath was expelled. A weight came on him causing pain in his shoulder and his face was being pushed into the wet earth and grass. "Why do I do this?" he thought. He opened his eyes and could see that he had been dumped to ground not far from the touchline where two attractive young ladies were smiling, clapping and enjoying the early spring sunshine. The blond in particular held his interest as she was slim with long legs, a short skirt and what Curly thought a roguish smile.

He forgot his pain and wondered if they were clapping him for his cheeky dash through the Malvil pack or applauding the great oaf who had managed to grab him and was now lying on top of him. He also considered their age and whether they would be interested in a 26 year old, scrum half if they were old enough. The weight eased from him and his mind returned to the game.

Just as he was setting the ball back towards his saviours there was a long shrill loud whistle. "Penalty, not releasing" he heard the referee say. "Who?" thought Curly. The heap of players climbed off him. "No damage" he thought. Then a huge pair of hands picked him up by the front of his shirt and held him off the ground. The usually smiling expression was absent from his friend Thor's face. "You bloody knob sack Curly. Right on half time. Can't you keep your bloody mind off wenches for eighty bloody minutes?" Curly was then flung back onto the ground like a rag doll.

Curly picked himself up to see a small group of his team mates staring at him with malevolent scowls. He couldn't make eye contact. He knew they were right. Nearly half time in the county cup final, against a team three levels above them and Haven had held them to nil, nil. Thor was right. Everyone's hard effort had been for nothing due to his loss of concentration. Malvil's skipper pointed at the posts.

The Malvil stand off was placing the ball on the kicking tee. Malvil had a proper kicking tee, not a marker cone as used by Haven. Despite being out near the touchline Malvil's kicker had gotten away with moving it ten metres infield to get a better position. "Sir! Is that the right place?" asked Curly. The look from the referee was enough to persuade Curly to let it lie. This ref had a reputation for not putting up with any nonsense.

Haven faced the kicker and stood stock still and silent as etiquette demanded. The crowd were hushed. Haven's players reacted differently, some scowled at the kicker while others feigned indifference. Prop Jim Cameron could be heard mumbling over and over "Miss ye Sas'nach bastard". Curly felt sick.

The ball arced perfectly between the posts and the referee blew a blast that signalled half time. A young boy from Malvil Tigers, the national league two club who were hosting the final here at the "Cheap as Chips stadium", slotted a number three next to Malvil on the scoreboard. Curly's morale sank lower.

A loud Northern voice bellowed "Right Haven, to me you buggers. Jog! Heads up! Now!"

Norman Arkwright had taken over as captain a year after joining the club some two years earlier. He was known as Northern Bloke and had bought a cottage fronting the little harbour in Haven four years ago. When in a conversation in the village pub he admitted to once having had a trial for Sale. He was plied with beer until he agreed to turn out for Haven. Despite not being outstanding it was obvious that Norm had been a decent player. He was six feet 2 inches tall, about 15 stone and since getting the rugby bug again had got himself quite fit. He had a round, honest face, brown eyes and a big smile. Except for his broad Lancashire accent there was nothing that would make Norm stand out in a crowd. Northern Bloke's enthusiasm had led to Tom Orre, aka Thor, asking him to take over as captain. Norm agreed if he was accepted in a vote. In a vote organised by Thor, who had been skipper for five years and was heartily sick of the task, Norm won unanimously. For some time Thomas Orre lost the nickname of Thor and was referred to as Mugabe or Rigger.

Northern blokes' achievements had begun with persuading the team members to have no more than four pints on a Friday if they had a game on the next day. The next season this was reduced to three pints on Friday and no beer at all allowed at lunchtime on match day. N B policed this by visiting both the Blue Bell pub and the Sailing club every Friday to catch offenders. After wins in the first two rounds of the cup. (well, as Northern Bloke explained, a bye in the first round counts as a win) Haven RUFC not only agreed to abstain from beer altogether from midnight on Thursday until final whistle on Saturday but decided to train.

This was a first for Haven as they had never trained since Thor's Grandfather, Evor Orre had helped found the club fifty years ago.

This regime had astounded everyone. The whole village was shocked to discover that practising moves, getting fit and starting games without a hangover had brought Haven here, to the cup final.

This was Northern Bloke's moment in History. Henry V had his at Agincourt, Horatio Nelson at Trafalgar, General Montgomery at El Alamein and now Norman Arkwright at the Cheap as Chips stadium.

"Right lads" bellowed Norman "Look at the scoreboard. Them buggers thought they'd have thirty points by now. They're shitting themselves."
Someone mumbled "could be nil – nil".

"I'm not having that" Northern bloke got louder. "What's done is done. Forget it move on. We've played well. If we stick at it they will begin to panic. They'll tire. Keep to our plan, hit em, hit em hard then hit em again. Forwards, no standing still, backs support. OK? I said OK ?
"Yes skip" came the unanimous reply.

"Anything to add Thor?" asked Northern bloke.

Thomas Henry Orre was a big unit by anyone's standards. He stood six feet six inches tall, weighed eighteen stone and was probably the fittest man in the team. He had a mop of blond hair that looked as if it had been cut using a basin that half covered his ears. There was a reason for this, it had been cut yesterday by his wife using just such a mixing bowl.

Thor's blond moustache came down to his chin on either side of his mouth. He had a face that went bright red as soon as he started to exercise but he was still going strong after the toughest test. He looked every inch like the Viking god of his nickname yet also managed to look like an impish schoolboy at the same time.

He took time to reply, looking them all in the face, one at a time. "Thanks Norm" he said "Firstly I must apologise to Curly and you all. I criticised Curly for giving the penalty away then in my anger I threw him to the deck." He paused "I could have put our best player out of the game, sorry" Thor pointed to the stand "See there! My granddad, our club chairman. He's pushing seventy, seems as fit as a fiddle and can sup most of us under the table but he's ill. Who knows how long he'll be with us? Our results this season have given him new reason to live, there's life in his eyes that I haven't seen since, well most of you know since when." Thor's eyes moistened and so did half of his team mates." I want to see him holding the county cup. No matter how tired you feel let's do it for Evor lads."

As if planned the whole team made a fist with their right hands, looked at the old man and shouted "Evor".

Evor sat in the stand and blushed. Another man, younger than Evor had just sat down next to him and proffered a hip flask. Evor looked at him, took the flask, sniffed and gulped deep holding the liquid in his mouth before swallowing with a satisfied grin. "You must want something Roger. It's not like you to give away a good Speyside single malt without reason." Evor was well dressed, wearing the club blazer and light flannel trousers. He still had plenty of hair, albeit pure white now and had a moustache in the same ilk as his grandson. This should have made him look ridiculous but with binoculars round his neck and a new trilby atop his snowy mane he reminded you of a retired colonel out for a day at the races. In fact he was a retired police inspector. His son Edwin, who had died at sea in a tragic accident some twenty years earlier, had been a policeman and now his grandson had just passed his sergeant's exam. The police service was in the family DNA, as was rugby, volunteering for the lifeboat service and ale.

"Evor, that's a slur" Said Roger, holding out his hand for the return of the hip flask. "No Roger" replied Evor before taking another, larger swig from the flask. "Dish ish a shlur". The two men giggled together despite having passed the same joke back and to for years. The flask was retuned, swigged by Roger and hands were shook with genuine smiles.

Roger was kitted out in similar dress to Evor, except that the blazer badge was not the bell and anchor of Haven but the Leaping Tiger of the club in who's stadium the game was being played. Malvil Tigers. The club had been Malvil West for years, changing its name some 8 or so years ago when a local supermarket owner had bought part of the pitches to build an out of town superstore. The remaining space was turned into a five thousand capacity ground with two thousand seats. The influx of money had enabled the club to attract and pay full time players and with four promotions, the Tigers were in national league two. With a top half of the table finish this year and the promise of more investment, Tigers hoped to push into the big time in the next couple of seasons.

Roger De Groot was proud of his club's achievements, even at the price of naming the ground "Cheap as Chips Stadium" and turning out a team with "Cheap as Chips" emblazoned across their shirts. The impromptu salute given to Evor by the Haven lads had brought it home to Roger just how far from the amateur ethos of the game he had come. Yes under his guidance the club had scaled the heights. They no longer competed in their own county cup as being full time professionals they would win every year. Roger envied his friend that spontaneous gesture from the Haven lads. How many of his players even knew his first name?

"Come on Rog" said Evor "What can I do for you?"
"All I want to know is are your boys going to keep this up. I've had a £10 bet with Phil Prior of Malvil Park that his boys would win by less than ten points. The first half has been even. Your lads have had to put more work in but that scrum half is causing them problems. Phil wants to double the bet. What's your advice?"

"My advice" said Evor "is not to gamble. But if you must...... Ok. They have a bigger pack but have only won their own scrums, not taken one off us. They haven't broken our line and don't look to have any magic up their sleeves. They're 3 points up, have five county players in their team but do they want it? That's the question."
"Well Evor. What's your decision?"

Just then the ref blew to start the second half. Malvil kicked deep into Haven's half. Father Devlin collected at full back and sprinted straight forward instead of kicking for touch. He made twenty five yards before the two Malvil centres grabbed him and tried to unload the ball. The Bennets grasped each other's shirts and drove in behind Father Devlin. They were joined by Thor and Chubby, pushing the Malvil pack back another twenty paces before the maul collapsed a ruck ensued and the ball spilled forward for a Malvil scrum.

"There's your answer Roger." Said Evor. Up the bet and see what odds he'll give against a Haven win. Here's a tenner."
"Ok. See you at full time." Roger made to go "Oh. Yes, I would like a word on another pressing matter. Catch you in the bar for a quiet chat."

Malvil Tigers normally filled the ground for their home games. Malvill Park would get around three to five hundred at their home matches. Haven however would only get wives, girlfriends and family members of players, a couple of dozen ex-players, some children and the odd person walking their dog. In bad weather this would drop to just a very few hardy souls as the rest would repair to the sailing club bar that sat adjacent to the rugby pitch.

Today there were around two thousand people in the Cheap as chips stadium, split loosely into four, even sized groups as follows :- Supporters of the Tigers, players and officials from other clubs in the county, supporters of Malvil Park and surprisingly, for a village of around 3,000 people, around 500, boisterous and noisy folk from Haven.

A young woman came to sit next to Evor. She carried two pints of beer and passed the black swirling glass of Guinness to the old boy. She took a good draught from her own pint of lager and gave Evor a big smile.

"Cheers lass" Evor said "did you know that husband of yours had planned that chant at half time?"
"No Pop." She replied "Did you enjoy it?"
"Hrmmphh!" was his response "I'll be having a word with him about that."

She gave him another smile and a cuddle. This was Pamela, Daughter in law to Evor, childhood sweetheart and now wife of Thor and mother of two rowdy children who were sat a couple of rows in front waving black flags with Haven RUFC splashed across them in bright yellow.

Pam was a plump lady, pretty but not beautiful or sexy looking. She had blue grey eyes, shoulder length blond hair, today in a ponytail. She was devoted to her man and her children and cared deeply for her father in law.

"I think we can do it Pop" Pam said. "I know we will" he replied.

Sure enough, Haven were having their best spell of the game. The standoff, Harry, had just sold a ridiculous dummy to The Malvil number 7 and had broken through their line. The veteran had this trick of dummying a pass that you would swear had left his hands. Then as you followed the ball Harry would pull it back in and leave you looking stupid. Fifteen years ago Harry would have cruised on towards the line but he wasn't quick enough nowadays and was unceremoniously decked by a Malvil centre. A ruck ensued which for some unknown reason turned into a brawl

The whistle blew and most players calmed down and stepped back. The vicar had just relaxed his grip from an opponent's shirt when someone threw a punch that caught him on the side of his head. That was it. The Vicar flipped and downed a couple of Malvil players before Thor pulled him away. Calm was restored. The referee called both captains to him along with the vicar and the Malvil flanker. "I'm not having that". Said the ref "This is supposed to be a showcase. There's youngsters here looking to you as an example. Captains, talk to your teams. That's the first bit of stupidity and it'll be the last. You two can have an early bath." The red card was flourished, the pair shook hands and walked off.

As they reached the touchline the Malvil lad asked Father Devlin what he wanted to drink and soon enough they sat down together with a beer. "I was knackered anyway" muttered father Devlin. "By the way, are you a good catholic boy or one of the other lot?" "I'm of the true faith. Why do you ask?" Seamus Devlin informed his new buddy that he was a priest. He apologised for fighting and said that he asked because he wanted to know if he should give himself a penance for hitting him or a stronger punishment for not hitting him hard enough. Two glasses clinked and two bruised and bloody, like minded idiots shared a moment of fun.

No one had noticed during the melee that the Malvil no 7 had sidled over to old Harry, said "don't take the piss out of me granddad" and given him what was known in these parts as a poachers kiss. IE a head butt. Harry was out cold.

Nipper, at inside centre was first to notice Harry seemingly asleep and drew the matter to Thor's attention. Thor in turn pointed Harry out to the referee who was about to restart the game. The ref held up one hand and beckoned the Haven Physio onto the pitch. This was the first injury of the game, now well over an hour old.

Havens Team Physiotherapist, and first aider was an attractive young woman called Mary Hynge. She gave her time freely on a Saturday as long as the team and all concerned solemnly agreed to only ever use her middle name which was Janet. The club enforced a £5 fine on anyone who called her Mary and a strict fine of £20 on anyone switching the H and M. As beer usually flowed well after a game Janet made more from giving up her time freely than if she had charged her hourly rate, as paid by her employers, the clinic in Castra where she worked.

Janet was in her mid twenties and a pretty girl Curly said he didn't fancy her as she had a fat arse. Indeed she was a bit pear shaped but everyone knew that Curly had made a play for her and been politely declined. The phrase "Fuck off Curly, you're a midget" was bandied about by his team mates. As

Janet was single half the team thought about "trying it on" but she only had eyes for one of them. Sadly, for Janet, the object of her desire, Thor, only had eyes for his wife.

Janet rushed on with her bag of tricks, a bucket of water and an inflatable pillow which she placed under Harry's head. After application of a cold sponge and a whiff of smelling salts, Harry opened his eyes. "Mary me darling. Did your mother not think when she christened you?" Splash! Harry got the full bucket all over him. He stood up and immediately fell down again. The referee declared him too concussed to carry on and he was helped off by Kieran and Chubby.

Haven only had one substitute or replacement as the referee quaintly referred to him. This was Eddie Khan, son of the owner of the Shere Khan Indian restaurants in Haven, Newport and Castra Juxta Mare. Eddies father, Mo Khan had three restaurants and three sons. Mo was a royalist and had named his sons after the English princes, sons of her majesty, Charles and Andrew managed a restaurant each and Edward was studying history at college in Castra. Mo sponsored the Haven shirts which bore "Shere Khan" across their fronts.

Eddie was nicknamed Teflon as his hands were said to be none stick. As Jim Cameron put it, "Yon young lad cannae catch a bus let alone a bloody rugby ball." Nonetheless, Eddie loved being part of the team. He loved wearing the shirt and didn't mind getting just his usual five or ten minutes on the pitch at the end of each game. His dad was proud of how English his youngest son was. Young Eddie was pleased that playing rugby impressed the girls. Not that he needed much assistance as Eddie was too handsome by far.

Northern and Thor put their heads together with their unofficial coach and owner of the team coach, the local taxi man Bill Davies. It was decided to move Nipper Shacklock to stand off, Haydn – Smythe from the wing to full back and have Teflon on the wing. This was thought to be the spot where he could do least damage and had less chance of dropping an important ball.

The referee had lost recollection of what the hell had occurred. He therefore gave a scrum for a. none existent knock on, with Malvil getting the put in. There were no complaints on the pitch but much jeering from the boisterous Haven villagers who were all enjoying their day out.

"I often wonder why you don't give that Hairy Minge a good wallop" The aside from Evor to his daughter in law was much louder than he intended and a lady sitting in the row in front of Evor turned round aghast. "Dirty old man" she exclaimed, moving herself and her daughter into empty seats further along the row.

"Oh Pop" said his daughter in law "I know I don't have any need to worry on that score. I find her gushing over Tom quite amusing as it embarrasses him. I love to see him outside his comfort zone."

Harry had come round with the help of a pint and large brandy which he had quaffed despite the disapproval of the team physio, who had wanted him to go to hospital for a check over. His wits had returned enough to hold up seven fingers when Thor had simply asked "Who?" when last passing near the touch line. A few minutes later Malvil had a line out just outside their own 22, following a long clearance kick from Haydn – Smythe. When play moved on the Malvil 7 was left stood holding his nose, from which blood was pumping all over his face and clean white shirt. Havens motto was "Subito Ulscici", Which Evor had chosen years ago and translated as "Retaliate swiftly"

Their first aider came on to treat the dazed number seven. The referee, on seeing the situation stopped play and insisted the player leave the field until the bleeding had been stemmed. A "blood replacement" was swiftly stripped and brought on by Malvil, wearing number 17 on his shirt. As the referee passed near Thor he bent down to tie his bootlace. "Your doing?" He enquired.

"Not guilty Sir," replied Thor, refusing eye contact.

The referee stood "I knew your father Mr Orre. He was like you, an honest man, a good back row and also a bloody awful liar. He gave a scrum just outside Malvil 22 with yet another Malvil put in.

Northern Bloke called the pack together while the opposition were bringing the substitute on. "This is our last chance lads. I want absolutely everything you've got left going into this scrum. Chubby, I haven't a bloody clue what goes on in that front row but get me that bloody ball. Ok and lads, no penalties. Keep it clean"

The two packs set themselves and crashed together. The Malvil scrumhalf fed the ball in, almost straight and sixteen bodies gave their all, eight pushing each way. No one had noticed that the Haven scrum half, Curly, wasn't sniping at his opposite number, as he had in every other scrum, This was because he had packed down at number 8. Curly and Thor had decided to gamble everything on this last scrum. This was a trick from their school days. How many times had Mr Blake, the P E teacher bollocked them for it? They were three points behind and a try would give them a five point to three lead.

The scrum groaned and grunted like a cow in labour. Against all odds the ball had been won by Chubby. He had swung forward with both feet, stealing the ball from between the startled Malvil hooker and his second row. The Bennet brothers grunted. That is to say one of them grunted, the other unusually wasn't talking. The Haven pack moved slightly forward and the ball rested at Curly's feet.

The Malvil scrumhalf was behind his own number 8, waiting to pick up the ball and boot it clear. Too late he realised that his pack had lost the ball. Everything seemed to move in slow motion as he also saw that Haven's big number 8 was stood in their scrum half spot, a yard or so behind the scrum. Curly was already bent low as he flicked the ball back on the command "Now" from Thor.

Thor already, moving forward to his right, collected the ball in his right hand. The Malvil number seventeen's first action in the game was to be flattened by Thor's huge left paw. Malvil's scrumhalf dived and grabbed a leg but this didn't slow Thor down. The Malvil eight was nearly as big as his counterpart from Haven but although he got a grip on Thor's left arm it slowed him but slightly. Thor dived for the line, carrying both players with him. Malvils fullback made a desperate lunge to get under the giant and stop him from grounding the ball but Thor reached over him and thudded the ball down firmly, well over the line.

Haven supporters went wild. The referee however had been unsighted and wasn't sure what to give. He ran over, looked Thor in the eyes "Well" he said. Before Thor could respond the Malvil number eight spoke "Sir! You can't make a decision based on his say so".

"You're right Peter" He paused "I'll make it on your say so. I'll assume that you're as honest as your father is. Was the ball grounded over the line Peter?"

The Malvil 8 felt the referee's grey eyes reading his soul. After what seemed like an age he replied "Yes sir" and walked away toward the posts. With the exception of the two number eights no one had heard this conversation. The crowd were making such a din. The referee raised his arm and blew shouting "try".

Evor and Pam hugged it seemed that every Haven supporter was hugging someone. Two small, blond children were screaming Daddy. Daddy at the top of their voices. It was pandemonium.

The try was out near the touchline and a difficult place to kick the conversation. Regular kicker Harry was off the field. "Who's having it?" asked Northern Bloke. No reply. "Come on. I've stopped the watch" said the ref.

Nipper walked over, picked up the ball and placed it into a little hole he'd dug with his heel. His team now lead 5 – 3. If he could make it 7 -3 it would mean that Malvil would need to score a try to win. At 5 – 3, a drop goal or penalty would put the cup in Malvil's hands. He was the only person in the ground not to have the jitters. He kicked. The ball soared towards the posts, clipped the nearest post and came back. No score.

Both skippers approached the ref with the same question. "How long Sir?" the ref heard in stereo. "Time to kick off and that's it. The next time the ball goes dead, game over. Northern Bloke and Peter didn't speak but looked at each both knowing how tight the game had been and trying to work out how to outwit the other for a few minutes more.

"Spread out" Shouted Northern Bloke "Catch it or trap it but don't knock on, Then boot the bloody thing into touch" "They'll kick short and high" muttered Paul Bennet. They didn't. Instead the Malvil kicker kicked it high and long right towards young Eddie Khan.

The ball seemed to take minutes to complete its trajectory. Both Malvil wingers had been tasked to chase it down and were dashing towards Teflon at full speed. "Oh no" thought Thor. He had made the scenario as had everyone in the team. Teflon drops it, scrum Malvil, drop goal game over.

Teflon stood still, his arms made a basket to take the ball. Father Devlin was crossing himself and murmuring "Please Dear Lord. I don't ask for much. I promise to burn them mucky magazines I confiscated from the choirboys"

Teflon caught it perfectly but then stood still. Shouts from every direction with advice. "Boot it out." "Call a mark." "Kick it". He did nothing. Just as the two wingers converged upon him he set off, towards them. They were as shocked as he was. He burst past them, skipped over the next two tackles and ran for his life. Boy, he was scared. He just ran, crying with fear and suddenly he knew he was through, no one in front of him. Yet he didn't dare slow down. He made for the posts went under them and stopped. He looked back and not one player on either side was moving. "What an anti climax." He thought as he put the ball slowly on the floor. "My first try. I thought it would feel better than that."

The referee pointed upwards and blew. Suddenly people were on him from all directions. The paperboy, Mr Davies, his mate Graham, his brothers, his team mates, the whole of the village it seemed.

It took ages for the referee to get people off the pitch so that Nipper could slot over the conversion thus giving Haven the Castrashire County Cup by twelve points to three.
"What a day" thought Pam "Did I lock the back door
On the way out?"

Chapter 2 – Presentation

Players from both teams were suddenly so tired. As always the losers are more tired than the winners. Many in the Malvil team just sat down on the pitch, some holding their head in their hands, others just staring into space. Their skipper, Peter pulled them up one by one. Some of the Haven lads reached down in a consoling manner to help up their opponents.

"Ard luck." Said Chubby to his opposing hooker "You couldn't have played any harder mate." "How the hell did you nick that ball off me in that last scrum" asked the bemused Malvil number 2 "Can you show me that trick"
"It's the first time I've done it." replied Chubby "I'm not quite sure how I did it but I tell you, I won't try it ever again, I think I've done my back in. I think I need a rub down from our physio." His oppo looked over at the Haven team physio "Do you think she'll give me a rub down too? I've strained me groin." The pair trudged over towards the stand together.

A few players had swapped shirts. The Malvil shirts were all white with a light and dark blue band. They were new shirts for today. In addition to the club shield they had "Castrashire County Cup Final and the date" embroidered on the left breast. Haven's shirts were the ones that they had worn all season. Evor had offered to buy the team new kit but the lads had declined the offer, feeling the tatty old shirts, all black with gold collars and cuffs, to be lucky.

Peter approached Thor with his own shirt in his hand. "Will you swap?"

Thor searched for a way to say no without causing offence. "I'm sorry Peter, I promised my son that he could have the shirt if we won." Peter understood.

"That was big of you by the way, you could have lied and told the referee that the ball was held up." "I was going to." Said Peter "Then I thought how I would feel picking up the cup, knowing that I'd cheated. Plus, my old man's over there." He pointed to the Clubhouse veranda "The first question he'd have asked is "Did he ground the ball?" The last time I lied to him, he just knew and belted me." Thor asked how old he was "Fifteen." Peter explained that he'd been seen smoking and drinking cider. Someone had told his dad and he was grounded for a month.

The loudspeaker system burst into life with an embarrassing jingle advertising Cheap as Chips. Then it was announced that the players should make their way to the clubhouse for the presentation on the veranda.

Both sets of players extracted themselves from the crowd that had run onto the pitch to congratulate or commiserate. Northern bloke shouted "There first Haven. Run you buggers!" The haven team made two lines at the bottom of the stairs. The chairman of Tigers, Roger De Groot now had the microphone. "I'm sure you'll all agree ladies and gentlemen, that we've been treated to a real cracking game of rugby here today. It's a shame that there has to be a loser but Malvil Park can hold their heads high. They've given all and played the game. Can I have up first the captain of Melvil Park and his team to collect the County plate and their runners up medals?"

Peter had exhorted his lads to go up holding their heads high. It was a big ask as they had come here today expecting to collect the cup as a formality. Everyone in the ground, including the Haven team and supporters had been shocked by both the effort and skill that Haven had sustained for eighty minutes. Peter led his team through the lines of clapping Haven players and up the steps. He shook the hands of both his own chairman and Evor, before moving along the veranda to shake the hand of Roger De Groot and pick up the large silver plate that was awarded annually to the runners up. As he had shook the hand of his own chairman, Phil Prior, Phil had said to him "Well lad, this is one trophy I never expected to see in our trophy cabinet." This had upset Peter who took it as a personal slight.

After all the Malvil players had left the veranda to the applause of supporters of all sides Roger De Groot called up the winners. "Now ladies and gentleman let's have a big hand for Haven's skipper."

Northern Bloke made to move forward but pulled up in agony. "Aaaagh cramp!" He wailed "Thor lad, you'll have to go up and get it for me while I walk it off." "No Norm. You'll be Ok in a minute." Replied Thor.
"We can't have a delay you big, daft bugger. Go and get me that cup!"
As Thor turned to obey, Norm turned aside and winked to his team mates.

Phil Prior congratulated Thor through gritted teeth. Not just because his team had lost but also thinking of the cash he'd be shelling out to Roger and Evor, he'd given them 10 to 1 on Haven winning

When Thor got to Evor they made eye contact and both immediately burst into tears. They had the same thought, how great would it have been if Thor's father had lived to see this day. Thor composed himself and looked behind, expecting to see his team following him up the steps. The sods were still at the bottom, looking up clapping and laughing. He noticed Northern bloke had made a miraculous recovery from his cramp and was jigging around with glee.

He reached Roger DeGroot who shook his hand and said "I'm supposed to be impartial but you'll never know how pleased I am that you won today." Thor thought he was really genuine. He was. He'd soon be picking two hundred quid up from Phil Prior. Roger passed him his winners' tankard then carefully lifted and handed over the huge, silver county cup. Thor was amazed at its weight. He turned slowly to the crowd below, searching for his family. He could pick out the voices of his children despite all the cheers as he lifted the cup high. There they were, with Kieran, their favourite. "Daddy, Daddy" they chanted as Pam appeared alongside them and blew him a kiss. Things can't get any better he thought.

Thor beckoned the rest of the lads up and they were lead up by Northern bloke. Thor was glad to dump the cup on him as he couldn't wait to get back down to embrace his wife and pick up the kids. He looked back up, one child on each of his broad shoulders and Pam arms around him. Remarkably, things <u>were</u> now even better!

Northern Bloke was now holding the cup up and receiving the accolade of the crowd. One by one the lads shook hands, received their tankard and held the cup up, until Teflon dropped it. Over the veranda it went straight into the safe hands of Malvil's captain, Peter. "Well if you really don't want it." He shouted and pretended to hide it up his shirt. The crowd roared with laughter and he got the loudest applause of the day. Eddie Khan sighed with relief.

The referee and touch judges had been up to receive their well earned mementoes of the occasion and Roger DeGroot picked up the microphone again. "There is just one final trophy to award, man of the match, sponsored by Cheap as Chips. The entire crowd shouted the words Cheap as chips with him. Damn, he thought, this is the price I pay for the thirty pieces of silver.

"I may have had a more difficult choice to make if Haven had brought on their secret weapon a little earlier in the game." He nodded towards Teflon "As it is I think all who know their rugby will agree that the outstanding performer out there today is the Haven scrum half. Please come back up, John Jones."

Despite being obviously the best player on the park, Curly was genuinely amazed to receive this accolade. He went back up the steps with a bemused expression and felt quite embarrassed. He shook hands again and raised the cut glass vase high, looking around for his wife, who was nowhere to be seen.

Despite the cheers Curly was upset and had to fight back the tears. He simply wanted out of the place. That morning Eloise and he had had a row. It wasn't a rare occurrence at Spring House, their five bedroom, upmarket detached with pool on the outskirts of Haven village. Today the bust up concerned dress. Curly had to be out to meet the team at 11 o'clock in the Bell. He was dressed in new club shirt and tie, black shirt with gold tie bearing the club crest of a yacht and a bell. Evor had paid for this out of his own pocket and had asked the team to wear it with black trousers and black shoes. The team were to have a light lunch before boarding a coach to get them to the ground.

Eloise had risen before Curly to go to the hairdressers. She had returned half an hour before Curly was due to leave. On her return she burst through the patio door, struck a pose and said "Da Dah! What do you thing dahling?"

Curly was speechless. At five feet 11 inches tall, Eloise was some 4 inches above Curly in her bare feet. The black high heeled shoes raised the difference to 7 inches. With her jet black, short hair, film star looks and slim yet curvy figure Eloise commanded attention. She wore a gold crop top and the shortest of black skirts over black stockings. She looked stunning. "Well Curly?" she asked.

"That." Curly waved angrily "is not an appropriate get up for a rugby match and you know it." Eloise flew into a rage "Not appropriate? What do you mean not appropriate? You asked me to dress in club colours and I've spent time and money to do your bidding. And you're still not happy. You little shit!" She picked up the nearest ornament, threw it at Curly, burst into tears and ran upstairs.

Curly had swept up and binned the pieces of the Royal Dalton ornament. "Fine start to today" He sighed out loud, shrugged and followed Eloise upstairs. "I'm sorry darling." He put his arms around her. "I'm a bit stressed and nervous today. What I should have said is that you look the sexiest woman in Castrashire but if you turn up dressed like this the whole team will lose concentration and it could be the end of Evor. Can you please cover up a bit? Please, for me."

"What is appropriate Mr Prudish?" asked Eloise, with an expression somewhere between scowl and a pout.

"Well, for a start I'd suggest flat shoes, so that you can walk on the pitch, without danger of breaking your heels and your neck, to watch us get our runner up medals. A longer skirt or trousers would be better. Why not nip back into the village shop and get one of the club T shirts, most players' wives will be wearing them, including Pam Orre"

"Most players' wives have no more fashion sense that cattle and Pam's a dear but she doesn't have much of a figure to show off, does she?" Eloise sniffed.

Curly looked at his watch, time to go. He kissed her on the forehead, ran down picked up his kit bag and wallet. Shouted back up "Please love. See you later."

"Right, I'll show you John David Jones." thought Eloise. She wiped her tears away ran down stairs, jumped into her Porsche roadster and sped down to the village shop to buy a T shirt. That was six hours ago.

As Curly reached the bottom of the steps he pushed his way through to the Orres. "Pam, have you seen Eloise."

Pam looked awkwardly from Curly to Thor and back again. "I'm not sure. I think she was in the club house bar earlier but it could have been someone else." Curly passed his trophy to her. "Look after this please Pam. I'm going to get in the bath before the big oafs get it too muddy." Curly padded off.

Thor looked at his wife "She's not turned up has she?" he asked.

Pam explained that Eloise had called round at lunch time to ask her to make some urgent alterations to a club T shirt that she'd just bought. Eloise had told Pam that she would not be going on the supporters' coaches as she intended to call into a beauty salon in Malvil before coming to the stadium. She had however asked Pam to save her a seat on the coach home.

"I'll tell you what love." Thor said to his wife. "You can't ever really answer I'm not sure, when the question is have you seen Eloise." Pam shrugged, kissed the big man and sad "You go and get in the bath too. You stink,"

On entering the changing room each player was given a can of beer by Northern bloke. "Right chaps. Clean up, spruce up and we all go back upstairs together. Ok?"

"Jawohl mein fuhrer!" was the response as half the men in the room threw him a nazi salute and clicked their heels. Thor looked round and put his arms round Northern Bloke "I don't know if I should thank you or bollock you for your alleged cramp. Thanks mate, it meant a lot to Evor." He paused "and me but I'd make sure your tyres are all legal. I'll get my revenge." Thor looked around "Where's man of the match Norm?"

"He came in, chucked his mucky kit in his bag, grabbed his can and buggered off for a bath without a word. I tried to congratulate him but he told me to piss off. You'd have thought that we'd been thrashed the way he was Tom." Norm's big face showed concern. "I couldn't help but notice his missus isn't about. Has she cleared off to mum again?" Thor said "Leave it with me." He stripped off and walked out to the bathroom, ignoring comments such as "Hey look at him chaps. He's got one of those things like a dick, only smaller. That was from the noisier of the Bennet brothers. The room laughed. The old jokes were the best thought Northern bloke.

Curly was the only person yet in the huge, steaming bath. The room smelt of disinfectant and the water in the two foot deep bath was white with the stuff. The room was modern by rugby club standards and well appointed. The bath was tiled and there was plenty of space with benches and towel hooks aplenty. He looked up as he sensed another person in the room. There was no need for either of the friends to be evasive.

"She's not come." Said Curly. "The biggest day in my life since our wedding and because it's not all about her, she couldn't be arsed to turn up. Cow! I'm finished with her. She can fuck off to mummy for good this time."

"I doubt that." Said Thor, tossing him another can. "She will be coming. I guarantee it. Now sup this, stop bloody whining and enjoy our moment. You're right, it's not all about her and it's not all about you either. It's about all of us, the lads, our little village, Evor and our parents who aren't lucky enough to be here to enjoy this day. Sort it!" He jumped in the bath with a huge splash. Curly was fighting back tears but was angry with Thor at the same time. "You're right. Why are you always fucking right?" He thumped the water in frustration. "Coz I is, massa." Thor sad putting on the voice of a negro slave and beaming his biggest grin. "coz I is."

Others had started to enter the bath, from both teams. A number of Malvil players had shouted congratulations to Curly, who was now responding well, enjoying the plaudits. Big Norm arrived, looked over towards Thor and Curly, judged all to be well and opened a bottle of malt whisky, passing out plastic cups to players of both teams. The bottle was tossed back and forth until, inevitably Teflon dropped it and the precious golden liquid mixed with the disinfectant. A huge groan went up from the now thirty plus, including referee and touch judges, crammed into the big bath. As if by magic a bottle of port appeared, courtesy of the ref. Good humour and much banter resumed.

Chubby had dived in the bath fully clothed, including his boots. Once in he removed his kit, one item at a time and proceeded to wash it in the bath. This was his usual modus operandi. The Malvil players were not used to this and one or two complained, words were exchanged and a bit of a scrap had begun. The referee got out and retrieved his whistle from a peg and gave one long blast that stopped them all in their tracks. "Stop this now." exhorted the referee.

Somehow, sir did not have the same gravitas stood totally naked with dangly bits on view, as when on the field in referee gear. When Thor came up behind him, picked him up and threw him back in the bath joviality was restored and arguments forgotten. The ref didn't complain. He had achieved his objective of preventing a great day turning sour.

After a while and a couple of songs Northern bloke got his team back into the changing room, reminding them to hang on and all go up together.

Meanwhile Roger Degroot walked over to where Evor sat, at a table with Pamela, Bill Davies and a couple of other wives of the players. "Excuse me folks. Congratulations by the way but I'd like a private word with Evor. Have you a moment please?" Evor stood up and followed Roger through a door marked committee members only. Inside this inner sanctum it was plush. Thick carpets cushioned the pairs' footsteps as they walked over and sat at one of the dark green, leather sofas that lurked beyond the oak table with matching green leather, high backed oak chairs.

Just above them on the wall there were three huge carved wooden boards. The first board listed the trophies won by the old Malvil West and new Malvil Tigers. There were many, particularly in recent times. The second board bore the names of club members who had lost their lives in the service of their country. The third gave the name of every person who had captained both the old Malvil West and new Malvil Tigers clubs. Both men looked at this third board and both recorded the fact that the names of Evor Orre and Roger DeGroot featured more than once on that board in times gone by. That was before a falling out had resulted in Evor leaving to form Haven RUFC in his own village.

The row was over a woman. Both men had proposed to a girl called Susan, she had chosen Evor, despite him being older.They had married and had one son, Thor's father. Roger had never married, throwing all his energy into his beloved rugby club and rising to his present position of deputy chief constable in Castrashire constabulary. They had not spoken for many years. Susan had died along with their daughter during child birth when Thor's father was about ten.

A couple of nights after this tragic event Evor was awoken by banging at his front door in the early hours of the morning. It was winter. A foul night. Snow lay on the ground, a North Westerley wind attacked across the inlet and the hailstones cut into the skin. There on Evor's doorstep stood Roger, soaked, frozen and in shirt sleeves. "I've just heard tonight." Roger said "I'm so sorry." He looked terrible. He held out a bottle of malt. "Can I come in please? My car wouldn't get me all the way here and I've had to walk the last couple of miles."

The men had sat in silence in front of a gas fire for two hours. Nothing was said but tears were shed, smiles were exchanged and whisky was drank. Sleep eventually came. Come morning wounds had been healed, friendship resumed, hands were shaken, embraces made, Paracetomol taken and a huge breakfast shovelled down. There was a bond between these two that few will ever be able to understand.

Roger looked seriously at Evor. "I have three issues. Firstly, the good news. Here's one hundred and ten beauties. It broke Phil Priors heart giving me that" He smiled as he handed Evor his winnings from the bet with the Malvil president. "Second a little more serious and please don't be offended."

Evor nodded.

"As you know I chair the county selection panel."
Another nod from Evor..

"You came up to the match against Cheshire at Christmas. You know what our biggest problem is. We aren't very creative at scrum half.

A grunt of agreement from Evor followed.

"Well the county scrumhalf was out there today and your lad made a fool of him, again and again. He missed the trick with the last scrum because, I think, he was not physically but mentally worn out, trying to work out what your nine was going to do next. Evor the county needs your lad to play at nine."

"Well." said Evor "I'm sure he'd be excited at the prospect and of course at Haven we'd all be behind him and over the moon to get our first county cap."

"Roger looked long at his old friend "and there's my problem. How the hell do I get the panel to back selection of a scrum half from, don't be upset, but you are the lowest ranked team in the county. You don't even bother to train, you don't have a club house and you play on a scrap of land, covered in dog shit and loaned by the sailing club. Here at Tigers we can't release full time players for county games, Hell, we don't like having to let the odd one go for international camps. A few of the club representatives would put their own man in the frame to gain prestige. You know what I'll be up against. Yet I know Jones is the best scrum half I've seen for years."

"I don't see how I can help then." Said Evor

Roger took in a deep breath "Next season Evor, I'd like Jones to go and play his rugby at Malvil Park. I approached Phil Prior at the same time he paid up. He said that he'd be more than pleased to accommodate Jones. Evor, you know it's in the best interest of the county and the player. Sorry."

Evor looked at his feet for a while before replying "I know you're right Roger. I certainly won't attempt to stand in Curly's way. There's a couple of things that you've overlooked though. Firstly Ok, we are a minnow club with no facilities but don't forget we are the county champions, as of today. Secondly, have you seen Curly play without my grandson at number eight? He's not the same player. He seems to lack confidence. I can't explain it."

Roger looked into Evor's eyes. "I've been told that by a number of people. Peter Craddock is a bloody good county number eight but again the battle of the number eights today was won by your man." After a pause a very red faced Roger shuffled uncomfortably before saying "Phil would take Thor too and play Craddock at flanker. Oh and don't forget they'd get paid a bit for playing semi – pro at Malvil Park." Evor looked as if he'd been stabbed. He was in shock. "I'd be

pleased for my boys to do well Roger." He choked, holding out his hand. "Naturally it's up to them."
Just then a loud cheers erupted from the main hall.

"What's the third issue Roger?" asked Evor.

Roger thought for a moment. "It's a bit contentious Evor. Can we leave it for today? How about I buy you supper at that pub in your village one night in the week?"

"Contentious? What, more contentious than decimating my rugby club? Bloody Hell Rog. What do you want now, a kidney?"

"It's actually advice on a police matter I'm after. Oh and by the way, not a word to anyone. You're still bound by the official secrets act even though you're retired. Come on. Sounds like your boys are about to start a long night of celebration. Let's go and enjoy it."

With his arm around Evor, Roger led him back into the hall towards the bar. "Now did I lock the committee room? Oh to hell with it" thought Roger. "Two very large Speysides please Eric."

Chapter 3 – Celebration

Evor swept the upset look off his face and replaced it with a huge moustachioed smile. It was a trick he'd become very adept at over the years. How he would love to see his grandson in a county shirt, even at the price of not seeing him wearing a Haven one. "Right me boyo's." bellowed the old chap "Let's show em how we celebrate in Haven. Get some bloody jugs filled. I'll open a tab."

There were two main rooms in Tigers clubhouse. The larger room was the public bar and concert room. This was wooden floored, trestle tabled and had bench seating, filled to the brim with rugby followers. The second room, occupied by the teams and their selected guests, was known as the president suite. On Tigers match days this room was used only by club officials, players, commercial sponsors and their guests. This room was carpeted and had tables and chairs that would be acceptable in most country pubs. Today admission to the president suite was by ticket. A hundred had been issued to each participating club and a small number to each other club in the county. The two rooms were separated by ceiling to floor partitions that could be opened for large functions or other fundraisers.

Roger looked around and thought the room seemed fuller than usual. He knew the number of tickets printed so he walked over to where the entrance doors were guarded by two trusted Tigers committee members. "Anyone got in without tickets?" He asked. The duo replied "No Roger." He shrugged. That was good enough for him.

Evor went to commiserate with Phil Prior. He bought Phil and his wife a drink and made the usual pleasantries. Mrs Prior went to powder her nose. "Powder her nose?" said Phil once she was out of earshot "These buggers," he thumbed towards the wives and girlfriends from Haven, "have been pouring lager into her. She'll be pissing all bloody night. As if I haven't got enough to sulk about eh." No mention was made concerning Curly and Thor's future, Evor noted this.

Eloise still hadn't turned up so Curly's attention naturally drifted towards any attractive, eligible ladies in the room. He was discerning. That is to say that he was discerning at this point. In an hours time the eligible criteria would be dropped and forty minutes later the need for them to be attractive would have greatly diminished.

Curly was a good looking man it could not be denied. His jet black, curly hair was always tidy, except for the long curl that he encouraged to fall over his left eye. He was fastidious, always neat, well dressed, tanned and vain. He had a way with the ladies, always did. He would fix the target with his deep brown eyes and lavish the girl with compliments, just enough to seem sincere. He was unfortunately short and not particularly strong. These potential inadequacies had never seemed to hamper him and he did indeed have a trophy wife, a good job, big house and a fast car.

All this he had been thinking to himself while the others around him had been telling each other about their part in the game. "Sod it." he decided "Bloody trophy wife's not here. I'll dispense with my usual plan and go ugly early." Just then he caught sight of the long legged, short skirted blond girl who had caused his attention to wander during the game. She was still with her mousier chubbier friend. He slid towards them "Hello ladies. Are you enjoying yourselves?"

Father Devlin nudged Thor in the back and nodded behind him towards Curly. "I think your skills will be needed ere long skipper." He said.

"Two things Vicar. I'm not skipper, haven't been for ages. I'm not Curly's keeper either. He's a grown man and would tell me to bugger off if I tried to stop him. Sorry Seamus if you're offended but you can sort it if you want."

Father Devlin was about to go over to Curly when Mike Bennet passed him a jug. He took this to be a sign from the Lord to keep out of it, filled his glass and passed the jug to Harry.

The girls looked at Curly "Your glasses are empty. Can I get you a celebratory drink?" He asked "WKD please." answered mousy girl. "We don't know you." Pointed out the blond "We're not in the habit of accepting drinks from strangers." The put down was not accompanied by a, Clear off expression though.

"Wise." Said Curly. "I'll introduce myself then. I'm John Jones, aka Curly to my friends, scrum half of Haven RUFC. Now will you have a drink?"

Mousy reiterated WKD. "I'll have a rum and coke, ice and lemon please." Said Blondie. They giggled together like plotters.

Curly returned with their drinks "I don't know your name." he enquired of the blond girl. "Samantha aka Sam to my friends." She informed him. "Agnes" said mousy.

"I'm very pleased to meet you." Curly smiled into Sam's eyes while just gently touching her waist. In order not to be rude he turned to mousy, raised his glass with neither eye nor physical contact "Agnes." He nodded.

"It may seem a strange thing to ask Sam but what shade of lipstick is that you're wearing? It's stunning." Sam replied that she wasn't wearing any. Curly responded, quick as a flash. "Wow that's amazing. Just goes to show that it's hard to improve on natural beauty." Sam smiled. Mousy made a fingers down throat gesture behind Curly's back.

"I saw you both clapping just before half time. I couldn't help wondering if it was because of my side steps or if you were supporting the other team."

The girls giggled again and explained that it was neither. They were both at college with Eddie Khan and he had got off the bench to run up and down. They were clapping because "he is so fit."

Just then Teflon spotted them and came over "Hi Sam, come over and meet some of the lads." Sam flashed an expression to her friend that said "Lucky me! See you later." And waltzed off with Teflon, holding his hand.

Curly and Agnes stood in momentary silence. Both felt that there must be a huge flashing sign with an arrow pointing at them and the word uncomfortable wrote large. In fact no one noticed.

Curly broke the silence "So then Agnes, what's your surname then?" The reply came back in a Brummie accent that Curly hadn't noticed before "Grimsby." Curly necked his large full glass of red wine in one "Oh well, any port in a storm. I'll get us both another drink eh Agnes?"

Agnes looked up at the skylight "There's now storm mayt. It's luvlay and sunnay, but I'll have another. Rum and cowke, this toyme, with oyce and a sloyce" Curly had two wry thoughts. Firstly, that's how market forces work. Price varies due to supply and demand. Secondly, he must stop thinking out loud.

Thor Grabbed Teflon by the ear as he was passing. "One. Warn yon chubby girl about Curly. Two. How have all these bloody students got in?" Teflon responded "One. You need to warn Curly about her. She drinks like a fish and is rumoured to have crabs. Two. Speak to Shallcock about the tickets See you."

"It's time we sang." Yelled Jim Cameron. This was seconded by Red Rod, the only Welshman on the planet who wasn't an opera standard tenor. "If we're going to sing, it's only fair that we share our talent with everyone." said Paul Bennet, while undoing the fasteners to the huge wooden partitions that split the room. The bar manager rushed over to put a halt to this. Roger DeGroot stopped him "Let it be Eric. They deserve freedom of the borough today plus, if they cause damage it may help a project I have up my sleeve.

The doors opened with a huge cheer from the public bar and there was a quick mingling of folk, with much patting of backs and clinking of glasses. Northern bloke had soon got his team on the stage and Nick Haydn – Smyth settled at the piano. On a nod from Red Rod, who had set himself up as conductor by virtue of his welsh ancestry. They began.

"Oh there was a young sailor who sat on a rock. A waving and shaking his big hairy ...(pause)
Fist at the ladies who worked in the Ritz. Who taught all the children to play with their ...(pause)

Kites and their marbles and all things galore. When along came a lady who looked like a ...(pause)...

Decent young lady. She walked like a duck. She thought she'd invented a new way to ...(pause)...

Bring up her children to sew and to knit. While the boys in the stable were shovelling ...(pause)...

Paper and litter from yesterdays hunt and old farmer potter was having some

...(pause)...

Pie in the fields while singing this song. If you think we're barmy you're bloody well right.

As the cheers were dyeing down the double doors at the entrance to the room swung open and there stood Eloise Jones.

"Holy Mary mother of god." said Father Seamus Devlin "Please forgive me for my present thoughts."

She struck a pose. One hand on hip, the other spread out wide and high. "Have I missed it all?"

Eloise had, had her hair changed to a black bun on top. Below this her heavily lidded eyes had gold eyeshadow in the style of an Egyptian queen. She wore a black necklace, again in Egyptian style. The black Haven T shirt, bought earlier, still had the word Haven, in gold, with RUFC underneath in smaller letters. Otherwise it bore no resemblance to the T shirts worn by other Haven supporters. For a start it was a child size, Cut in zig zags just below the bust. The arms had been removed and the neckline plunged down to symmetrically fit the V of Haven. It was all too obvious that Eloise wore no bra. She had swapped the short black skirt, as instructed. The soft, low waisted, pedal pusher, leather trousers must have been sprayed on. Her strappy sandals almost matched the gold of Haven's kit. The Nail varnish on fingers and toes matched the kit exactly as did her eyeshadow and even lipstick.

"Chapel hat pegs." Squeaked Chubby.

"Organ stops." Argued Paul Bennet.

"No. Blind cobblers thumbs." Chubby and Paul looked at Father Devlin with shocked expressions.

Many a chap in the room at that moment suffered frostiness from their partners for some weeks afterwards. Even Thor got a firm prod from Pam and was advised to close his mouth. Four beer glasses were dropped and one man from Malvil Tigers walked into a post and needed first aid, in his own clubhouse. Thor had been right, you can't ever really answer I'm not sure, when the question is have you seen Eloise.

"We're over here." Shouted Pam to break the spell.

Eloise moved across the room in a fashion that defies description. Mike Bennet prodded his brother. "We were wrong about The Saint." He said, pointing to where Bob Church was stood with the obvious signs of a "movement south of the equator" in his trousers. Since Bob had moved to the area a couple of years ago many unattached, local ladies had made a play for him, without success. This had lead to a rumour that he was gay, that rumour now looked unfounded. "She's certainly had an effect." Said Paul "You actually spoke first for once and nearly smiled. Pass that jug"

Eloise sat down and reached into her tiny gold handbag, pulling out a king size cigarette. "I'm very sorry my dear, but I'm afraid you can't smoke inside the club. Terribly inconvenient but it's the rules It would put me in an embarrassing position" Said Roger Degroot from the next table.

Eloise took in his dress and the way people around him acquiesced. Slowly, she returned the cigarette to her bag. She fixed Roger with a smile "I'd hate to put you in an embarrassing position. Who won by the way?"

"You don't know?" Roger sounded dumbfounded "Why, your team. Haven."

"Good." Eloise responded making the word sound joyous but managing to look indifferent. "We need champagne. Is there a waiter?" Jim Cameron's wife exchanged a glance with Chubby's partner. No words needed. They hated her.

"We had champagne after the presentation." Roger explained "But if you'll allow me, I'll get you a bottle." On receiving a smile from Eloise he shouted Eric to get two bottles of champagne. Good stuff and to put it on the club entertainment account. Roger counted people on that table, Eloise, Pam Thor, Bill, two other ladies. "Seven glasses Eric. That's if you don't' mind me joining you for a while." Please do." They all mumbled and smiled. The other Haven lasses were happier with Eloise as she had brought with her two good bottles of champagne.

"Not for me thanks sir." This was Thor. "I'm not keen on the stuff. If you'll excuse me for a moment I'll fill my beer glass."

"Please, call me Roger. We're not in work at present and we should get used to meeting as social equals. I feel you've a good future ahead both professionally and in rugby. Tom isn't it?" Thor grunted and started to move away with his empty glass.

"Stay where you are Thomas Orre." This was a loud order from Eloise "I have noticed the absence of a certain John David Jones and I want to see him return without a warning from his friend. Here's Evor, he'll fill you up. Evor padded across with a full jug of beer, filled his grandson's glass and asked if anyone else wanted a beer. No one did.

"C 27 black" said Thor quietly to Evor, nodding towards the committee room door slightly as he spoke. Evor looked puzzled then a slow grin of recognition came across Evor's face. He winked and moved away, in the opposite direction from the committee room, filling glasses in a nonchalant manner as he went. Fortunately Thor had remembered sitting on his grandfather's lap as a youngster and listening to old rugby stories. He had been told by Evor that if an opponent had committed foul play, sufficient to warrant retribution, then the replacement would call out the number of the man's shirt in code. Evor would then take appropriate action. This code system worked perfectly, unless the chap on the subs bench was a certain fisherman who's maths weren't that good. Many an opponent had gone home wondering, why the chap with the blond moustache had given them a good thumping.

C is the third letter of the alphabet. Thus Evor would divide the 27 by 3 to reach number 9. Hopefully he would pick up that black meant Haven and understand the message. "Get haven number nine from the committee room." Thor had noticed Curly slip through that very door with a plump. Mousy young woman while the team were singing away and before Eloise had arrived.

Evor had reached Northern Bloke. He explained the predicament, namely that Curly was in the committee room with some bird and Eloise fully suspected jiggery pokery, who could blame her with Curly's track record?

Northern Bloke thought for a moment then sidled away in the direction of the committee room. On reaching the door he bent down to tie the shoelace on his black slip on shoes. Whilst down and thus out of sight, he tried the door knob, found it to be open, slipped inside and closed the door silently behind him.

Judging from the noise coming from behind the back of the green leather settee, either a pack of hyenas were having an argument or Curly was as good as he bragged he was. Norman had only thought the plan out to this point. He now wished that he'd delegated the job to one of the youngsters. "What is the correct etiquette for interrupting a couple making love?" He thought. No inspiration came to him. "Curly! Your wife's here." He bellowed in a voice that he had made as un northern as possible. He was back out of the room before a startled Curly black head popped up over the back of the settee. Half the room looked as Northern Bloke slammed the door shut behind himself. "Sorry, thought it were bog." Now in as strong a northern accent as he could muster.

John David Jones was in panic. He now broke his own world and Olympic record for getting boxers, shirt, trousers, socks and shoes on. He knew that he couldn't go out of that door. He tried a window, it opened. "Please, give me five minutes." He implored Agnes "I'll make this up to you, honestly" He climbed out of the window and dropped onto the pitch below. Agnes was still too shocked to move. She'd never had this happen to her before. He was certainly a good lover but an even better liar she mused. How had he got dressed in such a blur of motion and disappeared?

Agnes looked out of the window, expecting to see him lying injured but Curly was long gone. He ran around the corner, back into the dressing room corridor, up the stairs and then calmly through the double doors where Eloise had made her entrance fifteen minutes earlier. He pulled Nipper Shallcock away from the crowd of teenagers he was with, thrust some notes in his hand and said "Kieran, any minute now a chubby bird will come out of that door over there. I know she's not up to my usual standards but I had my reasons. Here's some dosh. Just keep her well away from me and I'll double it tomorrow and I'll keep schtum about your forged passes for that lot. Deal?" Nipper looked at the money "Is it Aggi Grimsby?" Curly nodded "Double it? Treble it!" Curly was in no position to argue "Deal."

Curly walked over to where Eloise sat with the Orres, Roger DeGroot and friends. "Darling, I'm sorry I wasn't here when you arrived. I needed a few moments by myself. It hit me today, you know winning the cup and how proud my mum and dad would have been, Brought memories back, sorry love. Wow, you look absolutely ... Wow! That's cheered me up. Wow!"

Eloise had been expecting complaints. She'd dressed this way to provoke him as much as to tease every man in the room. He had taken the wind from her sails. Of course he would be upset. Thor and Pamela would be the same, as all three had lost their parents in the same tragic sailing disaster. "Oh Curly, you poor thing. Sit here and have some champagne." She insisted, pulling up a chair and stroking his curly locks

Pamela leaned across to Thor "He's missed his way in life. He should have been an actor. Even I believed him for a moment." Thor looked across towards the committee room door to see Nipper swoop on the upset looking young girl who had just come out. He noticed Nippers body language and the fact the he had slipped his arm around her and guided her towards the bar. "He may have got away with it." he said to his wife. "I'd cut his balls off." Was her reply

Evor had got hold of a microphone. He was mellowing slightly as were many now present. "I'd like just e few moments to say a few thanks if you don't mind. Please raise your glasses to Malvern Park, they gave us a great game today and did their chairman and supporters proud. Lads you displayed the spirit of rugby that is sadly dinishim... dishinin..... going."
Glasses were raised and a cheer went up. "Thanks to the match officials and to Roger DeGroot and his members for hosting the event at this magnicifent ground."

"Cheap as chips" roared the Haven supporters and players. Roger cringed.

"Finally thanks to the Haven team. The village will never forget this day." Another huge cheer went up.

"Oh, Oh and very finally, thank you Mr Arthur Guiness for inventing this stuff." Evor held up his glass of the black liquid and the crowd roared with laughter.

The crowd was thinning out now as some of the Malvil Park players and supporters had made their way home. Thor didn't miss much and indeed he had noticed that Nipper had just slipped into the committee room with a chubby mousy haired girl and a large bottle of cider. Should I warn him about the potential of crabs, he thought. He considered how he could possibly go about that and decided to give it a miss.

Peter Craddock came over. He introduced his wife, also called Pam to Pam Orre. He also had two children of about the same age as the young Orres. Craddocks junior however seemed quieter and polite whereas the Orre offspring were running amok chasing around with other kids from Haven.

Thor had liked Peter although this was their first meeting today and he was pleased that the girls seemed to get on. So much so that Pam, Orre had invited them over next weekend. Thor shouted his son and daughter over to meet the Craddock children, explaining that their daddy had played for the other team. He regretted it when his pair chanted "Losers, losers." at them.

Pam apologised but the Craddocks just laughed and told them not to discipline their children as it was funny. Thor got up and walked to the door with them. He shook Peters hand and said "Look forward to you coming over. Both nodded and Thor returned towards his wife.

Half way across the room Curly tugged at his sleeve. He had a concerned look on his face. "Tom, I need a favour old friend. See that guy there? That Roger the Goat fellah. He's all over my Eloise like a rash."

"Curly, you've ignored her as usual. He's just keeping her company. What's your problem?" said Thor.

"Look, look he's got his arm around the back of her chair and he's pouring more champagne. Thor I want you to deck him."

"What? Are you insane? You can't just deck somebody for talking to someone else. You're always at it. How about if people wanted to deck you?" Argued Thor.

"This is different. He's an old lecher. How would you like it if he was sniffing round your missus? Deck him!"

"If you're so bothered about it you deck him. It's your wife." Thor instructed.

"I know he's getting on a bit but he's a big lad, he might just deck me."

"Apart from the fact that Pam would go mad if I just decked someone for no cause there's a very good reason why I can't deck him, He's the Deputy Chief Constable."

A muscular tattooed woman of about mid thirties spoke to Eloise "Hi, this is the second time we've met today. I see your team won but you must have missed the game."

Curly and Thor had now arrived back at the table. "Is this your hubby?" asked the newcomer pointing to Thor. Pamela coughed and spilt her drink laughing.

"That's mine." Said Eloise, pointing at Curly. She introduced the newcomer as Sindy from the beauty salon where I got my nails and make up done this afternoon.

Pam asked "Is that the place with the sign that says ears pierced while you wait? The kids and I always laugh if we park in the car park across the road.

"That's the place." Confirmed Sindy "Have you seen Janet? I'm here to give her a lift home."

Janet bounced across "Hi Sind." This is Thor. The big hunk I told you about. Isn't he gorgeous? Oh, Sorry Pam didn't see you there." Janet was molesting Thor who showed his obvious discomfort. Pam just laughed.

Just then Eric the bar manager announced that the supporters coaches from Haven were ready to leave and asked passengers to make their way to the car park. Bill had brought in hire coaches from all over the county and had been asked to get them back in Haven while it was still light as, win or lose, a reception had been planned for the unsuspecting team coach that would leave fifteen minutes later.

"Can I trust you to be left with her?" asked Pam, laughing as she gave the big man a kiss. "See you soon."

The room emptied leaving just the players and officials of Haven, one or two stragglers from Malvil Park and the Tigers bar flies.

Evor came to sit with Curly, Thor and Roger. Northern Bloke walked across carrying the cup "What are we going to do with this." He asked. The group sat there looking bemused. Before anyone could think of an answer the door of the committee room opened and a very sheepish looking Nipper came out. "Is it time to go fellahs?" He asked. Before he could be answered he was followed out by Agnes.

"Yow said yow' d make it up to moy Curloy. Taxi fair howme'l do. Call it twentay quid eh?" An embarrassed Curly rummaged in his wallet and gave her the note. Agnes made to go then picked up a half full jug of beer. "Thanks for the drink." she said, tipping the contents of the jug onto Curly." Oh, and here's yer toy." She said throwing the bunch of knots that was once his club tie into Curly's lap. "See yer. It were fun." She walked out of the room laughing.

Curly looked pathetic. He was so embarrassed. Not so much because he'd had the beer tipped over him nor because he'd been bested financially but because the whole team had witnessed the fact that he'd stooped so low by his own standards. There was one more embarrassed than Curly though. Nipper. Not only his team mates but all the girls and lads he'd faked tickets for had seen him come out of that room with Agnes. He wasn't looking forward to college tomorrow.

"What a great day." Thought Bill Davies "I'll drive this gang back then get some beer myself in the Bell. I hope I locked the bus."

Chapter 4 – Home Sweet Home

The players had all retrieved their kit bags from the changing rooms and placed them in the luggage area under the coach. Everyone picked a seat. Most had a favoured person that they would sit next to but on the short journey back to Haven, people just sat anywhere. The coach passengers were entirely male, just the team, some ex-players, club committee and a couple of other villagers. This allowed for some bawdier singing than had taken place earlier.

The coach pulled out of the car park of Tigers RUFC and turned right. There were a few people outside the West Side pub opposite the ground waving them off, one or two being Haven folk who had spilled over into the pub from the Tigers club. The West Side was one of those hotels that were part of a local chain, specialising in decent, if somewhat unspectacular food and good beer, all for a reasonable price. This particular chain was part of the Cheap as chips group and like all other Cheap as chips pubs, had a larger than life sized plastic chef out front holding a plate of steak and chips.

Traffic was light and the coach had reached the outskirts of Malvil. The lads at the back were in good voice. They had just begun a rendition of a deeply moving song concerning a female offspring of the Mayor of Bayswater and the hirsute nature of her pubic area when blue flashing lights were spotted coming up behind. "Pull over Bill and let him past. He's after somebody," ordered Thor."

"No Bill, outrun him. Try and make the county line," yelled Paul Bennet from the back seat. His brother pointed out the he had bought Paul a boxed set of Dukes of Hazard videos, cheap off the market, for his birthday and apologised to all. Evor was pensive. Who could he be chasing? There had been no other vehicle in front for a while.

Bill pulled up in a lay bye and sure enough the police car pulled in behind. The noticeably short officer got out of the police car, put on his cap and walked to the passenger side door at the front of the coach. With a whoosh of air the door opened and the policeman climbed the steps. "Who's in charge here?" He barked. He judged by the vacant, mostly giggling faces that no one was in fact in charge Thor had kept is head down low but when the officer repeated the question and was greeted with a shout of "Mickey Mouse" from the rear of the coach, he had little option but to stand up and be recognised.

"Can I help Mike?" he asked.

"I might have known you'd be involved." Mike responded without an ounce of humour or friendship in his voice. "This won't go down well Orre. Just passed your sergeants exam and now involved in this fiasco."

The two men had joined the force in the same intake some seven years ago. P C Mike Hunt was a few years older than Thor and was jealous of the fact that Thor had been pushed towards promotion whereas he felt that he had been overlooked. He put this down to the Orre's family history in the force. It was actually, down to his own lack of empathy with the public and downright laziness.

"Would you mind telling me exactly what the farce is?" Thor had now sobered up rapidly and was fixing P C Hunt with a steely gaze. The uniformed man reached in his pocket for his notebook, opened it and quoted. "Earlier today a number of I C one males were observed stealing the figure of a chef from outside the West Side Hotel and bringing said statue onto a coach bearing the same registration as this one."

The rowdiest dozen or so at the rear of the coach began to chant "Mike Hunt." Clap clap clap, "Mike Hunt." Clap clap clap. "Mike Hunt." This obviously did not improve P C Hunt's general demeanour or attitude towards the passengers, especially as the H in Hunt was being dropped.

"Shut it, now!" ordered Thor. The coach fell silent. "Have you buggers nicked the chef?"

"Not so much nicked as liberated" shouted Father Devlin "The poor bugger was chained up outside in all weathers and we kind of thought this was an infringement of his human rights under European law." This brought guffaws of laughter across the coach and although Thor was annoyed he could not help smirking, biting his cheeks to stifle the laugh that was welling up in his stomach. "That's enough." roared Thor, pretending to cough to cover his jollity. "Where's the bloody chef now?" The chef duly appeared, bouncing about in front of the back seat. "Here I am. Free at last." shouted a northern accented chef. "Can I have a word in private?" asked Thor nodding to the door of the coach. "I'm not in the masons pal." Spat P C Hunt. "You surely can't expect any favours just because you're one of us?" He sneered victoriously at Thor. "I'm going to nick the lot of you."

At that moment another man in civvy gear mounted the steps of the coach. "Is there a problem here constable?" he asked politely. "What the ffff," P C Hunt stopped in mid sentence. "Nothing I can't handle Sir." He replied recognising his deputy Chief constable, seen out of uniform for the first time. "I'm just about to deal with these people who have stolen the chef from outside the West Side Hotel. You don't need to trouble yourself Sir."

"May I have a word constable?" asked Roger Degroot, walking off the coach. Hunt knew this was an order not a request and followed Roger off the coach. Roger reminded P C Hunt that his duty was to uphold the law and that of the many powers held by the police the most important was the ability to use discretion. He was asked that, if looking at the bigger picture, he thought the people of Castrashire would be best served by costly court cases taking up much police time. Could he consider that a rebuke would be the best way forward if some recompense could be made to the landlord of the West Side. Put like that Hunt had no argument. "Of course sir and thank you for those words of wisdom." He grovelled

P C Hunt climbed back into the coach. "OK driver, I've decided to let them off but only if the landlord of the West Side agrees not to press charges. Turn the bus round and return to the hotel." Bill looked at him for some time. "Please." Bill said. "What do you mean, please?" asked P C Hunt.
"I want you to say please." Bill said "I'm using extra diesel. I'd be doing you a favour mate. Otherwise you can ferry them back and to in your police car."

After constable Hunt had asked nicely, Bill had turned round and they were now on the pub car park. The landlord was in deep discussion with Evor and P C Hunt. Two of them were smiling the other wasn't. P C Hunt walked over to his car, got in and drove off the car park in a temper, straight into the path of a double-decker bus. Luckily nothing was coming the other way. The bus was able to swerve just clipping the wing mirror off the police car. The bus driver hadn't felt or heard the collision and continued on his way. P C Hunt got out, thought about giving chase then looked up and saw the CCTV camera outside the pub. He decided to let it lie. What promised to be a good shift was going rapidly sour. He drove off to find a quiet place for a kip.

Evor climbed back on the coach. "Right chaps the landlord's a decent bloke. I've got here a collection box for the local hospice. He says if we give generously he'll forget the whole issue. Say a fiver apiece?" The box was passed round the bus and duly came back stuffed with notes.

The landlord came out with two barmaids. They were carrying a couple of jugs of beer each and some plastic glasses. "Only fair." said the landlord "I've made a lot today, largely thanks to your fans. Fill up and off you go."

Five minutes later the coach was again passing the lay bye, just as the words "The Mayor of Bayswater he had a pretty daughter and the hair on her dickydido hung down to her knees" rang out from the back of the coach.

"Evor leaned over to his grandson "I'm having one of those déjà vu moments he joked.

Castrashire is one of the nation's smaller counties. It has only a short stretch of coast where the river Dee joins the sea. The town of Castra Juxta Mar lies some ten miles upstream of the mouth of the Dee. It was once a port in Roman times and as the name suggests was once nearer to the sea. Silting up over the years had caused the city to become defunct as a port and now only tourist trip boats made the journey from the coast up to the old city. At the estuary to the South lay the town of

Newport. Here there was a harbour that was used by fishing boats, a seasonal ferry to Ireland and smaller sea going vessels that carried mostly rock salt from a couple of mines inland and chemicals from various plants in Malvil, the largest town and rail hub.

On the North side of the estuary, hiding underneath a huge granite outcrop, purple and yellow with heather and gorse, lay the village of Haven. There was a small harbour here, used by just a couple of fishing boats, a ferry to Newport that could carry five or six cars plus foot passengers and a few dozen local yachts and motor boats from the sailing club.

There was only one road in and out of Haven, this joined the main Malvil to Castra highway about four miles east of the village. The population was swollen in summer by visitors to the caravan park called Sunset View, with around one hundred and twenty static caravans. To be fair the village did, on occasion, enjoy spectacular views of the crimson sun dipping into the silver sea out to the west. As the coach turned off the main highway towards Haven, anyone looking out of the left hand windows would have been treated to just such a sunset.

No one however was looking out of the windows as a usually quiet Mike Bennet, was shouting "Oi, oi, oi." He marched up and down the gangway on the coach, completely naked and making amusing scenes with his penis and scrotum. "Here gentleman, a yacht in full sail. Oi oi oi, oi oi oi and now sausage and two eggs on a plate. Oi oi oi, oi oi oi. Let's now visit Blackpool, here's the famous tower." He was just about to display a mole climbing out of the ground when the coach lurched to a halt.

A man in high viz gear had flagged the coach down. The yellow clad fellow walked over to the passenger door, which was duly opened by Bill the driver. "Hello Joe, this is it then?" Bill asked. "All players, off the bus now. Mike, get dressed will you."

Bill explained to all that Joe Nobbley, the local coalman, had cleaned up his truck and that the coach would continue into the village, followed by the coal truck, carrying the team and the trophy. A couple of players sounded none too happy about these arrangements but when Joe pointed out that it was a cup for the whole village to enjoy, they all trooped off. The coach drove on with Evor and everyone except the sixteen who had taken part onboard. The rest clambered onto the back of the ageing, flat bed truck, which now set off cautiously down the last half mile to Haven.

As they rounded the last bend a huge black and gold banner stretched across the road between the first two lamp posts. "Congratulations Haven RUFC" it said in gold on black. As they passed underneath a few of the lads looked back to see something was written upside down on the reverse side. No one was sober enough to discover it would have read "Hard luck boys."

Passing the Post Office and general store Jim Cameron fell off the back of the truck. He was unhurt as with luck he had landed on The Saint, who had fallen off a second before. It was discovered on the next day that Saint had broken his leg.

The whole village was out on the gardens between the sailing club and the rugby pitch. The cheering could be heard in Newport across the estuary. The floodlights were on outside the sailing club and a stage had been set up.

Music blared out. We are the champion by Queen. The crowd roared even louder as Northern Bloke stood on the top of the cab and lifted the cup high. The team just couldn't believe their eyes. This reception was not expected. A crescendo erupted when Northern bloke pulled the popular village bobby onto the cab with him and Evor was thrown up to them by the crowd. Children from the village school were climbing onto the truck and mauling their teacher "Mr Bennet you won us the cup." One child called.

"No Simon." Corrected Paul Bennet." "You mean "You won the cup for us. Let's not talk like yokels lad" The Queen song had now stopped and all was quiet, well as quiet as it can be with an entire village shouting clapping and cheering.

One by one the team were picked off the truck and carried over to the stage where Eddie Bennet, father of the two second row lads stood, bass guitar in hand and announced the name of each player as he was unceremoniously dumped on the stage. Eddie had been at the game but had returned early to help set up the welcome. He was however at the beginning of that slippery slope that inevitably leads to drunken oblivion. Not many noticed that when announcing his own sons he got their names the wrong way round, not even the Bennet boys. When all sixteen were stood on the back of the stage Eddie called upon the captain, Norman Arkwright to say a few words

Northern Bloke took the mike, looked down at the crowd, paused, said "Sorry I can't do this." and started to cry. "Sorry. I wasn't expecting this. Thor. Help me out for Christ's sake." The ever dependable Thor stepped forward, Retrieved the mike from his skipper, looked down at his wife just below and also broke down in tears. For the second time that day, the youngest man in the team showed great maturity. Nipper put an arm around the sobbing Thor and took the microphone.

"Ladies and gentlemen, boys and girls, oh and you too Chubby." He said laughing at his club mate. "It's no wonder Norm and Tom find it impossible to do this, none of us were expecting to win the cup and for sure none of us were expecting this." He swept his arm across the crowd. "We were very aware of your presence today out there. The noise you made was fantastic. You should know that you all played a part in today's victory. When we were tired you lifted us. I bet Tigers would give anything for the support we had today." He paused and put on a serious face "I was too young to remember the sinking of the Bluebell but I understand the effect it has had on this community. Despite the sorrow it's made us come together. We are special, all of us. I think all the team would like to dedicate this win to those who can't be with us today. Thank you all."

The crowd were now silent, many people openly crying and hugging each other.

"One more thing" Said Nipper "let's get pissed. ......Now give me a cheer that'll wake the fuckers up in Castra!" He had judged the moment like a top rock star the crowd roared the loudest roar of the night. People across in Newport wondered what the hell was going on in Haven. Nipper's mother turned to his dad "I'm not having language like that from him. He can consider himself grounded for a week and he can wash his own kit."

Eddie grabbed the mike back and asked if the fellow members of snow cats, his band, could make their way onto the stage. The band was a four piece that comprised of Eddie, Chubby's partner Janice who played drums and sang. Nick Haydn –

Smythe on lead guitar and vocals and Joe Nobbley on keyboards. Three of them were raring to go but Haydn – Smythe, Posh to his friends had seen better days. He hadn't been warned that he would be expected to play tonight and was thus no more sober than his team mates. He accepted his guitar from Eddie and they started off with an easy number, Proud Mary by CCR.

Most of the team left the stage to link up with friends and families, all looking a bit zombie like due to the shock of the surprise reception.

Thor linked up with Pamela and the kids. "Are you OK?" she asked "I'm bloody embarrassed after that performance." He answered

"Everyone understands." She told him. "Are you famous daddy?" asked his son. "The most famous daddy in Castrashire." was his reply, as he picked them both up and danced with one on each arm.

Curly had found Eloise who was looking happy and enjoying basking in the reflected glory and the fact that most men were gawking at her. "Young Nipper was splendid. He should consider a career in politics." she told him. "Politics?" He queried "He'd sign up for any party that would banish tuition fees and take ten pence a pint off lager." They both laughed. He pulled her towards him and kissed her passionately. "How about a little political jerry mandering of our own?" he suggested. "Home sweet home?" she replied. "Precisement, Mon cherie." The pair looked around like plotters and slipped away from the crowd unnoticed.

They reached Spring House after a couple of trips and falls. Eloise was tipsy and Curly was tripping over. Curly gave the door paint a damn good scratching before Eloise took the key off him and found the lock. As she closed the door behind them she kissed Curly again, noticing that he was not responding as well as she had hoped. She whipped off her skimpy top and placed his hands on her firm breasts with their large, erect nipples. Curly responded with a loud snore.

When released by his wife Curly slid into an unconscious heap on the floor. Eloise removed his trousers and boxer shorts. Stroking his floppy penis she was talking dirty to him, telling him what she wanted from him. All this was to no avail. Curly was unconscious. She shouted at him and slapped him a couple of times Curly murmured but there was obviously going to be no action from him tonight. She put her top back on and opened the door, then stepped back in and booted him firmly in the bum before slamming the door behind her and heading off back to the party.

Red Rod had been living at the Bluebell pub for the past three years with a welsh lady who had come down one summer, from Swansea, to stay in the Sunset View caravan park with her divorced sister and her children. Myfanwy had fallen in love with this little patch of England, it reminded her so much of family holidays in Pembrokeshire as a young girl. On the last night of their holiday they had called into the Bell to treat the children to a meal. Rod was pleased to get visitors from, what he called, civilisation and treated them extremely well. The pub was busy and one of his regular barmaids had phoned in sick.

Myfanwy could see that the landlord was under pressure, so after finishing her meal Myfanwy popped up beside Rod, behind the bar. She was a brilliant barmaid, having done this work for many years in a busy working mans club back home. Some thirty minutes later her sister informed Myfanwy that she was taking the kids back to the caravan as they were tired. She was astounded when Myfanwy replied that she would see her later and carried on serving customers. Rod shouted that he would walk her back to the caravan after closing.

Myfanwy worked hard all evening. Eventually the pub quietened down, with just a few locals left in the bar. Rod asked Jenny, the barmaid, if she could close up. He asked Myfanwy if she would like a drink before he walked her home. They sat together, the only two people left in the lounge bar. Rod gave Myfanwy thirty pounds. "Don't be bloody stupid." She told him "I'm not taking it. We owe you for our food." She said, taking her purse from her handbag. "Don't you be bloody stupid" Said Rod "The foods free and I owe you wages." When Myfanwy asked if he wanted thumping he guffawed with laughter, which Myfanwy couldn't help but join in.

They sat and talked for what seemed like minutes but eventually Rod noticed that the bar side was in darkness, Jenny had locked up and gone home and it was coming daylight. He apologised walked Jenny the half mile back to the caravan, holding hands. They seemed unable to say goodbye at the gate as if some magnetic force was preventing their parting. Eventually Myfanwy shivered, kissed him on the cheek and walked slowly away. Rod stood there for minutes, only when the electric milk float came along and the driver said "What you doing here Taffy? Jump on I'll give you a lift to the pub." Did Rod wake from his trance and climb aboard.

The rest of the day was the strangest day of Rod's life. He seemed to be watching the day pass from a distance as though he was not part of it. He watched the coach pass the pub, heading for the train station in Malvil. He shook himself and got the Hoover out, ready to clean up before opening the pub at noon.

At five past twelve he heard the bar door open. "Here we go." He thought "Some sweaty sailor with a thirst." The shock of seeing Myfanwy stood in the middle of the bar, suitcase at her feet was beyond description.

"I can't go." She said. They looked at each other and slowly tears began to run down Rod's face. Myfanwy joined in and ran across to hug him.

Jim Cameron burst in the bar. He took in the situation, hit himself across the face, turned round and walked out. Down to the harbour he went, deciding to jump on the ferry to Newport and read his paper in the Sailors Arms there.

On this great night in Haven Red Rod had made a decision. The band had just finished their version of White Wedding by Billy Idol. Rod jumped on stage and asked Posh Boy if he could have the mike. Haydn – Smythe duly obliged and passed the Mike to Rod. "Myfanwy, Mwfanwy my love, where are you?" She waved at him, jumping up and down so he could see her.

He "Myfanwy, would you like to get married?" The crowd Oooed.
She "Yes Rod but not to you, you idiot." The crowd cheered.
He "I'm being serious Myfanwy. I love you. Will you marry me please?"
She climbing on the stage and grabbing the mike "Of course I will you great oaf." She dropped the mike and kissed her future husband. The crowd roared out loud again. People in Newport searched TV channels to find out what on earth was going on over the water.

As the pair left the stage Posh Boy picked up the microphone, amazingly it still worked. "How the hell are we supposed to follow that?" He asked. A few bass notes were played by Eddie Bennet. The band quickly picked up his idea and gave the crowd Queen's, another one bites the dust. A couple more songs and it was getting past nine O'clock. Eddie announced that the band would have a half hour break and come back after food and beer. The crowd cheered, a few of them chanting "Monster, Monster." This was the bands signature tune and had become a bit of an anthem to both the village rugby club, football club and sailing club.

Simon Spencer, one of the quiet men of the team, unless whisky had been had, buttonholed Posh Boy. "Nick, do you think that the band could have a go at that song Northern played before the game today? If you were to tell the crowd about it, I think it would be nice." Posh said that it might be a toughie but promised to have a word with Eddie to see if it could be done.

Northern bloke had taken to bringing a CD player into the dressing room and playing a piece of music loudly before the team ran out. He would give them a pep talk, play the tune then out they would go. Some of their opponents had laughed at this but this season few were laughing at the end of the game. His choices had been as varied as the classical Tanhause from Richard Wagner to Immigrant song by Led Zeppelin. Simon and most of his team mates had been moved and spurred on by today's choice, Broadsword by Jethro Tull,

After they had done their warm up exercises, Norman had sat them down in the changing room and spoke to them, gaining eye contact with every player. "Imagine that you are the head man in your village, in Saxon times. You are warned that a Viking ship approaches full of wild men who want to steal everything you own, rape your women, take your children as slaves and kill you." The steady beat of one drum started softly and got louder. "He knows it's too late for flight. He needs to rouse every man in the village to stand firm and give their all on this day. He asks his steward to fetch his broadsword and he leads his force determined to win out against the stronger foe." The drum beat increases, and quickens Ian Andersons voice cuts in with song and guitars join in. At the end of the song Northern Bloke looks at them all again. He pauses. "This is your day. The foe is greater. Will you stand up and give your all?" The response was affirmative "Will you?" shouted Northern Bloke. "Yes." Bellowed the team. "Come on them."

They had all cheered and followed him onto the pitch. As they appeared the rousing cheers and waving black and gold flags had served to reinforce their resolve. Man is tribal and Northern Bloke knew it. Thor thought "That's how Adolph Hitler got millions of Germans to back him. I hope Norman doesn't have a downer on blond moustaches."

Evor had fallen asleep sat on a bench with a gang of his old cronies. They had been talking about their days of playing and passing hip flasks up and down. They had eventually agreed, that even on their best day, they couldn't have taken the physical beating that the Haven lads had dished out earlier.

Pam had told Thor that the children were getting tired and she was going to take them home to bed. "Please Daddy, can we stay at least until after Monster?" They asked. Thor looked at his wife, not wishing to tread on her toes. Discipline was primarily her area as the kids could wrap the giant round their fingers, "Oh alright." Said Pam "but home to bed straight after Monster OK?" They agreed, thinking that they had won a great victory themselves that day.

The band came back on and burst straight into "What's that coming over the hill is it a monster? Is it a monsterrrr?" The crowd roared. One hundred percent of the people still sober enough to stand were bouncing up and down making monster like hands in the air, even the folk old enough to know better. Harry Thelwell turned to his wife "Remind me to get some boxes of Radox bath soak out of the back in the morning. I can sense a run on it," Every youngster in the village was busy chasing their friends around and growling. Eventually the song ended as suddenly it had began to yet more wild cheers. "Fat chance they've got of going to sleep now." Pam said. "Right, come on you two bedtime. Don't get too drunk love." Thor smiled. "I already am." He thought.

The band started to quieten things down a bit with Lola from the Kinks and Sergeant Peppers lonely hearts club band of Beatles fame. Just then a flustered Pam returned, dragging two crying children behind her. Without drawing too much attention to herself she sought out Thor, who was talking to Northern bloke and his partner, Eva. "Tom. Oh Tom, there's someone in our house, downstairs. I can hear them."

"Stay here!" ordered a suddenly sober Thor as he dashed off up the road.
"Go with him Norm!" ordered Eva "I'll look after Pam and the bairns. Her partner was soon chasing after Thor and reached the garden gate about the same time. Thor could see that there was a candle lit in the front room through a gap in the curtains but that was all he could see. He tried the front door gently. It was firmly locked.

Round at the back he tried the back door, which opened in silence, He put his index finger to his lips and beckoned Northern bloke to follow him in. They crept through the kitchen, into the hall. There was a definite whimpering sound coming from the lounge and a slight light showed under the door. Tom bunched his big left fist wrapped his right hand around the door knob and burst in. He wasn't sure what he had expected to see but it wasn't this.

Sitting astride someone on the floor, totally naked and covered in sweat was Eloise Jones. Two of Pam's candles flickered on top of the fireplace. Tom couldn't see the face of the man beneath Eloise as his view was blocked by a chair arm but there was no doubt that this was the source of the whimpering.

Eloise turned towards the noise of the door opening. Norman thought she looked unworldly, like a ghoul from a gothic nightmare, beautiful but ghoulish none the less. Tom thought she looked feral as she snarled at them, not unlike a cornered wildcat, He stepped back into the hall and quietly closed the door, behind him. He turned the hall light on and he and Norman stared speechlessly at each other with mouths and eyes wide open. Thor had seen Curly and Eloise slip away together. "Only another hundred yards and they could have shagged on their own bloody carpet." He whispered.
Norman sniggered boyishly. "I'm glad you find it amusing." said Thor. "I'm going to dismember the little fucker, one piece at a time. Pam was saving those candles until my birthday."

It suddenly dawned on them simultaneously that the noise hadn't stopped. In fact it was reaching a crescendo. "That's the height of bloody cheek." Whispered Thor "They've not even had the manners to stop. I will do him some serious damage. I swear I will."

Then, silence. Neither Thor nor Northern bloke knew how to proceed and were almost grateful when the door opened and a now dressed Eloise stepped out. She smelt of sex and stared at them both as if challenging them to speak. Neither did. She walked past them towards the back door Just as Pam and Eva arrived with the children. Thor heard Eloise say "I'm sorry." to Pam, then, she just drifted away as if nothing had happened.

Thor prepared to read the riot act to Curly but was stopped in his tracks as he burst through the door to see Nipper Shallcock, now fully trousered, bend down to pick up his shirt. Thor, Norman and now Eva could clearly see the scratches all over his back and teeth marks that had drawn blood on his shoulders. Once more Thor and Norman gaped at each other like imbeciles. Neither picked up the expression on Eva's face, which was pure lust,

Nipper put his shirt on, looked very guiltily at them all and shuffled out. He paused by the back door. "Please Mrs Orre, don't tell my mum. I'm already in trouble for swearing over the mike." With that he was gone.

"Poor lad." Said Pam.

Thor and Northern bloke exchanged glances that summed up their feelings of disbelief, annoyance and envy. "Well I never." said Eva.
"I'll speak to the lad, severely, tomorrow." Norman promised. A puzzled Thor told him to leave it as it wasn't a rugby club matter. "Of course it's a rugby club matter." Insisted Norman "He's a Haven player, in club tie no less, who's shagged the wife of a team mate. As captain I can't just let it lie mate."

"Norman, we're good mates. It took place in my house with my best friend's wife. I guess that Nipper wasn't the instigator. You can't get involved. Your responsibility ends at final whistle or at latest when we leave the changing room.

- 73 -

You should not get involved in peoples private lives beyond that point. If you do people will fall out with you, at best. At worst, you'll go mad."

Northern bloke was about to argue but Thor said "Norm. That's my final word on the matter." Norman grabbed Eva's hand and stormed out. "Thanks buddy." shouted Thor after him.

"Have Aunty Elly and Nipper been robbing us Mummy?" asked the eldest.
"No dear. Aunty Elly was playing a game and that was Uncle curly in a wig. Now come on. Up the wooden hills to Bedfordshire." Then, aside to her husband. "They're so tired they won't remember this with all that's happened today. You follow Norman and make sure all's well."

Northern Bloke was for going straight home to sulk. He wasn't used to having his authority challenged even by such a strong character as Thor. As he reached the bottom of the Hill however, he could here his name being called from the stage. He and Eva ran across the grass. The crowd had thinned but still half the village and most of the team were here.

Eddie was on the Mike. "Here he is folks just in time for our last song of the night. Jump up on stage Northern Bloke, you'll enjoy this." Norman jumped up as did Teflon, the Bennets, Red Rod, Grandad and eventually Thor. "Tell us the story please Dr Jekyll, or is Mr Hyde yet?" Chubby tried to climb up but fell unconscious, losing a very large spliff that he had just lit up in the process.

Simon told the crowd about Northern Blokes motivational piece today and how this plus their cheering had motivated the team to glory. The players linked arms and swayed as the band made a fairly good fist of the piece. During the instrumental part Thor switched places to go next to Northern bloke. Thor Smiled. Northern Bloke nodded and smiled back. Fall out forgotten.

At the end of the song Eddie said goodnight and the crowd began to disperse, some towards home, some towards the Bell. Thor carried Evor to his cottage, took his shoes off and laid him out on the sofa with a duvet over him. "G'night Grandad. Hope you've enjoyed it and thanks for everything." He squeezed Evor's hand and went to have a last one in the Bell with the lads.

Eventually there were only the dregs left in the pub, in various states of inebriation. Thor and Northern Bloke had walked out arms round each other. Myfanwy and Red Rod had gone to bed after putting the record takings in the safe and leaving an honesty box on the bar for anyone who could squeeze any more drink in.

Red Rod was dozing when the thought struck him "Did I lock the safe?" He made to get up but wasn't up to the task. It worried him for another three seconds before he was away to the land of nod.

Chapter 5 – Monday, Monday

The day was dull and overcast, albeit mercifully dry. It was hard to believe, that after the sun and warmth of yesterday the weather could be so un-obliging. At least the wind was light and the sea like the proverbial mill pond. Mike Bennet was glad of this as his alarm roused him for duty in the lifeboat station. The station was in Haven rather than Newport as the prevailing wind and current would either sweep any craft this way or Northwards up the coast. In a life or death situation the time saved by launching the boat from this shore could be vital. Mike felt rough.

The first ferry left Newport for Haven at 7am, sharp, every weekday.   Today was no exception. The ferryman had onboard two vehicles, the electric milk float that crossed every day except Sunday and Thursday and the Post office van that crossed every day except Sunday. The post man would return on the same ferry, at 7-20am, having emptied the post box and dropped off the morning papers at Harry's shop. The milk man would return on the 8am ferry having completed the part of his round this side of the water. Neither the postman nor the milkman had ever paid the £1 fare on the ferry. It saved them a long drive round to the main road where there was a bridge. The ferryman had never paid for milk nor had he paid to have any letters delivered in this particular postcode. That's how things work round here.

The two drivers had left their vehicles today and were in discussion with the skipper through his wheelhouse window. "Bloody strange." said the postman. "There's no one waiting to cross." Usually there were three or four cars and a handful of foot passengers waiting for the ferry. Today the harbour was void of people, no ferry passengers nor any sign of the dog walkers that usually waved from the field next to the harbour. "Mind you." said the skipper, "Did you here the row from over here last night?" "I did." said the milkman "They're strange over this side the water. They've probably burnt somebody in a ritual, like in that film The Wicker man." All three laughed at this as the ferry reached the slipway.

The skipper tied up as both of the others returned to their vehicles and drove off. Milko started his deliveries on this side at the highest point, a farm halfway up towards the main road. From here he would turn back, delivering at a couple of other farms and cottages, then the caravan park, the small council estate and the village proper. His last drops were at the lifeboat station and the sailing club/harbour office. Often the duty lifeboat man would greet him on arrival and take their two pints as he left the boat. Not today though.

The ferryman looked at his watch. He had two barrels of beer onboard for the Bluebell. This was a frequent occurrence on Monday and usually Thursday. He was expecting Red Rod to be on the key with his wheel barrow to take them the hundred and fifty yards to the pub, one at a time. What should he do? Without Rod's signature he shouldn't just leave them on the quay but he certainly wasn't prepared to roll them up to the pub. "Ah well," he thought "I'll be back in forty minutes. Here's Postie, safe and sound."

The post van drove back onto the ferry. Postie got out and informed Skipper of his findings. He had driven past the pub. The bar door was open but no sign of life. At the shop he was amazed to find it closed and knocking brought no answer. He had left the papers by the door and retuned without seeing a soul. He did notice the peculiar matter of an alarm clock that lay on the road having been flattened by the milk float. On the plus side, he reported there was no sign of a fire or smell of burnt flesh.

"Do you think we should run up to the bobby's house?" Postie asked. Skipper replied that as he had to keep to schedule, he'd better cast off now but would reconsider on his next trip across. This was agreed but after pushing off both men looked at each other. "Do you think Milko'll be OK?"

Myfanwy had woken as the post van had driven past, by the time she had come round enough to resemble a human being, the post van had passed on its return journey and the ferry had cast off.

"What's that over by the door?" asked Rod. Myfanwy walked over and picked up a second hand envelope that had been pushed under the bedroom door. It had the name and address of Leo Antony on the front and inside was the safe key. On the back was a message. "Rod. You left the safe unlocked with the key in it. I've locked it for you. PS I've taken £20 for being honest. Leo."

Leo Antony was the village thief. Everyone new he did a bit of poaching, nicked vegetables from fields and allotments and had to be watched. He had been suspected of the occasional theft from parked cars but nothing had ever been proved. "That's decent of Leo." said Myfanwy. "Oh yes. If he says he's taken £20 it means he's taken £40. Still, we must have made a fortune yesterday." said Rod. "I suppose we'd better rise and survey the damage."

Ten minutes later he and Myfanwy went down stairs, slow but functioning. They were surprised to find Jim Cameron, Chubby and Simon Spencer fast asleep in the bar along with one of Evor's chums Ian Tomkin. They were aghast to find the bar door wide open and stunned to find over sixty quid in the honesty box. "That wouldn't have happened in Wales my love." Rod said. "I love my country as do you, but we are the tightest buggers on god's earth." "No were not." said his bride to be. She took the money and split it between the three charity boxes on the bar, the lifeboats, Malvil hospice and Salvation Army. "My, I love you." Her fiancé replied. Ian Tomkin had witnessed this act of charity and the whole village soon got to hear of it.

Harry Thelwell had heard the alarm, seen his wife try to turn it off, fail and throw it out of the open window. She turned over and went back to sleep.
Harry thought about getting up. He had dreamt of loud knocking. He turned over and went back to sleep.

In the Jones house, Curly awoke at the bottom of the stairs. He found his trousers and boxers on the floor next to him. He vaguely recalled Eloise being in a very frisky mood, stripping her top off as soon as they were home. He climbed the stairs. "My bum's sore." He thought. He opened their bedroom door saw his wife scrunched up under the sheets, took off his socks, slid into bed next to her and embraced her from behind. "You were fantastic last night sexy." He whispered in her ear. "I most certainly was." She replied. The tired couple were soon fast asleep.

Just down the road Thor had woken up. It was amazing but he never seemed to have any after effect after a drinking session. Many thought he was a beer god. In fact he had been given the secret by Evor. He only drank real ale, He drank a pint of water, in one, every fourth pint. He ate all food available and went to the toilet at every opportunity. He was awake at normal time, 7-30, but even he felt a little slower than usual today. Pam was still asleep. He left her in bed and looked in at the kids, both still snoring. He decided to wake them all at 8-20. What if they were late for school for once?

Thor showered, dressed in jeans and T shirt, as he wasn't on duty until eight this evening and made himself a coffee. He looked out of the window and noted what a dull day it was. As he sat drinking his coffee the memory of Eloise and Nipper came to him. What to do about this. Curly was his best mate, had been since nursery school. Should he tell him? That would be wrong. What then? No answer came and that was a very rare thing indeed. Despite not being academic by nature, Thor was practical, pragmatic and discreet, the person most people would approach, in private, if they had a problem. If he had ever had a problem he would usually talk to Curly but for the obvious reason this option was not a runner.

He took Pam a coffee up, as he did 364 days a year. On his birthday Pam got up first and made him a coffee. He kissed her gently on the forehead. She opened her eyes and smiled. He returned her smile and padded out, like a great polar bear, to wake the children. There was a loud banging at his front door. He looked at his watch, "8-05, what can the matter be?" He thought.

Upon opening the door he was confronted by a jigging milkman "P C Orre. Thank god you're still here. Everyone has disappeared. The village is a ghost town."

"Come in sit down have a cup of tea." said Thor, leading him into the kitchen and pulling out a chair. He gave the shaking milkman a cup of tea and asked if he could tell him, calmly what had upset him.

Milko explained that he had completed his round and not seen a single person. The shop was still shut. The pub door was ajar and no cars had turned up at the ferry. Just then a shout through the open front door proved Milko wrong. It was Ann Tomkin. "Tom, Tom Ian has not turned up at home. I've been to his sister's house and Evor's but no reply at either."

The detective in Thor came to the fore. It did not take the genius of Sherlock Holmes or the little grey cells of Hercule Poirot to work this one out. "Back in five," he shouted up to Pam. "Come on you two follow me. He marched down towards the Bell. Sure enough there was Ian Tomkin and the three from the front row union, tucking into bacon butties and sipping from big mugs of tea. "Thank God," said the milkman "but what's gone on here?"
"We won the county cup and the whole village went berserk." Thor informed him. Red Rod popped his head round from the kitchen "Bacon butty mate?" he asked. A big grin came across Thor's face as he took the sandwich from Rod.

"Ian, why couldn't you call me?" asked Anne. "Sorry my dear, I got in with bad company," he replied, pointing to his three drinking buddies. He got up and ambled towards the door. "What do I owe for tea and sandwich Rod?" The reply was to forget it.

When the Tomkins had left Jim Cameron turned to Thor and said "That bugger's dangerous. Man he can drink." Praise indeed from one who was no stranger to the bottle. Thor explained that the Tomkins had worked abroad and as part of a thirsty ex-pat community had drank to high levels. So much so, that they had both been advised to return home and reduce their alcohol intake for the sake of their livers. "Well why haven't they?" asked Rod, who knew how much custom they gave him and the village shop. "I'm told they have." replied Thor.

"Awesome." Was Chubby's only word.

Back at home Thor found that his wife had got the kids ready for school. Thor explained that there had not been an alien abduction but the village was operating a bit behind time today. Pam took the children to school where she found a group of mothers at the gate, with most of the thirty or so children that attended the village school but the door was not open.

Haven school taught children from five to ten. After this the children went on ferry across to "big school" in Newtown. Usually this batch of kids caught the 8-00 ferry. Today it went empty and these older children were starting to arrive for the 8-40 boat. Still no cars had left the village, either by road or ferry. Thor was pleased that villagers had the sense not to drive after yesterday's session.

At just before nine O'clock Mr Bennet came hurtling down the lane on his bicycle. He apologised to the parents and children outside, opened the door and ushered the children inside. He explained that Miss Bewick, the only other teacher at the school was a little poorly and would be along later. Anna Bewick who had become the fiancé of Paul Bennet since arriving at the school, was in fact still at their cottage having been violently sick.

Pam gave up a couple of hours per week to act as an unpaid classroom assistant at the school. A few other mums did this too and frequently those who weren't due to help that day, would meet round at someone's house for a coffee and gossip before going home. "You coming round for a drink Pam?"

asked one of the mums. "Sorry, not today, I've got to see to himself."

She actually meant that she needed to get home to discuss Eloise and Nipper with her husband.

Back at home Thor had a cuppa ready for her and a huge mug of tea for himself. The pair sat on the sofa, cuddling together and chewing the fat over how to proceed with what Pam had dubbed the Nipper business. It had been decided by senior management, Pam, that nothing would be said to either Nipper, Curly or he rest of the village. Thor was to speak to Northern Bloke and Eva, stressing the need for absolute secrecy as a marriage was at stake. Pam insisted that Eloise owed an apology, not only for the cheek of entering their home uninvited and using it as a knocking shop but for lighting her special candles. Pam would speak to Eloise next day as Curly went to London early on Tuesday and returned mid afternoon on Fridays.

Just as this accord had been reached there was a knock at the back door. Pam answered and brought a nervous Nipper into the kitchen. "They say criminals like to visit the scene of their crime" said Thor, putting on his sternest face.

Nipper said "I'm sorry Mr Orre, Mrs Orre." He handed Pam a box of chocolates as a peace offering and shuffled uncomfortable on his feet.

"That means the shop's open now," thought the policeman.

Pam gave her husband a stern look. "At least the lad's had the manners to apologise Tom. Cut him some slack and let bygones be bygones. Kieran, we'll not say another word about the matter but I do not want a repeat. Understand? Oh and cut the Mr and Mrs Orre business out OK?"

Kieran smiled said thanks and hugged Pam. "Bloody hell!" shouted Thor "He's trying it on with my wife now and I'm in the room." Kieran looked scared to death. "No, no Tom, it's not like that," he stuttered. Thor burst into laughter, "I know mate. Luckily for you or you would really get a scratching that would make last nights seem like a stroking. Pam's really violent you know." Pam thumped her husband hard in the stomach. "Ignore the oaf Kieran." She ordered.

"Seriously Kieran, I'd keep your shirt on in front of everyone for a while. We don't want people getting ideas do we?" Kieran thanked them both, promised there would not be a repetition and left a happier man than he had arrived.

Kieran hadn't slept well. He knew he had amends to make. He still had to face Curly. He'd decided not to mention Eloise to the scrum half but to let Curly off with the money owed for taking care of Aggi Grimsby. Kieran was genuinely repentant but he wanted Eloise and couldn't get that thought out of his head.

On leaving Thor's house he dithered, trying to decide whether to go directly across towards home, go and see Curly, just to tell him to forget the debt or head towards the Bell. The decision was made for him as just then a very buoyant Curly came round the corner "Oi, oi, Nipper. How goes it? I suppose you're coming to chase me for the wonga I owe you eh?" Nipper told him to forget it as mates shouldn't take advantage. "Ah ha," said Curly Aggi must have been a bloody good shag then? I suppose that's payment enough eh?" He asked putting his arm round Nipper and walking down towards the Bell. "I'll buy you a couple of beers and lunch then. Eloise has told me she's not cooking today." At the mention of her name Nipper blushed. "Sorry Curly but I've promised Mum I'd eat at home," he said dashing off across the road.

"Now that's weird," thought Curly, a student refusing money, beer and food!"

"I fancy one of those tinned steak and kidney pies for lunch, with chips." Thor informed Pam who said there were none in the cupboard, so he'd have to nip to the shop. Thor was down one of the isles in the shop when he heard Northern Bloke having a bit of banter with Harry. "Please don't say anything about Eloise," he thought, crossing his fingers, a strange thing for such a pragmatist to do. He needn't have worried they were just telling each other how well they had played yesterday.

Teflon came in "Twenty Bensons please Harry." Northern pulled at the youngsters arm. "What are you doing? You don't smoke Eddie." Teflon said that he'd decided to take it up. What Teflon didn't say, was that yesterday he'd felt really accepted by his fellow students after the game, particularly Samantha, who was a smoker.

Northern Bloke became angry. "Eddie, are you fucking mad? Smoking is for idiots. Why would you want to start something that will get you addicted, take all your money, kill you off early and is a bloody disgusting habit?"
"Steady on Norm. I smoke, am I an idiot then?" asked Harry.
"There Eddie. I rest my case. Harry smokes. How old do you think he is? I'll tell you. He's about the same as me and look at the state of him. Jim Cameron, older than me and drives a battered old Mondeo because he spends eighty quid a week on fags. Simon Spencer. Do you ever see him run? No he can't 'cos his lungs are knackered. I'll tell you Eddie, with the team

- 85 -

being so good, more players will come in and if you're going to start smoking there'll be no shirt for you lad."

Eddie put the cigarettes back and walked out shell shocked.

"Well thanks for losing me custom, questioning my sanity and abusing me in general," said Harry.

"Sorry H. I've just come for my paper." Northern Bloke picked up the Telegraph and walked out with a cheery wave. "Put it on my tab."

"Phew!" said Thor, emerging from round the isle carrying his tinned pie. "I don't know what to make of that outburst Harry. I'm not fond of smoking myself but I wasn't aware it was a capital offence."

Harry took the money for the Pie and forced a smile for Thor, "Northern twat!" he said.

The village gradually came to life, although few went to work today. The rest of the day passed without event. Light squalls came in from the West Mike Bennet handed over the responsibility for rescue coordination to a colleague The skipper of the little ferry settled into the Admiral Benbow for a game of dominoes. It was his turn to play but he was deep in thought. For some reason he had the idea that he'd left the padlock on the ferry's mooring chain unlocked. He felt the keys in his pocket and dismissed the idea, playing a hasty double six that brought a kick under the table from his partner, who had no sixes.

Chapter 6 – Ruby Tuesday

Thor was on the beat in Newtown. He had parked up his patrol vehicle and was having a stroll through the deserted shopping precinct alone. There had been a run on gangs trying to smash into bank teller machines in the East of the county at Winscorn and recently an attempt had been successful nearer to home in Malvil. Thor thought sooner or later it would be tried here so he visited the banking area more frequently than usual. It was just gone 1-20am and nothing was happening tonight. Suddenly, Boom! He looked skyward and could see the purple light that had followed the firing of the rocket to summon lifeboat crew.

Damn, he was on the wrong side of the water to be of assistance but he ran down to the harbour instinctively. Looking across the estuary, he could see lights on in the lifeboat station. He took in the lack of breeze and the fact it was a strong ebb tide. He thought it strange for something to get into trouble on such a night, unlikely that a vessel would be carried onto the rocks, more likely if an engine had failed it would be drifting slowly out to sea.

The searchlight came on aboard the inshore boat, a fast Atlantic class RIB with two 75 horsepower outboard motors it could hit 32 knots in these calm conditions. Just as Thor was admiring the boat take off across the water his radio cackled into life. The incident concerned the Newport to Haven ferry which was drifting out to sea. Could he call at the harbour to see if anything suspicious had occurred?

Thor ran the couple of hundred yards down to the ferry slipway and sure enough he came across the source of the incident. Five men from inland, on a stag party, had undone the ferry chain, placed a comatose stag aboard and let it drift. They had, for some unknown reason expected it to drift across to Haven. As one of them said "That's where it always goes officer." They hadn't the sense to take tides into account. Fortunately one of them had the enough intelligence to realize that something wasn't going to plan and had dialled 999.

Thor read them their rights and arrested the lot. No point bollocking them now as they wouldn't take it on board. The Newport police station was only a couple of hundred yards from the harbour so he marched them off along the quiet streets. Back at the station he would hand them over to Sergeant Taylor and find out if the ferry had been collected safely.

Newport was a small, satellite station to the district Head Quarters in Castra. It consisted of a front desk, an office, an interview room, a mess room and three cells. Usually there was a sergeant on the desk and between three to six community support officers and constables out on the road. Thor was worried to find the place empty "Sarge," He shouted. No reply but he heard a moan coming from behind the desk. There lay Sergeant Taylor, in a pile of vomit, groaning and holding the right side of his stomach

He pressed the emergency number on his radio and got straight through to control room. "Ambulance, Newtown nick, urgent. Sergeant Taylor unconscious, suspect appendix," He barked. "Right you lot. Through that door you'll find some cells. I'd normally lock you in but this man could die. Get in the cells and I'll see to you later.

"Should we do a runner? One of the men asked. They all thought about it, then the ringleader said "Don't be daft. They'd soon find us, plus there's Oscar to think about. He could be in mid Atlantic by now." Oscar had in fact just arrived back in Newport harbour, still fast asleep. As luck would have it, the lifeboat had found the drifting ferry fairly quickly, they had left a man on board who tried to wake the unconscious chap he'd found there without success. The lifeboat had radioed for an ambulance to meet them at Newport harbour.

Sergeant Taylor couldn't have chosen a better moment for the upset stomach to turn into a ruptured appendix. Thanks to the drunks there was an ambulance actually thirty seconds away from the police station when the 999 call was received by the driver. Thor had cleared his sergeant's airway and positioned him in the recovery position just as the paramedic burst in through the door. He quickly checked the details with P C Orre and took over. The ambulance driver came in and was instructed to radio for a theatre for appendectomy. The two medical people obviously knew their job and moved round Thor as if he were surplus to requirements. In no time the ambulance had cleared off with blue lights on but no siren. It was now 2-30am and the roads were empty.

Thor called the control room and the two other constables on duty to put everyone in the picture. He asked both police officers to return to the station. He then opened the cleaner's cupboard, found disinfectant and a mop and cleaned up the vomit from behind the desk. Just as this task was completed the door to the cell corridor swung open and the ringleader of the drunks handed him a mug of sugary tea. "You're supposed to be in the bloody cells," roared Thor. The man apologised, informing Thor that his four friends were fast asleep and that he had found kettle and teapot in the mess room. "I thought you deserved a cuppa and hope you wouldn't mind me making one for myself." Thor shook his head in disbelief, then patted his captive on the shoulder and with a grin said "Thanks, I do need a cuppa."

Constable Cynthia Young opened the doors to the station. "What's going on Tom? How's Sarge? Who's this bloke?" She asked, pointing to the other man in the room.

"There's been a lifeboat launch to recover the drifting ferry. I think Sarge's appendix has burst. He's been taken to Castra in an ambulance. This chap, sorry I don't know your name, is our new tea boy. Happy?" On her nod, he went on "Cynth, how do you feel about getting down to Southwyche, letting Mrs Taylor know the score and taking her to the hospital? I'll understand if you don't fancy it and I'll go myself."

"Not a problem Tom. If it's OK, I'll have a brew and a wee first, not necessarily in that order."

"I'll make you a brew. Oh, and I'm Gary De'Ath by the way." The stranger held out his hand and shook both police officers. "Can you make two more please?" shouted Thor as he heard another police car pull up outside.

Constable John Smith was known as Badger Smith. His once jet black hair had a white streak on either side of his temple. He'd been in the police for ever. Although pushing forty he was as fit as anyone in the force and a natural sportsman, having played a bit of rugby in his time he now ran marathons and played squash.

Before he could ask, Tom informed Badger that a cup of tea was on the way and updated him on Sergeant Taylor's sudden illness, the reason for the lifeboat launch and introduced him to Gary who had brought the tea, along with some chocolate digestives that he had found in a cupboard.

The four drank their tea and ate a full pack of biscuits between them. "Right I'll be off then," said Cynthia. "I'll let you know how things are doing when I get to the hospital Tom." "Cheers Cynth." was his reply. Gary said "If it's OK with you officer, I'll go back to my cell for a kip" and off he went.

"What would you like me to do?" asked P C Smith. "I was about to ask you the same question Badger." Thor replied, then after a quick thought, "How about you trying to find out where the drunk from the boat has ended up, start at the harbour, if no joy there, try a call to Haven Lifeboat station. Oh, and could you just stick your nose into the area where the banks are? Thanks John. I'll stay here and have a think about Gary and his mates. I may take a bit of advice from t'inpector when he gets in."

Inspector Hardy was a Yorkshireman. For some reason he used one less letter in the alphabet than everyone else as never in his forty four years had he been heard to use the letter H. He had no sense of time, being late for every appointment or meeting he'd ever had. He was however a good copper with a nose for criminal activity said to be second to none. The shift mimicked him behind his back. "Ope Eel be ear on time t'day 'appn," said Badger. Thor Replied "Eed betta be in arf an owr before seven, I want to go ome." Joked Thor.

Sure enough, dead on time, just twenty minutes late in walked inspector Ardy. "Ey up Thor, where's Sergeant Taylor?" Thor updated him, filling in the extra news that the drunken stag was sleeping it off in a bunk at Haven lifeboat station. And that Cynthia was still at the hospital with Mrs

Taylor, where she was happy to stay until Mrs Taylor's sister in law arrived about 9am. Sergeant Taylor was stable but an appendix lighter than when he went in. "Aright Tom, you did well. Now get y'sen off ome." instructed the inspector.

"I'd like some advice please Sir about the gang I have got in the cells. What should I do, arrest them or caution?" Inspector Hardy thought momentarily "What's yer instinct tell yer Tom?" He asked, fixing Thor with his beady inspector eyes.

Tom sucked in some air through his moustache. "Well, I know it shouldn't cloud the issue but if these idiots hadn't misbehaved, who knows, Sarge might be dead. Putting that aside they actually stole a ferry, caused the call out of a lifeboat and risked the lives of three crew members plus their friend. They've had a night in the cells and I believe them to be genuinely remorseful. They do need a lesson however. I think perhaps a serious ticking off from a senior officer might prevent a recurrence,"

"I'll go along with that. Wheel em in and look bloody stern man!"

Five very subdued men were paraded into the inspector's office. They stood in silence, hands behind their backs or by their sides, not in pockets. This was noted and appreciated by t'inspector. He got up from his desk and walked along the line looking each man up and down. Then he returned to sit behind his desk and opened a manilla file, shuffling pages of forms in it and periodically tutting. The tension built in each of the prisoners

At last he spoke "Professional men, married men family men. There's a combined age of over undred and fifty years stood before me. Yet the charges on these sheets surely belong to young teenagers with the combined IQ of a cornflake." His fist hit the table. "We add a man fighting for is life last night and my officers add to waste time dealing with naughty children. I ope you're appy." He paused and shuffled through the papers again. "What do I do about you? P C Orre ear is for giving you a bloody kicking and letting you off with that. I'm inclined to set you all adrift in a bloody boat and see ow funny that is." He paused again "To Ell with you. P C Orre, give em their toys back and get em out of ear. Now! Before I ave a change of art." He winked at Thor as they paraded out.

Thor caught the 8-40 ferry home. And shook hands with the stag, who was waiting to board the ferry back to Newport. He arrived at home just in time to see Pam and the kids on the way out to school. "Wake me when they get back in later love." He kissed all three and went to bed

Curly had got up early, as usual on a Tuesday. Eloise had given him a lift to the station and they had kissed passionately before saying goodbye. "I'll have a special dinner for you on Friday," Eloise winked. "Mmmmm," said Curly, having retrieved his case from the boot. "My favourite, steak, chips and jiggy jiggy?" Eloise smiled at him. It was an unusual marriage but there was a genuine love for each other and somehow it worked.

Evor had a lunch appointment, Roger De Groot had asked him to meet in Castra, as "walls have ears in Haven." Evor wore sports jacket, shirt and tie as he knew Roger would be smart. He decided not to drive but crossed to Newport by ferry and took a taxi from there. He could have got Bill the bus to take him, as he also did a bit of taxi work, even though not strictly licensed. Evor thought there would be many questions and as he could not guarantee sobriety on the return journey, he had opted for deception.

He met Roger in the Centurion, an olde worlde, up market hostelry built into the remaining Roman walls of Castra. "Thanks for your time Evor. What'll you start with? The Legion best bitter is on song old friend." Halfway through their second pint Roger called the waiter as they were ready to order. He had a mushroom starter followed by a Sea Bass, good for his cholesterol he pointed out to Evor. "Bloody Cholesterol," said Evor, "It was never heard of until a few years ago. I don't recognise it as a problem. May I have the black pudding and cheese starter and the large fillet steak with chips for main?" He'd decided if Roger wanted a favour, in addition to Curly and Thor leaving Haven RUFC, then he could pay for it."

The two chatted throughout their meal, downing a decent bottle of red wine as they ate. Evor asked if Roger was working today. "Yes and No." was the reply. After a fruit salad dessert for Roger and spotted dick with lashings of thick custard for Evor, they left the table to sit in cosy chairs by the window. The pub had emptied out and to all intents they were just two old friends catching up and yarning about days gone by. Both men had the ability to remain sober despite their alcohol consumption so two large brandies were called for.

"Well Roger, are you ready now to tell me the purpose of the hospitality that you have lavished me?" asked Evor. Roger dropped his voice, pulling his chair in closer to his old friend and reminding him of the need for absolute secrecy concerning the conversation about to take place. He received assurance from Evor that he would not tell a soul, not even his grandson.

Roger looked at his brandy glass, swirled it in his palm and took a gulp. The warm liquid ran over his tongue which picked up the subtlety of the concoction at the rear of its sensors and allowed him a moment of pure enjoyment before the tough stuff.

"Evor, I have information that suggests a large quantity of heroin is due to reach Castrashire in the next two weeks. This has been the case over the last few years. A consignment has come into, what is our, fairly lowly populated area at this time. Maybe it's not great on the national scale but forty to fifty kilograms of the stuff brings down the price to almost pocket money level round here. I would love my information to be wrong but I am told that this year the quantity will double. I am also given to understand that the heroin will come in via your club's rugby tour."

Evor had listened to the first part in silenced but now roared his disagreement, "No Roger. That must be wrong it's a slur!" Roger lowered his head, not cracking the usual age old joke, When he lifted it he had water in his eyes, "Old friend, I hope it is wrong and believe me I have debated long hours over whether to inform you or not. You realise I'm finished if this gets out? But I had to tell you. I'm sorry but on checking prices over the past two or three years they have dropped just after Haven came home."

The pair sat in silence for some time. Eventually Evor spoke. "What do you want from me Rog?" He asked in a hushed tone, "Shall I call off the trip? You know I hate the bloody stuff and the lives it has ruined as much as you do. I'm your man. You can trust me."

"I know," Roger replied, motioning to the barman for two more brandies. "I want it to go ahead. If you cancelled it would put whoever is behind this on their guard and probably delay the inevitable. Please let it go ahead, I hope to get the gear and the carrier or carriers," he paused again debating if he should divulge more. "Evor, I have a man on the inside, playing for your team and trusted by all. You'll understand I really don't want to tell you his name but if you insist, well, I couldn't refuse." Evor thanked him for the trust he had already placed in him but said that he wouldn't push the matter further.

"Before we close the matter," Roger said "I don't want you getting involved. Your family has seen enough tragedy over the years. I want you to enjoy your retirement years and I want Tom and Pam to have you there. Understand?" Evor gave a small chortle "You have my word old friend."

The second large brandies arrived and were gratefully received by the pair. "I've worried more about you falling out with me than about the bloody heroin," said Roger, half in jest. They clinked glasses "Oh, on a much happier note I hear your grandson took charge last night. Old Taylor had a burst appendix and Tom got him sorted and organised the shift like an old pro. His inspector has been singing his praises to anyone who'll listen. He could be in for a commendation, deserved too. By the way that's also secret."

"Would that be t'inspector Ardy?" Evor asked. "App'n it would." said Roger laughing out loud.

Evor got a taxi back to Newport, took the ferry across to Haven and sat in the late afternoon sunshine, outside the Bell with a mug of coffee. He always had tea with Pam and family on a Tuesday and although he felt sober, he thought it bad form to turn up stinking of brandy. The landlord, Rod came and sat with him, enjoying a bit of peace before the next ferry brought workers and students back to Haven, many of whom called in for a quick drink before going home for tea. "Did you hear that Bob Church broke his leg on Sunday? Seems he did it when he fell off the coal lorry. He didn't find out until he woke up in pain Monday morning. Bloody idiot cycled to Castra hospital, said he didn't feel sober enough to drive."

Evor laughed at this but pointed out that this would leave them only fourteen players to go on tour. Dominick Daly would still be away, serving a stint with the Territorial Army, Father Devlin thought it would be wrong to go away after missing mass last week and now Saint broken leg. Rod said that Saint would still go, just to spectate, as he put it. "I'll see if any of the footy lads fancy a couple of days fun and I'll phone Newport rugby, they might have somebody who fancies a drink." Evor pointed out. "The trouble is," said Rod "We'll be overrun with front row forwards. They're the same in every club aren't they? Chance of a booze up and they sign up without a thought."

Evor said goodbye and headed off towards Thor's house. Just as he reached the gate Norman Arkwright pulled over in his car and wound down the window. "Still on for our Wednesday committee meeting tomorrow?" He asked making a drinking motion with his right hand. When Evor nodded Norman informed him that he had received an interesting offer and would put it to the committee tomorrow night. The committee met every Wednesday in the snug bar of the Bell. The room was small and used infrequently. It just about fitted in the usual suspects. Viz, Evor, Iain Tomkin, Bill the Bus, Captain Scarletti from the boat club, an old boy called Bill McClaren, Mo Khan, Red Rod, Northern Bloke and Thor.

Northern Bloke drove off, waving and leaving Evor in suspense. "It's not a dull place to live," Evor thought as he opened the gate to Thor's cottage.

"Here's Grandad," shouted two exited young voices. Then two children ran out from the back of the cottage and grabbed Evor by the hand, dragging him round towards the back door. "Daddy's got good news but we can't say it's a secret." They told him. Evor couldn't help but marvel at the volume of intrigue in this part of the world. He wondered what it must be like living in a big town.

Pam greeted him with a big hug. "Afternoon Pop," she said "Lamb curry Ok for tea? Fried rice and my home made naan bread. About forty minutes away."

"That'll do nicely Lass," Evor replied. Although he had eaten well at lunch, Pam's curry was a favourite and despite his years he still had a healthy appetite. The children stood looking at him. "Have you two been well behaved?" Evor asked. When he was greeted with nods from the kids and Pam, he rummaged in his pocket and pulled out two bags of sweets. "Not until after your tea mind," He warned. Next he pulled out his wallet and gave them a pound each. They both kissed him said thanks and ran upstairs to put the pound in saving boxes.

"What's the good news?" Evor asked. "Wait until Tom gets here please Pop. He'd like to tell you himself. He'll be in soon after he's fed the chickens." Evor had another cup of coffee and played Ludo with the kids while Pam sorted the food. Ten minutes later a beaming Thor came in. "Hi Pop. Do you want some fresh eggs?" Evor said he'd take half a dozen, grinding his teeth and waiting for the news. Thor asked him if he'd heard the lifeboat call last night. He had. Thor went on to tell him the story of the night. They had a giggle together at the expense of t'inspector and Thor was pleased when his grandfather said that Roger de Groot had mentioned him.

Unable to stay calm any longer Evor asked "What's the good news then? Come on lad tell me."

"Ok Pop. Two things really, firstly Inspector Hardy phoned and woke me up this afternoon. I wish he could tell the time. He tells me I'm up for a commendation for saving Sergeant Taylor. I was just nodding off again and he called back to inform me that as of now I'm acting sergeant. He's going to move Dave Higgins from D shift with one of his lads into my shift and I take over D shift with immediate effect. This means I don't have to go in tonight but start afternoon shift again Thursday to Monday, 2pm to 10 pm."

"My lord, it's not like our lot to act decisively. I'd expect at least three meetings to make that sort of decision. You've not joined the masons have you? Only joking. I'm very proud of you lad and your mum and dad would have been too." Evor stood up and embraced his grandson. "One little piece of advice, don't let it change you. Remain your own man Thomas."

"Curry up everyone." Pam shouted from the dining room. There was a rush of feet and by the time Pam had brought the tureens through to the table, her four eager diners were set ready." "Ruby Murray," shouted Orre junior. "Yippee," chimed his sister.

After the meal more Ludo was played and Pam took the children up for shower and bed. "Fancy a wee one before you go?" asked Thor. Evor eagerly agreed to the idea. They sat down together with a glass of malt. "Oh, I've got a bone to pick with you my lad," said Evor. Thor looked worried. "So has my doctor told you something he hasn't told me?" Evor asked. "I'm not with you," responded a puzzled Thor. "You may not have noticed but I took my binoculars to the final. You may not know it but I did a course in lip reading when I was a detective. I'm talking about your half time pep talk to the lads last Sunday. Who knows how long he's got, you said." Thor was as red as a Newport shirt. Evor burst out laughing. "Don't worry lad. The end justified the means I'd say. Cheers."

Thor told his granddad that he wasn't aware of his lip reading skills but would speak with his back to him in future. He asked how he had learnt to lip read. "In my day," said Evor "you were sat in a room with other bobbies trying to make out what people were saying on the other side of a glass partition to the next room. Every so often the actors next door would turn on a microphone and you could check what you'd written down. When you got used to the actors, they'd bring fresh ones in with different accents or dialects. I suppose that nowadays they'd just stick you in front of a Video or DVD."

Pam came down and joined them in a drink. Both men complimented her on the curry. "Better than Mo Khan's." They agreed. Evor informed Thor about Saint's broken leg and the measures he intended taking to fill gaps. "Why don't you see if Peter Craddock is free?" asked Pam "He's a good player, should be able to afford it and he was saying that he has holidays to use? Plus you seem to get on so well." Thor asked Evor his opinion and he agreed it was a good idea.

Thor asked if she'd heard from Eloise. "I called round while you were asleep," said Pam. Her car was there but I think she's avoiding me."

"What's that about?" asked Evor. Pam said it was just a girly squabble. They sat in silence for a while, had another drink and Evor decided to get home in case in rained. "Sergeant Orre," said Pam it sounds just right.

Later as they were in bed dozing off Thor had the idea that he'd left the chicken coop open, listened, all was quiet, so he went to sleep.

Chapter 7 – Wednesday's Child

The Orre household awoke and went through their morning routine as usual. The day was sunny, with a pleasant breeze so Thor decided he'd spend the morning in the garden. He had a patch to manure and dig over and was ready to plant potatoes in a bed prepared a couple of weeks ago. It was Pam's day to be in school and she had volunteered to go with Anna Bewick and the older group of children, to visit the Roman museum in Castra. She was looking forward to her day out as she hadn't been to the museum for years. She also enjoyed Anna's company and could have a good gossip on the coach.

Just before Pam was ready to leave two bells rang at once. Pam picked up the phone and shouted "Tom, Jim Cameron for you." Simultaneously, Thor opened the front door to be greeted by a man behind a huge bunch of flowers and shouted "Pam, flowers for you." The couple passed in the hall, Thor pausing to pat his wife on the bottom on her way past.

Jim Cameron wanted to know if Thor could play squash at 10-40. The sailing club had one court and it was Jim's only exercise. He played the Saint once a week, on Wednesday morning. Saint's broken arm precluded this and Jim wanted a game. Thor said "Ok see you there."

Pam returned to the kitchen with the flowers. They were a huge arrangement, set in a glass bowl and were obviously very expensive. "If Curly is trying it on with you, I'll wring his neck," jested Thor. He'd already recognised the hand writing on the accompanying envelope as Eloise's.

Pam opened the envelope, read and then passed the note to Thor. It read.

"Dearest Pam, I can not apologise enough for my actions on Sunday. I can put it down to the drink and the excitement of the occasion. You are my only real friend in the village and I hope you can forgive me. If not I'll understand. Please give me a call and we'll have coffee. Love Eloise." Pam phoned her and left a message of thanks, pointing out that she'd not be available today, due to her trip to the museum. She kissed Thor, as did the children, and left him getting ready for an hour and a half in the garden.

Pam hadn't been gone ten minutes when there was a knock at the back door. There stood Nipper Shallcock. "No college today?" asked Thor. Nipper replied that he was due in this afternoon but wanted to see him about a problem. Thor put the kettle on and motioned him to a kitchen chair. "What's up Nipper?" Thor asked. Nipper explained what had happened in the boardroom at Tiger's clubhouse, including the fact that he had dallied with Miss Grimsby at Curly's behest. He went on to say that Agnes had been stalking him at college and he'd had to tell her that there was no way he wanted a relationship with her. She had been upset and he now felt bad. What should he do?

"I'm a bloody copper Kieran, not an agony aunt. I'm useless at matters to do with the part of the population that hasn't got a Willy. You might do better speaking to Curly, he's home on Friday." Nipper said that he wouldn't be able to look Curly in the face and that the matter was worse. He'd been itching for a couple of days and was pretty sure he'd caught crabs.

"You Muppet Nipper!" exclaimed Thor. "That means you'll have given them to Eloise, who'll have given them to Curly.

What a bloody mess and you come to me. Who are you? Curly's bloody apprentice?" He paused then went on "Curly will know he's got them from somewhere and he'll question his wife. Eloise will crack under pressure and you're then in the shit, up to your neck. Oh yes and I'll be in the shit too for not telling Curly. What a bloody mess." Nipper asked if Thor thought Eloise and Curly might not have sex as they were obviously not getting on. He seemed dejected when Thor put him right on that score, informing him that although they had a strange relationship they were very much in love.

"Curly won't question Eloise." Nipper smiled triumphantly, "Curly was bonking Miss Grimsby before me. Curly will keep bloody quiet. Also Eloise has a Brazilian, there's not much house room for crabs. There is another complication Thor," He paused, "there's also the matter of Harry Thelwell's eldest daughter, she approached me on my way from here and one thing led to another...."

"Did I say Curly's apprentice? You're bloody worse than him." Thor raised his voice "Who else have you shagged? You need gelding. I've a bloody good mind to call the vet now. Three women in one day? Despite you being bloody ginger. I don't even know where to start with this one." Nipper began to whimper, then sneezed a big blob of snot onto Thor's kitchen table. Both of them looked at this aghast. It lay there motionless asking the question "Well what are you going to do about me then?" Eventually Thor laughed at the absurdity of the situation, got up, found a bottle of disinfectant from under the sink, found some kitchen towel and cleared the snot into the bin.

"Bad things always seem to happen on a Wednesday," Nipper blubbed, "I was born on a Wednesday."

"Don't go bloody sulking lad. You caused this mess and you'll have to dig your way out of it. Firstly get to the Doctor's in Newport and get a prescription for Lice shampoo. Then I suggest you make abundant apologies to Eloise and Harry's daughter and suggest they do the same. You'll not be popular but you owe it to them."

Nipper looked horrified "How do you go about telling a woman that you've given her crabs?" he asked. "I haven't a bloody clue mate, I've never had to do it. My brains are in my head not in my knob. Here goes, spin em some yarn about forgetting your towel and borrowing someone else's on Sunday." Thor was surprised at how devious he could be. He put it down to hearing so many poor excuses in the course of his job.

Nipper cheered up. He could now see a way out of his predicament without his mum finding out. "No point gardening now," thought Thor, he was due to play squash in just over forty minutes, "I'll settle down and have a relaxing cuppa," just as the front door bell rang. "P C Orre, there's chickens all over the road. If I catch em all, can I have some eggs?" There stood Leo Antony, ne'er do well of these parts. "Leo, if there's twelve chickens back in my pen when I get back from squash, you're on for a dozen eggs."

Jim Cameron was always early for Wednesday morning squash. Eloise Jones had the court before for a weekly game with Myfanwy from the bell. Neither of them played particularly well or even tried to. It was exercise, albeit mostly exercise of tongues as they frequently stopped during the game for a discussion about TV, celebrities or some other pressing matter. Their game started at ten but they often got going earlier as no one had the court before theirs. Both women liked to finish the game early as they agreed that when Jim appeared on the balcony overlooking the court, they could sense him mentally undressing them.

Jim was on the balcony at ten thirty, sharp. He arrived in kit as usual and began his stretching exercises, stopping to glimpse over the balcony. Jim wore oval shaped spectacles, His eyesight wasn't great and he was too squeamish for contact lenses. He got by on the rugby pitch by taking little part in open play. Jim was there to scrummage. In his book, running with the ball was for idiots and Nancy boys. He needed his specs to see a squash ball though.

Myfanwy was wearing track suit trousers and a light blue T shirt. She had a sweat band on her head to keep the hair from her eyes. Eloise was wearing the shortest white skirt, white sleeveless top and matching white sweat bands on each wrist. For Eloise this was more of a fashion statement than a competitive game. Jim went down the stairs as the court lights went out and asked his usual Wednesday morning questions. "Good game girls? Who won today? Either of you fancy a rub down in the shower?" He received the same answers as every week. "Yes thanks. We don't really count the score. Jim, you're a dirty old man."

The girls actually showered back at home, not being comfortable at being naked in front of each other or with Jim in the building. They did however always go into the ladies changing room. Sit down to recover and have a five minute natter before going home.

Thor came through the door with Captain Scarletti who said good morning to Jim and informed him that the gents changing room was out of action today as it was being tiled. Just then Eloise and Myfanwy came from the ladies changing room. Eloise had overheard the conversation and said "You can go in the ladies now Jim, it's free the rest of the day I think." She saw Thor and blushed, not knowing if she was out of favour with the Orres or not. Thor smiled. Seeing her discomfort he said "Pam's left you a message Eloise. She's on a school trip today but normal service will be resumed don't worry." Eloise was relieved. Thanked him and followed Myfanwy outside.

Thor opened the door to see Jim kneeling down and sniffing the bench seat. "What the hell are you doing?" Thor enquired. "See these fancy squash shoes?" Asked Jim, pointing to a pair of designer pumps under the bench. "They're Eloise's. She's forgotten them. She's been sat sweating right here. You can smell her. Thor didn't know whether to laugh or be appalled. The choice was made for him when the door burst open again. "I've forgotten my trainers," said Eloise, "Jim what on earth are you doing?"
Jim was totally taken aback "I'm err, well, err, looking for my glasses," he stammered. "That'll be the pair on your nose Jim will it?" asked a disgusted Eloise, before bending down to pick up her trainers, shaking a disapproving head at Jim and storming out.

Thor burst into hysterical laughter and eventually changed, went on court and thrashed Jim, who had a total collapse of concentration. After the game a chastened Jim asked Thor to keep quiet about the sniffing incident as he was only doing it for a joke. A sceptical Thor replied "I'll never mention it but it's going to cost you a beer. See you in the Bell in five minutes."

Evor had seen his grandson coming out of the squash court and walking over to the Bell. Chubby had just had a chat with him, informing Evor that he was just going out in his boat to check a couple of lobster nets and asked if Evor wanted one, for free. Evor had declined on the basis that rarely was anything free in Chubby's case. Chubby had informed him that he was expecting a few quid to come his way shortly after returning from tour. "All above board I hope?" asked Evor. "Certainly Mr Orre." replied a respectful Chubby.

Myfanwy had just pulled a pint for Thor when he was followed in by Jim Cameron, who in turn was followed in by Evor. Jim ordered two more beers and asked Myfanwy to put it on his slate. "You need to speak to me about your slate, it's growing at a fast rate Jim Cameron." said the landlady. "I swear that by the end of the month I will clear it and possibly have a little party in here. I'm hoping for a deal to come off that will see a few grand coming my way." Jim replied. As Jim wasn't one for making idle boasts or wild promises this statement seemed to appease Myfanwy, who served him the drinks, adding just one word "Pervert!"

"Thanks for keeping that quiet Thor," Jim intoned sarcastically. Thor pointed out that He hadn't had time to snitch on Jim and reminded him who had been playing Eloise. "What's this all about?" asked Evor, who chuckled with mirth when Jim recounted the story. Jim's beer hadn't touched the sides. He ordered and downed a second one then said he had to leave as he was meeting someone. "Very strange, that's the second pauper I've met today who expects to be solvent on return from tour. What's going on Tom? Any idea?" asked Evor. "No idea Pop. Fancy lunch, on me?"

The pair both had steak and kidney pie, mash and peas. After another pint they went their separate ways. Thor to his garden, Evor for an afternoon nap and to ponder over the coming fortunes of Chubby and Jim.

Pam arrived home mid afternoon to find her husband digging manure in.

"Hey stinky, how's your day been?" She asked. Thor told her he'd seen Eloise and that all went well. He told her about Jim Cameron and his faux pas. Pam was aghast but pointed out that he may have just been joking. He informed her about the chickens and the fact that although Leo had recovered eleven there was still one good layer missing. "I wouldn't be too astonished to find that the shifty sod is having chicken for tea tonight." Pam opined.

"Was your day good?" He asked. Pam in turn informed Thor that Paul Bennett had proposed to Anna Bewick in a drunken stupor on Sunday evening then swore him to secrecy as neither of them had mentioned it since and Anna thinks he may not have meant it. "Oh I bumped into Pam Craddock in the car park in Castra. She's invited me over tomorrow for lunch. Is that OK with you?" Thor said of course and that he would try to catch up with his gardening.

When the children came home from school Thor took them onto the rugby pitch as they wanted to fly kites. Mr Bennet had been teaching them about kites in school and there was just the right sort of wind. If Daddy would take them to fly kites they would be able to draw a picture and write half a page about it. After a lot of running up and down Thor finally got two kites up in the sky and handed them over to his children. When Paul Bennet cycled past Thor jogged over and thanked him for his days work, with a very sarcastic smile.

"All going well Paul?" Thor asked. "Oh yes. Your kids are a credit to you both. I don't know what I've done wrong at home though. Can I ask some advice? Strictly confidential though?" Paul asked. When he received a smile and a nod he went on, "I have asked Anna to marry me. She said yes but hasn't mentioned it since. She's being a bit sulky and I don't know if she wants to marry me or not or even if she remembers me asking. What do I do?

Thor was amazed at how people who live together can fail to communicate and thanked his lucky stars for having married Pam. In their relationship there was none of this trying to second guess what the other persons thoughts and desires were, yet it seemed so common with many couples he knew.

"What would you do? How did you get Pam to marry you? If you were Anna would you want to marry me?" Paul questioned. "Slow down Paul. Before I can answer one question you've asked me about five more." Thor paused for a while before delivering his verdict "Grasp the nettle mate. These things are best not put off. Just walk in, kiss her and ask what she thinks will be the best time of year for your wedding. My guess is she'll run into your arms and tell you what a wonderful man you are. If I'm right, I'll be at the committee meeting in the Bell tonight and I'll want a jug sending into the meeting room. OK? See you later Mr Bennet." The Orre children waived and their kites became tangled and fell to the ground. It had started to drizzle so Thor untangled the kites and walked home with a child in each hand. When he walked in Pam queried his smug expression. He told her that he'd spoken to Paul Bennet and said "Thomes Henry Orre, Police Officer, husband, father and relationship counsellor at your service ma'am." He smirked.

With the kids in bed and evening meal inside him Thor trotted off down to the Bell with a rucksack on his back. As he walked in Myfanwy informed him that everyone was already in the snug and that the schoolmaster had left two pints apiece in the pump for everyone but refused to say why. She was distraught when Thor denied any knowledge of the reason but walked off grinning like a Cheshire cat, pint in hand.

"Ah here's Tom 8pm on the dot," said Evor as Thor walked in and sat down. "So we're all here. I'll pass out the agenda." He gave them all a sheet that said:-

1 Cup final review . *2 End of season do*

3 Tour timetable *4 Touring party*

5Tour rooming arrangements *6 Treasurers report*

7 Normans proposal *8 A O B*

"Ok," started Evor "Not much to say about the cup final except that it was one of the happiest and proudest moments of my life. Bill can you minute the result, team, scorers and attendance also can Ian, as treasurer, contact the county to ensure that we get our 25 percent of gate money. It'll be a bonus for us. Anyone got anything to add? No. Ok, moving on"

"Just a moment." Red Rod butted in, "Where are we going to keep the cup? I thought of having it displayed in a locked cabinet behind the bar in the Bell. Chubby will make me one for £100. Naturally, I'll pay for it."

"Sorry Rod," said Captain Scarletti, "The clubs home is at the boat club. It's only right and proper old chap that the trophy be held there. That's where we entertain our opponents immediately after each home game. It's where the team shower and eat after the game. I've already given Chubby a £50 deposit for a new trophy cabinet to match the rowing and sailing ones."

Mo Khan chipped in "I have sponsored the team shirts for three years now. I feel it only right that the cup should be on display at the Shere Khan. I would propose to keep it in the window. Of course it would be alarmed and I have already had a quote for this."

"Let me guess," said Evor "a quote from Chubby? I thought as much."

"Hang on, why not settle this squabble? I'll keep it on display at my office next to the harbour. Chubby can double glaze the small window that looks over the slipway then everyone can see it." Said Bill Davies.

Five minutes of argument followed and tempers began to fray. This was only brought to an end when Thor stood up and slammed his hand down, hard on the table. Everyone shut up and looked at the big, red faced man. "I have three things to say. One, Norman can you press that buzzer for more beer please? Two, if I had foreseen the trouble it has caused, I'd have thrown the game and given the blasted cup to Malvil." He sat down.

"What's the third?" asked Northern bloke.

"The third," Thor paused "the third is, does anyone know where the cup is at this moment?" Silence! This was followed by more silence then a longer thoughtful silence. "Great," said Thor "we've lost the fucking county cup!"

"You took it home Evor" said Bill McClaren. "I did hell as like. I saw Rod with it. It's in the pub Rod. Get it will you." Rod denied having it, accusing Chubby of being here late on with Jim Cameron and Jekyll & Hyde. Accusations flew back and forth and panic increased.

Once more Thor stood and demanded silence. When he had everyone's attention he told them in straight terms that he would not tolerate squabbling and that they must not fall out over this matter. "I have a confession." Thor told them, "On the morning after the cup final the milkman knocked on my door worried about the fact that no one was alive in the village. He also gave me this," he paused, reached into his rucksack and pulled out a dented silver cup. "He found it on the edge of the green. It's no use speculating how it got there. It's also no use arguing over who gets the cup, is it?"

A group of chastened men, allegedly adults, sheepishly agreed. Thor proposed that Evor, as chairman, founder and elder statesman decide the keeper of the cup. This was also agreed. Evor gave his judgement. "Mo, I'm very grateful for the support that you give to the club but I think you'll agree that it's not right to keep the cup over the water in Newport my friend." Mo acquiesced. "Bill, I know you'd look after the cup but it is nearly a hundred years old and solid silver. You'd be gutted if it were to disappear and it could, particularly in tourist season." "Aye, you're right." Said Bill

Both the Bell and the sailing club are secure and have a strong connection with the club. I propose that you alternate, six months apiece. In the winter the cup lives in the Bell, in tourist season it moves to the more secure sailing club. Whoever doesn't hold the cup has a big team photo with the cup, in lieu of the actual trophy"

This idea was unanimously agreed and more beer was buzzed for. "Bill, minute that but no mention of the falling out or loss of the cup please." Evor moved on "Item two, end of season do. This event normally involves about one hundred to one hundred and twenty people and fits nicely into the concert room at the sailing club. This year I expect demand will exceed supply and propose to hold our end of season dance in the village hall. This will hold in excess of two hundred. I suggest Rod does the drinks and Captain Scarletti the food. Comments please."

Both Rod and Captain Scarletti agreed to this and the committee passed the idea

Evor continued "Item three, Tour itinerary. The coach will leave here Friday morning 9am. Not 9-10, not 9-05 but 9am. Due at Ramsgate for the Ostend ferry at 11-15 am. Everyone to ensure they have an up to date passport. On arriving in Europe the coach will then take us to our hotel where we will behave impeccably. Food, day one will be bacon butties here, get your own on the ferry and evening meal in the hotel at 5-30pm. Saturday we have breakfast in the hotel and an early kick off against RFC Panthers at 1pm. Our hosts will feed us on Saturday. Sunday we breakfast at the hotel, then travel to Bielefeldt, where we will stay in barracks courtesy of the Yorkshire regiment. We were due to play the Yorkshires on Sunday afternoon but they have mostly gone to the Middle East and can't raise a team. They have managed to get a few local lads to join in and will offer both sides Yorkshire hospitality, on base, on Sunday evening. Monday morning means an early start at 8am. Due back here eightish Monday evening."

Bill agreed to minute that and to produce an itinerary that could be given to all players.

Evor pressed on. As in all rugby clubs, finer details can be left to sort themselves out as ordering more beer became a priority. No one mentioned the famous tour to Skegness that Evor had arranged many years ago. Coach, hotel and food were sorted, he'd just forgotten to fix up any opponents.

Haven came home, after a weekend on the lash, with clean rugby kit.

"Right Chaps, touring party. I have the eight of us here plus Saint, who can't play. Then there's Jim Cameron, Chubby, Simon Spencer, both Bennet boys, Curly, Harry, Nipper, Farmer Brown, Posh boy and Teflon. That's just fourteen players. There are two lads from Newport RFC who say they'll come, Nigel Royd and James Pyle, Anybody know them?"

Red Rod chipped in "Yes Evor. They're both prop forwards, good lads on a piss up but neither of them very fit. They'll do though."

Evor went on "A mate of Teflons, called Lee Washbrook. Anyone?" Thor said that he knew him. He played in goal for the football team so his handling must be better than Teflon's. He was also a cousin of Chubbies.

"Now here's a real surprise," said Evor "Malvils number eight, Peter Craddock is up for coming with us. That's a real bonus."

"No! Never!" This was a shout from Northern bloke that shocked all present. No one spoke for a while and then Evor pulled himself round. "What's the objection Norm? He's a damn good player and a nice enough bloke."

"I just don't think we should be getting too many players in from other clubs, that's all. This is a Haven tour after all." Evor said that he could see the point but with two games in two days the more the merrier. At this point Myfanwy brought in another round of drinks and left in silence.

Norman looked uncomfortable and said "I don't think he'd be right for us. I'd rather he didn't come." The other seven looked at him and each other with puzzlement. "I'm sorry mate," said Thor, "Can you be a bit more specific about your objection?"

Norman reddened "Alright, alright I'll tell you. You must have noticed? He's bloody black. He's as black as the ace of spades." Seven men were speechless.

Eventually Mo Khan spoke "Norman, you have probably overlooked this but neither I, nor my son Eddie is of the rosy cheeked variety of person. I thought we were friends." He had moist eyes as he realised the connotations of Norman's outburst.

"No Mo, you're fine. Your family are fine. This chaps different. His wife is a white girl and that's just not right." Norman said this as if he now expected everyone would now understand. No one did.

There they sat, seven men who had suddenly discovered something terrible about a man they had called friend. Each of them tried to make sense of it. Some of them were convinced that they must have misheard. Ian Tomkins had an urge to strike Norm as did Evor. Rod felt sorry for mankind but couldn't articulate his thoughts into words. Bill Davies put his head in his hands and studied the table top intensely.

Thor spoke, quietly. "Norm, my friend. When I scored the try on Sunday the referee was unsighted. He didn't see me ground the ball and could have disallowed it on the basis of that. Peter Craddock was honest enough to tell the referee that it was a try." He spoke even quieter but all could hear "That is how I judge a man Norman, not by his wealth or his religion and certainly," he now raised his voice "certainly my friend not by the bloody colour of his skin." He paused "I have invited Peter and as much as I value your friendship I will not withdraw my invitation."

"Is that the opinion of you all?" Norman asked. "It most certainly is." Ian Tomkins responded. "I must bow to the democratic process. You'll hear no more of this matter. I apologise if I have caused offence. It's the club that must come first." Northern Bloke stood up and moved towards the door. "I'll be back soon for item 7. You can manage without me for a few minutes. I'll send some more drinks in." With this he left the room.

"Do you think he's OK?" asked Mo Khan. "Leave it Mo. I'll speak to him at some point." Thor replied.

"Ok," Chirped Evor, as if nothing had happened. "Rooming arrangements. It's probably not the best idea to room Northern bloke with Peter Craddock eh." The remark was intended to lighten the mood. It failed. Some discussion took place over who would share the twin rooms in the hotel. Mike Bennet had asked for a break from his brother's constant questions. No one wanted to share with Saint as despite the fact he was a gentleman he snored like Farmer Browns pig. Thor normally roomed with Curly but he thought it best if he went in with Peter Craddock. Eventually a sensible list was drawn up, version 11:-

Thor & Peter Craddock	*Evor & Mo Khan*
Ian Tomkin & Bill McClaren	*Bill Davies & Harry Thelwell*
The two from Newport	*Lee the goalie & Teflon*
Saint & Tom Brown	*Curly & Nick Haydn Smythe*
Paul Bennet & Nipper	*Red Rod & mike Bennet*
Jim Cameron & Simon Spencer	*Northern Bloke & Chubby*

In addition to the above, team physio, Janet would be coming to the games to look after the team. As she had for recent years, she would travel with her friend, Sindy, by motorbike. They would come over on the Saturday and leave after the game on Sunday. The team would carry Janet's kit bags and treatment gear on the bus. She'd drop it off on Thursday evening and collect it on return on Monday evening.

"Evor, I have a question," this was Rod, "Do you think the two girls are on the other bus?

"Pay attention Rod boy," said Evor "there is only one bus and I've just told you that they'll be travelling on Sindy's motorbike. Very nice it is too, big shaft driven, water cooled BMW."

"No. What I meant Evor is, do you think they wear comfortable shoes?"

"Don't be bloody daft man. On a motorbike? I should imagine they'll be wearing leathers and biking boots. Why are you concerned about this?"

Thor butted in, "What he wants to know granddad is whether you think they're lesbians." Evor looked at Rod. "Why didn't you just ask if they were carpet munchers? That's what we called em in my day. No beating about the bush with pathetic euphemisms. How the hell do I know? What do you think Tom?" A good ten minutes was wasted while the committee of Haven Rugby Union Football Club debated the sexual preference of two young women. Evor finally brought the group back to more serious matters. "Don't minute any of that for god's sake Bill. Let's move on. Ian, how do our finances stand?"

Ian Tomkin was a former player, one of the originals who'd set up the club with Evor. He was a big man, had played the game to a high standard and had something about him that commanded respect. He began his report. "The clubs bank account has a healthy £2,140-57p in it. Mo Sold all 250 T shirts for the final and each one made a £1 profit for him and £2 for the club. Great idea Mo, I propose a vote of thanks." This was seconded and agreed unanimously. "The club tour fund stands at an amazing £1,832-57p. This is entertainment funding only as the lads have already paid in for transport and hotels. The fund has been boosted by a gift from Mary Hynge, I can say that name in committee I understand. She has donated £100 from the fines received throughout the season, mostly courtesy of Harry and myself I'll add. The villagers had a collection after the game and raised £1204-57p. This was as a thank you for winning the cup. I gather Leo Antony organised it. All outstanding bills are paid. Are there any questions?"

Thor wondered aloud how much Leo had pocketed but pointed out that the club should acknowledge the thanks and generosity of the villagers. "Minute that but don't mention the bit about Leo." said Evor. "Thank you Mr Treasurer. I propose we spend a little of our funds on a round of beer. This was agreed and Thor buzzed Myfanwy for another round.

When Myfanwy arrived with the tray, Northern Bloke returned with her. He had composed himself and sat down with a fresh pint as though nothing had happened.

"Good timing Norm," said Evor, "We've just come to this proposal that you have but first have a look at the proposed rooming list. Are you OK with Chubby?" Northern Bloke surprised them all again. He couldn't room with Chubby as Chubby smoked and occasionally had been known to use whacky baccy. Norman was very anti smoking so it was agreed that Rod would swap with him and Norman could have the quieter of the Bennets.

Norman was asked to outline his proposal. He said that he had spoken to a local businessman who was interested in linking up with Haven RUFC. The offer was that he would sponsor the team in the following way. Norman hung a prepared flip chart on the coat pegs next to the door. It read:-

1. The club committee to remain in situ and current club rules retained.
2. Acquisition by purchase or long term lease of a pitch on the Haven side of the estuary. Said pitch to belong to Haven RUFC.
3. The funding of purpose built changing rooms, possibly with a club house
4. The building of a covered standing area for spectators.
5. A promise to pay all costs for 5 years. IE Gas, Electricity, Council rates and RFU membership.
6. Funding of all away travel including two continental tours per season, with a provider of the clubs choice.
7. Special offers to all club members using the benefactors company.
8. A £1,000 donation to this year's tour fund, as a gesture of goodwill irrespective of whether these proposals are accepted. Or not

Northern bloke then hung a second flip chart on a lower peg, outlining what was expected in return. This read:-

1. The rugby ground to be named after the benefactors company
2. The benefactor to be allowed to bring up to ten associates to each home game free of charge.

3. The benefactors company name to appear on all club shirts, other clothing and literature.
4. The change of club colours to reflect the corporate image.
5. A new club crest incorporating the bell and anchor with the benefactors logo
6. The mention of the benefactors company in all Media interviews.
7. The benefactor to be given the title of president, but not to have voting rights on the committee.

"That's it in a nutshell," said Norman, "You'll no doubt want time to digest the offer and then I'll take any questions."

The committee were astonished for the second time that evening. Everyone looked at Evor for guidance. "At first glance it looks an exceptional offer Norman. What's the catch?" Norman replied that there was no catch, no tricks and that he had put much thought in before coming to the committee with these proposals. "I don't know where we go with this," Evor said, "I'll need time to consider my stance." Norman said of course and that tonight was not expected to be for deciding, just the beginning of a discussion.

"Who's the kind benefactor?" asked Thor. Norman said that he was not at liberty to divulge that information at the moment, as the person did not want this becoming open knowledge until at least an agreement in principal had been reached.

"What's your opinion Norman?" asked Bill Davies, who had already seen a better income as he would charge normal prices for coaches rather than his usual covering of costs. "I think it's above board and an opportunity to consolidate the long term future of the club. The sailing club have been great letting us use their facilities as has the pub but we have to plan for the worst. What if the sailing club changed tack, Excuse the pun, or if a new landlord came to the Bell who wasn't a rugby fan?"

"It would be nice to have a dry spot to stand and watch from." This was Ian Tomkin. Bill McClaren chimed his agreement.

"I'm firmly against it. I want no part of it." Thor's blunt opinion caused more surprise on what had been an evening for surprises. "May I ask why so?" asked his grandfather.

Thor outlined his reasoning. It went thus:-

- He assumed the benefactor to be Sir Christian Penhale. Member of Parliament for West Castrashire. Owner of business interests in the form of Hotels, Spa resort, golf course, Beauty and tanning salons and night clubs.
- He assumed the name to be used would be Penhale Enhancements. Not as bad as Cheap as Chips but the beginning of rot setting in.
- Haven had always played in black and gold and he did not want to change this to light green and very light green.
- Most of all though he considered Penhale to be a crook and Haven should have nothing to do with him.
- Finally he applauded the current total amateur stance of the club and did not think that Haven should go the same way as Tigers or Malvil West.

The group looked at Northern Bloke for confirmation of Thor's surmising. "Well," asked Evor, "what say you to Tom's assumptions?"
"I am unable to confirm them but am also unable to deny them." This was understood by all to be a confirmation of

Thor's opinion. A heated argument then ensued, some being for, some against and some changing sides faster than a French general.

Evor again took control. "Gentlemen, gentlemen. Please! I propose that we should not dismiss this proposal without due consideration. I suggest an extraordinary general meeting of all club members at which the proposal can be openly debated. First however I propose a letter to all members setting out the Pro's and con's of the proposal, I take it that you Norman and you Tom will be prepared to draft this under guidance from Ian?" All three nodded. Evor continued. "There must be no mention of any assumptions. You must stick to the facts as we know them. I will not have this club put in a position where we can be prosecuted for libel. Agreed?" This was agreed and a date set one month hence in the big room at the sailing club, there being in excess of seventy paid up members.

Evor buzzed Myfanwy for a bottle of good single malt and nine glasses. "It's been a hard session," he said "Is there any other business?"

Red Rod apologised and said that he had. It seemed a trivial matter, after what had gone on earlier but Spoddy Brown had asked him to bring the matter to their attention. Spod is a local slang term for someone of less than average intelligence, in fact it equates roughly to halfwit. Spoddy's wife, June, disliked the term being used to describe her husband and Spoddy had asked if the club could stop it, as they had with Mary Hynge.

"Not feasible," said Bill Davies, "His father has always been called Spoddy and his father before him." I have an idea," said Thor, "leave it with me."

"Don't minute Spoddy. Meeting closed, 10-46pm."

On the way out Thor made to speak to Northern Bloke. He didn't want to fall out even though they were in opposition over the proposal. As he approached, Northern Bloke looked at him and said one word before walking away. "Luddite!"

Everyone else had gone. Thor said goodnight to Rod and Myfanwy and left the pub. Outside an arm came round his shoulder. "We need to talk lad but not tonight. I'll catch you over the weekend."

"OK Grandad, goodnight."

Just round the corner stood a weary looking Bill McClaren. "I must have left the key in the lock on my bike." He said. "It's still here." Thor pointed out.

"Aye the bike is, it's not worth pinching but some bugger's nicked my cycle lock."

Chapter 8 – Another Day, And No Gardening

The alarm clock went off in the Orre household. Pam was already up and brought a cup of coffee for her husband. "Are you Ok love," she asked "you didn't sleep well last night, tossing and turning you were." Thor apologised and told her of the goings on at the rugby club committee meeting. He was worried about the direction the club might go in and very worried about Norman Arkwright's colour prejudice. Pam put her arms around her man. "Look my love, you can't be all things to all people. You have to accept that people will see things differently and at times you must respect their right to be wrong. At the end of the day your kids are healthy and you have my love for always. I know how much you love the club but sometimes you have to let go."

Thor smiled at his wife and got up and dressed for breakfast. They had cereal with the children and after playing for a while they all walked to school together. Pam then went off for a coffee with Eloise as planned. And Thor went to call on Evor.

Evor's white painted cottage overlooked the harbour. It held many happy memories for Thor, as after losing his parents in the sinking of the Bluebell, he was brought up here by his grandad. He found the back door unlocked and walked in. "It's me Pop," he shouted upstairs to where he could hear the old boy in the shower. "You should know better than to leave this door open. I'll put the kettle on"

Five minutes later Evor stamped down stairs. "Who's going to break in here lad? There's only Leo and he wouldn't bloody dare." Thor pointed out that someone from afar could drive into the village at night and take anything. "If anyone broke in Tom, they'd probably feel sorry for me and clean the place."

They sat over a big mug of tea. Evor said that he knew Tom would come to chew the fat today then gave him almost word for word the same advice that he'd received from Pam earlier. "Well Pop, if we're going to chew the fat how about bacon butties eh?" Thor asked. A few minutes later they felt happy, having downed some good local bacon on Evors own home made bread.

Thor told Evor that he was very worried about Norman Arkwright. He told Evor about his outburst with Teflon over cigarettes and mentioned how appalled he was about the racist comments last night. He then went on to tell Evor about his concerns over dealing with Sir Christopher Penhale in any way. He informed Evor that, to his knowledge Penhale owned Beauty salons or tanning shops in Newport, Malvil, Castra and Winscorn. In total at least 9 shops. In Thor's opinion these places could not make a profit as not that many women wanted regular sunbed sessions. He admitted that he could only speak for the one in Newport but said that there seemed to be very low footfall and he was suspicious that they were used to launder money or worse. Finally he mentioned that Northern Bloke had attempted to get involved in someone's private life. He swore him to secrecy and told him that Nipper had been caught with a team mate's wife. This was known to Norman who wanted to take action within the club. Thor had vetoed this and had to speak with Norm about where the boundary of team captain had to stop.

Evor topped up the mugs, more to buy time to think than to quench thirst.

"Phew. A few days ago the club reached the heights and less than a week later I sense a rift between the man who has captained us to glory and the man I love and admire more than any other. I am torn between the desire for progress and the need to retain your affection. I thought it was my generation who were supposed to find change difficult lad." He looked quizzically at his grandson who responded that he was not against change totally but was against knee jerk reactions and getting involved with crooks.

"The question of sponsorship can sit on the back burner for a while," Evor said "The two things that worry me are the need to stamp out any racist behaviour before it takes hold. Secondly I'm beginning to worry about Norman himself. Is he losing the plot do you think? We mustn't rush to judge him if he's becoming ill. Are things OK between him and Mrs Northern? I know she has a job up there somewhere and comes down most weekends but Norman is now ensconced here."

Thor asked if Evor thought Thor should have a heart to heart with Northern bloke. A thoughtful Evor replied "Not yet. You have enough on your plate at the moment, you really must try to lose the roles of village agony aunt and confession taker. Isn't it enough to look after your family and build your career lad?"

"I know what you're saying but look at my role models. People were always coming to dad to sort things and when I moved in with you it was the same. The village expects the Orres to be able to sort anything. Hey when I was young you could even mend burst balloons, sometimes even magic them into a different colour or shape. Look! Here I am now coming to you for advice. It's what we're good at" The old boy laughed at his grandson's recall of those days. He reached across and patted him with affection, as though he was still a toddler.

Evor gave Thor a plan. He wanted Curly to talk to Norman about prejudice. This surprised Thor but the old boy tapped his nose and said "Trust me, he's the man for this job." Evor said that he would make a few subtle enquiries about Northern Blokes well being and relationship with Mrs Northern. He suggested that Thor keep his opinions about Sir Christopher Penhale to himself, until he had something firm enough to approach his inspector with. "Don't forget lad, this is the United Kingdom. A man is still innocent here until proven guilty, except for Leo Anthony perhaps. Oh, one more thing. I'll support you within the club no matter what."

Thor was moved by that but told his granddad that he would still love him and that he was free to vote with his conscience as to what is best for Haven RUFC. They shook hands and Thor ambled out like a huge polar bear.

Evor thought how his son would be so proud of Thor. Thor thought that Evor had just manipulated him but walked away smiling none the less.

Thor saw a spotless yellow and green tractor coming up from the road from the small beach. It towed a trailer full of sand. Here was a chance to have a chat with John Brown about the Spoddy business. Thor out his hand up and the tractor came to a halt. Thor was surprised when, instead of the big frame of farmer Brown, down jumped Chubby. "Morning Mr Orre. What can I do for you?" Chubby asked. He was always respectful to Thor as he was a policeman and Chubby liked to keep on the right side of authority, just on the right side.

Thor asked what Chubby was doing with the Brown's tractor and was told that Spoddy and Mrs B had gone over to Newport to shop in the supermarket there. Chubby had asked to loan the tractor to take a load of sand from the beach, up to Captain Scarletti's house at the top of the cliff. Thor wasn't sure what the legal position was concerning the bulk taking of sand and made a note to ask t'inspector later. Chubby informed Thor that Mrs Scarletti had read a piece in the Mail about global warming and Captain S was paying him a hundred pounds to fill two hundred and fifty sandbags. Thor told Chubby that he should be ashamed of himself for conning the Scarletti's into having needless sandbags filled as the water will never reach so high. "I know that Mr Orre and I've told the Captain so but he insisted, honestly." Thor said that he'd check with the Captain and padded off down towards the sailing club

Thor found the captain painting the railings that separated the club from the harbour. Sure enough, Chubby had told the truth. It seems that after much discussion with Mrs Scarletti, the captain had decided it was easier to have a supply of sandbags ready than to convince Mrs S of the fact that if the sea reached up to their home it would be best to simply get out in a boat. A hundred pounds for peace seemed a good deal to Captain S.

On leaving the sailing club Thor noticed the ferry coming over from Newtown. He decided to hang about to see if the Browns were on it. His patience was rewarded as he saw Mrs Brown was a foot passenger. He waved to her as she got off and asked where John was. He nearly said Spoddy but managed to stop himself. He was informed that she had come over with the shopping and that John would come over on the next ferry, after calling into the National Farmers Union office to pay their insurance.

"Of course," said Thor, thinking that for NFU office, read Sailors Arms. "I can't help but notice that you haven't got any shopping bags June."

"Oh no," She put her hands over her mouth and started to hyperventilate.

"Don't worry. Sit on this bench," said Thor, pointing a few yards away. "I'll run down and shout the ferry back. It's only just cast off." He ran down, along the harbour wall and bellowed at the ferryman to stop. Luckily Thor had a voice that could be heard in Newtown itself. The ferryman recognised that it was the local bobby and pulled in next to the harbour wall. Thor jumped down, picked up four plastic bags of shopping and climbed back up a rusty ladder set into the harbour wall.

He reached June and sat down beside her. "Here you are." He placed the bags beside her. "Oh thank you so much PC Orre, I feel so foolish. I'll tell John how good you've been and ask him to drop you some lamb steaks down after our next sale." Thor thanked her but said there was no need as it had cost him nothing. He was pleased however when she insisted, the local lamb was gorgeous.

"I hear that you're upset about John's nickname?" He asked. She replied that she was and didn't like it being suggested that John was in any way simple. He was a good man, a good farmer and hard worker. Thor looked shocked and said that he knew nothing about anyone thinking her John was anything other than an intelligent chap. He said that his Grandad, Evor had told him that John's grand father, also John, was called Spoddy due to the American civil war song.

He sang, "John Brown's body lies a moulding in the grave, John Brown's body lies a moulding in the grave. That's where it comes from June. It's not Spoddy but S'boddy from the song. Your man is the third generation of Brown boys called S'boddy, along with his father, grandfather and brother, John. It has nothing to do with their intellect. It's tradition"

June smiled at him, "How nice. I'll let him keep the name if you like. It's a bit confusing though both John and his brother, being called John and both known as S'boddy." Thor said he agreed and told her that he liked her name, June. "Oh thanks PC Orre. It's 'cos I was born in the summer. 12th August it was. Bye now." Off she went. Thor called her back for her shopping bags then turned towards home. "What a perfect couple," He thought, "hardly a brain cell between em."

On arriving home Thor went into the kitchen. There was a note from Pam on the table. It read. *"Been to see Eloise. Strange encounter. You haven't forgot I'm meeting Pam Craddock for lunch? I've gone on bus as you'll need the car. ..... Love Pam XXX"*.

"What's the time?" thought Thor. "Bloody hell! 1-10 and my first day on shift as a sergeant." He flew upstairs, got changed into his uniform, ran out, jumped in the Ford Mondeo estate and just made the 1-20 ferry. When he finished shift at 10pm the ferry will have stopped running, hence Pam leaving him the car so that he could drive round the long way. He got out of the car and had a chat with the ferryman. "That bird who left her bags on today, is she with that dopey farmer?" the ferryman asked. Thor confirmed this and enquired as to why he wanted to know. "Only because the pair of them are dense. They came over early morning, together in their car. They returned separately as foot passengers." Thor told the story of John's nickname and how June had believed it. "It's a bloody good job that breathing is an automatic reflex," he added "or they'd both be long dead.

At the station he had managed to get in before the rest of his shift and knocked on the door of t'inspector. "Come. Oh it's you Tom. Ida thowt you'd a gotten in a bit early, bein your fust day wi stripes." He tossed a set of sergeant's stripes to Thor, one to sew on each arm of his number one uniform and six clip on sets of stripes for epaulettes on shirts and jumpers. Thor apologised unreservedly and admitted to having no excuse. Inspector Hardy appreciated the honesty. He genuinely liked Thor as he knew him to be absolutely straight. "Do you want me t formally introduce thee t shift or do y'own thing?" Thor thanked him for the offer but said he knew them all anyway and would let them know his feelings on policing from the start. He was informed there was one new recruit, a young lad who had impressed all and come out with top scores for teamwork during his acceptance tests. He had only started at the end of last shift and had been buddied up with P C Mike Maddox who was on holiday today. Inspector Hardy also said that they were one short on shift but he would let Tom settle in before looking at a couple of Bobbies who had asked to transfer in.

Thor shook his bosses hand, thanked him for his support and promised he wouldn't regret it. "Advice Sergeant Orre. Dunna make rash promises, they come back t ornt yer." He went out to the mess room where two Bobbies were having a cuppa. "Hello Sarge," said P C Danny Daniels, "congratulations." "Same from me." said P C Tony Taylor, offering his hand. "Congratulations?" asked Thor "Is that for getting my stripes or getting you lot?" he joked. The two officers laughed. Tony told him that it was a good shift and that he'd been lucky. He smiled at them. "Can you get the others to stay in here please?

I'm just nipping to the desk to see what C shift have left for us."

Sergeant Bent looked up from his computer screen when Thor walked in. "Tom. Pleased to hear of you getting stripes and even more pleased that you're staying with us. You've been lucky getting D shift, they're a good lot and I hear, that they're pleased to be getting you." Thor responded that they had already told him how they were the greatest. "Anything bubbling that I need to know about Dave?" Dave Bent told him that it had been a quiet afternoon. It wasn't market day so no drunks. The cells were empty. Only one job on, a report of a car being stolen. "It's over your side of the water Tom. Some farmer's wife called Brown phoned about an hour ago." Tom thought "what a great start. His shift hadn't even started and he would be able to clear up one job already!"

Back in the mess room two more P Cs had arrived Sonia Smith was a tall lady of about thirty something. Policing was her life as, like Thor her dad had been a copper. "Welcome to D shift Sarge." She greeted him warmly with a hug. "Bloody currying favour already." Shouted P C Simon Smith. He was no relation to Sonia and his comment was purely in jest. "Who's missing," Thor asked. "The corpse," replied Simon, "P C Lucy Lamont. She's never on time and is known as the late Lucy Lamont or the corpse."
"There's also the new lad. He's getting a lift in with her as they both live in Malvil." Danny told him.

Just then the door burst in and a small, pretty woman in police uniform burst in. "Hello Sarge. Sorry I'm late, there was a traffic jam on the main road in. This is Graham, our new recruit." Thor looked up. The lad behind Lucy was taller than him and in proportion.

"Jesus," said Thor, looking at the monster. Like Thor he was a big red faced chap with a big grin. "Do you play rugby Graham?" Thor asked. Before Graham could reply the others burst out laughing, Danny opened his wallet and passed a five pound note to Tony. "What's that all about?" asked Thor. Sonia told him that Danny and Tony were always having daft bets with each other, today's was on Thors first words on meeting Graham. Thor smiled, shook his head and said he'd try to be less predictable.

"I'm Graham Gascoine," said the big lad "I haven't played rugby since school. My sport is boxing Sarge. Nice to meet you. Everyone says you're the perfect bobby." Thor flushed and told him not to be bloody stupid, then gave him a wink the others didn't see, "there'll be a few perfect Bobbies on D shift though Graham. Make sure you're one of them."

Thor ensured everyone had a brew then detailed them to go out to keep Castrashire safe. Sonia was to contact Mrs Brown about the, not so stolen car. The team were surprised when their new sergeant told her that she'd probably find it on Cheap as Chips car park. Tony and Lucy were asked to have a drive around the harbour and down the docks area. He asked them to make a list of all vessels that weren't local and their nationality. Danny was asked to have a ride around the Mount Pleasant estate with Graham. He was to point out the addresses of known villains and sit outside the school later to show him some younger suspected ne'er do wells. He asked Simon to take a turn round the shopping area on foot then to pop back in about 6 to 6-30 to look after the shop while Serge went out on the patch. They were also told to pass the banking area at the bottom of town as frequently as possible.

A titter went round the room and Tony passed the five pound note back to Danny. "Ok guys, let's have the story," insisted a weary looking Thor. "Sorry Sarge," said Danny "I'd heard you had a bee in your bonnet about the banking area and bet Danny a fiver it would be a priority."

Thor put on a stern face and was about to give the shift a ticking off but he couldn't hold laughter back. When he had regained control he said "Here's the deal. I'll not stop you from making these bloody daft bets as long as it doesn't affect performance but you must agree not to settle up or mention them in my presence. I'm getting a bloody complex and I've not been in D shift for an hour yet." Both lads nodded agreement. Thor went on to tell them why he was interested in the banking area. He instructed the team that if they saw a JCB or any suchlike vehicle around the town centre after 6pm or before 9am, they were to notify him immediately. IF he called out JCB JCB at any time whoever was driving the BMW should block the main road to Castra and the officer in the Ford Focus should block the coast road to Gunnerscliffe. Any other officer on foot or in the unmarked patrol car should get to the ferry.

When asked if there were any questions Sonia asked the reason for listing vessels and their nationalities. Thor scratched his neck and said he thought it might come in handy. He'd always done this when on the beat and once or twice it had come in handy when coming across a drunken or troublesome foreigner who couldn't speak English. He would read out ships names until they recognised one then either take them back or put them in the cells as appropriate. "Good idea," said Simon. As the shift left Thor said "Lucy, can you give me a minute please?"

Lucy hung back and Thor asked if she had a nickname within the shift. She blushed and said that she was called the late Lucy Lamont or the corpse. Thor asked why. Lucy replied that she was sometimes late for work as she had a long drive in from Castra. "I'd like you to get a new nickname," Thor said "Lazarus. He rose from the dead. Ok?" Lucy said that she didn't understand. Thor informed her "You'll no longer be late so you won't be a corpse you'll have risen from the dead Lucy." He smiled at her but said, "Also, I don't like piss poor excuses."

"Sorry Sarge." A chastened P C Lamont made for the door.

"Oh, one more thing." Lucy looked worried. "I hear you're a damn good copper." Thor turned away to look at the computer screen. Lucy left feeling pleased but determined not to be late again.

Just before 3-30pm Sonia radioed in that she'd found the missing Land Rover on the supermarket car park, as Sarge had suggested. She'd phoned Mrs Brown who would come over on the next ferry to pick it up. "How did you know that Sarge," she asked. Thor told her that if she was pleasant and built up a rapport with people and then if she kept her eyes and ears open, information would drop into her lap.

At 5-40 it began to drizzle, heavily. The Scots called this weather Dricht, the Shipping Forecast named it Precipitation. Simon Smith called it Pissing down and decided to return to the nick as his sergeant had suggested.

"So, you're a fair-weather bobby then Simon?" his sergeant asked. "I'm a bit early Sarge. Do you want me to go out again for a while?" Simon offered this while making a mental note that there's no fooling this fellow and crossing his fingers at the same time. Thor told him he could stop in as long as he made a cup of tea and found something to dunk in it. He had his brew, informed Simon that nothing was happening and asked him to radio any problems. He grabbed his heavy coat and helmet telling P C Smith that he would wander off to see the pair at Mount Pleasant.

As he neared the shops on the rough estate he noticed a gang of six or seven lads kicking a ball against the wall of the end right hand shop. He strolled over "Hey fella's, he said "what have I told you about playing footie against the wall? You know the man in there rings up and complains. I have to take you all down to the nick, caution you, ring your mums who have to come and get you, then you get nagged at and I get paperwork." The lads stopped. Their main man spoke up. "Y'see copper, the lights out at the other end and I know you told us to use that 'cos the shop's empty but it'll be dark soon. It keeps us out of trouble" Thor told him that irrespective of that they mustn't play against this wall.

Thor looked at their ball. It was threadbare and didn't look as if it would last much longer. "I'll tell you what. I'll get that light at the other end fixed tomorrow and get you a decent ball if I don't get any mither. Is that a deal?"
The lads said OK and trotted off. Thor heard one say "Let's go and play on the green, the lights are on there." They then changed direction and ran off. This rang alarm bells with Sergeant Orre as an old boy with a bungalow on the green had, in the past, burst their ball if it had gone over his fence. He radioed Danny to meet him at the green ASAP and walked off that way himself.

Danny and Graham were there first and the police car was surrounded by the same bunch of lads, plus a couple they had gained on the way. "Clarky" Thor shouted over to the gang leader. "Come over here please." He had found that kids responded far better to a polite request that a direct order. Clarky sauntered over, taking his time, looking big in front of the lads. Thor dropped his voice. "Clarky, if you play here the old bugger in the bungalow will end up bursting your ball, you'll throw mud at his windows, he'll phone me and we're in the shit again." Clarky said this wouldn't happen as Happy Harry, their nickname for the bungalow resident, hadn't been seen for a while. "'S'funny though," he added "his kitchen light is always on."

Thor pondered this for a moment. "Do me a favour please Clarky? Get this lot out of here for tonight eh. I'll keep my word on the light and ball." He made a bunched fist. Clarkey did the same and they touched their fists together. "Ok P C Orre," said Clarkey

"Do you want us Serge?" asked Danny. "Serge?" said Clarky, "You've been promoted 'cos we don't give no bother eh?" Then he saw Graham get out of the car. "Phew, said Clarky, "won't give him no bother. He's a beast." With that he called the lads together and they meandered off.

Thor asked Danny to call at number 5 and Graham at number 9. They were to ask if anyone had seen the chap from number 7, find out if he was away or in hospital. Five minutes later Thor was looking through the letter box of number 7. Both constables had reported back that Happy Harry hadn't been seen for a week or more. Post had built up and light was coming from under the kitchen door. There was no reply to knocking or shouting. "Right Graham," said Thor "reckon you can open that door?" Ten seconds later the door was matchwood.

Danny was about to go in when Thor pulled him back. "Go on Graham, go and see what's to be found." Danny looked reproachfully at Thor who said "He's got to do his first stiff

sometime Danny, better tonight when he's got support."
Danny nodded.

P C Gascoine returned. His face was held low and his cheeks were pinched between his thumb and forefinger. "Sorry Graham, it's not easy your first time. Are you Ok?"

"I'm fine Sarge. I don't mind the dead. I'm trying not to laugh." Thor and Danny looked at each other aghast. "You see Serge, he's sat in front of the telly. He'd been watching a video. Here's the box. He's sat with his trousers round his ankles, his knob in his hand and a box of tissues on the chair arm. Probably a heart attack I think" Serge and Danny looked at the video box "Fanny Fest 3" was emblazoned on the box. "Well," said Thor, "He'll have died happy!"

Sergeant Orre left Danny, an experienced Bobby, to tie up the loose ends and took Graham for a drive round in the car. They had a good chat and got to know each other. "Have you ever noticed Serge that estates called Mount Pleasant are seldom actually pleasant. They are always the roughest area in a town, it seems to be where councils herd their black sheep all together." Thor agreed but pointed out that he mustn't judge people by their address. "There are some good people on mount pleasant Graham. Look at tonight. A lad who likes to be thought of as a bit of a tough nut gave us information about a death. These kids Graham aren't bad, they're bored."

Thor drove them back to the nick and swapped back with Simon for the last couple of hours on shift. Nothing much else happened. Tony and Lucy had returned a drunken Pole to his ship. Graham had chased and caught a shoplifter on Mount Pleasant who was now in the cells. Thor had handed over to A shift at 10pm, having given Sonia some money to buy the shift a round in the Ferryman, the nearest pub to the police station.

He had explained that they would call for just one drink to celebrate him surviving his first stint with D shift.

In the absence of their Sergeant the shift naturally discussed him. Most had changed into civvies. Tony and Danny, like Thor, tended to travel to and from work in uniform, perhaps because they lived nearest. The verdict on their new boss was good. Danny said that he'd learnt more today than in his previous four years as a bobby. Sonia considered that he may be just lucky, citing the stolen car incident. Graham's opinion was that it wasn't luck it was common sense, just as he had shown with the lads. Lucy said she could tell he was a bloody good judge of people but he wouldn't put up with shoddy work. Simon was pleased with his new boss trusting him to be left in the office. Tony said that he seemed as though he'd always been a sergeant,

Thor, pausing by the bar door was more than happy with these comments. He waited for a lull then burst in loudly "Right where's my pint Sonia and my change? I know what thieving buggers you coppers are."

An hour later, after driving home Thor lay in bed cuddling Pam. Pam was telling him about her strange meeting with Eloise and how pleasant her lunch with Pam Craddock had been. She had chatted away for over fifteen minutes before she heard the first of many snores from the Polar Bear next to her.

Chapter 9 – Rainy Day

Curly woke in his own bed. It was comfortable, huge and expensive. When his alarm went off a door slid open at the bottom of the bed and a TV popped up out of the sumptuous leather upholstery. On TV at this moment was the local weather forecast, A storm was brewing in the Atlantic that could end up hitting these shores late afternoon to early evening. "Are you doing anything later?" Curly shouted through the open French windows, "It's set to howl a gale later on."

Eloise was sat out on the balcony, enjoying a cup of Arabica filter coffee and a cigarette. Curly would not allow smoking in the house despite the fact that he himself lit up occasionally when drunk. Eloise was not a heavy smoker, often only having one per day but she did enjoy this moment of decadence first thing in the morning. She enjoyed it particularly after a night of passion which often occurred on Curly's first night home. Yesterday evening had been no exception. She had picked Curly up from the station and given him the message that Evor needed to talk to him urgently. On arriving home Curly had said "Bugger Evor woman. Get Upstairs."

The rear of their house was not overlooked as it faced the gorse covered hillside, being sheltered from the wind that often blew in from the estuary. It was just warm enough to be outside without a robe so Eloise was naked, except for the fluffy pink slippers on her feet. On a hot morning, Eloise had to consider that Jim Cameron might just be sat in the gorse "bird watching".

On occasions she had spotted him and either covered up quickly or stood up and stroked her nipples, depending on her mood. Today the hill was empty.

"Today depends on you my love," She responded, getting up and walking slowly inside. "If you have to work I'll potter about the house. If your free then," She delayed her suggestion until she had sat next to him on the bed, smiling suggestively while continuing to play with her nipples, "then, I could fetch us up breakfast in bed and maybe give you your favourite treat for afters" She slipped the duvet down below Curly's waist and stroked his penis until it stood to attention. Curly could not repress the boyish grin no matter how hard he tried, especially when his wife's head disappeared beneath the duvet.

"Perhaps my darling," Eloise said on her return to the light "we could go to Castra later and you might want to buy me a little treat from the jewellers on the quay." Curly told her that they weren't made of money and he couldn't spare much at the moment. He knew he was fighting a lost cause and soon gave way. In the war for control of John David Jones, between his brain and his knob, his brain had lost every single battle in his twenty six years.

An hour later Curly had showered and had left Eloise to get ready for a drive to Castra. He was walking down to Evor's, having promised to be back by 11-30am. The first indications of the coming storm were beginning to show. The estuary was becoming choppy and the birds had gone quiet. Even the gulls had disappeared from the harbour wall. He walked in through Evor's open back door to find the old man kneading dough for bread. "What ho Evor!" Curly jovially exclaimed, "I understand you want to see me? My professional fee is one mug of tea and a bacon sandwich." Curly's promised breakfast hat not transpired.

Sitting in the kitchen, Evor had given Curly the full story of the committee meeting. Curly approved of the tour arrangements and didn't mind swapping his usual room mate, Thor, for Posh under the circumstances. He was surprised by the offer of serious sponsorship and like Thor a bit sceptical of what Penhale really wanted in return. "I suppose," Curly said "that he will get a certain amount of Kudos from being the president of a rugby club in his constituency. It may bring in votes but why not go for Newport or even Castra? In any case this must be a safe seat for him."

Curly was a joker, always the one with a prank or a quip to turn a potential argument into idiocy. Many thought him the club clown, despite his legal qualifications. He was proud that Evor had asked him to speak to Northern Bloke about racism rather than entrust the task to his grandson. Evor was no fool and knew that Curly could be statesmanlike when it was required. He also knew that Curly had an experience of racism in his youth that he could recount to Northern Bloke.

Curly agreed to plan a discussion and see Northern bloke before returning to London on Tuesday. "Thanks John," Evor hugged him and let him go home.
Eloise was ready, looking stunning as always in a short red coat with matching hat and shoes. "New coat?" asked Curly. "I've had it for years." Eloise replied, turning aside to tug off the price tag.

It had been a quieter morning in the Orre household. The kids were looking forward to school as Mr Bennet had told them there was a competition today. Everyone would have to draw a member of their family and write a bit about them. Young Tom was going to draw his father but couldn't decide whether to dress him in rugby kit or police uniform. "Why not draw him in the bath?" suggested his mum, "It'll be easier." His sister told him that he mustn't as it was rude. She had decided to draw Aunty Elly, the family name for Eloise. As she said "Aunty Elly is like a film star. I'll win the prize.

Once the kids were off to school, Thor apologised to Pam for nodding off halfway through her story. They sat together in the comfy settee in their front room. The room was quite old fashioned and could have been used as a set for an Agatha Christy play, nevertheless it was warm, comfortable and always used for serious discussion. Thor and Pam had been sweethearts at school and Pam had told Thor that they would be married one day, when she was nine or ten. Thor looked at her now and she didn't really look much different. Obviously she was a woman now but her blond hair and smiling face seemed just the same to him and he loved her deeply. "Tell me about your day." He asked her.

Pam told of her visit to Eloise, who was really pleasant on her arrival. Eloise had been casually dressed for once, in track suit bottoms and one of Curly's rugby shirts. She had embraced Pam and made a fuss of her, telling her how glad she was to have her as a friend. Pam said it seemed so genuine that she was taken aback when after a bit of pleasant gossiping Eloise had become spiteful saying that because the Orre's had never experienced big city living and had little in the way of possessions, they had missed out in life. Pam had pointed out that they were both happy with their life and didn't feel that they had missed much. Eloise had asked Pam why she didn't make more of herself, she could lose some weight and buy some more modern clothes. She suggested that she should be flirty with men as it was fun. Pam had got upset and asked Eloise to accept her as she was.

There had been an embarrassing period of quiet, then, Eloise had been nice again, asking about the children and saying that they could use the Jones's pool anytime if they wanted, as long as someone could ensure they were watched. She had given Pam a key to the patio door that led to their small but luxurious indoor pool. Again they had chatted pleasantly for a while then, unexpectedly, Eloise had asked her why she didn't get of her arse and get a job. If she got a job they too could afford luxuries like a pool. She had then got quite angry when Pam had pointed out that she had a job, it was full time being wife to Thor, mother to Tom and Penny and cook cleaner and gardener as well as volunteering at the school. Pam regretted that she had also pointed out that Eloise didn't work and whilst Eloise had a pool, she couldn't swim. Eloise had flown into a rage and said "It's not about swimming you stupid cow. It's about people knowing that I can afford a pool."

As quickly as she had got angry, Eloise had calmed, apologised hugged Pam and said how much she respected her and what a good mother and member of the community she is. They had another coffee and all seemed OK but Eloise drifted away and seemed elsewhere. Pam worried about her and asked if she was OK. Eloise had replied "Ok? Yes I'm Ok. Not as perfect as you and your perfect husband and two perfect children but I get by. Even though My John is small and no one likes us we can buy you if we wanted and Curly is a better rugby player." Eloise had then burst into tears had apologised again saying that she didn't know what was wrong with her today. It must be hormones. Pam had reassured her of her friendship and had gratefully left to get ready to visit Pam Craddock.

Thor got up and tapped the barometer. It fell. "Well you seemed to have had a stormy day yesterday love. We're all in for one today. Look I know we grew up with Curly but it's probably best if we back away from the Jones's for a while. I don't want you being upset." Pam disagreed. She pointed out that if Eloise was having problems, true friends wouldn't walk away, they'd be there for them. Thor had to agree "I suppose that's one of the reasons I love you so much. How did you get on at Pam's?"

Pam explained that she'd taken the ferry across to Newport then got the 14 bus which passed by the end of the Craddocks road. Pam had made her welcome and had made lunch for them both which they ate in a conservatory. The food was good and Pam went on to describe the décor of Chez Craddock to her husband, who switched off during the description of the first room. There's something about the phrase "with beautiful swags in Fuschia deva" that switches the male auditory system off.

The blow to his arm brought Thor back into the room. Pam's father had been a decent amateur boxer and had taught his daughter to put her shoulders behind a punch. "At least pretend to listen, you bloody great oaf!" she chided her husband. Peter Craddock had been very pleased to be invited on tour. Pam had discovered that he was a bank manager and had met his wife at University. "Do you regret not going to University?" she asked Thor. His reply was "The only way I'd have got to university my love is in a jar, as a specimen. Being serious, I regret nothing. I wouldn't swap my life with anyone." Pam asked if he was disappointed with her being a bit chubby. "Look Pam, don't let Eloise sew seeds of discontent in your head. I wouldn't swap you for her. You are my love and your not chubby, you're cuddly."

He grabbed her and kissed her but was interrupted by a loud clap of thunder.

They had lunch, although in these parts lunch is dinner and the evening meal is tea. Thor got into uniform and said "I hope this rain keeps up." Pam queried this and he told her why. Newport is a town that attracts stag and hen parties at weekend, due to its pubs and clubs. If it's raining hard it keeps the revellers indoors and stops stupidity on the streets, making a slightly easier Friday and Saturday for the police. He gave her a kiss and said that two ten was his least favourite shift as he doesn't see much of the kids. She watched him drive off in the Mondeo. "He's right," she said to herself "I am loved and I'm so lucky. I wouldn't swap my lot either Tom, but you're so confident you don't ever need to ask."

Thor had left a note for the day shift Sergeant to contact the council and ask them to fix the light, for security purposes, at Mount Pleasant shops. There was a note for him saying the job had been done. He popped his head into t'inspector's office to let Mr Hardy know he was here, early. He then checked with Sergeant Bent if there was anything bubbling on handover. There wasn't. Despite it being market day, the rain had kept things quiet.

In the staff room Mike Maddox was in early to greet Thor. Mike was early fifties and coming up for retirement. He'd never had the ambition to get on in the force but was a good old fashioned beat bobby. "Hi Tom. You're the second sergeant Orre I've worked for. I hope you're as good as the first one." Thor took his outstretched hand "That's a big ask of me Mike but thanks. I'll do my best. I'd appreciate it if you gave me a little nudge if I start to lose my way." Mike replied, of course he would.

The rest arrived all in by 1-55, even P C Lamont, who Thor whispered a quick thanks to, unnoticed by all." He assigned them tasks, fairly mundane stuff but he asked Graham to be up on the Mount Pleasant around four. He was instructed to pick the best football out of lost property and to give it to young Clarky.

Across the water Curly had jumped into the driver's seat of Eloise's Porsche. It always annoyed him that he had to manipulate the seat forward so that his feet could reach the pedals, a subliminal reminder of his lack of height that nagged at him every time they had swapped cars. He had asked her to always move the seats forward and explained his feelings, which were as usual ignored. He brought it up again today and was dumbfounded by her response, "At least we have two cars unlike the Orre's who just have that tatty old Ford.

As they parked up near the quay in Castra, he heard someone shout John, John Jones. Curly had seen this man before but couldn't place him. He was getting on a bit, say mid fifties, well dressed with hair coloured dark brown, obviously from a bottle, and a moustache that made him look a bit of a spiv. "It is John, the scrum half isn't it? I'm sorry for butting in but this is fortuitous, I was going to get in touch with Evor later to get your phone number." He looked at Eloise and gave a greeting as cheesy as Curly would have done himself. "And your beautiful wife, Eloise isn't it?" He asked kissing her hand. Eloise judged him for what he was but enjoyed the flattery none the less.

Phil Prior introduced himself as president and owner of Malvil Park. This wasn't strictly true as he didn't actually own the club but Curly wasn't to know that. He went on to say ask if they would be offended if he offered to buy lunch, in return for a quick chat about rugby, Curly looked at Eloise who offered to meet him later if he wished. "No my dear lady I would extend my invitation to you as well. I'm well known around town and if I'm honest I would enjoy being seen in the company of such a goddess. Would Eduardo's suit you both with a good wine to wash it down?"

Eloise was nobody's fool but she could take free food and compliments all day, particularly at the best restaurant of many good eateries on the Quays.
Eloise accepted the invitation on Curly's behalf and of the three went.

After a rather good meal the trio sat comfortably together in the window of the restaurant, finishing the second bottle of Barberesco, a dark red from Piedmont with violet hints. Neither Curly nor Eloise were wine experts but both enjoyed this wine and both were impressed by its price.

Phil had told Curly that he wanted him to play for Malvil Park next season. He held out the virtual certainty of County selection and the offer of some financial reward for each game he played as well as a lump sum for signing a three year contract. Curly had naturally been flattered but at the back of his mind was the fact that he needed his trusty childhood pal on the field to look after him. When you're a small chap, no matter how skilful, it can be rough out there when the big boys in the pack get hold of you.

Eloise was ecstatic. This would certainly get one over on the Orre's and would elevate their social standing with Curly playing for the county. She would need new outfits and the bit of money coming in would pay for them. She was picturing herself making entrances, making the acquaintance of celebrities and being pictured in Castra County magazine. Then she heard something that she hadn't considered.

"I'd like to make a similar offer to the big number eight. Not as much mind, so I'd appreciate figures being confidential." Phil said "I also worry that the big lad will dismiss my offer out of hand so I'd like you to make the approach on my behalf. I understand that you have a special relationship with him. Do you think you could persuade him to accept?"

"You don't need Thor, Mr Prior," she heard herself saying. "Don't you already have a good number whotsit at Tigers? You just need my Curly."

It was Curly who explained that Mr Prior was not at Tigers but at the team Haven had beaten last Sunday. You are the world expert on fashion and make up my love but you don't know too much about rugby now do you?"

She gave a smile that to Phil Prior meant "Of course you're men and you know best." To Curly it meant "Don't patronise me you twat. You're in the spare room."

Curly thanked Phil for lunch and his offer. He asked for a couple of weeks to chew it over, pointing out that he works away half the week and goes on end of season tour next Friday. Phil agreed but made the point that he must keep in touch with the county selectors who will want to plan well in advance for next season.

The men shook hands. Phil accepted the chance to peck Eloise on the cheek. He then asked the Maitre De to put the meal on his business account and left.

Eloise told her husband that he must accept the offer, with or without Thor. "We're upwardly mobile and think how proud your dad would have been to know his son was a county player." This was a despicable ploy, she knew it was but also knew it would work. "Leave it for now my darling," Curly said stroking her hand "let's go and look in your jewellers shop, no going mad mind." Forty minutes later they sat in a bijou little coffee shop. Curly was eighteen hundred pounds worse off but Eloise was happy.

Thor looked out of the window, looked at his stripes and thanked his lucky stars that he could choose to be inside rather than on the beat. The wind had got up and this, along with the rain should keep the revellers off the streets but what a bloody awful night to be a beat bobby. T'inspector had just said goodnight. Thor leaned across to look into his boss's office through the window in his door. The big clock that was on the wall, just to the left of a portrait of a young Her Majesty the Queen, said 6-25. Thor's conscience got the better of him

He got on the radio and called P Cs Smith, Smith, Gascoine and Lamont back into the station. On their arrival He asked Sonia Smith to watch the shop for an hour or so and Simon Smith to have a ferry trip across to Haven for a walk about. He apologised for the lousy weather but said a cup of tea could be had if he knocked at Thor's house. He asked Graham and Lucy to accompany him down to the railway station. This was a new one on Lucy Lamont so she asked if there was any special reason. Her sergeant explained his thoughts. There will be two local trains and three trains from further afield coming in within the next hour and a half. On a Friday these would often contain stag and hen parties. He liked to show a police presence, maybe have a jovial word with each group of males himself and Lucy could have a friendly chat with the hens. "You know, ask who the stag/hen is and who is best man/ Chief bridesmaid. All was to be done with a friendly smile from Castrashire constabulary.

"What am I coming for Serge?" asked Graham Gascoine. "You my friend will stand back, put on your sternest face and hopefully put the shits up them." The two PC's laughed "I can do that," said the huge constable, practising a scowl.

The first train was local, containing workers coming home, no large groups. The second train had started in London there were six young men from Swindon. The stag was already comatose and the rest seemed harmless. The third train had a respectable looking group of mature stags who carried golfing gear. They had intentions of a good meal tonight, eighteen holes at the Penhale club tomorrow and try the "Gentleman's club" on Saturday night. Thor informed them that they should get discount at the club as it was owned by the same group as the golf course. The best man thanked him and shook his hand.

The fourth train was local again just a gang of real ale fans from Malvil out to pub crawl in Newport and catch the last train home. Thor warned them not to climb statues and recommended the Gunpowder mild in the old castle inn to start as it was top of the hill and therefore they would be going downhill all night after that.

The final train contained his worst nightmare. A gang of lads from up North who were mostly members of a rugby club could be heard singing before a single door had opened on the train. Thor could tell straight away. There is just something about the demeanour and body language of a rugby club He called them over, asked what club they were from and where they were staying. He'd never heard of Northwich but it turned out they were from Cheshire and played in the same colours as Castra. They weren't on tour but on a prop forwards divorce stag do. When asked who the lucky lad was, Thor was told that he wasn't here as his new girlfriend had banned him from coming. "Have a great time fellows but don't cause me any paperwork eh."

P C Gascoine stepped forward to reinforce his sergeant's comments. He said nothing but even the tipsy lads were awed by his presence and left the station quietly.

The rugby lads were not Thor's worst nightmare. The train also contained two hen parties. One, a gang of seven girls mostly in their twenties who came from the Midlands and an older group of six ladies in their forties and fifties were from London. The two groups left the train from different carriages but were shouting abuse at each other from down the platform. The two brides to be were the loudest and most abusive. "He must be blind to marry you, you old bag and have no sense of smell" Shouted the younger of the two. "You've no room to talk, you fat slapper." The younger looked around for a missile, unable to find one she threw her shoe which went under the train.

Thor had radioed Sonia to close the police station and get here quick. He also called Tony and Mike down from Mount Pleasant. In the meantime he intended to keep both groups apart. Lucy and Graham had read the situation and had positioned themselves between the two groups. "Now then ladies," said Thor approaching the younger group on his left with a big smile. "What's all the fuss about? You're here to have fun aren't you?"

All seven surrounded him at once pointing at the other group and calling them a bunch of effing tarts who aren't effing fit to be called women and who should be arrested for being effing old and effing ugly. "Girls, girls," Thor pleaded "firstly cut out the bad language there are children on this platform and if I hear any more effing, I'll be forced to spoil your weekend by making an arrest. Secondly, it is not an offence to be old or ugly. If it was I'd probably have to arrest half of Castrashire." Most of the girls were won over by his use of humour but the bride took off her other shoe and threw it. The shoe hit P C Lamont on the back of the head. Lucy drew her baton and turned round furious. She had intended to take revenge but was stopped by a brusque order from her sergeant "Lamont. Stay there! I'll deal with this you calm that lot down."

Lucy stopped in her tracks, returned her baton to her belt and turned back to the group of older women. "Aren't you going to arrest the scrubber who threw a shoe at you?" One of the ladies asked. "Your name is?" asked Lucy.

"Tracy but never mind that. The effing little tart should be locked up. If you're not going to do it then I'll do a citizens arrest." Tracy moved towards the other group. Big Graham blocked her path. "You're effing big enough to arrest em all. Get your act together you effing big soft git." P C Gascoine repeated word for word what he'd heard his sergeant say a minute earlier, omitting the bit about it not being an offence to be old or ugly. This didn't appease Tracy at all who pushed at P C Gascoine. The platform was starting to empty of all but a few curious bystanders, the two groups of hens and Castrashires finest.

Sonia, Tony and Mike arrived together with blue lights flashing but no sirens. They read the situation and quickly placed themselves between the two groups Thor split the younger bride, also called Tracy, away from her group and asked what had caused the fracas. He told her to answer calmly or he wouldn't listen. Her story was that her hen party, were having a good time with the rugby lads, singing and playing drinking games. The older women had come in from the next carriage and enticed most of the rugby lads away by pulling up their skirts and even going so far as to flash their tits. This had led to an exchange of insults and drink being thrown. He called Lucy over and told her to keep Tracy apart for a while.

He walked over to the older group and took another Tracy, who was the chief bridesmaid, aside. Her story tied in roughly with what he knew already. He beckoned them all towards him, keeping the four P Cs between the two groups, in case of trouble. "Right," he shouted in his sternest voice, "You're all here to have a good weekend but haven't got off to the best start. Your options are as follows. A, Get on the next train out of here and have a bloody good fight all the way home. B Start trouble in Newport, get arrested and have a night in my most uncomfortable cells. C Keep out of each others hair and have a bloody good time. There are plenty of men to go round. There's the rugby lads, some posh golfers who came in earlier, a bunch of decent young lads from Swindon who may be scared to bloody death by the lot of you and a fair amount of local chaps. The locals have six fingers on each hand but they'll be more than pleased to be spoken to in a civil fashion by such attractive ladies as you. You'll be a pleasant change from sheep.

The hens laughed and agreed to behave. P C Gascoine had retrieved the brides shoes and gave them back to her Thor demanded and received apologies for the throwing of shoes and the pushing of P C Gascoine. Thor was asked if the brides could have a picture with him, which he agreed to do, one at a time. The girls were then sent on their separate ways.

"Sorry Lucy," Thor said "but if you had hit her all hell would have broken loose." Lucy said that she was at fault and apologised for her loss of patience.

The sergeant asked P Cs Gascoine and Sonia Smith to meet the next train. He asked P C Maddox and Taylor to have a look around the banking area and P C Lamont to have a quick drive along to the docks. He would return to the station.

The kettle had just boiled when he got a call from Danny Daniels. "Hi Serge, I've just pulled up a young chap in a Honda sports car. I pulled him because he just looks too young to be able to afford this car. On questioning he says that he's a student. Normally I'd have brought him straight in but he claims to know you. His name's Nicholas Haydn – Smythe. Does it mean anything to you?"

"Ask him to drive into the station in front of you please Danny. I do know a chap by that name but like you, I'd be surprised if he could afford this car."

Thor was just finishing his cup of tea when Nick came in with P C Daniels.

"Hello Nick," said Thor, "Sorry about the inconvenience, I hear you've got a new car. I have to ask how you can afford an S2000. I know you do a bit of bar work at the Bell but Red Rod doesn't pay that much does he?"

Nick wasn't at all put out by this and explained that his parents had money and he had touched his father up for a new motor. He'd picked it up from a garage in Malvil today. He rummaged in his wallet, passed Thor a business card and said he could phone the salesman if there's any doubt. "No need for that," said Thor. I'll catch you in the Bell for the last pint all being well." Nick left and Thor heard the powerful engine roar away. "Sorry Serge." Said Danny. "You did the right thing Danny," his sergeant replied. "It's right to be suspicious about a young lad in a car like that. I'm a bit suspicious myself now and I've known him a couple of years."

Just before 10pm his D shift drifted back into the nick in ones and twos. Their sergeant had a brew ready for them and with a wicked smile said that he was looking forward to handing over to A shift. "I wonder how they're going to cope with the lovely ladies that are visiting our fair town tonight."

P C Taylor whispered to P C Daniels "A fiver says no arrests."

"You're on." Replied P C Taylor.

"Me too." Whispered their sergeant.

Chapter 10 – A Knight On The Town

Eloise had been getting ready for over an hour. It was just gone 9-45am and Curly was impatient. They usually went across to Newport on the ferry to shop on Saturday morning, not at "Cheap as Chips", Eloise couldn't be seen dead in there. "What's the delay love?" Curly shouted upstairs "If you're not quick The Orres will have gone across and I thought you wanted to see Pam, though I don't know what's so important."

Eloise struck a pose at the top of the stairs. She could never just come down. She would wait until Curly was pacing the wide hall space and appear on the balcony above, look down and utter "Well?" To which Curly would reply "Stunning," or some similar compliment. Eloise needed compliments, like the rest of us need oxygen. Today Curly's response was different. "Are we doing something in addition to shopping?" He enquired. When asked why he stopped himself from saying that she was overdressed and managed to turn it into "You're overly beautiful today my darling."

Eloise wore rich cream, high healed shoes that matched her tight knee length skirt. She had poured herself into a tight black top with a cream bolero over it, matching her skirt and shoes. Curly had noticed that her new earrings and necklace, bought yesterday, were getting an outing. He now understood the delay. This was in order that Eloise could show off her jewellery to Pam Orre. Pam would make appropriate noises out of politeness but Curly knew Pam just wasn't the jealous kind. He'd wasted eighteen hundred quid.

The seat was still forward in the Porsche. They jumped in and drove the short distance down to the ferry. They were the only car waiting which pleased Curly as he could roar off on the other side. The car park wasn't far from the harbour and by the time they arrived home, they wouldn't have travelled a mile. Tom, Pam and the kids were sat on a bench near the harbour. They would walk to Cheap as Chips and fill their rucksacks and shopping bags for the week. If the kids had been extra good they would have dinner in the Lobster Pot Café on the harbour, this was preferred to McDonalds as it had many fish tanks that the kids liked to look at.

After the weather yesterday, today was tropical, well as close as you get to tropical in England at the end of March. The estuary was like a mill pond and already a few yachts were going out from both Haven and Newport, trying to make something out of the light breeze.

Curly had dropped the hood on the Porsche and young Penny Orre came running over dragging her mum along. "Aunty Elly, you look fabtabulous," she shrieked. She told Eloise that she had drawn a picture of her and written that she was a film star. There would be a prize but it had been delayed until Tuesday and a real artist was coming to school to decide the winner. Aunty Elly asked what her brother had drawn. "He's done dad scoring a try. It's nowhere near as good as mine and he's not written much, he doesn't like writing. Wow! Your necklace is fabtabulous. Did it cost millions of pounds?" The Ferry approached and Curly drove onboard. "Well at least one of the Orre ladies noticed your new jewellery love." He smirked.

Pam wore old jeans and a jumper with a picture of Bagpuss on it. Despite this, in her own way, she was at least as beautiful as Eloise. There was a certain glow of contentment that she seemed to carry around and spread to other people. The Ferryman had a quick chat to Pam. Eloise couldn't hear what was being said but she was furious when they both laughed and he patted Pam's bottom. Thor was telling Curly about the two hen parties. "I might see if Jim Cameron fancies coming over for a bevy later." Curly stated. Thor warned against it but he could see Curly's mind putting a plan together.

The Ferry had filled up, mostly with locals from Haven going shopping. Just before they landed Eloise gave both Orre Children a pound coin each to treat themselves to sweets or something. They thanked her. Penny was already thinking about how many sweets she could get for a pound. Young Tom asked his dad to swap his pound for change as he would spend some and put some in his saving box.

Curly drove off and the Orres walked off towards the supermarket. They were just about to cross the road when there was a commotion coming from the direction of the harbour gardens. This was a two hundred yard long area with lawns facing the road, flower beds facing the estuary and a footpath between the two. The gardens were currently awash with crocuses in yellow and purple. The central bed was raised to face the harbour and spelt out Newport in flowers, purple on gold. Tearing along this path at speed, came a young man in jeans and T shirt, carrying a police helmet. Some thirty yards behind him ran a police officer who was looking out of puff. Strollers scattered as the young man made towards the market square, knowing once in the maze of alleys beyond he would probably escape. He jumped the central flower bed and turned onto the grass. He then hit the floor with a thud that totally knocked the wind out of him. He had been tackled perfectly from the side, put down and held fast. The policeman arrived out of breath and got the cuffs on him before he could recover. "Tom, good tackle," said the bobby, "This bugger just nicked the helmet off my head and did a runner." Even the culprit said "Good tackle mate, I never even saw you coming."

"I know this chap," said Thor, "You're from Northwich Rugby club aren't you? By the look of you I'd say a second row, a particularly daft second row at that as I told you not to cause me paperwork"

"I am," said the runner, "and you're the sergeant from the station who had a bit of bother with the hen party. If you hadn't tackled me I'd have got away and there'd be no paperwork. In any case you're off duty so he'll have the paperwork" The lad nodded towards the policeman, who had regained his helmet and his breath. "What shall I do Serge," asked the bobby, who replied "I don't care. Lock him up. Throw him in the harbour. Give him a good pasting. It's your call." Thor replied.

The second row was apologetic and promised no more stupidity if they didn't charge him. Amazingly he asked if he could take the option of a good pasting as his clothes were too expensive to be thrown in the harbour.

Both policemen had to laugh at this and the constable decided to let him go if he would care to contribute towards the RNLI charity. The lad agreed as he might need a lifeboat one day and offered the constable twenty pounds. "Don't be silly lad. There's a box on the harbour wall over there. I'll be watching mind."

Pam and the kids came over and young Tom was pleased. "Well done Daddy, another baddy caught eh?" The constable thanked Thor again and promised to leave a pint in the Ferryman for saving his embarrassment of losing his helmet.

Halfway round the supermarket Pam bumped trolleys with Mary Hynge, AKA Janet the physiotherapist. She was with her friend who had come to the rugby game. "Hi Pam," said Janet, cooing over how cute the Orre children were, "Are you by yourself today?" Pam told her that Thor was over near the tools counter. There were always special offers on that he couldn't resist. He would buy things that they neither needed, nor would ever use, Pam told her. "I've banned him from buying any more hooks, we've kitchen cupboards full of them and he's screwed the so called useful hooks all over the house. He's a one for screwing."

"Lucky you." Said Janet. The three women laughed just as Thor came back grinning like a Cheshire cat and carrying a huge sledge hammer with a long handle. "Look at this," He said, "twenty eight pound in weight and only sixteen pounds in money, too good to be missed." Pam looked at the other two girls and said "See what I mean." The girls laughed again as did Penny Orre. Young Tom just said "Wow dad let's see if I can lift it." He couldn't. Janet asked Thor if it would be OK if she gave the kids a pound each. Thor told her to ask senior management, nodding towards Pam. Pam gave the OK but told the children they mustn't spend it all on sweets.

Thor asked why they were shopping in Newport when they had a Cheap as Chips supermarket nearer home. Janet's friend, Sindy, explained that the group that owned the beauty salon and tanning shop that she worked in, had recently bought one in Newport and she had been asked to manage it and set up a tanning parlour. Thor asked if it was Penhale Enhancements. Sindy confirmed this but asked him to keep it under wraps for now or she might get into trouble. The two girls said goodbye and pushed off, literally as their trolley was quite full and heavy. Penny and young Tom shouted their thank you after them.

"Sugar must be going to be scarce Tom," said Pam, "Did you notice that the girls were stocking up on it? They had bags of sugar in their trolley. We must get some more. I remember your mum telling me about a sugar shortage in the 1970's." She guided the family back three aisles and put six bags of sugar in their trolley for themselves and another two for Evor. Other shoppers remarked on this and took extra sugar. By 3pm there was no sugar to be had in Newport and shoppers had started to drive to Malvil and Castra for the stuff.

The Orre family were blissfully unaware of the run on sugar as they sat in the Lobster Pot café, tucking into fish and chips.

Thor commented that he should really bring his uniform over when working 2 to 10 shift on a Saturday as it would save him having to travel back again to Haven to change into it. "You can forget that," Pam said firmly, "how would I carry all this shopping plus your stupid big hammer up from the harbour without you, especially with all this sugar?"
Northern bloke had met his wife in Newport station and was a foot passenger on the same ferry back as the Orres. He sat down next to Thor. "Sorry about the other night mate. I hope that there's no hard feelings about things. I shouldn't have called you a Luddite Tom."

Thor told him he hadn't been offended by that and said "look Norm, we are bound to disagree strongly about things over the next month or so. I propose that we play fair and be honest with the members and each other. You want what you call progress, I want the status quo. We do need to keep our friendship no matter what. If we both agree to abide by the majority decision and never mention it again, we'll get by. Agreed?" Norman agreed.

"One thing Norm. I'm sorry, but I found your racist stance difficult to swallow. I won't mention it again but can you keep your opinions to yourself on that issue please? You are a good bloke and I don't want you to put yourself in a bad light." Northern Bloke stroked his chin then looked Thor in the eyes, smiled and said "Agreed. You fancy a pint?" Thor replied "You'll never know how much I fancy a pint but I'm in work in an hour and a half. I'll buy you a beer in the week mate." Thor showed Norman his new sledge hammer Norman was suitably impressed.

Pam turned to Mrs Northern. "Boys and their toys." She said.

Curly and Eloise had just missed the Ferry. "That'll put us late for lunch now," Curly grumbled, "It's your fault spending so long in the bloody make up shop. You don't even need it, you're so attractive." He added the latter remark to get in good books. He was a man with a plan.

Alighting from the next ferry, the Jones's decided to drive the hundred and fifty yards to the pub and have lunch in there. Sitting outside was Norman Arkwright, waiting for Mrs Northern to meet him for lunch. Curly nodded a hello and went to the bar. He bought a pint for himself, one for Northern bloke and two gin and tonics for their respective good ladies. "Here you go Norm," said Curly, handing over the ale. Eloise had gone to the ladies so Curly tapped his nose in the age old sign for, keep this secret. "I need a chat Norm, in private. How about popping over to the Sailors Arms over the water early evening. We can speak in confidence over there."

Norman promised to clear matters with Mrs Northern who was coming down the lane.

The four sat in the sunshine enjoying their drink and perusing the simple but sumptuous menu. There was nothing particularly sumptuous about it except for the words "Enjoy our sumptuous menu," typed at the top. All were surprised when Nick Haydn – Smythe turned up, waiting at table. He explained that funds were short as he'd bought a new car and he was putting in a shift to reduce his bar bill.

The four enjoyed their meal. Mrs Northern gushed about Eloise's jewellery and her outfit, this put Eloise in a good humour and she didn't complain when Curly mentioned on the way home that he needed time to speak seriously with Northern bloke, in private about his racism. Eloise knew that Evor had tasked Curly with this and was pleased that he was being treated with this amount of respect. "At last they were being valued appropriately, wait until he's a county player," Eloise thought.

The beautiful spring afternoon drifted into becoming a beautiful spring evening. Most of the sailing craft in the estuary drifted back towards harbours and sailing clubs and in the village of Haven, all usual suspects had drifted into the bar of the Bell. Evor sat with Ian Tomkins, Bill McClaren, Jim Cameron, Eddie Bennet and Bob Church. At the next table were the younger element, Paul Bennet, Nipper Shallcock, Chubby, Teflon and a couple of lads from the football club.

The younger gang had eyes glued to the football results on the television. The mature gentlemen's eyes were glued to Myfanwy's low cut blouse and much banter went back and forth. Evor was at the bar when Harry Thelwell popped in. Seeing Evor's chair empty Harry said "Bloody hell! Has Evor kicked the bucket?" I'm here," said Evor from the bar "what you drinking you cheeky bugger?"

Harry asked for a guest ale and said "Being serious for a moment Evor, can I have your golf clubs when you do croak? Your Tom doesn't play and Tommo here will probably go before you." This was all meant in jest and others soon joined in. "I'll tell you what," said Nipper. "It'll be a great night in here when Evor does shuffle off this mortal coil. He's a great man and I'm sure he'll have left money for a damn good drink behind for his friends."

"You cheeky bastards," shouted Evor, "I'll see you all out. Yes, I will leave a good drink for my friends but there's no bloody friends of mine in this bar tonight." A cheer went up as Evor had taken the bait once again. "Tell you what Evor," said the saint, "you're easier to catch than a bloody mackerel." More cheering and banter ensued. The few early season tourists thought how cruel to bait an elderly chap about his demise. Evor enjoyed every minute of it.

From 6-30 to 7-30 the chaps would go home to partners and continue with the plans for the weekend but the Saturday teatime in the Bell was a ritual that was rarely missed. "Thor working today Evor?" Asked Paul Bennet. Evor confirmed this. "Your brother on shift Paul?" Teflon asked. "No. He's out drifting the currents as usual." Paul replied. Mike spent hours out in the estuary when not on shift as coxswain of Haven lifeboat. Although he was only thirty, no man knew the tides, currents and winds of the estuary like him. "Where are Curly and Northern Bloke then?" asked Paul, looking at Evor. "Paul, I'm not the village keeper," was his reply.

Speculation took place as to the whereabouts of the two absentees. It was eventually decided that Eloise had made

Curly an offer he couldn't refuse and that, as Mrs Northern had arrived that afternoon, Norman was also "emptying his tanks" as Chubby succinctly put it. Jim Cameron stated that Eloise wouldn't have to ask him twice and made a thrusting movement with his hips. Most agreed and laughed, except Nipper who stated that in his opinion it was out of order to say things like that about a club mate's wife and left for home.

As Nipper barged out of the bar he was surprised to see that Curly and Northern bloke had slipped past the pub and were boarding the ferry as foot passengers. He almost went back to tell everyone but hunger got the better of him and his mum had promised stew with dumplings for tea.

Twenty minutes later Curly and Northern Bloke were sat in the Sailors Arms in Newport. Norman's first beer hadn't touched the sides so he nudged Curly to hurry up and refill. "Oh, was this a wise idea?" thought Curly. Although Northern Bloke wasn't a real big drinker like say Thor or Evor, he could be a dangerous quaffer when he had his beer head on. Tonight looked like being one of those nights.

The Sailors was one of five or six pubs in the market square that overlooked Newport harbour. Only a short walk from where the ferry landed and not much further, from the railway station it was the first call of many a thirsty traveller. The pub had seen better days but the beer was good and the atmosphere friendly. You could also see all the other pubs in the square from the front window and Curly had positioned himself in order to look out for the hen parties. Norman disapproved of Curlys philandering. Well disapproved when sober that is. Curly had three skills, rugby, womanising and the ability to lead good men astray. First however he had to tackle the difficult issue as he had promised Evor.

Norman had outlined the proposed sponsorship deal. He was fair and also pointed out the fact that Thor has misgivings and listed them for Curly's benefit. Curly listened intently. He immediately saw a possible trade off with Thor, his support against the proposal for Thor's agreement to play for Malvil. Norman asked what Curly's stance would be, informing Curly that he, Norman Arkwright, loved the club as much as anyone and intended to move here permanently with his wife, who had informed him today that she had agreed to such a move soon. He opened his heart to Curly and told him that one day he would like to hold the position of high esteem that Evor currently held. He naturally promised not to usurp Evor, who he loved dearly but to wait until Evor wished to step aside.

Curly saw an opening here, for despite being the club clown, he was no fool. "Norman, I understand how you feel and although I need time to think over my stance. I appreciate your frankness and hope to be able to support you. I may even be able to win Thor over but no promises yet." Two more beers were called for.

Curly unknowingly slipped into his legal persona. "I have heard tell my friend of your issues with black people." Curly paused and grimaced. "You must know that to espouse these feelings in public may prevent you from achieving your goal of holding any position of high esteem. Indeed Norman it may even put your present position in some jeopardy. You need to grasp that the days of racism, colour prejudice, call it what you will, are gone. If you really do hold such feelings, you must bury them in the deepest chamber of your soul. To make them public will turn the majority against you. Do you see?"

Norman looked shocked. "I hadn't bargained on everyone being such mealy mouthed liberals John. What are your true feelings on having black chaps playing for the team?"

Curly hadn't really thought about it and said as much. "It's not something that I've ever given a lot of thought to. I wouldn't object and if I didn't like it I certainly wouldn't shout it from the rooftops in the current climate. I need to understand your feelings here a little better."

Northern Bloke sighed but had anger in his eyes. "I don't see why I should cow tow to blackies, wogs or any other bloody foreigner John. I'm English and proud like you. Don't you feel that you're superior?"

Curly had teased him with the bait and he had taken it. "Norman your argument doesn't stand up. Look at me, I'm short, brown eyed, with Mediteranean skin and black curly hair. Thor calls me a Moroccan camel herder. In truth, were it possible to trace my ancestors. I'm probably derived from a centurion of the XIII legion in Castra nearly seventeen hundred years ago. I'm not from these islands any more than a man from Jamaica is. The only difference is that I've been here longer. You're proud of being English, you say? England is named after the Angles, also not from these islands. This country of ours is named after a Germanic people who turned up here some twelve hundred or so years ago. Do I feel I'm superior you ask. I do feel superior to many people, that is to say intellectually superior to anyone daft enough to believe himself to be superior merely because of his skin colour. I don't mean to offend you Norman. You're a friend and a highly intelligent and likeable human being but it's not because you're white that I like you. Do you really, I mean really in your head, think that you're a better man than say, Nelson Mandela?" Curly had looked pained and raised his voice a little for effect.

Norman said nothing for some time, then, quietly "You don't understand John. You don't know enough about me or my background to grasp how I feel "Curly responded quietly "Then tell me Norman. Tell and I'll try to understand but first I'll get two more beers."

Curly returned from the bar. He noticed his friends shoulders had dropped. You get to be an expert in body language in Curly's line of work. Norman took a gulp of the malty brew, looked at Curly and began. "My father was a diplomat. He served mostly in West Africa. He met my mother during a flight, she was an air hostess with BOAC. They married and had a child, me. Two years later they had another, my sister Andrea. I was sent to school in England and suffered the usual bullying etcetera that goes with an all boys school. Andrea went to a local school and lived with our parents as it was deemed unnecessary to educate her so well. I loved my visits back to Africa and I was loved, if at a distance by my parents and my sister." He took out a handkerchief and wiped some moisture from his eyes. "John, please. This is for your ears only." Curly nodded.

Norman continued "One day, when I was fourteen, I was called into the headmasters study. My uncle was there and told me, in a matter of fact way, that my father was dead." He paused again, "I was informed that mother had left him and gone to live with our black gardener, Joseph. Father had been shunned by the ex pat community. He had taken to the bottle and one night shot himself through the head on the veranda of our house. Uncle Derek took me back for the funeral. My mother didn't even turn up and I've never seen her since. Uncle Derek and Aunty Judith took us in and brought us up in Lytham St Annes. I finished school at eighteen and was about to join the army, who were to sponsor me through university," Here Norman burst into tears.

When back under control he looked at Curly "At sixteen years old my sister hanged herself. I came home one Saturday and she was missing. We found her at the bottom of the garden. Now do you understand John?"

Curly put his head in his hands and breathed deeply for some time. He was thankful that he had brought Norman over to Newport as this revelation could not have come about in the Bell. There would have been too many interruptions and the atmosphere would have been wrong.

"Norman, thank you for trusting me. I'm moved by your story. My lips will remain sealed unless you ask me to inform anyone." Curly paused. "I can understand why you are angry and bitter but should your anger be directed at black people or those imbeciles who shunned your father? Good men and women would have offered support, not turned away. Please Norman think on that point. I'm not a religious man and as you know I lost my parents at a similar age. I am angry at that loss but have nowhere to direct my anger. I know it was freak weather that caused their deaths but although I hurt like you do I don't hate. I urge you as a friend to change your stance, not just because it's wrong but because it will destroy you in the end."

Norman was silent for a while then patted Curly on the knee. "Thanks John. You're a true friend."

A moment or so later a handful of mature ladies, dressed in Can Can dresses burst into the pub and ordered a round of drinks in London accents. The pub had changed at the flick of a switch from quiet local to instant party. Curly thought "Well done girls. I couldn't have ordered it to be timed better. Now for some fun!"

It had gone dark and Thor was sat with Mike Maddox, in the police station, going through the file on open incidents. Graham was making a brew. It had not been too bad a shift but the police would doubtless get busier later when A shift had taken over. Mike and Graham had broken up a fight in the Crown Inn between two groups of lads dressed as children's TV favourites. They had calmed it down but as often happens, one on each side wouldn't stop and two arrests had been made.

Mike had low morale. "Here I am Tom, all my years in the job and I'm arresting bloody flower pot men." He had brought in either Bill or Ben and was ridiculed by other revellers at every pub he had to walk past. "You're lucky," said Big Graham, coming in with three mugs of tea and a packet of biscuits. "I had to drag a Telly Tubby, La La in, with his arm up his back. I was booed, spat at and called pig, all the way here."

"Are you daft?" asked his sergeant. "Didn't you think of making him take his suit off?" Graham replied that in his judgement it would have been worse. La La was naked under the suit."

The sergeant's radio came to life with a report from the operator at HQ that a man was being watched on CCTV, defecating into the hat of Stan Laurel outside the theatre. "Come with me Graham. Mike, watch the shop please." Then as an afterthought "You think you've had it tough? I'm a sergeant going to deal with incontinence problems." This cheered Mike Maddox up no end.

The theatre was in the square near the harbour. On the pedestrian area outside was a statue of Laurel and Hardy, holding out their bowler hats. Sure enough, in Stan's hat sat a couple of turds.

"That's him in the white rugby shirt outside the sailors," said the voice on Thor's radio. The two officers strolled over to where the stag group from the North were sat outside at tables. Thor tapped the man in the white shirt. He turned. "You again," said Thor. It was the same second row who had stolen the helmet earlier. "What are you, some kind of one man crime spree?" The chap responded that he hadn't done anything wrong. Thor pointed to a tall lamppost in the centre of the square then at the corner of the theatre itself. "See them lad? They are CCTV cameras. Our lady operative at HQ has had the dubious pleasure of watching you shit in Stan Laurels hat. This joy she has shared with many good citizens and guests of fair Newport."

The group laughed. The Second Row blushed and stammered an apology. He then followed the officer over to survey the scene of the crime. "Please don't arrest me. I'll lose my job and I'm due to get married myself in August," he wailed. "Don't think of coming here for your bloody stag do fellah." Thor told him. The lad looked crestfallen and Thor felt sorry for him but needed to teach him a lesson. He looked at his constable, who was just about containing his laughter at the absurdity of the situation.

"OK," said the sergeant, "I suppose, if there was no evidence, I couldn't arrest you." Second Row asked what he meant. "Well, if those turds were to disappear rapidly into the poop scoop bin over there," Thor pointed, "I'd have no evidence would I?"

It slowly dawned on the Northern lad that Thor wanted him to move his own mess. He searched his drunken brain for a solution. Oh, how he wished he had brought more socks. He'd been dancing in a fountain earlier and had only his shoes on his feet. Socks would have been perfect for clearing the mess.

A crowd had gathered and one of his mates was videoing the scene. He considered running but recalled Thor's tackle earlier and dismissed the idea. "I only have this shirt sergeant and my fiancé bought it for my birthday. It's a special edition." Thor shrugged "Ok. Arrest it is then," unclipping his cuffs from his belt. "No, no, no! Please," said the lad. Slowly he took off his shirt to the cheers of the crowd. He looked at the hat and with stuttering movements scooped the offending material into his shirt, took it over to the bin and deposited shirt and poo inside. The crowd howled with laughter he was aghast but pleased to have avoided arrest. He turned to walk away.

"What about that?" this was the sergeant again, pointing to a third stool that must have missed the hat and sat accusingly on the pavement. "Nooooooo!" the lad cried. "What can I do?" he looked at the sergeant imploring him for help. "Nothing has changed. Remove the evidence or face arrest."
The crowd was hushed and to be fair, neither protagonist in the scene was particularly aware of the crowd. "It's your shit fellah. I suggest you pick it up." The lad had no choice. He looked away, knelt down and felt towards the stool. He gagged as his thumb rolled it towards his reluctant fingers. Oh how he regretted his actions. Where were all the guys who had egged him on? He was betrayed, in his hour of need no one came to help.

Then it was up away and into the bin. He wanted to look at his fingers but didn't dare.

"Right! It's back to your hotel now and you can stay there until morning. If I see you outside your hotel, you're nicked. Understand?" The lad nodded said "No hard feelings," and held out his hand. Thor nearly took it. Instead he looked at it in disgust and said "You nearly got me. Now bugger off!"

"Sarge," whispered the big PC, "you deserve a knighthood."

On the way back to the police station Thor and Graham were joined by another Northern Bloke, Norman Arkwright. He had asked Thor what time he was finishing his shift. Thor looked at his watch "Twenty bloody minutes ago mate. I suppose you want a lift round?"

Thor handed over to A shift, describing the second row and stipulating if seen out he should be arrested. Mike told him that the Flowerpot man was claiming wrongful arrest, claiming that he was Bill and Ben was the culprit. "Tough," said Thor, "If we let him go we'll have to release La La as well or else Human Resources will be bollocking us for Telly Tubby prejudice."

On the drive home Norman had told Thor that Curly had gone off to the Travelodge with a chubby, middle aged scrubber. "I tried to talk him out of it Tom but his mind was set. He'd had a few pints" Norman stated. "Don't worry Norm," said Thor, "I've tried talking sense with him about women over a period of years. I've even tried when he's stone cold sober and guess what? He ignores me too."

As he snuggled down next to Pam Thor gave serious thought to moving elsewhere.

Chapter 11 – Sunday, A Day of Rest?

Thor woke to the sound of the vacuum cleaner. He looked at the alarm clock whose bright red digits indignantly proclaimed it to be 08-17 hours. "It is Sunday?" Thor questioned himself, "What's going on?"

He put on a pair of shorts, he didn't own pyjamas, and went down stairs. The kids were up and outside feeding the chickens. Pam was moving through the house like a whirlwind, pushing the vacuum cleaner in front of her. The place smelt of furniture polish that got at the back of Thor's throat, causing him to cough. He went into the kitchen and smelt the more pleasant aromas of fresh ground coffee and a cake baking in the oven. He noticed the baking bowl on the table and scooped a finger full of deliciously sweet mixture into his mouth. He hated the sound of the vacuum and Pam usually only used it when he was out but his second scoop of cake mixture made up for the hated din.

"Stop that now! It's unhygienic and I've told you about it many a time." Pam picked up a tea towel and lashed him hard across the buttocks with it.
"What a poor example to the kids you are. You should be ashamed." She shrieked, lashing him again, even harder.

He scratched his blond mop and asked if she had put the house up for sale or something. He recalled reading that the smell of real coffee and baking were supposed to entice prospective buyers. "You great oaf! Have you forgotten that the Craddocks are visiting today? They're due at ten so can you shift all the shoes out of the back porch for today, and cut the front grass. Then for gods sake, get showered and look respectable and that doesn't mean track suit bottoms and an old rugby shirt. "What shall I wear beloved?" asked Thor. "You're a grown man." Pam replied. "Anything you want as long as it's appropriate."

This is a dangerous moment for all males. We're bound to get it wrong and be told to go and get changed again but if we ask for more advice we look stupid. Thor didn't know what to wear. Then, as Pam moved away to vacuum the stairs his saviour appeared. Curly Jones didn't look like the messiah. He did look a mess however. His hair was bedraggled, he was unshaven and had red lipstick on his neck.

Curly stuck his head round the back door. "Tom," He whispered, "I need an alibi for last night." He smiled at Thor who scowled back. "No way mate I'm not lying for you again. You'll have to face the music."

"Shhh," pleaded Curly, "I thought you could say that your colleague found me drunk just after you left and he let me sleep in the cells. How's that sound buddy?" Pam shouted down to see who Tom was talking to. "It's only Curly love. He spent a night in the nick, having missed the ferry and a lift from me. You swine Curly! There I've bloody lied for you again. This is the very last time. Oh wash your neck" Tom whispered loudly. Curly looked in the mirror and wiped the lipstick "Cheers mate. If I can ever do anything for you, just ask."

Tom said that as a matter of fact he did need some advice. He explained the dress issue and accepted the advice from the only man in the team who understood what women really mean when they say "Anything you want".

An hour later Pam answered the front door and greeted the Craddock family. Tom had asked a favour of the sergeant on the shift before his. It had been agreed that he would cover for Tom until 4pm, Tom would do a night shift for him in three weeks.

Pam Craddock was dressed in jeans, a Malvil West T shirt and trainers. Peter's outfit matched hers as did the clothes of the two children. Pam Orre also wore jeans and a new white blouse. Penny Orre had a skirt and my little pony T shirt. Her brother had shorts and a Manchester City shirt. Pam ushered everyone into the front room and called upstairs to Tom. "Tom the Craddocks are here darling."

Tom bounded down stairs and burst into the front room beaming his biggest smile, which immediately dropped away. The two Pams looked shocked. Peter could not stifle a giggle. There stood Thomas Henry Orre, resplendent in best shiny black shoes, perfectly creased black trousers, white shirt, blazer and gaudy tie. "Have you done this for a joke?" asked his wife. "I'll bloody kill Curly Jones." Was Tom's response. "I'll be changed in a jiffy. Sorry Pam."

Thor returned, red faced to be given a big hug by his wife. "Well, he might be an idiot, as I was saying but he's my big idiot and I love him." She said.

Pete Cradock said "Don't worry Tom. That romantic moment won't be passed on to your team mates, well not unless I find myself with an empty glass at any time on tour." Thor grinned wider and went even redder.

After a coffee and some cake the Pams went for a tour of the house and Thor told his kids to show the young Craddocks the chickens then they could go across to play on the green for half an hour if they promised to keep clean. With a blur of movement and slamming of doors Tom and Pete were alone in the lounge.

"Thanks for inviting me on tour Tom. I'm really looking forward to it. I'm getting a bit of stick from my team mates, they're calling me traitor and turncoat. It's only in jest though so I've wound them up by telling them I might play for Haven next season. That should cause a rumpus at the next committee meeting." Tom said that he'd welcome Peter here but pointed out that he might not get picked for the county if he played for a little club like Haven. "That's not why I play Tom." Peter looked hurt at Thor's suggestion.

"Sorry Pete. No offence intended mate." Thor paused "Why do you play Pete?" He asked.

Pete looked at Thor, finished his coffee and explained why. "My dad played. He told me it was a way for us black guys to be accepted and make friends. I played at school and at Uni. It has helped me to be accepted, I have made friends and if I say so myself I'm not a bad number eight. At least that's what I thought until some big Saxon warrior played me off the park last week. Tom you're bloody good. If you had the right coaching who knows what you could achieve."

Tom reddened again. He wasn't good at taking praise. "Behave yourself Pete. You haven't come down here to try to persuade me to play for Malvil have you? I tell you I'm committed to Haven one hundred percent." Pete assured Tom that he had no ulterior motive and that the visit was purely to cement a family friendship that he had maybe taken for granted.

"Pete I'm only joking and you can take my friendship as a given." Thor held out a big white paw which was grabbed and held in a big black one. The two men smiled at each other. It was as if they had been friends all their lives

Thor shouted upstairs to Pam that he and Pete would stroll down to the green to keep an eye on the kids. Pam said that they would follow on after she had shown her friend the wedding photos. "Aaaargh !" went Thor "Time for us to leg it Pete or we'll never get to the pub."

The two men had settled onto a bench overlooking the green and the four youngsters happily tossing a rugby ball back and forth. Thor put on a serious face and asked his friend a difficult question. "Pete, there's something personal I want to ask you about."

"Fire away. Be as personal as you like but I'm not going to give you any advice on my renowned love making technique." Pete said with a cheeky grin.

"You touched on something earlier, in the house. When I asked why you played rugby." Thor paused, not knowing how to put his question. "Pete. Do you come across much prejudice? You know with you being black."

Pete replied "No Massa. I is one happy boy." Then he saw that Thor was asking out of worry and became sensible himself.

"There will always be prejudice Tom. It's part of the tribal nature of being a human. If it isn't for skin colour it would be for religion, sexuality, accent, upbringing or one of a hundred other things. I probably feel it less than my dad who feels it less than Grandpa Craddock did. Hopefully the kids will find it scarce as society adapts to change. I worry for Pam as she gets the occasional look or utterance for being married to me.

It's mostly from the older generation or the less intelligent. She says it doesn't bother her but it must hurt. I initially turned her marriage proposal down and tried to end our relationship, for her sake but she was strong, strong enough for us both. I can guess why you ask. I don't want to cause any difficulties for you or your beloved Haven Tom. I'd rather not come on tour with you than be a problem."

"Hell no!" Thor replied "I'll be honest and tell you that we had one dissenting voice about bringing a black guy on tour but if my club tolerated that sort of behaviour I wouldn't want to be a part of it and yes that is about the only way I would join Malvil. It's been sorted and you're definitely coming. It was a unanimous club decision."

Pete asked if he was sure. Thor promised he had told the truth.

"One more question Pete. Do you have a nickname? Everyone here gets called by something other than their real name. What's yours?"

Pete laughed aloud with a deep peel of laughter that seemed to echo across the water. "Well Thor, at school I was affectionately known as Nigger but you've made it clear that's not an option."

The two Pams rounded the corner to see their husbands sobbing with laughter, arms round each other. The kids had run across and joined the laughing for no other reason than it was infectious.

The men couldn't stop to respond to the questioning about their mirth. Eventually Pete recovered enough to run across to the shop. He returned seconds later still giggling. "I do have another nickname."

"No Pete. No!" said his wife.

Pete set off laughing again and despite being in obvious distress and having difficulty with speech, he squeaked through bitten lips "It's, cos, it's custard."

He produced a custard tart from a paper bag, held it on his palm and inserted the whole thing into his mouth in one. His cheeks bulged, Thors jaw dropped open, the kids looked stunned, Pam Orrs eyes popped out of her head and Pam Craddock removed a trainer and beat her husband around the head with it.

"You simpleton! Look how you've embarrassed everyone! Girls never marry a rugby player, their brains don't work properly." She hit him again.

Pete tried to swallow the custard whole, as was his custom when showing his party trick but the laughter could not be held back. He put his hand firmly over his mouth but custard snorted out of his nostrils and he began to choke while still laughing.

"Awesome Dad" was his son's opinion.

Everyone even Pam C had to laugh at this. Pam Orre had tears rolling down her cheeks. Eventually the laughter subsided and Pete was mumbling "Sorry, sorry love." While trying to clean custard from his shirt with a handkerchief.

"So Pete, why are you called Custard then?" asked Thor while holding his sides." Do you want me to show you?" asked Pete and the laughter started again.

Sometime later the two families sat in the pub, replete after a Sunday lunch and puddings all round. Thor was cursing about being on shift. This meant that he couldn't have a beer and had to drink orange cordial instead of the Robinsons bitter that Pete was enjoying. "I'll tell you what mate" said Thor "Beer drinking, it's not a spectator sport you know." Pete lifted his glass and drained it. "Aaaaah! That's so good. I think I'll have another."

"I'll get them in Peter and for you ladies, children and another orange for you Thor?"

Thor was stunned to turn round and see Northern Bloke. "Looking forward to touring with us Peter?" Northern bloke continued. Polite conversation was made as Norman Arkwright shook hands with Pete and Pam Craddock before going to the bar and ordering a round of drinks.

"Tom. Tom! You've gone into a trance. What's the matter with you? Are you OK?" asked Pam Orre.

Thor was not OK. He was wondering if he had dreamt about Northern Bloke's racism or if he was dreaming now. He shook himself and mumbled something about thinking about a police problem, then smiled again in time to thank Northern Bloke for his orange.

Pete thanked Northern Bloke and asked him to join them. "I'm in the bar thanks Peter, with a bunch of ruffians. We'll have plenty of time for a good chin wag on tour. See you again folks." With that he waved and was gone.

Curly and Eloise came into the pub. Eloise, as usual was dressed to impress. She wore pink leather trousers with matching shoes. Her nails and lipstick were the same shade of pink. It was obvious to every male in the pub that Eloise was braless under her tight white T shirt. Young Penny Orre shouted "Wow Aunty Elly, you look gorgeous. You are my famous Aunty."

Eloise warmed to Penny's praise and gave her a hug "You look lovely too my sweet. I like your little pony T shirt." Pam Craddock leant over to Pam Orre and whispered "There's a lot more material in Penny's than hers."

Thor introduced everyone, then Pam told Curly about Thor coming down in his best bib and tucker. Eloise apologised for Curly using the police station as a hotel. She hadn't given him a hard time as for once he'd done the sensible thing she said.

"Hell I'm due in work." Thor shouted. As Curly hadn't had a drink he offered to drive Thor round. Thor accepted saying that he would forgive Curly for his clothing prank in return for the lift.

Within half an hour Curly had dropped his friend off at the police station in Newport, had dropped the car at home and jogged steadily down to the pub. Pete Craddock's family were about to leave with the Orre's. The Orre children pestered Curly to do some magic. Their mother told them not to pester Uncle Curly but curly winked at Pam and asked them both to close their eyes and shout the magic word. "Aboodiboo" they hollered in unison. This caused a hush to fall over the pub which was followed by a peel of delight when Curly produced a small chocolate egg from behind the ears of both Penny and her brother.

The Craddock children clapped and Curly asked them to check behind their ears. There was nothing. "I know" said Curly "sometimes this goes a bit wrong. Stand up!" The children stood and Lo! On each of their chairs was a small chocolate egg. Everyone clapped and even Eloise, who was used to Curly's tricks, asked how he did it.

"Magic" said Curly.

Over the water Thor had thanked Sergeant Bent for delaying his departure and deploying his shift. He was a bit dismayed when Dave Bent informed him that a couple of the team had been mumbling their dissatisfaction with the fact that their new sergeant had called them stupid. "That doesn't seem like your style Tom. Did they upset you?" Thor replied that he genuinely did not know what he was talking about

"Well if you'll take a bit of advice from an old hand, I'd get them in and clear the air before it festers and you lose them." Sergeant Bent offered.

When Dave Bent had gone, Thor pondered on the matter but could find no sense in it. At the end of yesterdays shift everyone said goodnight in a friendly manner and he certainly hadn't questioned anyone's intelligence. He was happy with his shift, until now that was. He decided there was no point putting the matter off and radioed them to come into the station ASAP,

As the weekend revellers had all gone home, Newport had quietened down. Sunday night was often a light shift and with the exception of Danny Daniels and Lucy Lamont who were dealing with a domestic on the Mount Pleasant estate, the rest of the shift all arrived within ten minutes of each other. Thor made them all a brew and asked if anything was happening in the area today.

As expected all was calm. Graham Gascoine said that he'd heard that the transport police had arrested someone on the afternoon train going north from Castra for streaking naked through the train. "Any bets on this one folks?" asked Thor "I'll stake my pension on it being that bloody daft lad who shat in the hat."

The expected laughter did not happen.

Danny and Lucy arrived in due course and Thor made them a brew. "Right, I expect you're all wondering why I've brought you all in." He looked round at them but no one spoke "OK, from your reaction even I can work out that you're not happy about something. What is it?"

Again no answer.

"Mike?" Thor said Mike Maddox's name as a question. Mike shrugged.

"Look you're annoyed at something. I don't know what it is and if I don't know what it is how can I be expected to put it right? If I'm at fault give me a chance to correct it will you?"

After another, seemingly week long pause, Lucy spoke. "You think we're all thick. We're not and we don't like it. Can you blame us?"

"What?" asked Thor "I'm really sorry Lucy but I honestly haven't got a bloody clue what you're talking about. Please enlighten me?"

Lucy looked embarrassed and looked sheepishly at Danny Daniels who looked furious. Danny stared at Thor "Alright. Last night you and I were leaving and you said that we were all thick bar you." Thor said that he had said no such thing and that he had been happy, very happy with the shift until now.

"I wouldn't make this up sergeant Orre. You called us thick. Don't deny it." Danny spat.

Thor looked puzzled and then it dawned on him. "Danny, what were my exact words please?"

"Does it matter? You called us stupid and that's it" said Danny. Thor said that his exact words did matter as there had been a misunderstanding.

"Ok" said Danny "You said that we were all illiterate bar you. That's bloody nonsense as everyone can read and write as you well know."

Thor beamed "Danny firstly you owe me an apology. Secondly wash your ears out, a lack of exact understanding could one day create an inappropriate action, as it has in this case. Thirdly if any of you are ever unhappy, tell me. It works far better than sulking among yourselves. I didn't say that you're illiterate. I said that you're all alliterative except me. An alliterative name is one that begins with the same sound or letters. Danny Daniels, Tony Taylor, Mike Maddox, Lucy Lamont, Sonia Smith, Simon Smith, Graham Gascoine. Me? I'm Tom Orre. No alliteration there."

Thor watched as it sunk into his team.

Danny spoke first. "I'm sorry Serge. I must be thick and I take full responsibility for passing it on to the team. I should have queried it with you. Sorry everybody. It's my fault and I'm bloody embarrassed about it now."

"You know, daft as it sounds, I never noticed that we all had names like that. What a strange coincidence." Said Mike Maddox. Lucy and Sonia both said that they had noticed that the other female had names starting with the same letter but hadn't picked up that the men had too.

Danny continued to apologise to his sergeant.

"Ok everybody. I wish I'd never said it" responded Thor "but in a way I'm glad it happened as we've all learned something. I suppose I should thank you Danny for causing a rumpus. Now unless anyone has any questions or anything to add, back out you go and keep the streets of Newport safe." This last comment was said in an overplayed American accent that brought the hoped for laugh from the team.

Danny was the last to leave. "Thanks Serge." He said as he picked up his helmet. "History now Dan. Forget it mate. Oh, grab Graham and have a pass down by the banking streets please." Was Thor's reply.

As Danny opened the door to leave both he and Thor were stunned to see Inspector Hardy outside. He never came near on a Sunday. Danny saluted t'inspector and Thor stood up to salute but was waved down again. Danny got out as fast as he could.

"Sergeant Orre." Inspector Hardy mused "If that wasn't the best example of man management I've seen in all my time in the force, then I'll be a Chinaman." There wasn't a hint of northern accent in the sentence. T'inspector smiled "See thee Monday lad." And with that he was gone.

Thor made another cup of tea, looked at the clock which read 6-40pm and settled down for a quiet shift. Twenty minutes later he got a call from Danny. "Serge, I did as you asked. We parked up and had a good walk around but nothing going on and no one about. We got back in the car and were going up to Mount Pleasant. This is probably nothing but I thought it a bit odd to see a large JCB digger going into the town centre at seven o'clock on a Sunday."

Thor jumped up spilling tea all over his desk. "Get back into the square Danny. Park up out of the way and just observe. Let me know what's going on but don't, repeat do not take action. Do you understand?" Danny confirmed that he understood.

Thor radioed the rest of the shift and instructed them to get out to the main road to Castra, before the roundabout. They were told to take no action for now but to prepare to set up a road block, using their cars, if instructed to do so. Next Thor contacted Headquarters. He explained that there was a possibility of a bank robbery taking place in Newport and requested that the force helicopter and an armed response team were readied for immediate deployment if required.

Thor tapped his fingers for what seemed like hours. Had he overplayed this? He would look a complete fool if it turned out that it was just some farmer lending a machine to his mate. The clock seemed to have stopped.

Thor was beginning to despair when his radio burst into life. A very excited Danny shouted "Fuck me Sarge. You were right. The JCB has just smashed into the wall of the Shire

Building society and tried to dig out the cash machine. It hasn't come clean and he's setting up for another go."

"Stay clear Dan. They could well be armed. Your job is to stay calm and observe. No heroics! Understand?" Danny said "OK"

Thor was straight onto Headquarters. "Robbery in progress Shire Building Society. JCB and probably another vehicle involved. Request Helicopter and armed response team deploy immediately. I have set up a road block on the Castra road."

"Orre this is DCC DeGroot here. You had better be right about this. I've been dragged away from a damn good hand of bridge for this."

Thor ensured the DCC that it was really going off and was informed that the helicopter was already airborne and that armed officers were converging on the roadblock from all over the county.

"Serge, Danny here. They've got the whole cash machine out and pushed it into the back of a Mercedes van. There's a big hole in the wall where the hole in the wall was. There's four of them and they're all piling into the van. The JCB has been abandoned and they're away. Shall we follow?"

Thor could hear the banks alarm going off in the background and said "You've done a great job boys but your best help now would be to secure the site and keep people away from the hole and the JCB. Tape it off please. They can only go one way, back towards Castra."

Thor relayed this info to Mike Maddox and his colleagues who had stopped any traffic from entering the Newport road. He gave the registration number and description of the van as given to him by Danny and instructed them to set up a road block using their vehicles. Anyone leaving Newport was to be allowed out except the van. He hoped that the road would be empty, as usual at this time on a Sunday, out of season.

He passed this info on to HQ and sat looking at the map on his desk. "Oh shit!" He exclaimed. He had been thinking what he would do if he were the gang leader who found his route out of Newport blocked. He made a very quick phone call and then returned to the map.

He had decided that there were two options for the robbers. They must turn around and head back towards Newport. Then, either turn up one of the farm tracks going uphill or look for an exit in Newport itself. The worst case scenario was an armed gang driving around the town. He had to prevent this somehow.

"Danny, Serge here. Can either you or Graham drive a JCB? Ok I'll be their in two minutes. Get any civilians the hell out of it."

Neither had ever driven a JCB so Thor was off. As he burst out of the station doors he knocked over Inspector Hardy who was coming in at the same time "Sorry Sir." Thor shouted as he sprinted off down towards the square. On arrival he swung straight up into the cab of the digger. He was just about to wrench the wires out from under the dash board in order to hot wire the beast when he saw that the keys were still in the ignition. The machine coughed into life and he was away heading out of the square down towards the harbour and the road out of town.

"Stay here" he shouted as he passed Danny. "No one's to come down the Castra road No one"

He could see the police helicopter hovering further down the estuary and surmised that the van had turned. Immediately he got radio confirmation of this from Mike Maddox "Van's turned Serge. Coming back to Newport. The driver nearly dropped it on its side. He must have forgotten the weight of the cash machine in the back. Two cars of armed Bobbies have just turned up and we've sent them both in pursuit."

Thor thanked him and knew that the sirens would be heard and the helicopter could be seen from over in Haven. He knew Pam would be worrying and wished he worked further away from home. He pushed the accelerator pedal to the floor and the machine rattled up towards the high thirties MPH. He had to reach a point just on the edge of town, where the road narrowed and the promenade began, before the robbers. If he failed they would be able to cause mayhem in the town. The helicopter was getting awfully close and he could hear sirens but there it was, the narrowest point. He'd made it.

As he switched off the engine and pulled on the brake, the white van swerved around the corner only one hundred and fifty yards in front of him. It sped towards him, seemingly in slow motion. He heard the squeal of brakes, saw the smoke from the tyres and registered the shock on the drivers face as the van lurched towards the upraised shovel. It pulled up five yards short and the four men jumped out two from each side.

Immediately the two pursuit cars screeched round the corner and armed policemen had deployed. The helicopter was above. It sounded like Armageddon. The noise was deafening. Then, a loud hailer from the copter. "Police. Stand still! Drop your weapons!" This was repeated and three of the robbers did just that. The fourth was being blown by the wind from the rotor blades but he decided to make a run for it. He had a shotgun and sprinted towards the promenade. Thor was the nearest police officer and without thinking he leapt from the cab and gave chase.

Once again life seemed to be in slow motion for him. He could feel the warmth of the evening sun and took in the beauty of the sun dropping into the sea as he gave chase. He thought of his family and the common sense side of his brain issued the instruction to stop the chase. This instruction was overruled by something else in his intellect and he continued after the armed quarry.

The robber had opened a gap of some hundred yards on Thor and he jumped the promenade fence into the water. The tide was going out with a strong current. This helped the robber as he waded through the near midriff deep water towards a small boat with an outboard motor that was moored to a buoy, swinging with its stern pointing towards the sea.

Thor ran along the promenade and got in front of the boat by about twenty yards. The robber was now shoulder deep in water but had reached the boat, one of many small boats, moored outside the harbour that were used to access larger craft further out. The robber had held the shotgun high to keep it dry and on reaching the boat had tossed the gun aboard and climbed in. Thor had followed the rope from the buoy to the point where it came ashore. He now reached down and began to haul the boat in. The villain finally realised what was happening and drew a knife that he used to cut the rope.

He was now free of the land and began to pull on the cable that started the outboard motor. The outboard coughed and spluttered but would not start. The helicopter had landed, the crew not having picked up the fact that one villain had got away. Thor took in the situation and could not help but chuckle as he watched the robber frantically pulling again and again on the starter without success. "Obviously a townie" thought the big policeman.

Even without motor power the boat was being pulled out to sea by the tide and Thor had a decision to make. He felt that the robber couldn't escape but despite that common sense took a back seat again as Thor ran out along a jetty and dived into the estuary. He was a powerful swimmer and began to gain on the drifting boat.

The ebb tide was now pulling both boat and Bobby at quite a pace. Thor was hoping to catch the boat before being seen by the robber, who was still pulling at the starter, stopping occasionally to call the outboard motor some very rude names and to beat his fist down on the casing. When Thor was about twenty yards from the boat, the robber caught sight of his pursuer. He left the outboard stumbled forward and picked up the shotgun, aiming it at Thor.

Thor dived under water but wasn't quick enough to miss hearing the bang that was followed by a splash. Thor felt no pain and surfaced to see the boat a little further away but empty. He swam fir it and hauled himself aboard. Here was the shotgun but no robber. Looking seaward Thor saw the man splashing about just a way from the boat. "Help! Help me! I'm going to drown." Shouted the robber. Thor looked at both banks of the estuary, they were a good way off both, "I'll be there in a minute calm down." Thor said calmly.

The robber splashed even more and pleaded to be saved. "OK," said Thor "Stand up." The man looked puzzled. Thor repeated "Stand up!" The man stood. The water here was just above waist high as there was a notorious sandbank. The boat drifted towards the robber and Thor uncoupled his handcuffs.

The man shied away. "Look pal," Thor spat "It's the cuffs or I'll leave you here 'til next high tide. Your choice." The robber meekly held out his hands. He was cuffed and dragged unceremoniously aboard the boat where he sat shivering.

"If I were you I'd consider a different career," Thor smiled at the robber "You're fucking useless at this. You choose to rob a town that has one road in and one road out. You pick the nearest cash machine to the police station, you smash it in broad daylight then choose to go for a swim. Best of all you treat an outboard motor in an unfriendly way. You have to talk nicely to em. Watch this." Thor patted the casing of the outboard motor said "come on now, there's a nice little motor." He then gave two slow pulls on the starter followed by one quick pull. The outboard roared into life.

The robber didn't look impressed. Thor laughed out loud. The robber hadn't seen Thor turn the stop cock on the fuel line. He could have pulled the motor for a week and it wouldn't have started without fuel.

Just then a high powered engine drowned out the robber's one word reply. The Haven lifeboat roared into view and then cut engines to drift alongside. "Want any help buddy?" asked Mike Bennet.

Thor responded "Too late Mike but thanks for coming over." The quick phone call Thor had made before leaving the police station had been to ask the RNLI to put to sea and be ready for any eventuality.

As Thor steered the boat back towards the promenade he was aware of four guns trained on them by the armed police officers. He waved and shouted Sergeant Orre and one unarmed prisoner. From the shore he heard Inspector Hardy shout. "Put bloody guns down lads. He's one o mine. If anyone's goin t cause im any arm get in t queue be'ind me."

When Thor had landed and handed over the unfortunate robber, t'inspector put his arm around him "Come on lad, let's get you ome you can dry out and call it a day f t'day.

Pam was glad to see her husband at the door, even if he was soaking wet and had t'inspector in tow. "Inspector Hardy isn't it." asked Pam "would you like to come in and have a coffee, or something a touch stronger if you wish."

T'inspector thanked and said that although he never drank on duty, he wasn't on duty and after this evenings goings on he deserved a good whisky. Inspector Hardy gave Pam a rough outline of the action, sipping at his drink and grinning from ear to ear.

Thor came down after a hot shower and a change of clothes. He was still hyperactive but trying his utmost to look calm and composed. Pam told him to get off down the pub. She didn't want him banging around the house, waking the kids up and thought he thoroughly deserved some quality wind down time.

"Fancy a beer Sir?" Thor asked his boss.

"A do Tom but a've a home to get to, thanks for the offer. Do you mind if a tell y shift where y'are. Newport 'lll be crawlin wi Bobbies an a should be able to let em go?" Tom pulled a fleece on gave Pam a kiss and grabbed his wallet. T'inspector thanked Pam for the drink and left with Thor.

"There's just one thing sir." Thor asked "I'd like to put forward Danny Daniels for a commendation. It was his quick thinking that led to our result tonight." T'inspector mused as he closed the gate behind him "Good idea lad. I dunno see why you shouldna ave as much paperwork as me." Thor said that he didn't understand. The inspector was off duty and took no part in the arrest.

Thor blushed in the dark when Hardy responded that he would have reams of paper to fill in as he intended to recommend Thor for an award. He was aware who instigated the constant checks on the banking area. He knew who's quick and decisive action got air and armed support on the scene. To say nothing of arranging the road block, which prevented the crooks from escaping. On top of this there was the quick thinking, albeit not standard procedure, using the JCB to prevent the Crooks return into Newport. The call to the RNLI as a safety precaution and finally the brave act of swimming after an armed man.

"A can forgive thee f shoving me on me arse Tom but a curse the bloody paperwork lad." Tom sheepishly told him that he'd rather skip any award for himself, thus saving the inspector the paperwork. "A think not lad. See thee tommorra." Hardy winked at Tom as he climbed into his car and drove off

Chapter 12 – The Morning After The Night Before

Thomas Henry Orre had seen better days. He had come alive, just, when his wife left the bed to get the children ready for school. Pam had been as quiet as possible knowing that it was late when her husband had arrived home and had brought, what seemed like, half the Castrashire constabulary with him. In fact it was just D shift who had all come to Haven in a minibus that had returned to pick them up at around 2am. Somehow the kids had slept through the noise of eight drunken coppers, each recounting their part in the capture of the most dangerous gang since Genghis Khan's Mongol Horde.

Pam had asked the children to be extra quiet as Daddy wasn't feeling too well. Normally if Thor had overdone the booze, Pam would encourage as much din as possible from the kids to teach him a lesson. Today was different. Pam was so proud of the part her man had played in the operation and was delighted with the praise heaped on Thor by T'inspector.

Thor had washed, put on a pair of track suit bottoms and an old rugby shirt and made his way downstairs. He held on tightly to the banister as the staircase was swaying for some reason. He didn't feel too bad but couldn't fathom out why his home was behaving like a ship forging through a heavy swell. His blue eyes were red rimmed, he was unshaven and his hair, that rarely looked tidy, was like a hayrick in a gale.

He opened the kitchen door, fully expecting a full broadside from Mrs Orre. He was pleasantly surprised when she pulled a chair out for him, sat him at the table, placed a big mug of sweet tea in front of him and asked what he'd like for breakfast. He wanted a full English but thought it would be cheeky to ask for one. His sluggish brain was trying to work out what to say when the Orre children couldn't hold their peace any longer.

"Daddy did you see the police helicopter over Newtown yesterday? It was flying round for ages. There were blue lights and sirens. Were you chasing baddies Daddy? Mike Bennet sounded the lifeboat hooter and roared across in the RIB. Did you see it Daddy? Lots of people over here ran down to the harbour to see what was going on but Mummy made us go to bed. We sneaked into the bathroom and opened the window so we could see. Don't tell Mummy. Daddy tell us all about it. Ooh you do look a funny colour Daddy are you alright?"

Thor gulped a pint of water down. He mused as to why it was fairly easy to drink a pint of beer in one but damn difficult to get a pint of water down. In a sheepish voice he asked Pam for a full English and winced, ready for the lash of the tea towel. Instead she smiled and asked if they could break a family rule of, no TV in a morning, to see what was on the local news. Thor grudgingly acquiesced and Pam turned on the kitchen television, switching channels until the adverts came on followed by the tune announcing the Castrashire Today programme.

The newsreader opened up with the robbery in Newtown as the first item "Last night Castrashire police arrested a gang that have made a number of robberies in and around the county by forcing automatic teller machines from the walls of banks. Acting on information received a road block was set up outside Newtown and armed officers captured the armed gang on the Castra road." During this there was archive footage of police cars, with blue lights flashing and of the police helicopter taking off.

The newsreader continued "One of the armed robbers made to escape by boat, firing his shotgun at a brave officer who gave chase. He eventually had to be rescued by the same policeman, who he'd tried to kill moments earlier, after falling into the river Dee at ebb tide." This was accompanied by fairly clear film of these events with the words "Amateur video footage" at the bottom of the screen.

There followed an interview with Roger DeGroot, wrongly described as the Chief Constable by the lady interviewing him. DeGroot waxed lyrical about the behind the scenes intelligence work his force had undertaken and how the bravery shown by Sergeant Orre was only to be expected in such a well trained and lead police force.

"Oh my god" shouted Thor. "He's not only trying to get some praise himself but the bloody fool has just named me. My life will be a misery for a while as every bloody idiot in the county will want to shake my hand and my real mates will take the piss without mercy."

"Thomas Henry Orre. Do we use that sort of language in this house? It might be OK in the rugby dressing room but I will not have it in the family home." Pam nodded towards the children. "I think we all deserve an apology. Don't you children?" Penny answered her "Yes Daddy you're very naughty. I think you should be put to bed early tonight." Pam said that the moment Daddy came home from work tonight she would make him go straight to bed. She gave her husband a look that told him he wasn't really in bad books, rather the opposite.

After Thor had eaten his huge breakfast of bacon, black pudding, sausages, eggs, tomatoes, beans and toast he felt one hundred percent better. Pam asked if he could take the kids down to school while she washed up. This seemed a good deal to Thor as after a full English breakfast the kitchen resembled an operating theatre after a bomb blast. He put on a pair of jeans and a decent rugby shirt, checked his offspring had everything that they needed and said "See you in ten love" before pecking Pam on the cheek and setting off.

Twenty five minutes later Pam was starting to worry when a troubled looking Thor crashed in through the back door. "I was right. I was right. Penny's friend's granny grabbed me and told me what a wonderful job the police are doing. Some bloke I don't really know told me he was proud to know me and pumped my arm up and down until I was nearly sick. Two of the mums kissed me and even Anthony Leo shouted "Well done Mr Orre,"then road off on a bike that I'm sure isn't his. Oh and young nipper wanted me to have my photo taken with him to show his mates at college. Harry Thelwell said some woman who looked like a reporter had been in the shop first thing and asked where I lived. He told her to try Malvil. Good old Harry. If this is my fifteen minutes of fame, I'll be bloody grateful when it's over."

Pam laughed at her husband's troubles. She knew he hated the limelight and recalled how nervous he had been about having to speak at their wedding. She wasn't laughing an hour later when she had to take the phone off the hook and closed the curtains. Before that however they had been visited by Evor.

"Thomas lad, what the hell were you thinking of? You could have got yourself killed man. Are you bloody stupid?" Thor replied that he didn't have time to think and that he couldn't have people with guns on the streets of Newtown.

"I don't give a toss about Newtown lad and neither should you. It's only a job, not worth risking your life for. The people you should care about are this lass here." Evor hugged Pam "and those two rascals." He pointed to a picture of the young Orres. "Understand you big lump?"

Thor responded "Grandad, you know how it is" Evor cut him off in mid sentence. "I don't give a shit son." This at the top of his voice. Then he quietened down "I'm sorry Pam, sorry Thomas. Losing your Dad and your mum hurt me deeply. No one is supposed to outlive their children and certainly not their grandchildren. When I saw the news this morning I thought of how it would be for your two without you."

Evor suddenly looked old and tired "I'm sorry Tom. It's just that I love you all so much and although I'm so bloody proud of you, well I had to be strong for your sake all those years ago and I don't think I could do it again."

Thor stood up. He walked over to the old man and hugged him. "I love you too Grandad. And yes, I'll take your advice." Pam eased out of the room and gave the two big masculine men a moment to cry together. She cried herself, with happiness, at the thought of how much she loved them both.

The door bell rang. Pam answered it. There stood a female, circa thirty, plenty of make up but dressed like someone who lacked a decent salary. Behind her, sporting a worn jacket and holding a huge camera, stood the perfect caricature of a freelance photographer, which in fact is what he was.

"Hi Pam. I hope you don't mind me using your Christian name? I'm Janet Warren from the Castra Chronicle. My friends call me Bunny. Can we come in and have a chat with you and Sergeant Orre?

Pam had never closed the door in anyone's face in all her life. Her mother had brought her up to befriend anyone and to assume the best in people unless she had reason to think badly of them. Pam thought for a moment, smiled said "No!" and slammed the door in Bunny's face. She did so with a pleasant smile and justified her action to her Mum by whispering, "It's the lipstick Mum. No one who puts her lipstick on so badly can be anything but bad. Sorry".

Before Evor had finished his second cup of tea two more newspaper reporters had called at the door and received a similar, smiling rebuttal from the lady of the house. "I'm not putting up with this Grandad. I'll get my uniform on and go and bollock the next lot." Evor pointed out that this would be playing into their hands. He had a better plan. Evor would leave by the back door go through the allotment and return with his car, to the rear of the house. Thor and Pam could drive off in it while he offered a cup of tea to the reporters of which four were now outside the front gate. "You can go down to my place" Evor enthused.

"That's a great idea," Thor replied "Better still I'll drive off in the opposite direction, turn into Curly's gates, they're electric and if Curly closes them quickly behind us then by the time the press round the corner they'll assume we've headed out of town and hopefully bugger off.

After a phone call to Curly to ask for his help the plan was put into action. Evor's 1962 Morris Minor was the most unlikely get away car ever. But the plan worked better then could be hoped. Evor had invited all the reporters in for tea and by the time he'd told them who he was and got them sat down at the kitchen table, listening to old rugby stories, Thor and Pam were happily ensconced in the Jones's house telling Eloise and Curly all about it.

Pam complemented Eloise on her diamante slippers that perfectly matched her sparkling fingernails, the brooch on her expensive dressing gown and shiny eye make up but wondered why the hell bother to go to such a length to sit around at home. What Pam didn't know was that Eloise had been asleep when Thor had rang and had moved like a Dervish to be looking this way on their arrival.

Curly brought in a tray coffee with home made shortbread biscuits. Pam looked at Eloise's figure, with well disguised jealousy and noticed that she didn't eat any of the biscuits. Pam then looked at the shortbreads made a promise to herself, that one day she would get slim and enjoyed every mouthful. Eloise looked at Pam scoffing the shortbreads. She too was jealous, jealous that Pam didn't have to worry about how she looked as she was so confident, happy and contented. Eloise longed for contentment but didn't know which shop you got it from. Heaven knows she'd spent a fortune and still hadn't found it.

"Pam" asked Eloise "I don't understand why you don't want to be interviewed by the press. You could be all over the papers and when Thor goes for his commendation you could get a ball gown and maybe even be in Castrashire Life. It would be fantastic. I'd absolutely love it if Curly did something to get us noticed."

Pam said that Eloise was so stunning that she was noticed everywhere she went and didn't need any additional publicity other than her looks and dress sense. Eloise loved this sort of conversation and milked the adoration, not seeing that Pam was just mollifying her. Eloise made a few modest remarks and then asked to be excused while she went upstairs to shower and dress.

Curly thanked Pam with a knowing wink. A happy Eloise made for an easy and often cheaper day for him.

"Here's an idea" said Thor. "I've got my uniform in Evor's car. If you give me a lift round to Newtown, you can call into the Bell, with Eloise, on your return and tell the reporters that you know me. I'm sure Eloise will love that." Curly agreed that she would but wondered at the wisdom of such action nevertheless agreed to giving his friend a lift round.

"Something I've always wanted to ask" Curly prompted after a while. "Why is Evor called Evor? It's a bloody strange name mate."

"It's been in our family for generations" Thor replied "It's usually given to the firstborn male. My dad was Evor but used his second name. He also decided not to burden me with it and I've also broken the tradition. There is a reason for the name but I don't really want to go down that road just yet if you don't mind."

Thor Curly and Pam chatted about trivia for a while and it was soon gone noon when Eloise returned. Dressed in her finest and suggested a walk to the pub. She was disappointed when Thor vetoed the idea, reminding her of the reason for them being here. She perked up again when Pam outlined Thor's idea that she and Curly could call down later and maybe bump into some reporters.

The sun had come out and Eloise had rustled up a light lunch. The friends had all moved to the patio at the rear of the house, overlooking the pool. Pam was enjoying the chicken salad and commented well upon the dressing. Thor asked if there was any bread as he was "Hank Marvin". He couldn't understand why this had brought a sharp elbow into his ribs from his wife and gave a little boy lost look. This made Pam giggle

Curly had another question for his friend. He asked who he would be sharing with, as it seemed appropriate for Thor to share with Custard Craddock, as he had invited him. Thor confirmed this arrangement and said that Curly would be in with Posh Boy, Nick Haydn – Smythe. He asked if this was OK.

Curly looked uncomfortable and eventually said. "Look buddy, I understand its right for you to room with Custard but I'd rather not have to share with Nick. Can't I go in with one of the Bennet boys instead?" Thor was aghast. "What? You'd rather be in with either the silent one or his brother who never stops asking questions. Jesus John, Nick must have upset you. What's he done? We thought you two would be Ok as you're both intelligent men and are clean. You're both known for being a bit fastidious. In any case, Evor said he'd OK'd the arrangements with you. What's the problem?"

Pam looked surprised and Eloise looked as if she knew the answer already.

"I'll not beat about the bush" Curly answered "I've found out something that I didn't know when I spoke to Evor. I think Nick's a bloody poof." Thor laughed "No come on mate. What's the real reason?" he asked.

"I'm telling you Tom. He's an uphill gardener and I don't want him in my room."

Thor's laughter stopped. For the second time in under a week he'd found some totally unexpected prejudice right on his doorstep. "Curly, are you being serious?" Curly said that he was and when asked for evidence he said that he'd seen Nick's S2000 in the car park of a gay club in Castra when shopping or visiting the beauty salon with Eloise. "You saw him coming out didn't you Elly?" Curly asked his wife. Eloise was obviously uncomfortable but confirmed that she had seen Nick leaving the Bon Homme club and furtively looking up and down the street.

"Curly, he's shagging Jenny from the Bell, Jim Cameron's daughter. Do you see her looking like anything other than a happy young woman who's being well serviced? Ouch! The Ouch was in response to a rabbit punch from Pam that caught him unawares in the stomach and winded him. Thor got his breath back, apologised to Pam and Eloise, who was visibly enjoying Thor's discomfort, and carried on. "Posh has played with us all season. Have you ever seen him looking at anyone in the bath or having any movement south of the equator? No. He's as straight as you or I. In any case, even if he were a wussie, what makes you think he'd fancy you? Curly looked hurt at this and Eloise began to cry with laughter. Thor said that if Curly insisted he'd switch Posh Boy into another room but he offered Curly his absolute guarantee that Nick was not gay. Curly asked for time to think it over.

A short while later Evor rang to say that the press had left and gone to the pub. He told Curly that after two hours of Evor's old yarns he actually felt sorry for them. Thor asked Curly for the lift round to Newport, kissed his wife and said that he was sorry for all the inconvenience he had caused to Eloise and

Curly. Elloise pinched Thor's bottom and said he could repay her some other time. Pam laughed as her husband turned into a tomato once again.

The two men drove in an uncomfortable silence. On reaching the police station in Newport Thor asked if Curly had ever been molested or even approached by another man. Curly said that he hadn't.

"Why so homophobic then John?" Thor asked "You're intelligent and I consider this kind of prejudice is as stupid as colour prejudice mate. Nick's really not gay but why would it matter if he was? I've known you all my life and I am really surprised."

"It's like this Tom" Curly explained "A black guy can't help being black it's just the skin he was born with. Homo's, well they make that choice don't they?"

Thor got out of the car opened his mouth to speak but nothing came out. He closed the door, held up his hand in thanks and walked into the police station shaking his head.

He was in early. Sergeant Bent was surprised to see him. "Hello Tom, well done yesterday. My lot are gutted that it didn't happen on our shift. Me? I'm bloody grateful it didn't. I'd probably have reacted so slowly they'd have gotten clean away. T'inspector can't wipe the grin off his face. Mind you he's placing all the praise on you, unlike DeGroot, who's trying to steal your glory." Thor said that the DCC was welcome to all the praise he wanted and told Dave Bent about his troubles avoiding the press.

"Is that thee lad?" shouted inspector Hardy. "Come tha'sen here. A'd like a word." Thor went into his boss's office, sat down as he was instructed and informed that as soon as he'd set his shift up he would have to go to HQ as the DCC wanted him for a TV interview at 4-30 for the evening news. "Can't you go sir?" Thor asked politely. "Dunno worry. I ave t'go an'all. An I'm just as cheesed off as thee."

"You can drive Tom" ordered inspector Hardy, throwing the BMW keys to Thor. Once in the car Hardy gave Thor more advice "Say nowt unless you're asked a direct question, either by his lordship or the interviewer. Pause and consider if your answer reflects well on, A You, B The force in general and C Me. I understand there is some history between the lady interviewer and our beloved DCC. If his lordship the root digger gets himself in a muddle keep shtum. When he's suffered enough I may dig him out. OK?"

"Sir" was all Thor replied.

"Any question?" prompted the inspector. Thor said that he had one question but it was of a personal nature. "Go on then. I suppose you've earned the right. Just the one mind and my answer is strictly between us." The inspector obviously expected a question concerning the job. He was taken by surprise when Thor cheekily asked "Wots appened t'northern accent sir? It's gone"

Hardly burst into laughter. "You cheeky sod! I'll tell thee. I am a Yorkshire man and proud o'me accent. I can of course speak as I wish and do a bit of amateur dramatics as a hobby. I can lose my accent at will but listen to how reet broad a get wi DCC DeGroot. Av eard it pisses im off so a exagerats it all the mower." He paused "Strictly between us though Tom." His pronunciation swayed between tripe and onions and canapés on the lawn.

"Sir" was Thors grinning response.

They parked up and walked the short distance down the tree lined avenue to the front of head office. At the front desk the attractive receptionist was expecting them and informed them that the local TV people were set up in the police studio, a room designed into the building specifically for such an occurrence. DCC Degroot would like them to call into his suite first for a chat.

Thor had never been to the top floor of Headquarters before and was somewhat taken aback by the opulence. The carpets in the corridors were thick pile with the county crest inlaid every couple of yards. The walls of the corridor were adorned with paintings of local beauty spots, mostly by local artists but a couple by well known national figures. When the door Marked "Deputy Chief Constable Roger Degroot QPM" was opened by the root digger himself Thor was aghast. The room was splendid, antique furniture huge red leather chairs and more expensive artwork. In pride of place on the wall behind DeGroot's desk was a huge Photograph of DeGroot receiving his Queens Police Medal from the Duke of Edinburgh.

"Gentleman. Thank you for coming to help with the TV. I know you've done this before Inspector Hardy. Do you have any media experience Sergeant Orre? No. Well here's a little advice for you. Unless asked a direct question, say nothing. If you are questioned, then before replying think how your response will reflect upon, A me, B The police service as a whole and finally, C Yourself. Got that Orre? Good man."

T'inspector instructed Thor to phone home so that his family would see him on TV. Thor said he'd prefer them to miss it. T'inspector told him it was not a request. Pam was excited and said that she's tape it so he could see himself.

The three officers walked down to the studio and DCC DeGroot introduced his colleagues to the producer and the lady who would be interviewing them, Miss Teresa Green. Thor thought she looked as if she should still be in school. Some member of the TV crew buzzed around them with a light meter. Spot lamps were adjusted and the process repeated until the producer/ director was happy. Then a rather effeminate young man dabbed Thor's face with a powder puff. "Get off you Jessie." Shouted the Sergeant, pushing the chap away.

"That's enough of that Sergeant Orre." Commanded a flabbergasted DCC DeGroot. T'inspector was working hard to stifle laughter. Miss Green calmed things down by explaining that although she found Thor's boyish, bright red cheeks very attractive, their redness would be exaggerated on TV and a dab of make up would be required to improve his looks. Whilst explaining this to Thor she was patting him on the leg which made him even redder in the face.

After a few practice questions the director decided to go live. The interviewer introduced T'inspector and asked if he was pleased with his officers catching the felons red handed. T'inspector responded "Eeeh am right proud 0 my lads lass. T'were a good thing they catched up wi em afore they cud do summat worse. DeGroot was scowling off shot at his subordinate. It was now Thor's turn to fight back laughter.

There were a couple more innocuous questions for Inspector Hardy then without warning she pounced on DeGroot. "You have claimed Deputy Chief Constable, that your own intelligence work lead up to the arrests yesterday. Can you give us some background into this?"

DeGroot was not expecting this and said that he had organised an operation that had born fruit and that due to his diligence and that of his officers some dangerous criminals were now off the streets.

Refusing to accept this, the young lady continued "Come now Deputy Chief Constable, the word on the street is that this was just a chance arrest, not a planned operation in any way. Are you using this as an opportunity to enhance your own image, bearing in mind that the Chief Constable is due to retire next year? Roger DeGroot was caught totally of balance. He went purple with rage and began to stammer a response that began "Now look here madam".

"If I may interject" Inspector Hardy butted in and the camera swung towards him. "There are some circumstances where it would be inappropriate for the police service to say too much. This can be because disclosure may prejudice an impending trial or because of the sensitive nature of the intelligence work that has been carried out. In this instance both circumstances apply and naturally my superior officer feels it improper to comment on that particular aspect of the case. There was not a hint of northern accent here. Thor looked at his Inspector and was awestruck by the capability of the man.

Knowing that she had been outmanoeuvred Teresa's attention turned to Thor "I understand Sergeant Orre that you were instrumental in preventing the armed gang from running loose in Newtown and that a particular act of bravery on you part, resulted in the capture of the gang leader who had fired a gun at you. Can you explain what happened for our viewers please?

Thor's world had stopped turning. He knew he was live on TV with who knows how many friends and family watching and he couldn't think of a response. He recalled the day when he had officially become a police officer and taken his oath of allegiance. He thought of his father and Evor and inspiration came.

"I think enough has already been said about what happened and as my inspector has suggested, we do not wish to prejudice proceedings by saying any more. As for the capture of the gang leader, I did what any officer would have done in the circumstances." He thought that would be the end of his ordeal but no. "You're very modest Sergeant Orre but I doubt if many officers would have been brave enough to swim after a man who was firing guns at them."

Thor had had enough now. He was losing patience wanted to get out, wanted a pint. "I am fairly well paid for doing my job. I have sworn to maintain the peace and protect her Majesty's subjects without fear or favour. I was simply upholding my promise. That's all. Nothing special. Just doing my job, as trained and instructed by the senior officers of this county." He added the last sentence as a thanks to T'inspector with a nod in his direction.

"Wrap up!" came an instruction through the interviewers earpiece.

"Thank you gentlemen" Then turning to the camera "I for one will sleep safer in my bed knowing there are men like Sergeant Orre patrolling our streets." This was said part in fun but T'inspector caught the look in her eyes as she looked across at the young sergeant. "Jesus" He thought "She'll eat t'poor bugger in one."

The two senior officers picked up their caps and made for the door. Thor made to follow them but was accosted on his way to the door. Teresa fluttered her eyelashes at him and smiled a more provocative smile than even Eloise could manage. She passed him a business card and whispered "Call me! Soon!" then she was gone and he made his escape.

In the corridor the DCC invited both up for a drink in his office. Thor was grateful when T'inspector apologised, saying that they were so short handed, they had better return to Newtown. DeGroot patted T'inspector on the shoulder. "Thank you for today Hardy." He meant it.

"Oh Orre. Has your friend Jones had a word with you about rugby?"

"Sir?" questioned Thor. "Oh nothing" the DCC replied.

The inspector and his sergeant drove in silence for a while. "Sir" Said Thor, pulling into a lay bye. "This isn't what I signed up for." When prompted by T'inspector to tell him more he continued "I want to help, I want to lock up villains, catch thieves, guide my team. I can't be arsed with politics and cosying up to these bloody media types. Can you keep that side of the job away from me please?"

T'inspector thought for a while. "Lad, you dunno think I like it do you? I'm like you, a no nonsense copper. In your dad's time that was what was needed. It's changed now. I'm a bloody dinosaur. I'm trying t keep me nose clean 'til I get me pension. You? Well you've got years t go. If y just want to be a bobby then fine. Keep yer stripes and you'll be a bloody good sergeant. Trouble is lad you're better'n that. You can get to the top, be the man making the policy, making the job better for the coppers at sharp end." He paused to restructure his thoughts. "Your choice lad. You'll come to a cross roads. Do you take th'easy road or the less enjoyable route? Drop me at home. I'm knackered." With that he was asleep in the passenger seat.

Thor looked at him amazed anew. He slipped the car into gear and took the Malvil road.

Thor was totally cheesed off with the job. As he walked back into Newtown police station he was dreaming of handing in his resignation and taking up farming.

Mike Maddox beamed at him from behind the desk. "What a day Serge. You wouldn't believe it. People are smiling at us and being nice. Little old ladies have brought home made cake into the nick. We've had three unlicensed firearms handed in and even an anonymous phone call from the lad who has been throwing eggs at people promising to stop it for a week. Silly bugger rang on his mobile and we've got his details now. Shall we pick him up?"

Thor was about to tell him what a bloody awful time he'd had, then had a rethink. He could see that Mike was really buoyant, not bad for a cynical old bobby who's been in the job for years. "Tell you what Mike I'll make us a brew and you get me a piece of cake, then well have a think eh?" Mike reeled off the cakes on offer, chocolate, coffee and walnut, Victoria sponge, Apple pie. There had been a super Black Forest Gateau, Thor's favourite but big Graham Gascoine had scoffed the lot.

After a brew and cake Thor and Mike had decided that the best approach to the egg thrower was to get his name and address from the phone company, text him to thank him for owning up and saying that they wouldn't charge him as long as it stopped completely.

It was a quiet shift and as the A shift came in to take over and D shift coppers returned to base, Thor took a high amount of jokes as everyone had managed to be near a TV during his interview.

"Blimey Serge, you looked like a tomato." Said Danny Daniels.

"You did what any officer would have done?" asked Simon Smith. "I'd have kept out of the way and left it to the armed response Serge."

"Us girls'll all sleep safely in our beds tonight Serge" teased Sonia Smith, fluttering her eyelashes.

"Any of that gateau left?" Big Graham Gascoine asked.

"Bloody Hell! Give me a lift round to Haven Mike will you? You lot had better get this out of your system by tomorrow." Thor smiled knowing that to be given such a ribbing, he was accepted by his shift.

When Thor slumped into the sofa, at home Pam could tell that he'd not enjoyed his day. She went into the kitchen and returned pouring him a beer. "Remember Tom, me and the kids love you. "She handed him the glass, and cuddled down next to him. He took a big gulp. It was his favourite, Oakham JHB. He snuggled in next to her, took another gulp of his beer and suddenly all was well in his world.

Pam had things to tell him about occurrences this side of the water but that could wait until the morning.

Chapter 13 – Abandon Ship!

Curly woke to the sound of gentle tapping. He looked at the room, taking in the whiteness of the décor. This wasn't his room. He next noticed the chair jammed under the door knob, to stop anyone coming in from outside. This worried him greatly. Where was he? Who had he seduced now? What could his excuse be?

"Curly, you'll be late for your train. Please open the door. Little Elly is very sorry." He recognised his wife's little girl lost voice and his memory started to work. He wished it hadn't. He wanted to erase the whole of yesterday from his mind and also from the collective memory bank of the village of Haven.

"Get me a black coffee woman and a bacon and egg sandwich, done properly. I'll have a shower, get dressed and you can take me to the station." It was rare that he'd dare to issue orders to his wife but for once he was in the ascendancy and was going to make the best of it. Ok Eloise could sulk but on the rare occasion when Curly sulked, he was a master of the art, British Olympic Gold Medal Sulking Champion for over twenty years.

They had driven to the station in silence. Well silence except for Eloise's occasional apology and bout of sobbing. Curly had driven, too quickly. He wanted to get out of Haven without being seen but the Orres had all waved as they tripped down to school together. Curly had waved back but his wife had just increased the volume of her sobs. Curly almost felt a little pity for her, knowing how much she envied Pam for having the children. He then recalled the embarrassment that she had caused him and he felt good that she was suffering.

He was now sitting in first class of the London bound train, dressed in a dark suit with papers from his briefcase on the table in front of him. He needed to read through them on the journey but the pictures of his humiliation would keep breaking into his train of thought. The thought of having a train of thought, while on a train brought him a brief smile, very brief smile. How he deplored yesterday!

Having dropped Thor off at Newport nick, he had returned home yesterday as planned. Eloise had persuaded Pam to come to the pub for a drink with her and Curly, for a nosey at what the reporters were asking. She had lent Pam a dark wig and some dark glasses, intending to tell the locals not to mention that she was Thor's wife. Pam had gone along with the idea as she was a fun loving girl and hoped to get some stories to tell her husband later that day.

As they walked into the Bell, Curly recalled seeing that Myfanwy and Nick Haydn – Smythe were working behind the bar, which was quite busy for Monday lunchtime. Chubby was being bought drinks by a lady reporter. Evor and Ian Tomkins were on bar stools trying to rid the world of Glenlivet and Leo Antony could be heard telling one reporter how he might be able to get a photo of the Orre Family for a small fee.

"Here's the chap I was telling you about now" said Rod Davies, pointing towards Curly. "He grew up with Tom Orre and he and his beautiful wife are the Orres closest friends."

At this Eloise struck one of her poses. Her white teeth shone from between her shiny plum coloured lipstick, which was the exact match for the tight halter necked top that she wore with matching shoes and sprayed on white jeans. The four or five male hacks in the bar immediately dropped the local with whom they were conversing and stampeded towards Eloise, with offers to buy her and her friends a drink. The two female journalists had lost the rapport with the men that they had been conversing with as Chubby, Leo and Ian Tomkins had switched off and gawked at Eloise.

Pam had slipped unnoticed into a corner. Curly had got Evor to pass the word round for the locals not to mention Pam's presence, on pain of a serious discussion with Thor. As usual this threat worked,

Eloise had chosen the best dressed newspaperman to buy Pam and herself an expensive cocktail and Curly a best bitter. After the initial flurry of excitement a natural pecking order had been established by the members of the fourth estate and a babble of conversation ensued. Most questions were fairly innocuous and if anything was to be avoided a light tap on the shins, under the table from Pam, as arranged in advance, ensured that Eloise and Curly would duck that particular question

More drinks were brought over by Nick and as he put them down he winked at Curly. To Nick the wink meant, "You crafty buggers you're on free booze." To Curly the wink revived the thought that Nick might be batting for the other team.

When the same happened on the next round Curly leaned across to the reporter and asked "See that lad working the bar there? Do you think he's gay?" The reporter shrugged off the question and asked "Tom Orre's father was a policeman. Didn't he die in some boat tragedy?"

Nick had seen Curly looking at him and waved in a friendly way. Curly was beginning to mellow and shouted out "You can cut that out Posh Boy. I'm a happily married man." Nick thought this was a joke and blew Curly a kiss.

"He's a bloody Nancy boy he is." Curly exclaimed "come on Eloise we're going." Eloise refused to budge as she was enjoying being the centre of attention. There ensued a bit of an argument between them that quickly became a mini scuffle. The reporter asked Curly to stay and calm down and promised more drinks. Pam decided to go onto coffee as it would soon be time to collect the kids from school. Eloise tried a different cocktail and Curly shifted to gin and tonic. Double. He scowled at Posh Boy.

Rod Davies came over and asked if everything was OK. Eloise said it was. Curly said "Fine, but why do you employ a Nancy boy as barman?" Rod was taken aback as he realised Curly was being serious.

Nick stormed over "Who are you calling a Nancy boy? We're mates Curly. Pack it in! I'm not a Nancy boy Rod." Rod said that he knew that and told Curly not to be so daft. The attention of the entire pub was now focused on Curly. "Right" said Curly "Here's a question for you. Look at my wife here! Do you fancy her then?"

Nick certainly did, as would any straight bloke but how could he answer that question without causing offence and how could he say he did when word would get back to his girlfriend. "No I don't. Not really" Nick replied.

"Aha" said Curly "I knew it you're a shirt lifter, an uphill gardener. I'm not rooming with you on tour. You should have to change separately from the rest of us."

Curly suddenly realised that the room was silent and everyone was looking at him, in shock. Well everyone except Eloise who was looking at Nick also shocked that he had said he didn't fancy her. He must be gay, she thought.

"What?" Curly asked, looking round at everyone. There was more silence in the room than you can imagine.

To break the silence Eloise looked at Pam and asked if she fancied shopping in Castra tomorrow. Pam replied that she had already accepted an invitation to visit Pam Craddock. She was about to suggest that they go the following day when Eloise burst into an angry rant.

"Oh that's bloody typical isn't it? Curly and I have been dropped now you have friends with children. You just use us like this morning. Well that's the sort of people the Orres are. Self, self, self." Then she turned on her husband. "It's your fault Curly. You're firing blanks you useless little twat. That's why we haven't got kids everyone. My husband, the great Casanova Curly is firing blanks." Eloise burst into tears.

Pam put her arms round Eloise, gently lifted her and took her out of the pub. "Can you pick the kids up please Evor?" she asked. Evor nodded.

The silence in the pub had trebled in intensity.

"I'm really not a Nancy boy. It's not my fault I talk a bit posh and have a double barrelled name" Nick Haydn – Smythe insisted, looking very hurt.

Curly looked around, thought what have I done and walked meekly from the bar. He went home, locked himself in a spare room and went to bed.

He'd gone over the entire scenario three times on his journey and each time another titbit of memory would return that made the matter seem worse. The train slowed as it neared London. He hadn't read the paperwork. He wasn't looking forward to going into a high level legal meeting badly prepared and he certainly wasn't looking forward to going home or going on tour.

Back in Haven, Pam had seen the children off to school and had recounted the tale of the Jones's embarrassing time in the pub to Thor. She told how she had taken Eloise back to the Orre's house and let her sleep off the booze, under a duvet in the spare room. Later Eloise had woken up and apologised to Pam saying that Pam was her only true friend in the world.

"I suppose Curly will have gone to London today as usual on a Tuesday?" Pam asked. Thor responded that Curly had planned to do so but only for two days this week due to the tour.

"I never knew he was firing blanks though. I just assumed that they preferred having the money to having kids" Thor mused.

"Oh Tom" Pam answered "sometimes you're so bloody insensitive. Eloise isn't getting any younger and there comes a time when a woman feels the need to reproduce. It can be devastating when she finds it's not happening. Money isn't part of the equation you big lump. Mind you I'd happily have sold our two this morning. The Artist is coming in to school today to judge their paintings and they're both at fever pitch. At least the village is devoid of the press now. You're fifteen minutes of fame is over my love."

"On a different tack, did either Curly or Eloise mention anything about rugby yesterday?" Thor asked. His wife gave a negative answer. "Funny" said Thor "The DCC asked if my friend Jones had, had a chat with me about rugby. When I queried what about he said it was nothing. How strange is that? I think I need to sit down and have a talk to Mr John David Jones."

Pam agreed but told him not to mention infertility unless Curly brought it up first.

"That's the problem" Thor replied "Curly's not bringing it up at all"

The look from his wife told Thor that this was no laughing matter and that he was in bad books. He decided to stroll down to Evor's for a cuppa while Pam forgot his insensitivity about Curly's problem.

Walking down to Evor's place he came across Chubby, waiting for the Bell to open. "Morning Mr Orre. Saw you on the Telly yesterday. Hey! What about Curly being a Jaffa Eh? I didn't see that one coming." Chubby shouted.

Thor stifled the urge to make an inappropriate but witty comment and walked over to Chubby. "Look mate. I gather he's a bit upset about it, so best if we all just forget it for his sake. You know I've got kids and I understand that you've fathered half the under tens in the county. What do you think?"

Chubby thought for a moment "Yeh, you're right. He's a mate and I wouldn't want to upset him. I'll put the word out to keep quiet about it Mr Orre. Still bit of a shocker though eh, little Shagger being seedless?"

"You've got a bit of a wait until opening Chubby and it looks like rain." Said Thor changing the subject.

"No, I'm not after beer. Rod's promised me a bit of work varnishing some chairs he bought at auction. He'll knock some of my slate. I won't need to worry about that soon, I've got a nice earner coming when we get back from tour and I can clear my slate here and in the shop and have some left." Chubby looked pleased with himself.

Thor was just about to ask where the money was coming from when Rod opened the door and shouted Chubby to come in and get cracking.

Thor mused on Chubby's coming windfall as he strolled on.

"I caught you on the box yesterday Thor." This was Spoddy Brown who pulled up on a motorbike that Thor had never seen before. "Do you like my new bike? My cousin over in Castra said I could have it for nothing if I would take it away on a trailer. It hasn't gone for a couple of years and our Sheridan's missus is sick of it dripping oil on the hall carpet and having to squeeze past it to get in and out. It cost me nothing and I reckon it's worth five times that. Jim Cameron said he'd fix it for fifty quid. He's done it. It was just a blocked fuel line caused by not being used according to Jim."

Thor said that he liked the look of it, then he pointed out that the penalties for riding without tax and insurance would set him back a lot more than fifty quid. Not to mention the possible fine and ban for riding without a helmet.

Spoddy jumped off the bike like a shot and switched off the ignition. He reddened and looked very worried indeed. "Good job I'm not in work Spoddy. How about bringing it round to my place tomorrow morning? I can have a proper look at it and you can show me your tax disc, licence and insurance certificate. Oh and there's a sale on in the motor bike warehouse in Newtown, helmets up to thirty percent off. See you then."

Thor strolled on smiling. Spoddy pushed the bike the mile back home, just in case.

"Am I pleased to see you? I was going to call up to your place. We need a chat about Curly." Evor spoke in a concerned manner whilst filling the kettle to make his grandson a cup of tea.

"You're right Granddad. Who'd have thought Curly was like a panda eh?" Thor asked.

"Thomas. I would have thought you were above that. I'm not talking about his unfortunate infertility. It's the issue of homophobia Thor. Do you think he's serious?" Thor recounted his conversation with Curly on the previous afternoon. "It's come as a shock to me too and I've had words with him about it but he seems unrepentant. I would never have thought that he would have been so vehement about the matter but his outburst in the pub suggests otherwise. What should we do?" Thor responded.

The pair sat in silence for some time "I'll have another word." Thor offered.

"No lad. He may be reticent with you. I'll have a chat about it with him. See if I can get any sense out of him. If necessary I'll play dirty and bring up his parents." Evor replied. "Oh, we have another problem" Evor continued. "The two chaps from

Newport can't room together. They haven't spoken to each other for a couple of years. "

"What?" exclaimed Thor "They prop together, in the same team and they don't speak? That's bloody dafter than our lot.

Evor took a swig of his tea, looked at his favourite mug and told Thor the story. The loose head prop, Steve Royd was courting a girl called Emma. He asked her to marry him and she refused his proposal, not wanting to be Emma Royd. They split up and some time later she was asked out by the tight head, Simon Pyle. He proposed and now they're engaged and the lads don't speak.

"Well, that's women for you granddad. I can understand her not wanting to be a haemorrhoid but she'll end up a pile now anyway." Thor advised. "Back to Curly Granddad, we can't have that stance in the club but Curly is like a brother to me and like a second grandson to you, What if we can't get him to see sense. I think at the least an apology is needed with some form of discipline within the club if he continues in this vain."

Evor mused and agreed that Curly should apologise but pointed out that at present he hadn't done or uttered any indiscretion while in club colours so discipline for now was not appropriate. He sighed and suddenly looked his age. "You see Tom, we Orres have taken over the mantle of confessor, problem solver and crutch for the weak to lean on in this village. I suppose years ago the role would have been filled by the local vicar but our nearest full time clergyman is in Newtown and very few of the parish are believers anyway. I feel I let your dad down because he saw me in this role and took it on himself to do the same. You copied us as you assumed it was a normal thing to do. You need to accept that we can't cure every ill and we don't have all the answers.

We're just ordinary men Tom, don't expect too much of me or yourself."

He patted his grandson on the shoulder, hoping that his words had taken some weight off the burden that he could see Thor carrying.

It was Thor's turn to sigh. Then he smiled "You're right granddad. Thanks."

On reaching home Thor found a note. It read "Pie in the oven. Gone to see Pam Craddock. See you tonight. Love Pam XXX" Underneath she had written in a different pen "Eloise rang. Wants to speak to you"

Thor ate the excellent game pie, showered and changed into uniform. He had decided to go over on the ferry and get one of his shift to give him a lift home. He had plenty of time so he locked up and strolled up the road to see Eloise. He disliked talking much on the phone, preferring face to face conversations where possible. Strange, how women who live within a stone's throw of each other will call and chat for ages on the phone yet most blokes would only use the phone for brief imparting of information and would visit their friends for a longer chat.

The sky was as perfectly blue as Thor had ever seen it. It reflected in the waters of the Dee estuary, where looking back Tom could see the ferry shuffling into the Haven Jetty. A solitary yacht was attempting to make some progress in the lightest of breezes and the RNLI inshore boat was drifting further out with Mike Bennet at the helm making notes on his knee pad.

He buzzed the intercom on the gate and was greeted by a chirpy Eloise who told him to come round back by the pool.

Eloise was stood in the patio with one hand on the back of a chair and the other holding a long thin glass of Pimms and Champagne. She chided Thor for buzzing the intercom "You don't have to buzz Tom. You all know our access code. You wouldn't forget 6969 would you? So just come on in you silly Billy."

She wore a lightly shaded pair of sunglasses and a pale blue silk wrap that covered very little. Her finger and toe nails were the same shade of blue but Thor did not notice that subtlety. He was struggling with all his might to avoid staring at her nipples, which pointed slightly skyward through the silk.

"Can I offer you a drink dahling?" she pouted.

When Thor explained he was due in work she got him a glass of orange cordial as he had requested.

"Are you Ok to stay outside? It's such a lovely day. Come and sit over here." Eloise lay down on a sun lounger and beckoned him next to her. Tom sat a little further away, explaining that, being fair he preferred a bit of shade. Truth be known his increase in temperature was not being helped by the fact that Eloise's wrap was slipping open. Thor was sweating and as red as a ripe tomato.

"You wanted me Eloise?" he asked.

"Oh Tom. I've been so naughty. I was drunk, as you've probably heard and said some awful things about Curly but worse than that, I said things about you and Pam too. Pam was so good to me and she has accepted my apology but I wanted to say sorry to you too Tom." This was said in her little girl lost voice and accompanied by a pose and a pout.

Thor forced a smile, struggling to maintain eye contact "Forget it Eloise. We all say things we don't mean when we're drunk."

"Oh thank you dahling" she oozed. "There is one other thing that's upsetting me a little and I wonder if I could talk to you about it. It's a bit personal but I know you're a man of the world Tom." She leant across and put her hand on Thor's thigh.

Thor thought she was going to open up about the desire for children, her husband's infertility or maybe his homophobia. He thought this would be good as he might get an insight into how his friend was feeling He was not expecting what came next.

"That posh boy said he didn't fancy me Tom. Do you think I've lost my magnetism?" Once more this was the little girl voice.

Thor coughed out a mouthful of orange cordial. It was an involuntary reflex to the pose now struck by Eloise. He spluttered and stammered but finally calmed down enough to explain that Nick probably did fancy her but couldn't say so in public or his girlfriend would hear about it and Nick would be in the dog house.

Eloise pondered on this and Thor was congratulating himself for his diplomacy when the next question came. "Tom" pause, sunglasses off, flutter of eyelashes, pout "Do *you* fancy me?"

Shit!

He could hear his own heart beating. Hear it, he could feel it trying to leave his body.

The situation reminded Thor of an old black and white war film he'd watched as a child. A ship had been hit by torpedoes from a U boat. Sirens were wailing, claxons going off and bells ringing as explosions occurred all over the vessel and seamen jumped and swam for their lives Damage control reported extreme heat from the cheeks, legs turned to jelly, brain refusing to compute and most worrying of all, movement south of the equator had occurred.

He was about to shout abandon ship but heard himself say "You're my best wife's friend. I mean my best friend's wife and my wife's best friend. I err, well err. No! Yes! I can't think like that Eloise."

"Tom I'll never tell. It will be secret between us" She stood up slowly and ever so slowly the silk wrap slithered from her body.

She looked magnificent, a perfect shade of tan and no white bits anywhere. Her breasts were full yet pert with long dark brown nipples. Everything was in proportion, neither skinny nor plump. Thor's eyes were drawn to the subtle tattoo of a light green viper that slithered over her lower abdomen.

"Do you fancy me Tom?" She asked again, slowly. "Screw me Tom. You know you want to" She moved towards him, the snake swaying between her hips. Tom's snake was trying to break out, sending messages to his brain that were overriding the common sense driver. She rubbed against him and her hands moved over his shoulders and buttocks. She made a noise like nothing he'd ever heard, a kind of deep primeval rasping sound. He wanted to run but he'd never run away from trouble in his life. He knew he was losing the battle for HMS Thomas Orre.

The captain made one final attempt to save the ship. "Eloise. I'm in a terrible situation. If I make love to you, I'll never forgive myself. If I don't make love to you, well I'll certainly never forgive myself. You are so sexy, so bloody gorgeous, so desirable" He paused and looked at her in the eyes. He pulled her to him kissed her passionately, roughly on the mouth "but I made a promise to Pam who I love dearly. Today never happened Eloise." He dropped her from his arms, gulped the last of his orange cordial, bowed, turned and marched away.

As he turned the corner a half full jug of Pimms and Champagne flew past him and smashed against a tree. "Fuck you Mr bloody Righteous Thomas Orre. I hate you!" Eloise screamed after him as he reached the gate and slid through, marching towards the ferry.

"Are you alright mate?" asked the ferryman as Thor sat with a vacant expression on the port side of the boat, staring blankly into the distance. Thor nodded but said nothing.

Fifteen minutes later Sergeant Bent Asked "Tom are you OK? You don't seem to have heard a word that I have said." Thor nodded a blank faced response. He still gazed into space. Sergeant Bent thought he looked as if someone had removed his brain and replaced it with candy floss. "Tom! Tom! Can you speak lad?" Bent was worried. "Are you ill?"

Thor shook himself and poured water from a paper cup over his head. "Sorry I've err, had, well kind of a shock I suppose. Sort of err, nothing happened, nothing to worry about. I'll be fine" Thor wondered if he had said this for Sergeant Bent's benefit or to convince himself "Sorry, I was miles away. Can you go through things again please?" The ship was back under control. He was once more a professional officer of the law instead of a vacant hulk.

The shifts changed over and Thor designated his constables to their duties. There had been trouble between the lads from Mount Pleasant estate and teenagers from Greenbank. Danny, Tony and Sonia were to show a presence on Mount Pleasant, while Simon and Graham patrolled Greenbank.

Thor had been told that a cruise Liner full of Americans was in the port and most of the passengers had been bussed up to the Roman town of Castra. T'inspector had left word that a police presence would be desirable at the cruise dock as the Yanks liked to be photographed with a policeman. Mike Maddox loved this aspect of the job. He would put on his best uniform and be accompanied by Lucy who could remove any colonial ladies who became too attached to him. This pairing had worked well in the past Thor had been told.

Everyone had left the station and Thor settled down to a bit of paperwork on what promised to be a quiet shift.

The office phone rang. It was Pam. "Tom, Tom can you get over here please. I think Eloise has taken some sort of overdose. She's breathing but I can't rouse her. Oh Tom I'm so scared. The children went across to tell her about their artwork and came running back to say she was asleep and wouldn't wake up. I thought she was dead."

Tom calmed her down, called for an ambulance, asked Lucy to return to the station and ran down to the ferry. The ferryman had gone across at full throttle and Tom was in the Jones's garden in no time. Pam had forced salty water down Eloise, as instructed by her husband and the patio was now covered in vomit. As Tom suspected, Eloise had drunk herself into a stupor after being rejected. She was still out for the count when the ambulance arrived. Pam was back "Chez Orre" with the children and the ever reliable Evor.

When the ambulance had taken Eloise off to hospital in Castra Tom decided to clear up. He found a bucket and mop in the utility room and with some scalding water and disinfectant he cleaned the patio. He took the bottles and glasses inside and returned to wipe down the glass topped patio table when he noticed something that worried him greatly. A white powdery residue remained on the surface that had the unmistakeable smell, texture and taste of cocaine.

Chapter 14 – Midweek

Pam had awakened with the sun coming through her bedroom curtains. They were old and faded. She had a saving fund in a tin in her dressing table to buy some new curtains but she had just decided to give the money to her husband as a treat for his rugby tour tomorrow.

Thor had told her everything. She was both furious that Eloise has attempted to seduce her man, furious when told that he had kissed her but so pleased and proud of him for having the strength and love to resist. She looked at the great shaggy sheepdog of a man snoozing next to her. How lucky she was that Thor had chosen her. They had been friends at infant school, sweethearts in their teens, then lovers and now what? There isn't a word that she could find to describe her feelings for this man. She wanted to wake him and squeeze him and tell him how she loved him. Instead she just pictured him being Daddy, Mr dependable, always smiling always safe, always hers.

Pam knew that Eloise didn't really want her man, nor did Eloise really want to hurt her. Eloise just wanted to reduce her own pain by whatever means possible, even drugs it seemed. Pam wouldn't mention it to her or Curly or even Thor. It was an incident to be forgotten, in the same way that the Orre's had forgotten when Curly tried his luck with Pam some years ago. Pam should have felt flattered but when she told Thor he hadn't been annoyed. Thor joked that he would have taken offence if Curly hadn't tried it on with her, as he'd tried it on with every other woman in Castrashire.

The big lump next to her opened his eyes "I can feel you thinking" he said. He pulled her gently to him and they just cuddled in silence, enjoying the special feelings without words.

The alarm went off and the children burst into the room seconds later. "Has Aunty Elly woken up mummy? Did you tell her about our pictures? Have you told Uncle Curly? Is Uncle Curly in London? Why was Aunty Elly poorly?"

Thor muttered under his breath "Are you sure these two are mine and not Paul Bennet's? Listen! They're just like him, questions, questions."

Pam told the children to hush and reminded them to wait for an answer to one question before rhyming off more questions. She told them that Aunty Elly had been taken to hospital in the ambulance but would be alright once the nurses had looked after her. She explained that Aunty Elly had eaten something that made her poorly but they mustn't talk about it with anyone, even their best friends as Uncle Curly would worry when he came back from London tonight. Pam extracted a promise from them that it was an Orre family secret then promised to take them swimming in Newport after school. This took their minds off Aunty Elly as there were slides in the new pool complex.

With the kids fed, Thor took them down to school. His head was swimming with worry for his friends and anger at the cocaine. He didn't know how to proceed for once and was astounded to find himself at the school gate almost immediately after leaving home. "Hell I must have crossed the road in a trance" he thought. He had. He hadn't spoken to Myfanwy who had asked him what the ambulance was for. He hadn't noticed Spoddy, resplendent in a shiny new motorcycle helmet and waving documents under Thor's nose. On kissing the kids at the gate, he did notice the enormous diamond ring on Miss Bewick's engagement finger. "That must have cost Paul a fortune? Congratulations. You make a lovely couple" Anna replied that Paul was expecting to come into funds next month and she was surprised and a little embarrassed at the size of the diamond.

Once home Thor accepted a big mug of tea from his wife and they both went to sit outside in the sunshine. Pam had told him that the hospital had phoned and they would be discharging Eloise after the Doctor's rounds later this morning. Thor had left their number with the ambulance crew yesterday.

"How do we play this?" Thor asked. Despite being a decisive man of action, he knew his wife would have some better ideas than he could come up with. His mental pondering had swept back and forth from "pretend it never happened" to "Never having anything to do with Eloise again".

Pam mused for a while curling her hair with one hand. She often did this when perplexed, angry or tired, Thor knew better than to interrupt during this process.

After a while Pam spoke. "Well!" she paused "Stop me at any point if you disagree or want to ask any questions. Firstly we have to consider our medium to long term objective here. I think it should be a return to the status quo. IE Everybody happy and Eloise and Curly reconciled. Agree?"

Thor nodded

Pam continued "I'll collect her by myself and bring her back here to have a coffee with us both. A lot will depend of course, on her attitude towards me on the way back. You know she's swung from paying me compliments to being quite spiteful in recent months."

Thor pointed out that mood swings were probably caused by her use of cocaine and not just the usual woman's stuff. Pam frowned at his chauvinist attitude but when he looked hurt and asked what he'd done to deserve a scowl, she couldn't help but laugh at him. Strong, intelligent huge and occasionally clueless, she thought.

After a second mug of tea and home made scones. They had put a plan together. Pam knew that Eloise would have to have a way of saving face after her outburst in the pub and had the idea to roll the pub and ambulance incidents into one. The explanation would be a strong viral infection that had caused delirium, strange dreams and eventually a collapse. The villagers could be told this and that Eloise was on a strong course of antibiotics, having to stay indoors for a couple of days. They could then say that the business of Curly's impotence was part of the delirious babblings and the whole incident would be forgotten as, no doubt, someone in the village would do something dafter to move gossip on.

Thor liked the plan, especially as it involved no action on his part. Pam would sort it all out while he was on tour and keep a watch on Eloise.

They went for a walk down to the harbour and Thor told Pam about Anna Bewicks big diamond. "Where do you think a school teacher gets the kind of money for that?" he asked. Pam looked at her plain wedding ring. They never had got formally engaged as Thor couldn't see any point in wasting needed cash on a gesture. Momentarily Pam felt envious of Hannah Bewick's diamond but then looked at the man next to her. As if by telepathy he asked if she would like a diamond ring, pointing out that they were a bit better off now. She stopped in her tracks, hugged him and answered "I've got a huge diamond Tom. You and that's all I want."

"Phew" he thought, resolving not to be so bloody spontaneous in future, "that was a close one."

Mike Bennet was washing the RIB down and shouted across "Hey! We'll have no hanky panky in the harbour in public if you don't mind."

"You cheeky bugger." Thor shouted back "For that you can put the kettle on and get the biscuit tin open."

The three sat on a bench outside the lifeboat station and made small talk about the weather, coming rugby tour and state of the tide. Thor casually dropped in a question about Anna's diamond and where his brother was getting the money from.

"I've no idea Thor" was Mike's reply "You know him, he'll ask a hundred bloody questions a minute but never seems to answer a question you ask him. He reckons it cost about three or four months salary though."

Mike moved back to his favourite subject, the estuary and after a while the Orre's thanked him for the brew and headed home for lunch.

As they entered their home the phone rang and it was Eloise asking for a lift home. Pam looked at Thor and said "See you in about forty minutes, all being well."

Almost to the exact minute the front door opened and roused Thor from daydreaming. In came a smiling Pam and a wretched looking Eloise. Thor had never seen Eloise looking anything other than glamorous. She wasn't so much white as silvery grey. Her eyes, that were normally so alive, looked dead. Her hair was lank and lacklustre. She stood looking at Thor and burst into tears. Not her usual put on tears but the genuine article. Her whole body shook. She wore a plain, baggy grey jumper and a pair of tracksuit bottoms that Thor recognised as belonging to Pam.

He stood slowly, smiled and held his arms out to her in reconciliation. Eloise ran into them sobbing and shaking. After a moment she beckoned Pam to join them and held both Orres to her. "Thank you both so much. I'd understand if you hated me. I don't understand why you care."

"That's what friends do" Pam explained. "Tea is the thing methinks" she smiled.

The three sat quietly sipping tea. Well two sat sipping out of best cups and one gulped out of a large mug. "Tom" said Pam disapprovingly. He looked at her bewildered and took another gulp of his tea with a noise like a walrus.

"I'm sorry Eloise" Pam explained "He can't do anything quietly. When he's asleep every orifice in his body makes a noise, even his ears squeak!"

Tom looked hurt and Eloise managed a smile.

"Curly doesn't have to know about this does he? It would really upset him and I need to make him happy" Eloise pleaded. Pam assured her that they would never mention it.

Thor became serious "I'll need to know where you got the Charlie from Eloise, I'm sorry." Pam looked shocked and said "we didn't say that Tom we promised a secret."

Tom held Eloise's gaze "Secret it will be ladies but you must tell me where you obtained the cocaine Eloise. That's the deal. I don't like to ask this of you and promise I'll never reveal my source of information but I need to know, at any cost."

She told him what he wanted to know. She began to sob and rock back and forth gently in Pam's arms until she fell into a deep sleep. Thor picked her up, took her upstairs and laid her on the spare bed. Pam covered the sleeping Eloise with a duvet, looked at her husband and walked downstairs. The big man followed. "I had to know Pam. I have to stop this filth."

"I understand Tom and so will she."

Later that afternoon Thor was on his way to Newport to begin his shift when he was pulled over by a police car with blue lights and siren on. It was one of those strange days that can't decide if spring has come or if we should still be in the grip of winter. The sun shone on the estuary and looking back he could see Haven harbour enjoying spring warmth. Over on this side of the water the drizzle hitting his windscreen had an icy element to it.

Tom had left the sunshine behind and the Bobby who had pulled him over was about to feel a very icy element indeed if it wasn't for a good reason.

Thor wound down his window and recognised the policeman as a fairly new lad on Sergeant Bents shift. The Bobby could see that Thor wasn't happy at being stopped and looked a bit worried. "Sorry to be dramatic with the blues and twos Serge but old man Benty, sorry, Sergeant Bent said be sure to catch you before you get in. Some ginger bird has turned up at the nick, demanding to see you. She kicked up a fuss when Sergeant Bent refused to give her your address and she's refusing to leave the nick." He then innocently asked if Thor had been a little less than saintly.

A few choice words blasted the poor Bobby back to his police car, where he confronted the female driver. "You bloody set me up there Nicola. I daren't go in for change over or he might tear me apart."

Thor slipped in through the rarely used back door to the police station. He could see the flame haired Teresa Green sat in the foyer so he crept on all fours below the counter and hissed at Sergeant Bent who was clearing up the incident board, ready to end his shift. "Pssst Pssst"

Bent looked round and managed to contain his laughter at the site of his huge colleague crawling about. "Meet me in the cells as soon as possible please" Thor whispered.

As soon as the first of Thor's shift arrived, Lucy Lamont was left on the desk and Sergeant Bent shuttled off the meet Thor. He told Thor that Teresa had been in the Nick just over an hour. She refused to tell him anything and got so angry that he damn near put her in the cells. "I must admit Tom" he said "I'd never have marked you down as a philanderer. She is tidy mind you, jammy bugger."

Thor told him in no uncertain terms that he hadn't and wouldn't get involved with her but that she had made the offer to him. He asked Benty to get rid of her but Benty explained that he'd tried, to no avail.

"Oh well here we go then" said Thor. He took a couple of deep breaths then opened the door to the foyer. He took in Lucy on the desk and big Grahan carrying mugs of tea. Teresa Green looked stunning, her red hair standing out against a spring green blouse and darker green skirt.

"Miss Green" Thor smiled, "I gather you want to see me."

She stood up, smiled and said "I'm not used to being ignored Sergeant Orre. When I tell people to phone me I expect a call. Who the hell do you think you are?"

"I madam am a police officer. My duty is to the public of this county. I am not at the beck and call of the media. Furthermore I am happily married and intend to stay that way. I act as instructed by my superior officers, not by you. Good day." As he said this he gently moved her towards the door and pushed her outside. In a quieter, calmer voice she almost whispered. "I have information that I trust no one with. Please come to my flat 9pm. Please tell no one, especially police" With that she was gone.

Thor walked back in to the blank faces of Sergeant Bent, Lucy and Graham. A red faced Thor said "I don't know why I'm telling you this but that woman is nothing to me. She interviewed me on TV as you know and she's obviously obsessed with me. There is not now, never was or ever will be anything between us end of story."

Lucy broke the lengthy, embarrassing silence. "It's only natural Serge, you don't realise how hard it is for us girls to keep our hands off you." She said this with a sarcastic smile, pointing to the mirrored window in the door leading to the cells. Thor followed her gaze and saw a red faced, tangle headed, angry looking oaf with a moustache that badly needed a trim. He burst out laughing at himself "Tea wench" was his smiling order.

The shifts changed and his team went about their duties. Mike Maddox had agreed to come into the nick at 8-30, allowing Thor loose on the street. It was a quiet, chilly and wet evening nothing much going on. The only incident was at the railway station where one member of a religious group, who had been handing out leaflets, had taken offence at the T shirt worn by a chap getting off a train. The shirt bore a slogan "Blessed are the Cheesemakers" from the Monty Python film Life of Brian. The leafleteer had taken offence at this slogan and berated the wearer. The wearer, a man in his fifties had initially responded apologetically but belted the evangelist who had ripped his T shirt. As luck would have it big Graham was on hand and had hauled them both in. They were presently in the cells while Thor decided what to do with them.

Thor's thoughts were directed to the much more important matter of his visit to Teresa Green.

At 9pm precisely Thor pressed the intercom button to Teresa's luxury apartment in Castra. She asked if he was alone and if he had told anyone. When he answered yes and no in that order she buzzed him up.

When the lift doors opened directly into her sumptuous open plan apartment she stood there to meet him. She looked nervous but looked beautiful with her hair falling down to her waist over a lacy lime green top and matching wide trousers.

"Let's get one thing straight right now. No trying to seduce me Teresa or I will be annoyed."

She looked hurt and replied "I'll be honest with you Thor, why do they call you that? I do want you to make love to me but there are two reasons for this. I do find you strangely attractive but also I want to be sure that I can trust you. You seem trustworthy but I know something that scares me and I need assurances that I can trust you. The fact that your wife must be able to trust you helps as does the fact that you've turned me down but I just don't know you."

He sat down. Firstly they call me Thor because I'm Thomas Henry Orre. T H Orre, Thor. Secondly if you think that making love with a man means that you can trust him you should stop reading Mills and Boon romances. Finally, there's nothing that I can say to prove my honesty. I'm probably no better than any other man but I try to live my life to my father's standard. He died, at sea, when I was young and I never got to know him man to man. I never knew his faults. I put him on a pedestal and even though I know he can't have been perfect, I try to live to what I perceive as his standard. Why I'm telling you this I don't know. Can you trust me? I don't know. I'm just me Teresa. Father and husband first, police officer and fellow human being second."

Teresa looked shocked "Your father Tom, did he die in the boat disaster?"

Thor's eyes watered. "Yes." He bowed his head.

"I'm so stupid. Orre is such a common name around here" she passed him a tissue as he fought back his tears. She put her arm around him. Not in a sensual way but to protect him. "Tom, the information I have is about that sinking. It's about murder Tom. I can trust you."

Tom looked up "It was an accident Teresa. The inquest found open verdict. I was young but all the papers said the boat had probably hit a mine left from the war that had come up in the storm."

"No Tom. It was murder."

Thor asked how she could think that and if she could prove it. She answered that she had a signed statement from the man who had set an explosive device on the boat. The statement gave the number of the officer who paid for the job and the name of a rich man who was the target. Thor asked how she could trust the statement from some petty criminal, who would probably give any old yarn for cash.

She told him.

"The man who did it was a petty criminal. He had been in the army in his youth and had learned about explosives. He couldn't get a proper job and when his wife ran away he was left to bring up a child alone. He was a small time thief, always in debt. His child grew and did well at school. He had to find money for a university education and stooped lower than ever to achieve this. He was on his death bed, dying in pain from cancer when he dictated this story to me. How do I know it's true? Because I didn't pay a penny for it nor did he ask for any money.

That petty criminal was my father. Yes Tom my father was responsible for the death of your parents and others. I can't go to the police as you'll see when I hand you the file. The police were and probably still are in the pay of a mister big"

Thor could see it was true and they cried together holding tight to each other. There was a bond and Thor didn't like it but he knew he couldn't turn his back on this.

Teresa half whispered, half whimpered "Tom, take me to bed. Please. I need you so badly" She looked up with tears running down her cheeks. "Please Tom. Just this once. I need you."

Thor was in pain but it was a good feeling too. To be so wanted that a woman, a very attractive woman at that, was close to begging him for sex.

"Teresa. You are beautiful and I would love to hold you, to comfort you and yes to make love to you. I can't. My wife. I can't explain but it would ruin what we have together. Please try to understand."

"Ill never tell anyone. I promise on my dead father's soul" Teresa implored him with her eyes.

"You wouldn't have to tell anyone Teresa. Pam and I, well it's hard to explain but we're more like one person than two. We've known each other since infant school. We've shared tragedy and bliss. It's as though our brains have merged at times. We know how the other feels and what they're thinking. If I took you to bed Pam would just know and if she didn't it would play on my mind until I told her." Thor gave her a gentle smile, kissed her with love on the forehead and slowly stood and backed out of the room.

Teresa was shocked. She was in love for the first time in her life and knew it was hopeless.

Thor pulled over in a lay bye to take in the unusual sunset out at sea. The thin clouds made the sun look elliptical in shape and like larva slithering from a volcano. Thor felt as though he was watching the sun set of another planet. He cursed his stupid loyalty. In the past forty eight hours two of the most desirable women imaginable had asked him for sex and because he had to be as pure as he imagined his father had been he had declined. He thumped the dashboard in anger. Then he thumped it again and drove off

Thor was in the station just before the end of shift. He was a different man in a way that he couldn't explain. For the first time in his life he felt hatred and didn't like or understand it. He had to find the crooked policeman and he would take revenge. He couldn't tell Evor. He couldn't even tell Pam and he shared everything with her. He decided to park the matter until after the tour, when he would collect the evidence from Teresa, identify the bent copper and decide whether to go for revenge within the law or without.

A little earlier and on the other side of the estuary, Eloise was in no state to pick Curly up from the station and was grateful when Evor offered to drive Curly home. Pam had put both Evor and Eloise in the picture with the story that she had concocted to explain the ambulance and Eloise's "delirious outburst" in the pub.

"Heavens daughter. Does Thomas Henry know what a devious woman he has married?" Evor exclaimed as he hugged Pam. "Great idea though" Evor, not short of being devious himself saw this as an opportunity to talk to Curly about Nick Haydn - Smythe

Curly sat in first class. He was one of only two occupants, the other being an old lady who was asleep. Halfway through the journey Curly thought she had passed away as there was no movement and he couldn't see her breathing. Curly recalled seeing a TV series where a nurse had leant over a patient to see if she could feel the patient's breath on her cheek. After dithering for some minutes Curly tiptoed across and leant over the old dear. Just as he felt the slight breath on his cheeks she opened her eyes and screamed the place down. People came rushing from second class, followed by the ticket collector. The old lady was upset but Curly's explanation for his actions was accepted by a doctor and calm was slowly restored.

The incident had upset Curly who was already in low dudgeon as he wasn't looking forward to returning home to Eloise and the ridicule of the village. He sat, accepting the scowls that were cast his way from across the apartment and pondering if he should talk to Thor about all other matters.

The train pulled into the station, exactly on time at 7-45pm. Curly remained seated while the rest of the train emptied. He sighed, picked up his case and reluctantly left the comfort, albeit icy, of the train. Imagine his shock to see Evor, instead of his wife at the end of the platform. Curly always rang Eloise when away but this time, due to the circumstances before their parting, he hadn't bothered.

Curly dropped his case and his jaw. "What's happened to my wife Evor?" He implored.

"Nothing to worry about lad" Evor replied "She's had some sort of bug and isn't up to driving. Pam's looking after her and I've been commanded to pick you up. That's all." Curly was shaking and he was as white as a sheet.

"I'll tell you all the news in the car Curly unless you fancy a drink on the way home?" Evor asked. Curly took this opportunity to delay his return and accepted the offer from the older man

Fifteen minutes later Evor and Curly were sat in the lounge bar of a nondescript hostelry half way between Castra and Haven. Evor had chosen this pub as no one from Haven would be likely to use it. Anyone wanting a pint was only fifteen minutes away from the Bell and could then walk home. It was too close to home however for any Haven resident to use for a clandestine meeting.

Evor knew that Curly was at low ebb when he didn't even notice the attractive and well endowed barmaid. In normal mode Curly would be treating her to his dark eyes, irresistible smile and old fashioned compliments.

Evor told Curly that Eloise had been diagnosed as having some form of virus that had given pressure on her brain and eventually caused her to pass out. One of the symptoms, Evor explained, was mood swings. He asked Curly if he had noticed any. This ploy sold the idea, hook line and sinker, to the younger man. After some discussion the two men relaxed and Evor judged the time right to bring up the issue of homophobia.

"John" Evor began "I've known you since you were a wee lad. I went for a few beers with your dad to celebrate your birth and I cried with you and Tom when you lost your parents on the Bluebell. There's nothing you can't say to me. I love you as much as I love the big oaf. While we're here together is there anything you'd like to get off your chest? In complete confidence of course."

Curly thought for some time. He scratched his cheek and sighed. "Evor. Can I tell you I'm not firing blanks?"

This took the wind out of Evor's sails. "I understand John. We had all put that down to Eloise being delirious with the virus and just talking Gibberish no one thinks you really have a problem."

"No Evor" Curly became agitated "This must not be told to anyone. Please. Not even Thor." Evor nodded his agreement and Curly continued "Evor. I have a daughter. Oh it's so wonderful to tell you. She's two years old and is the most beautiful child the world has ever seen. Evor this must be kept secret. It's so good to be able to tell you"

Curly had become more animated than Evor had ever seen him. Evor must have looked sceptical as Curly again asked for a promise not to ever tell anyone what he was about to show him next. On Evors promise Curly produced a picture from his wallet of a little girl. The child was obviously of mixed European and Afro Carribean origin. She was laughing and had the whitest of teeth behind her full lips. She looked intelligent and well nourished with loose curly black hair, not unlike that which gave John Jones his nickname. She was as Curly had said a very pretty little girl.

Evor smiled to show that he was sharing Curly's joy. "Thank you for showing me this John. She is lovely. May I ask, if her mother is of African descent?"

Curly looked astonished. "No Evor" Curly was annoyed. "If you must know she's English but of an Irish background. She's a cleaner in our office and one thing led to another one Christmas and now I have a daughter. Roisin knows I'm married and that I have no intention of upsetting Eloise. We have an agreement that I will look after our daughter financially, see them both during the week and continue to live with Eloise. What made you think that she's African Evor?"

Curly asked this in an angry tone. Evor didn't know how to answer, as in his mind the child was so obviously Afro Carribean. Curly had been taken for a ride he thought but he didn't want to antagonise him further so he switched tack. "She is very pretty John. What's her name?"

Curly softened his tone. "Thanks Evor, we called her Treasure" He cooed, before lovingly sliding the picture back into his wallet.

Evor asked if he had a picture of Roisin. "Don't be daft. If Eloise found a picture of another woman in my wallet that would take some explaining" Curly told him.

Evor pointed out that if Eloise found the picture of Treasure in his wallet, then Curly would still have some explaining to do. After a pause Evor asked if Curly was sure that Treasure was his or if there was a chance that a mistake could have been made.

Curly exploded "Don't be bloody stupid Evor. Look at her hair" he pulled out the picture again. "She's obviously mine. Just look at her. I don't like what you're suggesting about Roisin either. She's not the sort that would put it about. Trust me. She even resisted me for well over an hour."

"Have you met her parents or any of her family?" Evor enquired.

"What the hell has that got to do with anything Evor? As a matter of fact I haven't. Roisin says that they are a rough lot and she's moved on now. She has a nice house in a better area. She doesn't want Treasure to know how common they are."

"Aren't you curious lad?" Evor asked.

"Drop it Evor. I wish I'd never told you. Why can't you just be happy for me? No one, no one is ever happy for me Evor. I have no family, no one who really, actually, gives a shit about me, except for Treasure. Her love is unconditional.

Evor's heart felt as though it weighed a ton. Curly's outburst had hurt him as he loved the man as much as his own grandson. Evor sat quietly looking at the table. Tears welled in his eyes. Curly saw them. "I'm sorry Evor that was unfair of me. I'll get us another beer. You'll be OK driving on two but no more."

"Another thing Evor" Curly sipped his ale "I've been asked if I would consider playing for Malvil Park next season. There's money on offer and I understand a county cap." Evor kept a blank expression. Curly continued. "Imagine how proud my dad would have been, me in a county shirt. I'm going to find it hard to say no and the money will come in handy. I've been struggling a bit what with Treasure to pay for plus Eloise's high running costs. I'm sorry Evor but unless you object I'm going to have to go."

Evor said that he was aware of the circumstances as Roger DeGroot had spoken to him, asking permission to set things in motion. "Go with my blessing John. I'll be as proud as anyone to see you in a county shirt and I'll come to watch no matter where you play."

Curly put two pints on the table. "It's not so simple Evor. They want Thor to come with me and play number eight, both at

Park and County level. I can't play without him. You know it's having the confidence that he'll get me out of the shit that allows me to be flamboyant. Trouble is, Thor won't leave Haven, unless maybe you persuaded him?"

Evor smiled to himself. "I'll tell you what John. I'll have a word with Thomas Henry Orre but the deal is that you come round to my place in the morning to discuss another matter. Agreed?"

Curly said they could discuss now but Evor pleaded the need to be in the Bell for committee night and in any case Curly should go to see Eloise. The two men smiled, shook hands, both pleased with how things could be going their way.

Chapter 15 – The Day Before D-Day

Thor sat at the breakfast table with his wife and their offspring. "No work for me today love" Thor said "Shall we pop over to Newport for lunch?"

Pam asked why not go to the Bell and was taken aback when Thor said that he'd prefer to go over the water for a change. "You see love" He explained "I'll be stuck cheek by jowl with the rugby lads for the next few days and a bit of time together will be nice." What he really thought was that Curly would be home and there was potential for another scene between Curly and Eloise, if they stayed on this side of the estuary.

The Children were eager to get to school as Mr Bennett had promised to get Farmer Brown to bring some new lambs in. After dropping them off at school Thor called into the village shop. He bought a jar of headache tablets, a box of pills for an upset stomach, sea sick tablets, a roll of bin liner bags, two toilet rolls, tablets to stop diarrhoea and a box of laxatives. "That should cover just about every eventuality on tour" he thought.

Harry Thelwall played the till like a virtuoso pianist. With a big smile he thought how good a rugby tour was for selling medicines. He also noted that unlike his four previous tourists, who shall remain nameless, Thor had not added condoms to his order. He thought at least two of his earlier customers were being very optimistic indeed but he would keep their confidence, at least until the tour court was in session.

Chez Curly everything was sweetness and light. Eloise was still poorly and Curly had taken her muesli and coffee in bed. She had apologised profusely for the outburst that Pam had told her about, claiming not to remember a thing. Curly always felt a pang of guilt on the first morning home after visiting his daughter in London and was therefore prepared to forgive and forget. He mused at how a man really could forgive and forget but a woman would forgive and lock, whatever the occurrence had been, away for future use.

Curly left it until after the school bell had rung. He kissed Eloise gently on the cheek and told her that he was off to discuss the matter of his forthcoming switch of clubs with Evor. Eloise had been pleased that her husband had decided to make the move and looked forward to boasting of the fact that her John was a county player.

It was one of those mornings when the weather seemed impossible to describe. There was a light southerly breeze coming off the sea that brought warmth. There was a spring smell in the air and the new season's greenery was pleasing to the eye and yet the clouds across at Newport had the look of late autumn and a threat of bad weather in them.

These thoughts were going through the mind of Mike Bennett as he began a service on one of the lifeboat's engines. He couldn't decide if he should go ahead, as planned or delay until the weather settled for certain. People thought that being a coxswain was an easy job but it was getting decisions like this right that mattered to Mike. If he decommissioned the boat for a few hours now and someone got into difficulty he would regret it. On the other hand he wanted both engines serviced before the tourist season began.

An hour earlier he had ducked behind the boat to avoid having to talk to his brother who was on the way to school. He loved his brother dearly but man, he could talk. Not so much talk as ask bloody questions. Mike always had things going on in his head, albeit mostly concerning the estuary. Very little ever came from his mouth. His brother was the opposite. Despite his university education there seemed to Mike that bugger all went on in Paul's head. He wondered how such an alleged intelligent man could ask so many bloody daft questions and not even bother to listen to the answers.

While thinking these thoughts Mike hadn't noticed Curly approach; going towards Evor's cottage.

"Morning oh great sailor" Curly greeted him thus often "How fares the river Dee estuary today?"

Mike had started to give a tidal report and wind direction but Curly hadn't broken stride. "Sorry chum. Can't stop to gossip about the weather. I'm due to see Evor."

"There's another University idiot" thought Mike "asks a question then buggers off before the answer. How did they ever learn anything?"

Curly's thoughts were of self reproach. "Phew that was a close one John" Curly said to himself "What have I told you about asking Bennet senior about the bloody sea. He could have had you in a coma if you hadn't kept moving."

Curly passed Chubby without noticing him. "I might not be the brightest in this village" Chubby said aloud to no one "but at least I don't talk to myself like the clever buggers."

The back door of Evor's cottage was open. Curly entered without knocking to find Evor ironing shirts and singing loudly to a Roy Orbison record. "Bloody hell Evor. I didn't know you did that sort of thing" said a shocked Curly. "That's women's work in the eyes of your generation isn't it?"

Evor looked up "Who else will do my ironing? I don't enjoy it but you may have noticed that I live alone and therefore have to do it. It came as one hell of a shock to me, when I lost my wife, to discover the rigmarole that occurs between throwing a shirt on the bedroom floor and finding it back in the wardrobe."

"I suppose I'm lucky, having Eloise to do my ironing for me" Curly opined.

Evor just smiled, at him, deciding not to enlighten him to the fact that Eloise paid Spoddy Brown's wife to do her ironing. He chuckled when he tried conjure up a mental picture of Eloise stood at the ironing board, actually doing housework. "What's funny?" asked Curly.

"Oh nothing" Evor responded. He couldn't tell his young friend that he was picturing his wife ironing in the most exotic of lingerie. "Have you had breakfast John?" Evor asked. He responded to Curly's grin by rapidly producing two plates of full English breakfast, two huge mugs of tea and shepherding Curly towards the kitchen table.

After Evor had lured Curly into a false sense of security Evor broached the subject that had intrigued Curly since yesterday evening. "John there's no easy way of starting this conversation so I'll just dive straight in" Evor sighed a deep sigh and continued. "There's no point in beating about the bush so her goes. Are you ready John?" Curly nodded eagerly.

Evor didn't speak. The silence grew heavier. Curly nodded at Evor smiling. Evor frowned and tried to begin "Look John, this isn't easy for me to begin but I have been asked to talk to you about a serious matter. So I'll just get on with it and then it's done right?"

"For god's sake man, get on with it!" screamed a now exasperated Curly.
Evor was taken aback by this, so Curly had to apologise.

The two men looked at each other. "Would you like another cup of tea John?" Evor asked.

"Evor, my friend, I don't take offence so please just tell me what's troubling you" Curly implored.

"Well it's about your homophobia John. In the same way that the club was concerned about Northern bloke's racial prejudice, you must know that we can not countenance any bad comments towards homosexuals. That's the official line from the club and I've been asked to speak to you officially. Unofficially I'm concerned on a personal basis." He made eye contact with Curly and held it. "John I've known you since you were a nipper and I care about you. I have to ask, has something horrible ever happened to you to make you so anti homosexuals?"

"Sorry Evor. I'm not with you" said a puzzled Curly.

"Well. Has anyone at any time done anything inappropriate to you, say in your youth?"

Curly responded a definite "No!" Evor pressed him further. "Why then do you have such a strong feeling against these people? Can you explain it to me?"

"I can" said Curly but you might not like it. "I am appalled by the thought of what they do. It's wrong. I find it abhorrent and I will never to be able to accept it as anything other than grossly obscene. It's not an illness. It's a choice they make and it's not right. End of story."

Evor opened his eyes wide. Not knowing how to pursue this issue. "Well lad I know what you mean. I went to Doctor Jennings's a couple of years ago and she checked my prostate. A finger up the bum was a shock to my system. When she'd finished she said that she'd check it again in five years. I told her in no uncertain terms that nothing would ever go up my arse again." He continued. "I get a bit annoyed myself with these people who are gay or lesbian and have to go on about it at every verse end. It's as though they want to boast about it and I find that just as annoying as I find people who attack them for just being themselves.

Evor paused as Curly sniggered. Then he continued "You're right about it not being an illness but you're totally wrong about it being a choice. It's just people being people. Curly anyone could be gay. What if Thor was gay? Would you just drop him as a friend? He would still be the same man, the friend that you grew up with."

"Don't be bloody silly Evor. There's no way Thor is gay." Insisted a red faced and annoyed Curly.

"Of course not" Evor agreed but what if he was? Think about it. Would you still be his friend?

After a pause Curly said that he would always be Thor's friend. No matter what. Curly looked upset and confused.

"Why John? Why not just accept that everyone is different and there's good and bad in all, irrespective of their sexuality?"

Curly looked in pain. "Because, because," Curly began to cry. "Because I think I might be bloody gay." He looked up at Evor with tears rolling down his cheeks. "I'm one of them Evor. I'm a bloody pooftah! I hate myself too."

Evor put his arms around the younger man. "You're not John. I know you're not."

Curly had snot ballooning from his nose that mingled with his tears and ran into his mouth making him cough and retch. Evor handed him a tea towel. He blew his nose into it, curled it into a ball and dropped it on the floor. He looked directly at Evor and then through decreasing sobs he spoke again.

"Evor. I'm in love with another man. There I've said it! So you see I am gay."

Evor paused, in shock, then a grin came over his face and his usual warm smile returned "John, do you want to have sex with this man?" Evor asked.

"Fuck off Evor, of course I don't." Curly responded in a hurt voice.

"Do you want to kiss this man John?" Evor earnestly enquired.

"No! No! I couldn't imagine...... Yuk ! Curly was appalled.

"All's well John. You really aren't gay. It wouldn't bother me if you were but you're not." Evor smiled at him. "You love another man but not in a sexual way. You admire him. You appreciate him I can't define the feeling or explain it but I too have felt the same. Despite these feelings neither of us two are gay. It's love but camaraderie is probably a better word for this situation. I can even tell you who it is you feel like this about." Evor paused again and beamed. "It's my grandson isn't it?"

"How do you know?" Curly asked.

"John you've looked up to Thor all your life. I've seen how you are, you were both the other's best man at your weddings you're brothers in everything apart from having the same parents. If you were actual brothers you wouldn't have any qualms about your feelings. The thing is John, the big oaf thinks exactly the same about you but because he is a different man to you, he doesn't even know it."

Curly snivelled and began to smile a little "Are you sure I'm normal Evor?" He asked.

"Whoa lad! I said you weren't gay. I didn't say you were normal. Normal is not a word that you can apply to people. When you get a minute have a think about all the people you know. Is there one of them that you can describe as normal? I doubt it."

The pair of them laughed a little at this.

"Thanks Evor. Please don't tell anyone about this." Curly asked "I need to apologise to Posh boy don't I?"

"Just buy him a beer and give him a kiss on the cheek." Evor joked.

Walking home a happier man, Curly came across Thor and Pam walking down towards the ferry. Two minutes later a bemused Thor asked his wife if that had really happened. Pam confirmed it had. Thor shook his head in bewilderment. "I think the bloody world's going mad except me and you love."

Curly had skipped up to them, kissed Pam on the cheek, patted Thor on the shoulders then hugged him. He then beamed at them both and strolled off up the hill towards home without a word.

They sat on the ferry waiting for departure and were joined by a worried looking Chubby. "Mr Orre" He said "I think your pal Curly has been on the wacky baccy. He's just thumped me on the shoulder and told me that he's normal. What do you think?"

Thor mulled this over and then told Chubby that it was his day off and that he wasn't going to think without being paid. Chubby wandered off scratching his head.

There was warmth in the midday sun and the estuary was like a mill pond. Not a craft was to be seen on the gently rippling water. Pam looked out to sea and then upriver. She sighed happily. "There's nowhere as lovely as England on a day like today. We are lucky Tom, living here. It's beautiful."

Thor was about to remind her that this river had caused a tragedy in their young lives when the boat had sank with their parents onboard. He decided not to spoil his wife's happy mood. He just hugged her instead and smiled.

The ferry chugged into the slipway and off came the Browns, their car loaded with shopping. Mrs Brown wound the window down and asked Pam how Thor was behaving. Pam replied that he was OK and was informed that

John Brown was impossible as he was excited about the tour. His wife described him as like a child on Christmas Eve. The Orres waved and boarded the ferry.

"You off on tour with em tomorrow Sergeant?" enquired the skipper from his wheelhouse. "Yon farmer has just been telling me that it's his first trip abroad and that he's learnt some French."

"Spoddy Brown speaking French? Now I'm getting excited for the tour. I can't wait to see him in action." Thor replied. His eyes widened when the skipper told him that Spoddy had said that Curly had taught him a few words last week.

Waiting to embark on the ferry over at Newtown was Bill Davies, committee man and coach driver to Haven RUFC. Thor leant on the roof of Bill's car. "Anything exciting happen at last nights meeting Bill? Sorry I couldn't make it." Thor omitted to say that after his news about the boat tragedy he just thought it best to stay at home and calm down.

Bill looked a little guilty and informed Thor that he couldn't remember as Evor had been wearing his drinking cap and everyone was pissed at the end of the evening. Evor didn't actually wear a cap but it was a local colloquialism to say that a person was wearing his drinking cap when they were "fast glassing".

Thor said that he'd call to see Bill McLaren's minutes if he got chance. A very sheepish Bill Davies told him that he thought that the other Bill had stopped taking notes after a lengthy debate, started by Evor, about whether, given the choice, the committee would choose to shag a young Sophia Loren or a young Brigitte Bardot.

Bill apologised to Pam for swearing. Pam laughed shook her head and said that the rugby club committee should consider going into politics as such important matters need sorting out nationally.

"What are you doing over here anyway?" Thor asked.

"Oh there's a queue on the Castra road" Bill told him "I've been to pick up the first aid and physio gear from Mary Hynge and decided it would be quicker coming home via Newport ferry. I'll tell you what Tom, I dunno what she's bringing this year but that big chequer plate box that we had last year is now two. Both weigh a ton. I joked that she was taking coal across and got my head bitten off. Apparently we've got ice packs, a defibrillator and loads more kit, just in case. Oh! Don't tell her I called her Mary Tom."

Thor waved him on the ferry, put his arm around Pam and asked her where she'd like to eat. Her reply shocked him. His wife had asked for fish, chips and a can of lager from the chippy near the docks and they would eat it on a bench at the end of the breakwater.

Thor pointed out that they were flush at the moment and that he had spare money as his tour savings were augmented by sponsorship and input from the village. "We can eat anywhere love, even in a posh restaurant if you'd like."

She looked him up and down and laughed so much that she cried with happiness. The big oaf had obviously made an effort to be smart as he'd put on clean jeans and a sports jacket over his comfortable, old England rugby shirt. His jeans were clean but they were a pair that had a back pocket missing that had been torn off while playing with the kids. His old shirt was spotless but had frayed cuffs and his footwear was an old pair of black shoes that Pam had thrown out at least three times.

"Sorry love." Said a sorrowful Thor "Have I got my clothes wrong again?"

"You're good enough to go in the poshest restaurant in Castrashire. I don't care. I love you so much. I want to eat like we did on our first proper date. Don't you remember we went to the pictures and had fish and chips one Friday evening and your dad picked us up later?" Pam grabbed her husband's hand and ran, trying to drag him along with her. She felt just like the young girl who had been the envy of her friends back then.

The fish and chips had been good. Fresh fish this morning and an extra large portion of chips. The only difference was that all those years ago Thor had nicked a couple of cans of his dad's lager. Today they had called into an off licence for two bottles of a top quality Belgian lager.

They were walking back towards the ferry when a police car pulled alongside. "Hiya Serge" said young Gascoine "T'inspector had asked me to find you as he couldn't get you on the phone. I called over at your place and some old bloke was just leaving. He'd put a note through your door. I'll tell you what Serge, he was the spit of you though."

Thor asked if he knew what T'inspector wanted. Graham said that he didn't and asked them to jump in and he'd give them a quick lift to the station. They jumped in the back of the police car and the few people who were walking along the front could be seen speculating as to why the policeman had arrested the young couple.

Pam looked disgruntled so Thor apologised and pointed out that it never was a nine to five job. She shrugged and gave him a smile.

Graham Gascoine dropped them off outside the police station and drove off.

Inside Mike Maddox was on the front desk. "Hello Serge, Mrs Orre. I'll tell T'inspector you're here."

"T'inspector already knows." Shouted a belligerent voice from behind the inspector's door. The door opened and a belligerent face popped round it. "It's Inspector Hardy to you Maddox or Sir if you're addressing me directly. OK?"

A much chastened constable replied "Sir!"

"Hello Pam" the inspector beamed at Mrs Orre "Sorry to spoil your day but if I could just borrow your husband for ten minutes, I'd be very grateful. Get Mrs Orre a drink please Mike. Tom and I will have a tea and you can share those chocolate digestives in your drawer eh?"

Thor and T'inspector shuttled off into the office.

"That was amazing." Said Pam "Where has his northern accent gone?"

Mike told her that when he's being serious it disappears. He said that he must have been annoyed at being called T'inspector. Mike took the tea and biscuits into the office and then brought a coffee for himself and Pam. He brought out a second plate of biscuits, this time of much better quality. "I've given them biscuits from Cheap as Chips. These are some from the bakery on Market place. Yvonne, who runs the place, gives me a packet every week and I save them for special guests."

Mike had been trying to repress a giggle since their arrival and Pam had noticed this. "What's tickling you Mike? You can tell me." She implored.

Mike looked bashful and said "Sorry Pam. It's Thor he always makes me laugh when I see him out of uniform. I know that he's always clean and tidy but somehow, well he always manages to look sort of scruffy. Sorry, please don't take offence." "Don't worry." Said a laughing Pam Orre "I know what you mean. I could dress him in a made to measure suit from Saville Row and he'd look like a sack of oats within five minutes."

The pair laughed together and Mike admitted that although his shift more than respected Thor, they had many a good laugh at the fact that he would check them at the start of every shift to see if they were smart with clean boots etcetera but he'd look like a bundle of rags.

Pam was crying with laughter now, so much that her make up had run. Mike was also near to hysterics when the door of the office opencd and Thor came out.

Thor took in the site before him and, as laughter is infectious started to giggle himself. T'inspector opened his door to see what was going on. "Wassis then?" He asked "School f'bloody laffin policemen is it?" He grunted then shut the door behind him. He sat in his chair and smiled to himself. He certainly had a happy crew aboard.

Inspector Hardy had told Thor that he had been visited by that bloody ginger wench from telly news. She had a file of papers with her and wanted to give it to Thor personally. She refused point blank to leave it with Inspector Hardy. She had stormed out of the office, indignant that the inspector would not contact Thor immediately. Forty minutes later she had stormed back in, given the inspector a deposit box key and her business card. She had told the inspector that if Thor contacted her by phone, she would give him and him only the location of the deposit box.

The inspector also said that she had asked him to tell Thor that it was vital he moved quickly.

"Reet lad. What the ell's goin on?" Hardy asked, back in Yorkshire mode. "You've got a bloody lovely wife out there an I'd not be appy if a thought you were cavortin wi carrot top. So you'd better come clean." He looked sternly at the sergeant who in turn reddened but gazed blankly back at him.

Thor was fairly sure that he could trust T'inspector as he hadn't arrived until after the boat disaster but he was still reticent to disclose what Teresa had told him so far.

"Come on Tom there's summot funny ere. I can smell it an a dunno like it." Hardy implored.

"I'll tell you what I know sir." Thor met his bosses stare with one that was just as steely. "Firstly you must know that I would never, never understand, cheat on my wife." This was delivered with some vehemence and Thor continued "I am annoyed that you even think that I could do that Sir. As to Ms bloody Green she tells me that she has some information that would be very useful to Castrashire Constabulary. I don't know what it is or even if she's serious. As you know she's a damn forthright woman with a busy schedule and I doubt if she's wasting our time but I'm wary of being used to get her some sort of news scoop. I intended to come and get advice from you on return from the rugby tour."

Hardy looked chastened. He looked down at his desk then back up to Thor "I owe you an apology Tom. Of course I know you're above board but that bloody woman seems to rattle my cage." He then became a northerner again. "Ere's t'key. Give err a bell and find out what the ell's it all about. Tell err mind if it's not kosher al do err f'wastin police time. F'give me lad?" He held out his hand in reconciliation.

Thor took it "Sorry sir. I got a bit heated there. Probably because she rattles my cage as well."

The Orres sat on the harbour wall, waiting for the return ferry. When asked what T'inspector had wanted, Thor answered honestly that an informant had been in touch who would speak to Thor and no one else. Pam asked if he wanted to go and sort it but Thor responded that it would keep until return from the tour.

They boarded the ferry and had a pleasant trip across the water on a lazy ebb tide. They were the only passengers this trip but as Pam noted, the next ferry from Newport would have sky larking teenagers on it and Thor would struggle to resist his natural instinct to try and make them behave. "Hey, is that Evor pacing about near the lifeboat station?" Thor asked. Pam confirmed that it was as she'd recognise that walk anywhere. It was the same as Thor's.

As the ferry docked Evor came nonchalantly along the quay. "Hello you two. Had a good time?" he beamed. Pam replied that they had lunched on fish and chips and had had a great time. "Is everything OK Evor?" She asked.

"Fine. Fine" Evor answered "I just fancied a bit of fresh air and caught sight of you both on the ferry so I thought I'd just hang about to say hello." He turned to go and half waved but turned back. "Oh Pam can you pop down later with your recipe for pasties, I'm going to bake a few tonight for the bus."

Pam said that she would send the kids down with it as they would be out of school soon. Evor was taken aback by this. "Err no Pam. I want a bit of technical advice too. Err about well, my oven. See you later." With that he turned again and made off at pace.

"Mmmm" said Thor "Grandad's up to something. He looked a bit like a toilet then." When Pam asked what he meant Thor explained that Evor appeared a little flushed. Pam thumped her husband on the arm and they walked off towards home, giggling at his childish joke.

After the Orres had finished their evening meal, Thor was helping the children to write and draw pictures about the new lambs and Pam put her coat on to visit Evor. She took the recipe with her, knowing full well that Evor must want to talk to her about another matter.

Evor was in his garden and beamed a huge but somewhat sheepish smile as he watched Pam approach. "Hello love. Thanks for coming. What would you prefer a cuppa or a little very nice Menorcan gin?"

Pam kissed him on the cheek and said that she was off cuppas for medical reasons. They went inside and sat at the kitchen table. Evor produced two gin and tonics. Pam wasn't one to beat about the bush and asked, straight away, what it was that Evor wanted.

"Pam" Evor began "I am fully aware that you and your husband are as open with each other as any two humans on this planet of ours. I have a problem that I don't know how to handle and you're the only person that I would dream of approaching with it." He paused and played with his moustache for a few moments. The matter is so serious that I must ask, no insist, that it does not leave this room. Not even my grandson can hear of it."

He looked at her sternly with eyes that telegraphed his love and concern to her.

"Are you ill pop?" Pam asked, grabbing his two hands in hers and with wetness showing at the bottom of her big, wide eyes.

Evor assured her that he was fine, in fact bloody excellent for a mature chap. Pam sighed with relief and smiled at him. Her look told him that she had promised total secrecy. No words needed to be exchanged to confirm that.

Evor touched her arm and went to refill their gin and tonics. He then told her, word for word, about his conversation with Curly concerning his daughter, pointing out that in his opinion the child simply wasn't Curly's and that Curly was being taken for a ride.

"Pop, Curly's an intelligent man. Do you really think that he would be so stupid as to be conned in this way?" Pam asked

"There are times my love that a man will believe what he wants to believe. Even the most intelligent person can be hoodwinked by the streetwise. How often have you read of some fraud or scam and thought, how could anyone have fallen for that?" Evor looked melancholy "The thing is Pam, I love Curly damn near as much as I love you and your family. What do I do about it? Do I do anything or forget it altogether?"

"It's what do we do about it." Pam pointed out "I'm involved too now Evor and I don't have an answer. Probably best you forget it until after the tour and I'll see if I get a flash of inspiration."

Evor seemed to shrink. He regretted involving Pam and apologised for sharing his burden with her. She smiled at him. "Pop, how many times have we come to you for help and advice over the years? Don't worry! It'll cost you another G and T though before I leave.

Evor pulled the bottles over towards them and held her hand, grateful that he had such a strong woman married to his grandson.

Chapter 16 – D-Day

At 7-30 am the tourists began to arrive at the Bell. Red Rod and Myfanwy had prepared a mound of bacon butties and some were making beer their choice for a breakfast drink.

Eventually all had arrived except the two props from Newport. Evor asked young Nipper to pop his head round the corner to see if the ferry was on the way over. Nipper returned with the information that the ferry would drop anchor in about five minutes and contained the milk float and the post van. There were also two chubby pedestrians, one sat at the prow and one at the stern. As both had a big kit bag he assumed them to be the missing props.

Evor grunted.

"We can't n have them not speaking to each other." This was Red Rod.

"I have a good idea" Evor replied. Then to all present "Everyone. Humour me with this will you?" Assent was given, as all who knew Evor trusted him implicitly.

Six minutes later the front door creaked open and a prop forward shaped person threw his kitbag down, beamed and said "James, loose head prop but I'll play anywhere. Thanks for the invite. Evor shook his hand and motioned him towards a seat, passing him a pint at the same time. James had no sooner sat down that the door opened again and a second newcomer beamed at the assembly. "Hello. I'm Nige Royd.

Tight head pleased to join you" Once again Evor shook his hand, gave him a beer and motioned to the empty seat next to James Pyle.

Nige scowled at James. "If you don't mind I'll sit over here". He edged past his club colleague and took a seat at the bar.

Evor raised his glass. "Here's to an enjoyable, safe and successful tour." All present raised their glasses and downed the contents. "I have a few words to say before we depart" Evor announced "So grab another butty and take another beer and I'll begin"

The beers had been stacked up ready on a table and soon everyone had a handful of ale and a plate of bacon sandwich.
"Sorry Myfanwy" Evor apologised "I must thank you for providing a breakfast but I must now ask you to leave as I have some solemn rugby club business to enact." Myfanwy accepted the applause of the men and left with a smile on her face and a pat on the bottom, from Curly.

"Right chaps" said Evor as he jumped, surprisingly sprightly for a man of his years, to sit on the bar. "Firstly can we have Lee, Peter, Nigel and James up to the front, please?"

The four came and stood to the side of Evor, who had now donned a black robe and a judges' wig. "Haven. I order that for the purpose of this tour these four men are treated as friends and club mates and shall be looked after as one of our own in every respect. Agreed?"

"Aye Evor" came the chant from all Haven players.

"In return" Evor proceeded, "I expect that you four will abide by my judgements, taking any penalties awarded with good humour and not taking any action to bring the club name into disrepute" He paused "Well, let's say not taking any action worse than anyone else here to bring the club name into disrepute. Agreed?"

The four looked at each other. The three rugby players smiling but Lee, being from a soccer background, looked frightened to death. Peter winked at him and all four responded "Aye Evor".

Evor pointed out that this year there had not been the usual auction of tour positions and sale of tour virgins. This was due to the sponsorship and collection received after the cup final. "Hey! Don't rub it in" shouted Peter Craddock. This was followed by loud cheers from the Haven regulars.

For Lee's benefit Evor outlined the usual pre tour auction that took place in many rugby clubs prior to a tour, to raise beer money. At some point during the day a court would be held and misdemeanours, both real and invented, on the field and off, would be heard by the judge. Fines, in monetary terms and other punishments would be handed out. The accused would always have to abide by the judgement or the punishments would be physically enforced. For example, it was better to strip and jump into a fountain than be thrown in fully clothed and stripped afterwards. The position of judge fetched the highest bidding as the "rule" was that a judge can not be judged. Bailiffs and advocates were auctioned as usually these positions gave some protection from the harsher punishments. Virgins, chaps who had not toured with this particular club before were sold as slaves and although they were not expected to pay their masters fines they could be forced to take at least one of their master's punishments.

"I'm off. You're bloody insane mate" said Lee, the goalie and he picked up his bag and made for the door. Thor grabbed him by the scruff of the neck, picked him up and returned him to his spot in front of Evor.

Evor looked at him very sternly. "Young man, as you are new to these proceedings I shall not be too harsh with you. When I am not in robes you may abuse me if you like. When I am the judge you will address me as your honour. There will be no sale of virgins this year so you need not worry but I can not let your impudence go unpunished. Do you like Irish or Scotch whisky young man?"

Lee replied that he did not like whisky at all as even the smell of it made him gag. As if by magic, a large tumbler of a cheap, blended whisky appeared on the bar. "In one!" Evor ordered firmly.

Lee looked at the glass. He scanned the faces of all present. At that moment he hated Eddie Khan for talking him into coming on this trip. He caught Eddie's eye, Eddie motioned him to knock it back. The room was silent as Lee picked up the tumbler. He tried not to breath but despite his efforts, somehow the sharp smell of the liquid assailed his nostrils. Lee looked again towards the door, only to see the huge figure of a Viking god snarling at him. He had broken into a sweat and was concerned about what they would do to him if he couldn't drink it. In a trance, the liquid was approaching his mouth. The hand holding the glass was his but he had no control of it. In slow motion it reached his lips and tilted. Aach! It was bloody awful but had gone down his throat, which felt as though it was being cut by a plethora of razor blades. He felt terrible but then a cheer broke out and people were patting him on the back. The judge was smiling. The big black guy said "Well done". The huge Viking who had picked him up came into view, grinned and said "You'll do for me Lee. Good man."

In a matter of seconds his outlook had changed. He was a frightened outsider only seconds ago and now, it slowly dawned on him, he was accepted, one of them.

When it had quietened down Evor spoke again. After a smile and a nod to Lee, his solemn face returned. "We have another matter to deal with before we leave these shores to bring fame and glory to Albion." He paused. Many looked puzzled. Spoddy asked Paul Bennett who Albion was. "Later Spoddy" was Paul's answer.

Evor continued. "We can not have disharmony in the club. We must all get on together. There is no sense in leaving and waiting for things to come to a head." Most people in the room didn't know what the hell he was talking about but the two Newtown props were looking at the floor.

"I understand," said Evor "That you two lads don't get on. In fact you don't speak do you?"

They looked at him and Nigel spoke first "That's fuck all to do with you. It's a personal matter."

Evor reddened in anger "Don't you mean its fuck all to do with you, Your Honour?" Nigel couldn't believe it. His private life was being brought up in a rugby club court. He was furious and decided to leave. He turned to go and was immediately pinned by Ian Tomkin and Thor. He struggled but to no avail. "I insist on leaving" He shouted. "You can't kidnap me."

Evor reminded him again that he must address him as Your Honour. He also reminded him that only ten minutes ago he had agreed to abide by Evor's judgement taking any penalties with good humour and not bringing the club name into disrepute.

The other Newtown prop, James, was enjoying his enemy's predicament. He was by far the more intelligent of the two but despite this, he hadn't grasped that the same would be applied to him.

"Bring them both here" Evor ordered. In a flash the pair were placed on chairs facing each other and held firm.

Evor spoke in a quieter, conciliatory tone. "Look chaps, I want you to come along and enjoy yourselves on tour but I can't have this not speaking nonsense. I don't know why they put up with it at Newport. You're right Nigel, I can't kidnap you. I can take you part way to the port, get you drunk, strip you and put you off the coach in the middle of nowhere in female underwear, with lipstick and eye make up.

James laughed at this, then, as they say, the penny dropped. He had the sense to address Evor correctly. "Your Honour. That would be judged as kidnap by the authorities and it would bring the name of Haven into disrepute. Surely you wouldn't want that?"

Evor was one step ahead. He pointed out that they had both agreed not to bring Haven into disrepute. He went on to ask how they thought that they would be viewed by all rugby men in the county and beyond if they had gone to the police over a rugby court judgement rather than accept the forfeit. They chewed this over for a moment or two and their eyes met and held. They might have the satisfaction of Evor being in trouble but they would be a laughing stock for all time.

A table was placed between them. Next two newly pulled pints of best bitter were placed on the table. These were followed by two other pint glasses full of liquid. Floating in each glass was a horror that made Lee realise how lucky he had been with the whisky. He could make out a sardine head, numerous fag ends, bits of seaweed, a slug and what could have been vegetable bits or human vomit floating around in each glass.
The props looked at the concoction and knew what was coming.

"Gentlemen" said Evor "It is the will of this court that you two shake hands and resume your friendship as befits the front row union. Should you agree and be genuine, the following benefits will accrue to you. You will have your beer and food paid for from tour funds, as will everyone else. The only outgoings you will have will be for any "cultural" expenditure should you choose to visit say an art gallery, museum or any other "establishment".

Spoddy looked bewildered. Paul Bennett leant over, "He means knocking shop."

"Right." said Spoddy, albeit none the wiser.

Evor continued "Furthermore, should you agree then you can choose which of the pints in front of you to down in one. Should you decide not to comply with the will of this court then you will be dropped off as intimated earlier and that pint," pointing to the foul mess before them, "will be poured into you. What say you?" The props looked at each other in horror, knowing that Evor meant to carry out the threat.

James spoke first. "Nige. You need to know than Emma has given me the elbow now. She told me on Sunday that she's taken a shine to some young copper, called Gascoine. She called me a fat loser and walked out. We're both better off without her mate." With this he held out his hand.

Nigel looked at him for some time, shaking his head. "I'd heard that on the grapevine. She's just used us both and will probably do the same to the copper." He took James's hand and held it for some time. "Tell you what though. She was right about one thing mate, you are a fat loser."

James gave him a playful punch under the ribcage and the pair laughed together.

"Good decision" said Evor. "Down the beer of your choice in one please. Then we can be on our way. That is if you still want to come?"

The pair stood up put one arm on the other's shoulder, picked up a beer each, clinked glasses and downed in one.

Five minutes later the engine of the coach began its rhythmic throbbing and it pulled gently away from the double yellow lines outside the pub. Evor and Mo Khan sat together on the left side front seats. Ian Tomkin was across the aisle with Bill McLaren, on the right side. The clock above the driver said 08-55.

"Evor" said Tommo "This must be the first time in the history of rugby union that a touring party has got away on time. All credit to you." Bill cut in "Aye and the way you handled those two Newport props was an exemplary example of diplomacy. I think you deserve an MBE or something." Evor pointed out that threats could hardly be counted as diplomacy.

Mo reached inside his blazer pocket and produced a hip flask. He gave that strange little shake of the head that despite being a cliché is nevertheless a habit that some older people with Indian sub-continent heritage cannot help. "Never mind Evor, it was bloody brilliant!" Mo stated. He took a swig from the hip flask and passed it to Evor, who gulped, smiled and gave it to Tommo. When Tommo and Bill had swigged it was returned to Mo. "I thought that you were tea total, Mo?" Tommo asked.

"You know I have to be, for religious reasons" Mo replied "Let's not forget the rules though chaps. What goes on tour stays on tour eh?" The four elder statesmen of haven RUFC laughed conspiratorially. The tour had begun.

The next row of seats consisted of Bill Davies and Harry Thelwell on the Left and Rod Davies and Norman Arkwright across the aisle. Bill Davies had hired a driver for the trip so that he could "enjoy alcohol responsibly", as he put it. Bill had arranged to pay the driver himself but Evor would not hear of this and the committee had unanimously agreed to fund this. Bill produced a couple of cans. The Tschhht sound was heard and Bill and Harry tapped cans together as a sign that they had started as they meant to continue.

Across the way, Northern Bloke and Red Rod had opened a newspaper each, The Daily Mail and Morning Star respectively. The pair often held political discussions and despite their self proclamation of being at far opposing ends of the political spectrum, they agreed on more issues than they differed on. They had made a pact not to drink until the half way stop as both suffered a touch from stomach acid. The sound of cans opening had tested their resolve, particularly as they had drank beer with their breakfast. On reaching the main road, just outside Castra, Norman looked at his friend.

"Rod, I think we have shown our will power to be immense and I propose that we reward our resolve with a bottle of Old Speckled Hen from the rack above."

The Welshman pondered this suggestion for a whole millisecond, raised his hand "Motion carried" was his response, whilst producing two bottles, two pint jugs and a bottle opener, seemingly from thin air.

The row behind was empty on both sides but contained various packs of beer, spirits and mixers. Behind this, on the left was Mike Bennett who sat alone fast asleep as he had been out on a false alarm call in the early hours. Someone had seen a body floating out on the tide and he had scrambled with his crew to search the estuary only to be called back as a fishing boat had reported a blow up sex doll in its nets. Opposite and also alone, so as to stretch his plastered leg was Rob Church. The Saint took time from reading his motor cycle magazine to beg someone to reach him a beer. Rod teased him for a while. "Skipper has said no beer for you as a punishment for injuring yourself in a drunken stupor." After a few minutes of begging, Rod caved in and poured him a perfect pint of Speckled Hen.

Continuing down the coach, on the left side one came to a pair of seats facing the rear, a table and a pair of seats facing forward. The rearward facing seats were occupied by Nige Royd and James Pyle. The other side of the table, the seats contained Jim Cameron and Simon Spencer. Had the four prop forwards planned to sit thus or, as so often happens, had the front rows come together by sheer magnetism? Who knows? In any case a pack of cards was opened and a game of three card brag had begun. Nige had passed out a can of Guinness to each player. He insisted that it was special "low calorie Guinness" that would never put any weight on them. Jim Cameron was scouring the wording on the can for confirmation of calorific content, when he failed to find evidence of this he simply lifted the can to his mouth and took a huge swig. "Amazing" he said "You can barely tell the difference." The four laughed long and loud. Truly the front row union will never be understood by the rest of us.

Across the aisle once more was a similar set up of seats with a table. On the rear facing seats sat Thor and Curly. Opposite them were Paul Bennet and Peter Craddock. Curly had produced a very nice bottle of red wine which he had decanted into top quality plastic cups bearing the Fortnum and Mason logo. The wine was tasted and had its merits appreciated by Curly Paul and Peter. Thor had knocked his cup full back in one. "I'm not supping this crap all weekend!" He informed them. Three mouths had gaped open in disbelief. "I never had you down as a Philistine Tom" said Peter Craddock. "He's not" Spoddy chipped in, leaning over from the seat behind. "He's a Castrashire lad born and bred, just like me."

Thor considered this and silently vowed to get to like wine.

Adjacent to Spoddy and also sat alone was Chubby, who was also leaning over the seat in front of him. The difference was that Chubby had a purpose. He was watching the game of three card brag, intending to ask if he could join in at some point. For now he was content to watch and work out who was a chancer and who only upped the stakes to support a strong hand.

Finally there came the back row of seats. The five seats were occupied by the younger element of the tour, Nipper, Lee, Teflon and Posh Boy. They had placed a sign board in the rear window that read "HAVEN RUFC on tour". They had dashed to this spot in order to kneel on the seats looking out of the window, alert for any attractive "totty" who they could make unsavoury gestures to. While they would publicly espouse politically correct behaviour and respect for the female sex in college, once aboard the coach they had reverted to type. Bottles of wildly coloured alco - pops were opened and packets of crisps chomped. "Whey Hey! Look at that babe in the Porsche!" Lee pointed with excitement. He did not expect the hard punch under his ribcage and the order "Behave you twat! That lady is Eloise, Curlies wife." ordered an angry Nipper.

The Brawl that ensued between the two friends was stopped by Paul Bennett. "Bloody Hell we haven't done ten miles yet and you're behaving like my school kids. Pack it in now or I'll split you up." His schoolmaster voice held such authority that the lads stopped scrapping immediately and Nipper even said a very genuine "Sorry Mister Bennet" The whole coach roared with laughter. "Time for a song" called Red Rod.

An hour from the port the coach pulled onto a motorway, then shortly after again pulled off again to a service station for toilet brake. As a few drinks had been consumed most ran off towards the toilets. The handful of tourists who smoked however had a more pressing priority. Chubby fell between two stools and came very close to peeing himself as he was lighting up a hand rolled cigarette that smelt suspiciously of "herbal remedy".

When everyone was back on board, Evor gave a stern warning that, on no account were any illegal substances to be brought onto the bus at any time. Failure to abide by this law would lead to serious consequences for any individual concerned. He laboured to point so much that even Northern Bloke, with his hatred of smoking, believed that he had gone a bit over the top.

When Evor sat down again Mo asked him why he had come on so strong as he had never mentioned drugs in previous years. "Trust me Mo. I have my reasons" said Evor, who had noted that both Chubby and Posh Boy had looked a little sheepish.

A few seat changes had taken place and now playing three card brag at a table were James and Nige with Chubby and Spoddy taking the vacated seats. Now Simon Spencer was spectating from the seat behind.

Over the way, Pete Craddock had asked Thor if it would be OK for him to change seats for a while. Thor had told him that of course he was free to change at will. Pete pointed out that he simply couldn't take another hour of Paul Bennet's constant questions. Pete threw in a quick impersonation "Do you think we'll win these tour games Tom? How good are the teams we're playing? Do you know how big the boat is? Do you think I should have brought a waterproof coat?" Peter said "Hell Tom, I was expecting an, are we nearly there yet. I could cope with it if he would wait for a bloody answer to a question before asking three more!"

"Thor said "See you later buddy" and Pete went to ask if Mike Bennet would object to him sitting alongside him. Mike smiled and made space. "You're the lifeboat man aren't you?" Peter asked. "That must be an interesting job?" Mike answered him. An hour later, Peter deeply regretted the question and was praying, silently for the journey to end.

Evor and Mo were playing chess. Bill McLaren and Tommo were sampling and discussing a box of miniature malt whisky that Bill had brought along. A few more were sensibly having forty winks but on the back row the youngsters had become very animated due to a coach full of young women who kept passing them and being passed by them. Nipper had concluded that the girls were also bound for the ferry. He understood full well that he was totally irresistible to the opposite sex, a delusion brought about by three or four bottles of WKD and high octane cans of lager.

Curly had also noticed the ladies and being sat in a window seat, had smiled and waved at them each time they passed. He was sure that a dark haired lass, with a sunbed tan had noticed him and undone an extra button on her blouse for the last overtaking. Thor missed nothing. "Here we go again. When will Curly learn?" He thought to himself.

Unlike the others Thor had also noticed a mini bus full of older individuals, some of whom were nuns and a couple were dressed as priests. They looked genuine and the placard in the rear window, reading "Saint Elspeth's pilgrimage" seemed to confirm this. After passing each other a few times Thor also noted that the curtains had now been closed in the mini bus windows. A glance towards the rear seat of the Haven coach provided the reason for the drawing of curtains. The faithful had obviously seen enough of the bare arses on view from the four lads on the back seat.

After half an hour they left the motorway and followed signs to the port. It was only just over a mile and the traffic slowed to a crawl as each vehicle picked the correct lanes to get through the custom booths and onto the awaiting ferry.

Evor stood up and shouted down the coach "Right lads get some covers over the booze supply. We're not supposed to have any onboard while travelling so all evidence away please and best behaviour for ten minutes in case some nosy jobsworth decides to board us."

The coach full of young women pulled alongside and the dark haired girl waved back in response to a kiss blown to her by Curly.

"Do you fancy her then Curly?" asked Paul Bennett "How old do you reckon she is? Where are they from Nipper? Can you see on the back of the bus? What do you reckon your chances are Curly? Don't you think you should behave a bit with women Curly?"

"Paul. For god's sake give it a rest will you. Why can't you be a bit quieter like your Mike?" was Curly's response.

There was a loud cheer from the back of the coach and Lee came running down the aisle with Nipper. "Bloody Hell! Did you see that? Two of them flashed their baps out of the rear window."

At this everyone jumped up and looked out of the right hand side of the coach. It had been a quick flash though and the girls in question had pulled their tops back down and were waving at the rugby team. A very guilty Mo had slipped back into his seat, concerned that his son would report home that he had jumped up as well. He need not have worried as young Teflon was far too enthralled with the activity on the other bus to have looked towards his father.

Another coach pulled alongside. This contained mostly men, with just the odd female person. The coach driver beeped his horn to get attention and most of his passengers held up a can of beer and gave a thumbs up, or some other friendly gesture to the Haven lads. The more sober occupants had noted that it was strange to see a coach from a rugby club without the rugby lads holding up cans in return. Fortunately everyone on the Haven coach had followed Evors instruction to hide their drink and behave for ten minutes.

"Hey they're from Castra" shouted Teflon "Castra Albion Football Club. It says so at the back."

"That's handy" thought Evor "With them waving their beer about like idiots they'll take the attention of H M Customs away from us."

The Haven coach pulled forward again to go alongside the coach load of girls. Curly was looking out for his dark haired girl. He couldn't believe his good fortune she had written on the window in lipstick "I'm Tracy. You?"

Curly breathed on the window and wrote, back to front so that it could be read, CURLY X. She smiled and blew him a kiss as her coach pulled away.

This activity sparked another set of questions from Paul Bennet. Curly didn't care. "I've still got it" He thought to himself.

Chapter 17 – Barnacle Bill The Sailor

The coach from Haven had been the first vehicle to board the roll on roll off ferry, on deck B.

As Evor had expected, the footballers had drawn the attentions of most of the port officers and port police were busy confiscating the copious amount of beer that was visibly on display. A lone member of Her Majesty's Customs and Excise had boarded the rugby bus and after receiving a polite greeting from Evor, Mo and Tommo, he made no more than a cursory glance down the aisle.

"I don't know" he said "Why can't the soccer fraternity behave like you rugger lads eh? That lot have gallons of drink on board and are all totally pissed. You guys are an excellent example of good behaviour, as are most coaches from rugby clubs." Evor thanked him for that and made a comment that they would soon make up for their "tea total" journey, once on the boat.

As soon as the coach came to a halt, the four elder statesmen, Evor, Mo, Tommo and Bill were off the bus like a shot. Their speed of movement amazed some of the younger element. "Where have they gone in such a rush?" Spoddy Brown asked no one in particular. "Look and learn Spoddy" Thor replied "Some of those guys know a thing or two about rugby tours. They'll be first at the bar and will have staked out an area for us to use as a club house on the boat."

"Come on lads. Let's get after them and help get a good spot" Northern Bloke urged. With that a disorganised scramble occurred as everyone tried to get off the bus at the same time. Peter Craddock made it off fairly quickly. As he told Thor later, after sitting next to first Paul Bennet and then Mike, he'd have fought the entire British army to escape.

Bob Church, The Saint, couldn't join in the melee due being on crutches. He sat back and watched the unruly mob, chuckling to himself. Lee asked him what he found so funny. "Look at this lot mate" Bob replied "If the Martians are watching from a flying saucer, then they'll return to base and report that there are no intelligent life forms on planet Earth."

Lee stepped back and took in the scene before him. Everyone was cursing and fighting to get off but in their efforts departure was actually being delayed. "I see your point Saint" said Lee "but it looks like fun." With that he dived over the top of Nipper and Teflon and grabbed hold of Paul Bennett.

Eventually, one by one they got out of the bus and ascended the flights of stairs that lead from the car decks to the passenger areas of the boat.

By the time Lee reached the bar area he found most of the tourists already seated. He was particularly surprised to see The Saint had got their before him. "How the hell did you get here?" Lee asked. Saint explained that he had left the coach via the emergency exit and instead of scrambling up the stairs with the rest, a crew member had directed him to a lift for disabled passengers. "Brains, Lee. When you get a bit older you'll start to use them too." That was Saints kindly advice.

Sure enough Evor and the mature chaps had selected a decent area, close enough to the bar but with plenty of seats. Being virtually first in the bar, except for a few foot passengers, they had been able to commandeer a good spot. Tommo had also spoken to the head barman and given him a good tip with the promise of more to come providing jugs of Grolsch were not allowed to run dry.

"Time for a song" shouted Red Rod. "What shall we begin with lads?"

"How about she'll be coming round the mountain?" asked Nipper. Evor pointed out that in mixed company with children aboard it wasn't really appropriate. "There's a cleaner version Evor." Nipper pointed out. "Aye lad there is" said Bill "but no bugger knows it."

"Why not start with that song, the one that you gave us after the cup final?" asked Peter Craddock. "That's clean." Thor told him that it was Haven's club song and a good idea. With that decided the singing began. "Oh there was a young farmer who sat on a rock a waving and shaking his big hairy, pause, fist etc"

The bar area was beginning to fill up with other passengers. These fell into two distinct groups. One group who were interested in where all the noise was coming from and wanted to take a look, possibly get involved in the fun. The other group knew precisely where and from whom the row was emanating. This second, much larger, group wanted to be as far away from the noisy area as possible. The song finished and received a deserved round of applause from the bystanders.

"Barnacle Bill The Sailor." suggested Evor. Everyone agreed even the Newport lads who knew this one. "Wait, wait" shouted Peter Craddock. "Can I be the young maiden please? I've always wanted to sing that bit."

After a moments shocked silence Evor produced a blond, curly wig from his rucksack and tossed it to Peter. "You'll make a fine young maiden Pete." Evor shouted and took a huge swig of his beer. This action was automatically copied subconsciously by everyone else.

By now the football lads had arrived and had gathered round near the rugby tourists. The sixteen or so girls from the minibus had also arrived. It later transpired that they were Castra University Hockey team, going on tour to Holland.

Peter had donned the wig and stood up holding his hands in front of his face in a parody of a shy young girl. Onlookers were already laughing before Thor shouted across "Are you joining in this one Curly?" A loud cheer went up as John David Jones already had the girl on his lap. He would find it very hard to sing as she was examining his tonsils with her tongue. He broke off for air. "I'm with you Thor." He said, sheepishly.

Peter began in a high pitched voice. "Who's that knocking on my door? Who's that knocking on my door? asked the fair, young maiden."

The loud, boisterous and deep bass response from the rest was "It's only me from over the sea said Barnacle Bill the Sailor. It's only me from over the sea said Barnacle Bill the sailor."

Peter feigned shock at the rough response "It's too late to let you in. It's too late to let you in. said the fair young maiden."

"Open the door you bloody great whore. Said Barnacle Bill the Sailor. Open the door you bloody great whore. Said Barnacle Bill the Sailor."

The crowd were enjoying it. It was harmless fun, as most of the tourists were sober enough to shout bleep or bleeping when foul language was called for.

Thor's second shout of "Curly! Come up for air man." brought laughter in abundance. Barnacle Bill eventually concluded, to much applause and Evor got the crowd to join in with "Swing Low Sweet Chariot" with all the actions. Evor demonstrated each action and got the onlookers to try them out in advance. "Are there any questions?" Evor asked.

A pleasant Lancashire lady, going on holiday with her chap asked for clarification. "I understand the swinging hands near the floor for swing low. I get the Italian touch of the lips for sweet and the shacking of reins for chariot but can you explain why we have to pretend to stab a cat on our lap to symbolise coming. Please can you explain?"

Evor thought for a moment before replying. "In a word my dear. No! Perhaps you could help Sir?" He directed this question at her companion who had begun to cry with laughter as had many of those present.

During the singing of swing low, one of the priests who had arrived in the minibus full of pilgrims had sidled over towards the noisy area and spoken quietly with a few of the rugby lads. While the priest was in conversation with Evor, one of the football supporters shouted "Hey! You lot might be good at singing but you're bloody rubbish at drinking. We got our drinks taken off us by the cops" This was said in a confrontational manner and sure enough a couple of the rugby lads took the bait.

"Knob off mard arse!" This was said in a very upmarket voice by Haydn – Smythe. "We'll sup you lot under the table Boyo"

Red Rod retorted. A few insults were passed back and to before Evor took charge. "Gentlemen, gentlemen! Some order please" he commanded. "May I suggest a contest? A boat race perhaps?"

"I'm talking about drinking old man, not bloody boat races" jibed the loud mouth.

Evor explained that a boat race was a drinking contest. Each side would provide eight rowers who would sit in a straight line alongside their opponents. Each man would have a full pint of beer on the floor next to him. On the command, "go", the first man would lift his pint and drink it as quickly as he could. When he had finished or had enough he would upend the glass above his head as a signal that the next man could then lift his pint and do the same. This would follow on down the line until the last man had an empty glass on his head. The winning team were the first to have all eight men sat with upturned glasses on their heads. The losers would pay for both sets of beer.

The football fans, for it transpired that the team had left yesterday and this group were their supporters, huddled together to discuss. "Agreed" said a more conciliatory member of the group, holding out a hand to Evor. Any hint of animosity between the two groups had now evaporated and everyone was laughing as they began to sit cross legged in two, side by side rows. Full beers were produced and the rowing eights were ready to go.

The Haven team had set up with Red Rod at number 1. 2 was the Saint, 3 Thor, 4 Spoddy Brown, 5 Jim Cameron, 6 Grandad Thelwell, 7 Evor and in bow position was Tommo.

"Wait a minute" called the football leader "We need a starter. Father would you do us the honour please?" The priest smiled and replied that while he didn't really condone drunkenness, he saw no harm in starting the race. "On your marks, get set, Go!"

To the cheers of a good sized crowd, Red Rod grasped his beer and guzzled as fast as he could. When he'd downed the pint he upturned the glass on his head and glanced across. His opponent had beaten him. That was rare.

Saint slurped well and when his empty glass was on his bonce he had drawn level. Thor took it steady, watching his opponent and keeping dead level. He could have drunk faster but he had faith in the legendary ale men who anchored the back of the boat.

Spoddy was so enthralled with cheering that he forgot to begin his pint when Thor had finished. A smack on the back of the head from Jim Cameron behind him galvanised Spoddy into action. He drank well but due to his delay his team were a full half pint behind. Jim pulled most of it back at no 5 but Harry was up against a good man at six and passed on to Evor still behind.

Evor had quaffed beer with the best of them. He was cheeky enough to hold his glass up and say "cheers everyone" before even starting. When the empty pint pot was placed on his head, Evor was a little surprised to see that the teams were neck and neck.

The two at bow paused, looked at each other, shook hands and began their own private race that would decide the outcome of the contest. The number 8 in the football fans boat fancied his chances. He knew he could sup. He was their best man by far. However he hadn't even got the beer to his lips when his jaw dropped open in amazement and he spilt half of his pint. He had never seen anything like what he had just witnessed. Ian Tomkin had simply opened his mouth wide and poured a full pint of beer straight down his throat in one go.

Tommo winked at his transfixed opponent and slowly raised the empty glass and turned it upside down on his head. "I think I deserve a beer for that" Tommo said to the cheers of both teams and onlookers.

After a bout of handshaking and slapping of backs the rowers stood up, slowly and refilled their glasses from the jugs of Grolsch. The money for the wager was given to Evor who offered to waive it as the tour kitty was bulging with funds. The football fans wouldn't hear of it and insisted on paying up. After a fair bit of argument Mike Bennett came up with a solution pleasing to all. There was a collection box chained to the bar for the RNLI. Everyone agreed that this was a worthwhile place to deposit the cash and applause rang out as the money was placed into the lifeboat box.

"Anyone seen Posh Boy?" Evor asked. "Never mind Posh Boy" said Thor "Where's that bloody Curly Jones?"

"Is Curly the cute little one?" asked a busty blond girl from the hockey team.
Kieran Shallcock pointed out that he was the smallest in the team but disputed the description as cute. "I'm far cuter" he asserted, smiling his best smile. "Would you like a drink?" he had noticed her empty glass and proffered the jug. The girl asked if he was old enough to drink. This was done in jest but raised a laugh from the rest of his team mates.

Another of the hockey girls bounced over and said "Right guys, we'll challenge you to one of your boat races if you're up to it."

Simon Spencer, who was bordering between being Dr Jekyll and Mr Hyde at that point, spoke out. "Don't be daft girlie. These lads are serious drinkers. You won't stand a chance."

She agreed with him and asked if they would consider it if the rules were altered to even things up a·little. When asked how, she proposed that the girls only had to drink a half pint while the rugby team had to down a full one. Jekyll agreed to this on behalf of his team mates. And the same crew sat down cross legged ready for action.

"Oh no you don't." chipped in a tattooed young woman, "We'll choose your team. OK?" As the crowd were looking expectant, the rugby lads couldn't really say no so Evor stood up, waved his hand towards the tourists and said "Certainly ma'am. Please feel free to choose any of my men, but what's the wager?"

The bubbly blond lass came up with a solution acceptable to all. "If you win then we'll take off our blouses and bras. If we win it's trousers off chaps and overboard they go."

The girls had obviously watched the first race and had thought out a game plan. The team they had picked consisted of :- 1 Mo, 2 Red Rod, 3 Spoddy, 4 Mike Bennett, 5 Paul Bennett, 6 Lee, 7 Nipper Shalcock and 8 Teflon.

The two teams sat down with glasses primed and ready. Evor was just about to count down to the start when the first girl shouted "Hold on! We need a referee." She jumped up and ran across to the priest again, asking him if he would ensure fair play. He reluctantly agreed muttering in his head "Holy Mary Mother of God forgive me for what I'm about to acquiesce to."

On the command "Go" the teams began. The first girl finished while Mo still had a half pint in his glass. The second was still half a pint ahead of Red Rod. Spoddy went a little further behind and by the time Mark Bennett handed over to his brother the rugby team were a pint behind at the half way stage. The girls were feeling assured of victory as their best drinkers were at the back and their captain had picked the four, who looked like weakest links, to sit in the last positions for the opposition.

The crowd had grown in size as word of the wager had spread around the bar .

At number five Paul Bennet fell a little further behind. Then on the shout of sixty nine from Evor, Lee tipped the full glass over his head, soaking himself in lager. Nipper immediately did the same as did Teflon. The three lads were soaking wet and smelling of beer. The last two girls hadn't touched their drinks but all were bone dry. The rugby lads were cheering and began to chant "Get em off, get em off" at the girls. The onlookers didn't know what to make of it. The girls were angry and appealed to the referee to declare them the winners and the rugby lads as cheats.

The priest stood up and appealed for quiet. When silence had been achieved the referee gave his judgement. "Ladies and Gentlemen. The rules were stated clearly at the beginning of the first contest. Insomuch as each rower has a full glass and after the number one has upturned the glass on his or her, head the number two may pick up their glass. This procedure to continue down the line, each rower must have his glass upturned on his head before the rower behind can begin. No mention was ever made of having to consume the contents of the glass, it merely must be upturned on the head of the rower in front before the rower behind can begin. I reluctantly have to say that the rugby eight complied fully with the rules and I have no option other than to declare them the winners of the contest." This having been said, the priest sidled off in search of obscurity and prayed for forgiveness.

The smiling rugby lads looked across at their opposite numbers, some of whom were angry, some indifferent and some simply couldn't have cared less. There was a period of total inactivity, a stand off.

Eventually the girl at the back of their line said "Oh sod it then." In a trice she whipped off her team polo shirt. She then reached behind her back and undid her bra, which fell to the floor revealing a fine pair of breasts with dark, erect nipples. "Well, come on then don't you want to play with them?" She directed this question to Teflon.

Teflon froze in amazement.

"Come on Teflon lad. You're not likely to drop them are you?" This jest from the Saint got a good cheer from his team mates but Teflon still didn't react. He was still sat with his mouth wide open with beer dripping from his hair when the girl dived on him. Four or five of the other girls followed suit and the rest scuttled out of the way.

"Just my luck" said the girl alongside Nipper. "I get the bloody ginger top. Come on then lad, get a grip of these." Her shirt and bra were off and Nipper didn't need asking twice.

Chaos ensued. Some passengers were trying to get closer to the action some were trying to get away. A handful of chaps were trying to get closer while pretending to be getting away. No wives were fooled by this.

A group of Morris Dancers had become involved and the music from their accordion enhanced the atmosphere. One of the younger Morris men elbowed hid way in and stole a pretty girl from young Lee. Lee took offence at this and said "Come back here love. You don't want that ponce with bells on his shoes."

The Morris man asked who he was calling a ponce. No one can be sure who threw the first punch but Jekyll had become Hyde and he certainly threw the second one. Hyde threw a fist at a Morris man who evaded the blow, which hit one of the soccer fans. In no time at all a brawl had begun. It was like one of those old, black and white cowboy films, where everyone joins in. Women screamed, hockey girls got dressed, Evor shouted "Stop this at once!" while throwing a crafty punch at a complete stranger who had Mo in a headlock.

Unbeknown to the protagonists, this melee was the cause of a divorce. A quiet chap from the Home Counties ignored his wife's order to keep out of the childish fight. He'd never been involved in a brawl in his life but was pulled towards it by a magnetic force. "Woman, you've bossed me around for thirty years. I've had enough I tell you. His pent up anger was meant for her but for some reason he chose to unleash thirty years of frustration into one big punch. He chose Thor.

Thor took the surprise punch full in the face and as his nose began to bleed he stood up looked at the little chap and just asked "Why? Why me?" The man froze, petrified at the size of the beast in front of him. Then a bell began to ring loudly and the crash of the shutters coming down over the bar brought the fight to a halt. Half a dozen sailors had placed themselves in front of the bar and an officer in uniform called for silence. Damage was not great, a couple of stools broken and some glassware smashed, nevertheless the officer, who had a powerful presence, surveyed the scene as if the ship would be written off.

"Right children," he shouted in a voice that could probable be heard on passing ships, "The bar is closed for the remainder of the trip. We shall shortly be docking and I would ask you to make your way to your vehicles, when your deck is called. We'll have no more trouble or I shall use my power of arrest, assisted by the crew." Amazingly he saluted, clicked his heels and walked away.

"Anyone seen Haydn-Smythe?" asked Evor.

"What's your problem Evor? It's my daughter he's engaged to," said Jim Cameron. Evor stammered that he was concerned for his well being. "Look Evor," continued Jim "We're on tour. What goes on tour stays on tour. I certainly shan't be reporting back to our Jenny and don't expect you to. Good god man, remember some of the things that we got up to in our day and let it go." Evor nodded "Aye you're right Jim."

Just then up popped Nick. He explained that he wasn't a good sailor and had spent the time outside leaning over the rail. He went on to tell the club elders that he had just overheard an officer of the crew telling another that the police would be waiting for both rugby and football coaches outside the port.

Curly also reappeared, blissfully unaware of the mayhem that he had missed, he and Nick were among the few without a mark on them.

Evor called the tourists together and explained the likely situation, namely the possibility of arrest. He asked if anyone had any ideas that could get them out of trouble.

"What started it?" asked Curly. Thor explained that one of the younger lads had called a Morris man a poof or something. "Bloody Hell!" exclaimed Evor. "What have I told you, many times? Don't get in a fight with Morris men and don't get drinking with bell ringers."

"Sorry Evor." Said Nipper "I told Lee and might have got it the wrong way round." "Don't worry chaps," said Tommo "already sorted it. I have a plan."

"It had better be a bloody good one" thought Thor who was shaking hands with the little man.

It was.

Tommo had paraded the tourists and had selected the ones with no marks and those who looked well behaved. "Come with me" He instructed. Tommo returned and when their deck was called for, his troops shuffled sullenly and silently down towards the coach.

Imagine the shock when the first boarders found the front couple of rows seats occupied by a few nuns and some of the pilgrims. The bewildered tourists waited outside not sure if they had come to the wrong coach, particularly as this one had a sign in the front window bearing the words "Saint Elspeth's pilgrimage".

"Get on" ordered Tommo "You young uns at the back, heads down and silent. Thor, get down there with them and clout anyone who so much as squeaks. In fact you can belt a couple of them now, just as a practice."

Thor growled at the lads on the back. He could tell from their faces that the point had been made.

A priest then boarded the coach. "Hey" said Peter Craddock "I know you. You're the one who was sent off in the cup final. What the hell are you doing here? Pardon the blasphemy father. That's if you are a real priest?"

"Father Seamus Devlin at your service, young man. Yes, I am a real priest, at least for the time being. My association with you lot may well get me defrocked." This was said only half in jest. He continued, "Surely the lord does indeed work in mysterious ways. I was approached by the Abbess here and asked if I could consider taking the place of father O'Donnell, who has taken ill. They felt it would be beneficial to have a French speaker on the trip, so here I am."

He went on to explain that the group were set to visit the shrine of St Dymphna, an Irish princess who had been martyred in Belgium and who particularly cared for the mentally troubled. He had convinced the Abbess that some of the rugby lads were, poorly upstairs, as he put it. She agreed it would be a kindness to help them out of their current predicament and to light a few candles for them at St Dymphna's shrine. Of course the rugby lads would want to recompense the pilgrims for their trouble by praying with the Abbess and making a pecuniary contribution to the pilgrimage.

Father Devlin smiled. The Abbess smiled and made the sign of the cross. Peter smiled as did Tommo and Evor. An understanding had been reached.

The Bow doors were open and the coach started up and left the boat. It turned slowly through the port, following instructions from a police motorcyclist to follow him. About half a mile after leaving the port the coach was instructed to pull across into a holding area. Evor shouted down towards the back of the coach "I suggest complete silence and a bloody good pretence at sleep. Sorry sisters."

Two vans of riot police in full gear were lined up ready to receive the trouble makers. The coach halted and the doors had given their whoosh from the compressed air system. A gruff looking Belgian policeman boarded and spoke to Father Devlin. A few passports were checked, specifically the nuns and a couple of respectable, older tourists at the front. To all intents this was a bus load of genuine religious types and nothing like the gang of hooligans the officer was expecting.

In the meantime the minibus with one nun, a few pilgrims and some of the rugby lads had sailed past, towards an agreed rendezvous. The police, as hoped, were only interested in larger coaches.

The Belgian policeman apologised to the passengers. "Please accept my sorry for zer inconweenience and ave an enjoy stay in Belgique"

He alighted from the coach just in time to have his attention drawn to the next coach to be escorted in. This looked more promising as it had red and white scarves hanging from the windows. As the new coach ground to a halt it had the full attention of the officers in riot gear. This was as well. Had any of them watched the departing coach they may have had suspicions raised by the four bare backsides showing at the rear window.

Lads can only behave for so long.

Chapter 18 – The Dutch Handkerchief

The journey from the port to the team hotel proceeded without further incident. A few miles further on from the port the rugby coach pulled into a service area and met up with the minibus. Rugby players and religious types returned to their respective modes of transport but not before all had knelt in prayer and given to a collection plate that was carried round by a pretty young novice. Curly smiled at her as she proffered the plate. She blushed as he took her hand, placed a decent sum into the plate, looked her in the eyes and asked if she was really sure that she couldn't serve the lord better outside of the holy order.

"Ouch!" Curly exclaimed on receiving a blow to the head from Father Devlin.

"I'll not have you corrupting this Lamb of God John David Jones. Avert your eyes from her this second or I'll do you some bloody serious damage" Father Devlin was aware of Curly's ability to win over the ladies by stroking their hand and hypnotising them with his dark brown eyes and he was having none of it. The novice moved on, with unusual feelings "south of the equator", knowing that she would have a difficult time at her next confession.

When the coach eventually pulled up outside their hotel Evor stood up at the front and appealed for silence. His loud bellow of "Shut up you bastards!" served the dual purpose of quietening those who were awake and waking those who were asleep.

"Right Haven. This is a respectable hotel that will have other guests, business people and families. I know we're only here for two nights but I insist that we behave while on the premises. Anyone out of order in the hotel, will receive a very hard time and a big punishment at breakfast court." Evor was serious and everyone knew it. He went on. "Club dress, shirts and ties at dinner tonight. That's at 5-30pm, sharp. No drinking until you've checked in and dumped your gear in your room. Comprendes?"

A mumble of acceptance went around the coach and Evor stepped off to allow his club mates to disembark. He felt satisfied that he had made his point strongly from behind an unforgiving moustache.

The tourists climbed steadily off the coach and one by one retrieved their bags from the lockers underneath. There was only one girl on reception and it would take some time to get the group all checked in.

Young Nipper Shalcock took in this situation. He also noticed a bar across the road. He quietly tugged the sleeves of Teflon, Posh Boy, Lee and Spoddy Brown. These four were youngest members and Nipper judged them to be the most easily led. He nodded towards the bar in a conspiratorial manner and his conspirators looked at each other, grinned and shot across the road.

The bar was dark inside and it took the lads a few seconds for their eyes to adjust after the brightness of the street. Their grins turned to horror as they came face to face with Tommo, Bill Davies, Red Rod and Evor.

Something wasn't right. Nipper couldn't put his finger on it but once he had recognised Evor he expected a bollocking from the tour judge, instead Evor's face broke into a jovial grin.

"Clever lads" Evor said, waving a welcoming arm towards some bar stools adjacent to where the older chaps were sat. "It will take a while to shift that queue at reception so you've also decided to call in for a coffee right?" He then held up his hand to the barman. "Four more coffees please monsieur"

Red Rod, who sat nearest to the lads, whispered something to the barman and at the same time moved his own coffee cup away from the newcomers.

Posh Boy was quick to make an excuse for coming in the bar. "Cheers for the coffee Evor. We actually came across here to use the toilets. There's also a queue for them over the way." With this he walked over to the stairs that lead down to where the toilet sign pointed. A sheepish looking Spoddy followed him as did Teflon, lee and Nipper. When they had gone Tommo looked at Red Rod. "Phew, that was a close call. I assume that you whispered to the barman to skip the brandy in the coffee for the lads?" Rod confirmed that this had been the case and agreed that it would have been bad for the four older chaps to have been caught with laced coffee after Evor's stern instruction to have no drink.

Meanwhile downstairs the lads were congratulating Posh Boy on his quick thinking. "Well done mate. You got us out of the shit there." Said Teflon.

"Tell you what fellas. There's something not right here. There's no piss stones in these bogs." A very worried looking Spoddy Brown had exclaimed "and another thing" continued Spoddy pointing at two vending machines on the wall. "I know that one's for nodders but what the heck is the other one selling? I've never come across anything like that thing in the picture."

Teflon looked as puzzled as Spoddy but said nothing. Nipper had an immediate look of mischief come across his face. Posh boy sighed and began to explain to his less well travelled team mate that in certain places on the continent things were a bit different from back home. He pointed out that, particularly in older buildings, there was only one loo, shared by both sexes. This was Ok, as like in this bar there was no urinal, instead there were four cubicles and men or women had sufficient privacy for this to work as the accepted norm. He then had to respond to Spoddy's next question, that the "accepted norm" had nothing to do with Northern Bloke, Norman Arkwright, but was the accepted normal situation.

Spoddy declared that he wasn't happy with the situation as he wouldn't feel comfortable performing on the big white trombone if a lady was in the next cubicle. He went so far as to say that he wasn't going to poo until he got home. This raised a titter from the other lads but Posh pointed out that modern places would have ladies and gents and in any case there would be a toilet in the hotel room. "Now my friend" Posh boy began. "I'll tell you all about the vending machine."

Posh looked annoyed when a voice from the doorway butted in. He didn't like being interrupted when speaking, particularly by a cheeky looking Curly Jones who, he recalled, had recently accused him of being gay.

"These things Spoddy old chap" Enthused Curly as he put some change into the machine. These things are Dutch handkerchiefs." The machine had come forth with its wares. Curly had unwrapped the sanitary towel and holding it by the loop at either end he proceeded to pull the item back and forth under his nose. "Of course" Curly continued "They are bloody useless at removing snot. These days they are used as a symbol of elegance. If you're sporting one of these." He waved the towel at Spoddy before placing it into the breast pocket of his club dress shirt. "Yes, if you're wearing a Dutch handkerchief then you're a man of means, a gentleman, someone to be held in high esteem."

Curly purchased a second sanitary towel, this time leaving it in its wrapper and tossing it towards Spoddy. "Save it until just before you come into the dining room later. Pop it into your top pocket so it can be seen and see how differently the locals treat you and I compared to the others."

Spoddy thanked curly and left the toilet, beaming from ear to ear.

The others looked at Curly in awe. Even Posh Boy was impressed and had forgiven him the interruption. "Bloody brilliant Curly." Said Nipper "but you do realize that he will probably beat you to a pulp when he finds out that he's wearing a fanny towel?"

Curly just shrugged, hoping that, as usual, Thor would save him. He left the toilets with the others having forgotten to have the pee that had been the purpose of his visit.

The mature chaps had left the bar but been replaced by Thor, Northern bloke and Peter Craddock. This group, along with Curly had been first to check into the hotel, had changed into club shirt and tie and crossed the road for a much needed beer. Actually none of them wanted a beer but on tour bravado overcame common sense and someone in each group would often suggest a beer hoping that a mate would say no. No one ever had the sense to say no to beer.

"You youngsters haven't been drinking before checking in have you?" Northern bloke asked. "You heard Evor spell it out."

"We were in hear with Evor and he bought us all a coffee. Honestly we haven't had a drink." Whined Nipper, fearing a fine and forfeit at breakfast court. "Well. You'll just have to watch us then." Said Thor, taking a gulp from his glass. "Mmmmm, this Dutch beer's good. Oh. By the way, why was Spoddy smiling like a Cheshire cat when he walked into the hotel?"

Teflon told the chaps about Curlys jest with the Dutch handkerchief.
"Quality." Said Peter Craddock, offering Curly his hand.
"He'll kill you." Said Northern bloke.

Just over an hour later the tourists had all showered and changed. The group began to assemble in the dining room. The Older chaps had club blazers as did Thor and Northern bloke. This was expected of anyone in the club who had captained the side. The rest were wearing black shirts with the club crest printed on the breast pocket. They also had Gold ties with "Haven on tour" and the year embroidered on the tie. The players who were guesting had all been given two shirts but had the option to wear their own club tie. Peter Craddock and the two lads from Newport did this but as Lee didn't own a tie he wore the Haven neckwear.

The hotel restaurant was half full with families and business people, pretty much as predicted by Evor. There was also a group of four young French ladies who were on a weekend party to celebrate on of them getting a place at Oxford University to study English. Most of the tables were round but over by the long windows that opened onto the terrace, a long table had been set out to accommodate the touring rugby club.

Already seated across the top of the table were Evor, Tommo and Northern bloke. The top two seats on either side of the long table were reserved for Thor, Bill Mclaren, Mo Khan and Red Rod as these esteemed individuals would hold a position at the morning tour court. As others arrived they were beckoned up the table and seated, this regime meant that the last to arrive would be at the furthest point from the top of the table.

Here lay a dilemma for the tourists. Being away from the eyes of the court officials meant you were unlikely to be spotted, say, drinking with the wrong hand or licking your knife, thus avoiding a fine. The downside was that if you were called to the top then you had to pass everyone and may suffer some indignity both on the way there and back.

The tourists began to file into the dining room, most looking very smart but no matter what he wore or how hard he tried, Thor managed to look like a haystack after a gale, even in his blazer. His arrival brought nudges and sniggers from most of the party. There were more nudges and a quiet cheer as Curly entered the room. He swiftly took in the four girls, detoured past their table, smiled at them all and said "Tres belle. Enchante." He then bowed and moved towards the rugby table with a look back and little wave just before taking his seat.

The young ladies giggled. Northern bloke leant over towards Evor and whispered "There's a twenty euro fine. He can't help it can he?" At the same time Peter Craddock passed a ten euro note to Thor in payment of a bet.

There was just one seat left at the far end of the table. The single waiter and two waitresses were hovering, eager to begin serving the soup. There was a hum of conversation, both from the touring party and other guests. The young French ladies were discussing which of the rugby chaps would be most worthy of their attention. Spoddy Brown then made his entrance.

He looked nothing like the red faced farmer that the lads were used to seeing. His hair was slicked back with gel. He was spotlessly clean, resplendent in club shirt and a rarely worn tie that Nipper had helped him with. Instead of his usual vacant or puzzled expression he looked aloof, a man of the world, assured, superior.

Spoddy walked slowly around the full table with head held high, apart from the occasional glance down towards his shirts breast pocket. By the time he reached his chair, in slow deliberate motion, he had the full attention of the entire dining room. He pulled out his chair, turned and nodded to the dining room in general and was just about to sit with a smug grin when Evor shouted. "Spoddy lad, what's that in your pocked?"

This pleased Mr Brown. He paused his sitting motion and stood up, removing the item from his pocket. "This Evor sir, as these good people are aware is a Dutch handkerchief." He had gestured towards the local area of the dining room whilst removing the object with a theatrical flourish. He paused then holding the item delicately, he pulled it back and forth under his nose, just as Curly had done earlier.

There were gasps from some of the residents, sniggers from some of the tourists but mostly the faces in the room were fixed open mouthed or grimacing. There was a crash as a waitress dropped a soup bowl which thankfully was empty.

Evor beckoned Spoddy towards him with his index finger. A pleased looking Spoddy strutted slowly towards the top of the table his grin widening with every step. As Evor whispered something in his ear the grin turned to horror and Spoddy threw the sanitary towel onto the floor. He stood stock still, wishing the ground would open and swallow him up. Laughter was growing both from the touring party and the rest of the room. Spoddy waited while his brain attempted to compute what had happened and what he should do to correct his actions but as often happens at times like this the old grey cells gave a completely wrong piece of advice. "Kill Curly!"

Curly could tell by the look on Spoddy's face that he might regret his joke if he didn't move quickly. Now Curly was no hero. He certainly didn't want to fight with Spoddy as he might not even come second. Curly was however quick and as Spoddy made to grab him he was off. Under the table he went with the big farmer in pursuit. He was out the other side and under the next table that was populated by some worried looking Dutch business types. Spoddy appeared and Curly was off again. Evor was shouting for calm, some were laughing, some ladies were screaming. There was a crash as the tables were tipped over by Spoddy in his rage. Spoddy was gaining on Curly who was running out of tables to hide under. He dived under the table of French girls, finding the time to wink at one and shouting "Je n'ai pas peur", "I'm not scared", he was on his way out of the room, through the hotel lobby and into the street.

Spoddy chased him for some time until he realised that he wasn't gaining and that he was totally lost in a foreign town.

Meantime back in the Hotel Evor and the other club officials had apologised profusely to the other diners and hotel staff. A generous sum had been handed over to cover damages, meals replaced and wine given to each table. Everyone seemed relaxed again as Tommo leaned towards Mo Khan and said "Good job we had the big tour kitty eh?"

Most of the other diners seemed happy and raised glasses towards the rugby team in thanks for the free wine. Laughter was building as people discussed the big Englishman who had waved the sanitary towel about and the tourists speculated what Spoddy would do if he caught up with Curly.

Bets were taken between the touring team so that when a smiling Curly appeared at the door money changed hands. Pete Craddock passed another note to Thor, Northern bloke paid a large sum to Evor and the two lads from Newport passed funds over to their neighbours at the table. No one who new Curly had expected him to be caught.

Curly strolled in nonchalantly as though he'd just popped out for some fresh air. His hair was in place and his tie perfect. He paused at the French ladies table and apologised for disturbing their meal. He walked to his seat with a smile shared with the whole room. "Sorry Evor" he said "I hope that didn't cause too much of a problem?"

Evor put on his sternest face, pursed his lips, twitched his moustache but he couldn't hold the act and burst into laughter. "I think that this is a matter for tour court in the morning Curly" Evor spoke while wiping tears of laughter from his cheeks. "You shouldn't expect leniency" he concluded while leaving the room close to hysterics.

The saint stood up to go to the toilet. Whilst adjusting his crutches he placed his foot on the discarded Dutch handkerchief, slipped and hit the floor with a thud. It was only on return to England when a visit to the local hospital discovered a broken arm.

Just over a mile away, in a maze of streets near the railway station, a very sad Englishman sat on a kerb and sobbed. He was bright red, covered in sweat with his shirt hanging out of his trousers. Some local kids had jabbered at him in a language that may as well have been Martian and he was thoroughly fed up. "I'm in this bloody foreign place. No bugger speaks properly, I've been made a fool of and I don't know where my hotel is or even what it's called. I want to go home." He wailed.

The tourists finished their meal without further incident. At the start of the meal Father Devlin, who had remained on the wrong coach, said grace and after the port had been passed round at the end of the meal, Mo Khan stood and proposed the loyal toast. "Gentlemen" said Mo. "The queen".

The tourists all respected these traditions despite some being atheists, others republicans and Jim Cameron, both. To a man everyone stood, raised his port and repeated "The queen".

The locals were amused by the quaint English rugby men. The French girls even more interested. "I will never understand these people" the girl due to study at Oxford commented. "One waves around a sanitary towel then for no reason at all he chases the little cute one. They pray to god, toast their queen but they are all insane and I have to spend three years among them"

One of her friends pointed out that the Germans call them "Insel Affen" and that this means they are like a tribe of monkeys that live on an island, all interbred and therefore quite mad. "They may be mad" said the first girl "but the little cute one? Well, he may be cured n'est pas?"

The girls all giggled and then blushed as Curly made his way towards them.

Curly introduced himself as John David Jones. He asked if he could join them and offered another bottle of wine to recompense for diving under their table and spoiling their meal. This was done in perfectly accented French.

The Lead girl introduced herself as Simone and her friends as Sabine, big Paulette and little Paulette. Sabine commented on Curly's excellent French but asked if he would speak in his own tongue as they were all trying to improve their English. The other girls all agreed and Curly called for another bottle of wine.

Little Paulette asked if some of Curlys friends would also like to join them. This was great news Curly thought. It looked like he was on a winner tonight, he just needed three helpers. "Is there anyone in particular that you'd like me to invite over" He asked the group. The girls giggled, got into a huddle and jabbered away too quickly for Curly to pick up much of what was said.

Simone told him, in a whisper, that Sabine liked the handsome eastern boy, Big Paulette liked the mature man with the strange accent and little Paulette really fancied the big Swedish looking man. "I like the man who ran away after waving the sanitary towel" Simone said.

Curly was crestfallen. His mouth dropped open. He was speechless. What could he do? She preferred Spoddy to him.

She laughed out loud and squealed. "I am joking only mon petit" She said, sliding onto his lap without seeming to move. She embraced him and kissed him passionately, leaving Curly out of breath and out of his comfort zone. "Go John David Jones and bring your friends!"

Curly was a bit worried that this wasn't a request, it was a direct command. He got some air into his lungs and informed the girls that he should be able to get Eddie Khan and Jim Cameron involved without any trouble but despite the fact that little Paulette was very attractive Thor would refuse as he would not even talk to other women. He offered Young Kieran Shallcock, extolling his virtues as an intelligent student and a great rugby player. Little Paulette refused point blank, pointing out that he was ginger. She looked around at the rugby lads still present and said that Paul Bennet would have to do or they would all be off to the nightclub near the station to look for Dutch talent.

Five minutes later Curly was in Paul Bennets room, pleading with him. "Paul I'm not asking you to screw her, just to talk to her so she can improve her English."

"It's not right Curly. I shouldn't be chatting to French birds. I'm engaged. Besides I wouldn't know what to talk about" Paul insisted.

Curly put his hands around his head and rocked back and forth. "You wouldn't know what to talk about? You never fucking well shut up! Please Paul, pleeeease." Curly begged. "I know. I'll lend you my Porsche for a weekend when we get back and you can take Anna away for a weekend in it. How's that buddy?"

Paul was giving due diligence to this idea when the bedroom door opened. It was Nipper Shallcock. "A few of us are thinking of jumping on a train to Amsterdam, just for a look see of course. The journey is only an hour and trains run all night. Either of you up for it?"

Curly cursed. This idea could trump his loan of a Porsche.

It had the opposite effect. To Paul, time spent talking to a French girl was less damaging than a trip to Amsterdam and all that it might entail. "Sorry mate" he said. "I've just agreed to step in with one of those French birds".

Curly beamed a great beam. "Nice one Paul. You'll not regret this."

Chapter 19 – Amsterdam

The older chaps were sitting in the bar of the hotel and took in the fact that Curly had been rounding up troops to help with his assault on the French. "Looks likely to be another victory for us Anglo Saxons" The Saint opined.

"Look boyo! You can't do it without help from the Celts" Red Rod chipped in "He's had to get Jim Cameron to help out"

Sure enough Curly had recruited Jim along with Paul Bennet and a very happy Eddie Khan. "I'd better go and remind my boy to behave like an English gentleman" Mo Khan made to rise but was waved back down by Evor. "Leave him Mo. If any of that lot can behave at all, my money would be on your lad. Mo was pleased by this comment and waved to the waiter for another round of drinks.

Mike Bennet was annoyed that his brother had become involved. "Our Paul should have kept out of that. It's not fair on the lovely Anna. It pisses me off that he can pull the women and I seem to have no luck in that area. It's not fair."

"Have you ever considered speaking to women Mike?" Bill Davies asked "Your brother has verbal diarrhoea and you are as tight with words as Evor here is with money." This earned a laugh from everyone except Mike Bennet and Evor.

"Bill's right" said Ian Tomkin. "You don't make any effort to find a woman. You can't expect one to bloody well swim out to you while you're out in the estuary. Why don't you try a dating agency?"

"Nah" said Mike "I'll settle with my beer tonight." He signified that this particular conversation was at an end.

Thor, Pete Craddock, Posh Boy, the lads from Newport and Northern bloke padded across and joined the group. They already had beer in hand, so they pulled up chairs and sat down. "What's the plan for tonight chaps?" Thor asked.

"We'll probably have a couple across the road and make an early night of it." Evor answered.

The newcomers agreed that that seemed like a good idea and the group fell silent, all taking liquid on board. They were so quiet that they could hear Jim Cameron chatting up one Paulette in the adjoining dining room. "Have you got any scots in you then girlie? No. Would you like some?" Paulette had not grasped the innuendo in this and said that she would like to try a Scotch drink very much.

The other Paulette had told Paul that it was too noisy in the dining room for her and had asked him if they could take their drinks up to her room. When he seemed reticent she suggested that they could sit on her balcony and chat for a while. As they passed the group in the bar Paul could be heard asking if she had trouble with hearing, or was she uncomfortable in big groups, which side of the hotel is her balcony, did she think he'd need a jumper?

"That's why I don't say much" said Pauls brother "Once he started talking at about age two, I could never get a word in."

The group were readying to move across the road when Nipper burst into the room. "We're getting a train down to Amsterdam. Any of you fancy coming?" He shouted to the hotel as a whole. In tow were Lee, Chubby and Simon

Spencer, who was on the edge of turning from Doctor Jekyll to Mr Hyde.

"No thanks lad, too old for that game" said Evor. The two lads from Newport declined, saying that they had a bit of catching up to do. Thor shook his head and Nipper was about to leave when Nick Haydn – Smythe said "Yes. I'll give it a look over." This was a surprise to all, even more astounding when a sullen Mike Bennet stood up and declared that he was also going.

The group left the hotel and turned left out of the door towards the station.

Evor looked nonplussed. He fiddled with his moustache, an action that only happened when he was troubled. He asked his mate, Ian Tomkin if he would pop outside as he wanted a quiet word. Once outside Evor heaved a heavy sigh and told Tommo that he needed to share a confidence with him.

"Tommo old friend there's someone in that group that I'd like to keep an eye on. Can't tell you why at the moment but I'm going to have to join them in Amsterdam. I could do with a companion. Will you come?"

Tommo laughed. "Whatever you say. It'll be like the old days. Remember our tour there, oh when was it?"

Evor said that he couldn't remember the year but he recalled a club called the Banana Bar. With that he put his arm on Tommo's shoulder and the two conspirators took off after the younger chaps.

Back inside the Hotel bar Thor had watched this activity with interest. He told the group that Evor and Tommo had buggered off after the young chaps and that he would have to go to keep an eye on his grandad. After all he was getting on a bit. The big man finished his pot of beer, stood up apologised to his mates and went out after the others. He hadn't gone fifty yards up the street when he heard a shout from behind.

"Hey! Big fellah! Do you need a deputy?" Thor laughed, patted Pete Craddock on the back and grinned. "Sure do partner. We'd better get a move on to catch up."

They soon caught up with Evor and Tommo and as they reached the station they joined the ticket queue behind the rest. Much joviality was had as the youngsters were pleased the other chaps had come along. As they crossed over to the right platform, the ever observant Thor noticed a dishevelled figure asleep on a bench. He shouted at him to come over to platform two and join them in a little trip. Spoddy Brown had never been so glad to see anyone before in his life.

The train was modern and not overfull as it sped through the Dutch countryside in the gathering gloom. Spoddy had gone to the toilet to tidy himself up and Evor suggested that they all be nice to him as he was obviously shaken by his experience. "He'll probably end up more shaken" said Tommo "Especially if we end up in that place we went to years ago Evor"

Lee and Nipper looked at the old guys in awe.

"We were young once you know lads" Evor said with a glint in his eye.

He was bombarded with questions about his previous visit but refused to answer, claiming the old adage that what goes on, on tour stays on tour. The lads who hadn't been to

Netherlands before were shocked at how flat the place really was. Evor explained that this area was largely below sea level. "I'm not falling for that" said a cleaned up Spoddy "If it was below sea level we'd be drowning Evor"

The train pulled effortlessly into Amsterdam main station and the, by now, very excited group trooped of onto the dark forecourt and onward into the city. "Bloody hell!" exclaimed Nipper "Every bike in the world must have been left outside here." Sure enough there were hundreds if not thousands of bikes chained up outside the station. Evor warned them all to watch out for cyclists as they crossed a busy road and were led towards the canals and red light area.

There was a slight drizzle and the narrow, mostly pedestrianised, streets were thronged with people, most of whom were there window shopping, IE here to gawk at the ladies of ill repute who were showing their wares in the many windows fronting the canals. The place had a seedy air that whilst being somewhat unpleasant, also had the feel of festival about it. As Thor remarked, it felt like the crowds shopping in Castra near to Christmas.

The smell of cannabis wafted from the occasional café and Chubby decided he deserved a little smoke. He asked Evor where they were heading for and Evor asked for patience as they would soon be there. They crossed another canal and up some stairs to enter a bar called the Lion. The young lads were glad to have someone who seemed to know the area and eager to gain knowledge. Evor informed them that this would be their base and gave them a time to be back here to return to Breda. He pointed out the area where girls could be hired, gave a rough idea of prices and recommended a club, the Banana Club opposite, for those wishing to be entertained without taking part themselves.

As beers had already been organised the group moved out onto the balcony area of the Lion. Here there was seating and a good view up and down this particular section of canal. No one else was out here due to the weather but an awning kept the area dry and it was an ideal spot to take in the sights.

Across the canal there were five windows, two at street level and three up an external flight of steps above. In each window a scantily clad woman sat, stood or jiggled in an attempt to attract custom. There were three or four other windows that could also be viewed from The Lion. "This is what I call entertainment." Remarked an excited Nipper.

A customer was talking to one of the girls opposite. He eventually went in to her room and the blinds were closed. Lee decided to time him. He emerged canalside a mere six minutes twelve seconds later to be greeted by loud jeers from the rugby tourists on the Lion balcony. This was a great game and Pete Craddock suggested it should be repeated when he spotted another punter going into a room a little further away. When he emerged after over twenty five minutes he was cheered and clapped by the tourists. He looked across, laughed, made a flamboyant bow and went on his way.

Chubby shot across the canal during this period, had a smoke in a café nearby, waving across to his chums He returned happy. Nipper, Lee, Posh Boy, Chubby and Spoddy decided to cross the canal by the nearest foot bridge and have a look at the Banana Club. They got a cheer as they paid up and went in. This left Thor, Pete, Evor, Tommo, Mike Bennet and Simon Spencer, sat on the balcony timing and either cheering or booing at customers of the ladies, depending on time taken to perform. It was a game that would keep them happy for the entire evening.

The five chaps in the Banana Club had taken a table at the front of the small, dimly lit stage, ordered a round of drinks that cost the earth and settled down for the one hour show. They had been given a share of the tour kitty by Tommo but told that any extra "cultural expenses" would have to be funded from their own pocket. Despite the kitty money, Nipper baulked at the price of his drink and suggested that they sip their beer slowly.

None of the five knew what to expect in such an establishment but all pretended to be worldly wise and sat with a nonchalant air waiting for the first act. Lee remarked that he was surprised that about ten percent of the seventy or so customers were female, mostly women with their partners. The other punters were either single men or stag parties. The latter included five lads from south Wales in uniform of the Boar war period, red tunics and white pith helmets. These lads said that they had been here before and informed the rugby lads that it would be a good laugh.

The lights dimmed even more and a trapeze was lowered from the ceiling with a very attractive girl swinging to and fro, dressed in Victorian costume. She sang a song as she swung and slowly undressed in a sensual but not sleazy manner. Nipper felt that this was well within his comfort zone and relaxed a little. At the end of her song the girl slid demurely from the swing. This took some doing as she was now totally naked. She came across to Nipper and asked "English yes?" Nipper nodded. "Would you care to come upstairs with me?" She then gave a price that was not within the gift of young Nipper to bestow. He was about to ask Posh Boy for a loan when one of the Taffies leant over and suggested Nipper give it a miss as he could get a shag for a quarter of that price at any of the windows outside.

The girl spat towards the Welsh lad with venom then resumed her coy expression and walked over to a few more chaps before finding an older man who slyly walked off with her through a curtain at the side of the stage.

Nipper, who was no longer within his comfort zone gulped down his beer and beckoned the scantily clad waitress for a brandy. To hell with the cost.

Banter was exchanged between the rugby lads and the Welsh stag party and the room fell silent when a nun walked to the centre of the stage. She was a young nun who, unusually for one of her calling had false eyelashes and make up. She walked around the stage berating the audience for coming to such a den of iniquity. She did this in English and a couple of other languages. Some people were laughing but Lee was feeling a bit guilty. She must have caught the guilt on Lees face as she strode over to him and gave him a personal telling off. She pulled him off his chair and onto the stage, bringing his chair with him.

She then instructed him to kneel on the chair, which for some unknown reason he did without thinking. She undid his belt and pulled it from his trouser loops. All the time she was shouting about what a naughty boy and a terrible sinner he was. In a flash his pants and undies were around his ankles and he was being spanked on the bare bum with his own belt. The audience were roaring with laughter but Lee's brain had still not worked out that this was part of the act. He was in total confusion which got worse when his shoes and the rest of his clothes were removed and he was now standing naked except for his socks.

The nun now removed her headdress to reveal long glamourous auburn hair. She disrobed from her habit and was wearing a basque, stockings and suspenders underneath. "On your knees!" she ordered, slipping the belt round Lee's neck like a dog collar and dragging him back and forth across the stage. "What should we do about him?" she asked the audience in what was now, unmistakably an English West Midlands accent.

The crowd were now howling with laughter and even Lee was laughing, not seeming to notice that he was naked except for socks. The girl addressed the crowd saying that he had been a good doggy and deserved a treat. She took him back to the chair and removed the belt from around his neck. When asked his name Lee gave it willingly. She then removed her basque and stood with well sun tanned breasts pointing directly at him. She produced a bottle of baby oil that had been concealed, god knows where, held out his hands, poured the oil into them and then suggested he rub the oil onto her breasts. Lee did this with a huge grin and the beginnings of an erection. "The lucky bugger." Said Spoddy Brown, as she pulled Lee's head forward, half suffocating him between her oiled bossom.

She then told Lee that she would tie him to the chair and give the crowd a little show. Despite the fact that she was stroking his penis at this point Lee felt he wasn't happy about being tied up. He told her so and she assured him all would be OK. Lee refused point blank. He stood up grabbed his clothes and left the stage. She was nonplussed. Stood momentarily with hands on hips then regained her composure. "What a wanker everybody." She shouted. The crowd began to chant "Wanker, wanker." As Lee dressed at the back of the room.

Still, as they say in theatre, "the show must go on." Within a couple of minutes she had a second choice tied firmly to the chair. Lee had now been forgotten by the baying crowd as the new chap, possibly a little high on weed, sat expectantly with oiled hands.

The girl was kneeling in front of him. She had placed a small bucket of water and a towel next to the chair. She then took his penis in both hands, bent forward and performed oral sex on him. "Lee. That could have been you." Said Nipper. The lads all looked at a dressed but newly crestfallen Lee.

She then rubbed baby oil into the man's pubic area. He was enjoying his moment of fame. "I've seen this before. Watch this!" one of the Welsh lads leaned over and said. The girl produced a cigarette lighter from her garter and seemingly set fire to the guy's knob.

The water bucket was obviously placed to extinguish the flames from burning pubic hair before any damage could be done. She had performed this trick many times. It was spectacular, there would be a quick flame that was put out before the participator was aware of the fire almost. She would then dry him off with the towel, bow and leave the stage. Today it went wrong. She had placed the bucket a little too near to the chair. The man had twitched at the sight of the lighter and knocked the bucket over, spilling the water. Too late! She had lit the hair and he was screaming. "Lee. That could be you." Said nipper again in a different tone of voice. Lee had gone white.

One of the Welsh lads reacted first. He ran on and threw a pint of lager over the man's knob which put out the flames. It had probably only taken two or three seconds longer than what the girl would have done had all gone to plan but the participant was not amused. A man who looked like a bouncer appeared, untied Mr Unfortunate and took him off stage while informing the crowd that he would be looked after. Chubby remarked that looked after could either mean that he would be given a free jump or slapped about and told to keep quiet.

During the commotion, no one had noticed that Posh Boy had slipped out.

The final act came on stage. She was a stunningly attractive, statuesque Afro Caribbean lady. She wore a flowery bikini and had a hat of fruit on her head, a la Carmen Miranda style. After a little song and dance routine, the hat of fruit was all she was wearing. The rugby lads were amazed when she pulled a banana from her hat, peeled it, inserted it inside herself then lay on her back with legs akimbo and fired the banana at the Welsh stag party. One of the Taffies caught the fruit and was motioned at by the girl to eat it. He did so to the cheering of the audience.

The girl danced a little more and reloaded. This time she pointed directly at Spoddy Brown, smiling at him. The banana fell short and landed on the edge of the stage. Undeterred, the girl walked over, picked up the banana and with a sensual wink offered it directly to Spoddy. The farmer was horrified. His mouth fell open. "I'm not bloody well eating that!" He insisted, looking at the Welsh lads with a frightened gaze. "It's been on the floor." With this he downed the remains of his drink and ran out of the club. He didn't notice the roar of laughter that erupted in the audience. The dancer laughing loudest of all.

The laughing group were spotted by their chums on the Lion balcony as they left the club. Spoddy was outside, leaning on a railing next to the canal. He expected ridicule from his mates for being so squeamish and was very pleased when Nipper, still chuckling, patted him on the back saying "Bloody brilliant

John lad. Bloody brilliant." This was followed by Chubby shaking his hand and telling him that he was now a tour legend. What a day of ups and downs for the country farmer.

The chaps returned to the Lion, still laughing and arrived to find Posh Boy already present but no sign of Evor, Tommo, Thor or Pete. Nipper shouted for a round of drinks and asked about the whereabouts of the senior chaps. Mike Bennet was explaining that Evor had tugged Tommo's sleeve and the pair had dashed out. Next Thor had tugged Pete Craddock's sleeve and they had followed. Just as he explained this Thor and Pete returned.

"What's going on Tom?" Nipper asked. Thor replied that they were keeping an eye on Evor and Tommo but they had just gone for a bite to eat in a café over the way. He pointed to the place and Evor and Tommo could be seen laughing in the window, eating baguettes and cake. Stories from the Banana club were shared and the group fell back to jeering or cheering at the punters across the canal.

"Look!" exclaimed Nipper some ten minutes later, pointing excitedly across the canal. Evor and Tommo were talking to a girl at one of the windows further down the street. Thor was aghast but relaxed again when the pair moved on. The old chaps were obviously in high spirits as they were laughing uncontrollably as they weaved between the thinning crowds along the canal. They stopped outside the two windows opposite, blatantly surveying the girls. They shook hands with each other, laughed again and split up.

"Noooo!" wailed Thor as Evor opened the door to a window occupied by a pretty Asian lady and after a brief chat went inside. The curtains were closed behind him. "Grandad. Don't do it." Thor for all his size looked like a small lost boy as he almost sobbed this request. The group were mostly laughing but Pete and Nipper empathised with Thor's anguish and moved towards him.

"Old Tommo's gone in too. The bugger." This was Simon Spencer. "He's gone for that big black lass with the huge knockers. Wow! Fair play to him if he survives." The blinds were closed behind Tommo and Mike Bennet shouted that someone would have to start a stop watch as he was timing Evor.

"He's out!" shouted Mike "Two minutes fifty three."

Thor lifted his head from his hands in time to see Evor return to the street, still laughing loudly despite being half naked. Evor was wearing his trousers and putting on his shirt. The girl threw his shoes after him along with his blazer and tie. "You disglace! You dirty man!" she shrieked, before going back inside and leaving the curtains closed. Evor just laughed despite the fact that one of his shoes had gone into the canal. He looked across and waved to the crowd at the lion. When he saw his shoe in the canal he just pointed at it and laughed even louder.

Eventually Evor reached his friends on the balcony of the Lion. When questioned about his dismissal by the girl a laughing Evor told them his story. Without any shame and through bursts of laughter he said that he had stripped and lay on the bed on his back. As the girl had come to climb on him, he had farted, followed through and made a mess. "In short chaps" he said "She threw me out for shitting the bed and got bloody angry when I asked for a refund" Even Thor had to laugh at this.

When the joviality has receded Chubby pointed out that Evor's pupils had dilated. He asked what Evor had eaten in the café and when a giggling Evor had answered that he had a baguette and three fantastic cakes. Chubby informed Thor that his Grandad was high on space cake. Thor sighed took the beer away from Evor and asked for a large jug of water. He told Evor that it was clear beer and Evor sat guzzling it down and praising the taste, between giggles.

"Here's Tommo." shouted Pete.

"Thirty four minutes exactly." Lee informed the group.

Tommo was cheered and clapped all the way back to the Lion.

All good things come to an end and the jaunt to Amsterdam was no exception. Nipper had counted his patrol and when all were present they made their way back to the train station. As soon as the train pulled out, Evor was fast asleep. The train proceeded to Breda without incident. Most of the group took forty winks but Nipper thought that he should stay awake as he felt responsible, having suggested the trip. When the train stopped in Breda everyone decamped onto the platform. The train was just starting to move off when Spoddy Brown shouted that they were at the wrong station. He ran and managed to open a door and scramble aboard a carriage. "Look!" He shouted "This isn't Breda it's Uitgang. You're at Uitgang you bloody idiots" he screamed waving his hand and pointing at the Way Out sign.

The train had gathered momentum and Spoddy couldn't hear Nipper calling for him to get off. In a moment the train had gone and silence reigned over Breda station. Everyone looked towards Thor for an answer. Answer came there none. The big fellow just shook his head, said that Spoddy at least knew that they were in Breda and had money. With that he picked up a sleeping Evor from a bench, threw him over his broad shoulder and ambled off towards the hotel. The rest of the very tired tourists followed in silence.

At the hotel, Thor was about to place his burden down onto a chair in the reception area when the burden spoke to him, coherently. "Tom, we need to talk in private. Please carry me round into the bar. It will be empty now."

Thor obliged but dumped his grandad unceremoniously onto a bench seat in the uninhabited bar area. Thor was about to speak when Evor hushed him and they watched the Amsterdam group troop past to either stairs of lift like a collection of zombies.

"Sorry Tom" the old boy didn't look too sorry, nor did Evor look drunk or drugged. "I know you're not happy with me but I had my reasons. You'll have to trust me for now but I don't want to fall out with you and certainly don't want to upset you lad." The old man looked pleadingly at his grandson who responded with an angry face.

"How am I expected to feel Grandad?" Tom asked. "You get drunk, take drugs then pay for a prostitute at your age. Worse you shit her bed get thrown out and then laugh about it. What would my mum and dad have thought? You've brought shame on the family Grandad. Yes, I am bloody annoyed with you. How would you feel if it had been me behaving like that?"

The old chap surveyed the empty, dimly lit room, playing for time to compose an answer. "Can you wait for my reasoning until we reach England Tom? It's important" Thor was too angry to accept this and assumed that Evor was playing for time in order to get excuse ideas from his chums. He accused Evor of this ploy and it was now Evor's turn to display anger.

Genuine anger. Thor was not expecting the lengthy dressing down that roared his way.

"You cheeky young sod. You need to lighten up a bit and stop putting people on pedestals. I'm just another human being Tom. I'm not a saint, your dad wasn't a saint and even the saint isn't a saint boy. Why should I try to live my life to the impossible standards of perfection that you set yourself? I hope that when your lad gets older that you let him see some fault in Mr perfect Tom Orre, or do you intend for him to labour under the yoke of the standards that you seem to think everyone should apply? Get bloody real man!" With this Evor stood up and left the room.

A few minutes later Peter Craddock popped his head round the corner to see his friend with head in hands sobbing. When he asked if Thor was OK, a seemingly little boy in a man's body looked up at him and said "I don't think my grandad likes me Pete."

Only later as he lay in bed did Thor review the evening. Pete was snoring but not too loudly. Someone in the next room however was doing a one man impersonation of a herd of Wildebeest. That's when it dawned on Thor that Evor had been play acting all through the evening. He found this hard to reconcile with the volume of beer that he'd witnessed Evor drink or the fact that Evor's pupils did seem dilated but he was convinced the old rascal had been putting on an act. Evor did seem genuinely annoyed with him however.

He gave up thinking, closed his eyes and slept.

Chapter 20 – Match Day One

or some reason continental Hotels just can't seem to do a decent English breakfast. This hotel was no different. The breakfast would be described by an Australian as "ordinary". It was described by Father Seamus Devlin as "pure bloody shite". Despite this he had piled his plate high and sat down near the top of the table. Ian Tomkin sat opposite the priest and his plate was even fuller, it would not have accepted one more bean. "You could go back for seconds you know Tommo" The priest informed him. "I fully intend to father" was Tommo's reply.

One by one the tourists assembled in varying states of distress. Teflon could not get the grin off his face, nor could Jim Cameron. Paul Bennett looked decidedly sheepish and Curly looked as if he'd lost a fight with a pair of tigers, which strangely wasn't far from the truth. Thor had returned to his usual cheerful self and Evor looked as if he'd stayed in, watched TV and had an early night. Of Spoddy Brown there was no news.

Many of the other guests acknowledged the Englishmen, wishing them good luck for the game and thanking them for the wine with their meal. None of the French young ladies had as yet surfaced for petit dejeuner.

During breakfast stories of the previous nights' escapades were exchanged. Despite the obvious immoral tales from Amsterdam, they were trumped by tales of Curly's daring do back in Breda. It transpired that despite being almost raped, Paul Bennett had escaped from the clutches of Little Paulette, who was certainly on heat. She had then interrupted her friend and Curly demanding that Curly also fulfil her needs. Curly had risen to the challenge, in every way and was absolutely shattered this morning, albeit very pleased with himself. The younger Bennett had taken some stick from his mates but had been quietly taken aside and praised by his elder brother.

Towards the end of breakfast time the French girls had arrived in the dining room together and had sat quietly away from the tourists without so much as an acknowledgement to any of them.

As breakfast drew to a close Evor produced a gavel and a judge's wig. With wig on head, he banged the gavel on the table three times and formally opened the session of the tour court.

The touring party sat in silence as Evor asked if there were any matters to be brought before the judiciary. He did this in the most solemn language. "On this day during the reign of her majesty Queen Elizabeth the second, I request and require that any person herewith, being aware of any misdemeanour pertaining to any other person herewith make said misdemeanour known to myself. Failure to comply with this request could have the most dire consequences for any none informant." Having said this Evor looked sternly in the faces of the entire party.

By now Tommo and Northern Bloke had donned shorter wigs, cheap curly nylon affairs, one bright red the other bright green. They looked comical characters in their respective roles of defence and prosecution advocates. Mo Khan and Red Rod wore paper tricorn hats, as befits court ushers and Thor, along with Bill McLaren had stripped to the waist, both wearing lone ranger masks and a single coloured feather at the back of their heads, this being the traditional headgear for Haven enforcers. Many of the other guests had moved their chairs towards the rugby lads as they knew this had potential for good entertainment.

Red Rod beckoned Paul Bennet to a chair in front of the judge. "I understand M'lud that this man has brought the reputation of Haven RUFC into disrepute by refusing the advances of an attractive young lady."

Evor tut tutted and asked the defendant if he wished to engage a lawyer. This gave Paul a dilemma, it would cost to hire a lawyer but could reduce the inevitable punishment and fine. He opted to pay for Tommo.

In flowery terms Northern bloke gave details of the charge without looking in the direction of little Paulette. Had he done so he would have seen her pink complexion turn scarlet.

Tommo then stood and pointed out that Paul was engaged to be married, that he held a responsible position in society and that he had never offended before. He then stated that in his opinion the defendant was some sort of deviant and should be shown no mercy. The place erupted into laughter with even Paul chortling at this unexpected turn of events from his own advocate.

The judge banged his gavel for order and when calm had been restored, Paul was instructed to pay a fine into a bucket held by Bill Mac and to drink a mixture of coffee, tabasco sauce, brandy and raw egg.

Next up was Jim Cameron who was accused of the exact opposite, IE bringing the club into disrepute by not refusing the advances of an attractive young lady. This time Northern Bloke waxed lyrical about how Jim had seduced a young virgin who knew no better in her innocence than to do his bidding. Jim again hired Tommo to defend him. Tommo's defence consisted of "M'lud, he's a lucky bugger at his age. I urge you to throw the book at him."

Evor agreed. A fine was extracted and despite Jim's protests he was pinned upright by Thor while Bill removed his trousers and scraped his breakfast leftovers into Jim's underpants. Evor pointed out that but for the moving words on Jim's behalf by his advocate, the punishment would have been worse.

Teflon stood up and said that he wished to submit himself to the courts mercy on the same charge as Jim. Evor thought for some time, took in the worried look on Mo Khan's face and gave a verdict with no further ado. "Young man, in all my years as a tour judge I have never known anyone split on themselves before. In view of your honesty and impeccable family, he gestured towards Mo, I shall let you off with a warning." Teflon looked disappointed.

"However" continued Evor "In view of your bloody stupidity in admitting this act I shall fine you, make you drink the mixture and have cold beans poured into the back of your pants." A cheer went up as the punishment was enacted and Teflon grinned throughout. He was one of them. He caught his father's eye and saw that dad was beaming with joy.

Some minor misdemeanours concerning spilled drinks and general silliness were quickly handled and Evor was about to declare the court closed when young Lee, the footballer asked if Evor should not come before himself on the charge of shitting on the tart's bed. Lee had expected to get a good laugh from this question but was astounded by the reaction of the entire group. Evor looked upset and everyone else took in a sharp intake of breath. No one smiled. No one even tittered. Silence reigned supreme.

"Young man" Evor gave Lee a look between a smile and a scowl that Lee thought no other person on the planet could match. It was at the same time a threat but seemed to contain some sympathy. Evor continued. "If such a comment had been made by any member of the rugby fraternity I would have taken extreme offence. As it is I must inform you that in respect of this court and indeed across the rugby brotherhood, a judge cannot be judged. Normally such lack of respect for my authority would ensure a severe punishment, even your dismissal from the touring party. I do however believe it to be a genuine mistake on your part and providing that an appropriate apology is immediately forthcoming you may be given a lighter punishment."

Lee railed at the injustice of the situation. Something inside him made ready to argue the unfairness of the situation but a glance at the faces of his friends and a worried shake of the head from Nipper persuaded him to comply.

"M'lord. I am an innocent abroad, in more ways than one" Lee responded "I offer you my unreserved apology and will accept whatever punishment that you see fit."

This was seen as the ideal answer by all present and after consulting with Mo Khan and Red Rod, Evor gave his verdict. "Lee, I have decided not to fine you as I believe that you genuinely were unaware of the finer points of rugby club law. I think that some example must be made however and with this in mind I insist that at all times, when on the field of play, you must dispense with shorts and wear this." Evor reached into a bag and withdrew a large pink ballerina's tutu. Lee came forward, accepted the tutu, removed his jeans and wrapped the tutu around his waist, securing it with the Velcro pads provided to ensure that one size fits all.

This action brought approval and applause from everyone in the room. Evor closed the court session and instructed everyone to be on the bus in twenty minutes. Just then the door to the dining room burst open and in strolled a certain farmer Brown, beaming from ear to ear.

As the coach pulled away from the hotel Spoddy explained his good fortune to Evor and those at the front of the bus. When the train reached the third station after Breda, the fact that every station seemed to be called Uitgang began to concern Spoddy. He alighted at station four, Uitgang, and finally realised that this couldn't be the station name but must mean something in Hollandish. He followed the Uitgang signs and found himself outside the station. It all suddenly became clear to him, these stupid Dutch didn't know the word exit and had made up a word of their own to describe the way out.
"Man they must be thick" Spoddy had thought.

Outside the station it had become light but Spoddy was not perturbed as he now had the hotel name and address written on a card in his wallet. This had been an idea of Thor's.

He spied a café across the road from the station and there outside the café was a motor bike with a British number plate. This seamed great luck to Spoddy as he would be able to get some sense out of the owner, who would speak properly. When he opened the café door he felt even luckier as there sat the fizzyo girl, Mary Hynge and her friend, both dressed in biking gear, drinking coffee and talking to some bloke.

Initially they didn't seem too pleased to see him but when he explained how he had come to be there Mary had shown sympathy and told her friends that all was fine. They had chatted to the bloke again, who Mary told him was the Dutch owner of the café and that they had never met him before. Despite this the bloke had driven him back to the hotel in Breda as a favour. Spoddy said that his chauffeur had driven in silence and when Spoddy tried to have a chat with him he just said "No speak English chum". Thor asked where the girls were now and Spoddy said that they were going to do a little shopping and then see him at the match.

The coach made its way to the outskirts of town, eventually pulling up at a sports centre with a number of soccer pitches and one set of rugby posts. A large marquee had been set up alongside the pitch and makeshift seating for about eighty people had been set up in front of the marquee. As Evor alighted from the coach he was greeted by a red faced, plump and very jovial Dutchman who introduced himself as Willem DeBruyne, club chairman of Panthers rugby. Willem pumped Evors hand up and down until Evor was nearly sick. He repeated this introduction to everyone getting off the bus. He stopped the hand pumping after Thor had gripped his hand so tightly as to make him grimace.

Willem escorted his guests to the changing rooms, where the players were left to kit up and have a light training session. He then took Evor and his none playing guests across to the marquee, where they were introduced to other Panthers officials and offered bitterballen and kroket snacks to be washed down with Jenever, a Dutch type of juniper gin, downed neat and in one. Willem made a short welcoming speech and explained that Panthers usually only had a handful of spectators but today they had the town mayor plus other local dignitaries who would attend. Tickets had been sold to see this top English side and the funds raised would keep Panthers going for the next two or three seasons. Evor looked very worried and explained to his host that far from being a top English side, Haven were just a bunch of drunks on tour.

"Ah, you not fool me my friend Evor," said Willem "Since agreeing this game I watch you team results. I know you county champions but we try to give you good game."

Evor looked to his friend Tommo for help but Tommo was holding a lengthy conversation with a very unusual looking glass of dark beer and waved Evor away.

Just before kick off a large and loud motorbike roared up and parked near to the tour bus. Spoddy Brown ran over to meet the girls as he had promised to help them unload the two cases of equipment. Mary Hynge, aka Janet, asked him to leave one near the rear of the coach as this was big stuff for serious emergencies and hopefully wouldn't be needed. Spoddy carried the other box to a point near the halfway line, opposite the seating, where each team had been allotted around a dozen plastic chairs for subs, and officials. A marching band was practising and the sun had popped out from behind clouds that were rapidly giving up the fight to dull the day for the spectators who were beginning to arrive. Spoddy laid down the box, sat on a chair and went to sleep.

He slept through the band playing three tunes while the crowd assembled and only awakened when given a sharp dig in the ribs by Red Rod. "Stand up man. It's our bloody national anthem" Rod ordered. The band struck up a lively version of "God save the Queen". The entire crowd stood respectfully and the Brits among them sang their hearts out. "Feels like I've been picked for England" the diminutive Curly whispered up to the blond giant on his left. "It's a better anthem at this pace" Red Rod informed Evor who didn't hear due to the bellowing of Mo Khan stood next to him. No one sang the national anthem as loud as Mo.

Next came the Dutch anthem "Willhelmus". This was a slow tune that made our own anthem seem almost exciting and it went on for verse after verse. "This is a plot to put our players to sleep" Evor confided to Mo.
"It's working Evor" Mo replied, pointing at Spoddy who had dozed off again.

The teams lined up tossed a coin for kick off and on the referees whistle the Dutch standoff hoisted the ball high in the air for his orange clad pack to chase. Curly was positioned perfectly and caught the ball, moving it out effortlessly to Nipper at inside centre who threw a long pass out to posh boy, who was playing at outside half today. Posh drew a tackle from his opposite number and slipped the ball to Lee, the footballer, who was outside him on the wing, looking unusual in pink tutu. The move looked quality and Willem said to Evor "Just a bunch of drunks eh?"

Lee caught the ball and skipped past the orange winger, setting off down the touch line at pace. All was going well until the Dutch fullback hit Lee with a perfect, text book tackle, arms spread, shoulder right under Lee's ribcage. The full back hadn't slowed his run whatsoever as he half lifted Lee forcing him into touch, dumping him on the ground and landing on top of him. A cheer went up from the crowd and even the Haven lads applauded the tackle.

The only person who hadn't appreciated it was Lee. He jumped up and threw a punch at the full back. "You can't do that you Dutch twat" he shouted, hitting the Dutchman with a second punch before the fullback had time to react. Orange players came running across to defend their team mate and Lee was soon floored by a prop forward. Thor dived in trying to separate the antagonists and someone punched him. In seconds it was like a re-enactment of the battle Agincourt, everyone on the field had joined in. The referee blew long loud blasts on his whistle and the fight petered out into a bit of pushing and slapping. A couple more blasts on the whistle and the scrap eventually ended. This left Teflon in a very embarrassing situation as he had just sprinted across from the opposite wing, pulled back his fist but had no one to hit. He seemed to stand for ages with his bunched hand ready to thump before letting it drop to his side and sidling away sheepishly.

"What the hell was that all about?" Northern bloke asked Lee.

"Did you see what he did to me?" Lee answered.

"I did" said Northern bloke "and it was a perfectly good tackle you'll have to get used to that lad. This is a game for men."
The referee called the two skippers together along with Lee and the Dutch fullback. Northern bloke apologised and explained that this was Lee's first game of rugby and thus his first tackle had come as a shock. The Dutchman had blood coming from a cut above his left eye and looked angry. Lee told the fullback that he was sorry and offered a hand which was taken.

When Thor suggested that Lee also apologise to the referee a bemused looking Lee smiled at the referee "Sorry ref. Misunderstanding. It won't happen again."

The referee was now furious "Sir! You call me Sir, young man."

"Eh?" Lee was even more bemused and half laughed. A smack round the back of the head from Thor persuaded Lee of the correct course of action. He put on a solemn face "Very sorry sir"

The referee spoke in Dutch to the orange men and then gave a translation for Northern bloke. Both skippers called their teams together to pass on the words of wisdom.

"OK chaps" said Northern bloke, "the ref isn't going to send Lee off as it's a friendly but has asked if I will substitute him to avoid any further trouble."

Lee said that this wasn't fair as he'd come all this way and only touched the bloody ball once. Northern bloke pointed out that although the referee had politely requested this course of action, it had really been a request that could not be declined and in any case Lee would get a full second game next day. The replacements were Jim Cameron, Simon Spencer, Spoddy and Father Devlin. Thor and northern bloke had a brief natter and decided to bring on the vicar at full back and move Red Rod to his usual position, on the wing. A disgruntled Lee skulked off to boos from the crowd and play recommenced.

The rest of the first half was a comedy of errors for Haven. Father Devlin caught a hoisted ball perfectly and called for a mark. As he was outside his twenty two metre line, a couple of Dutchmen hit him full on and he dropped the ball. From the resulting scrum the Haven pack were driven back over their own line to concede a try which was converted. Ten minutes later Curly made a long pass to Teflon, he caught the ball and sprinted past Dutch players, avoided the tackle from the full back and dived into the corner. He was embarrassed when the referee pointed out that he had over run the try line and made a spectacular dive to down the ball over the dead ball line.

At a later scrum both Haven props were violently sick due to too much "catching up" with vodka the previous night. They went off, their opposing front row changed to clean shirts and Haven looked to bring on Simon Spencer and Jim Cameron. Jim however was nowhere to be seen.

"Have you ever played prop before?" Northern bloke asked a fearful looking Spoddy Brown. Another long drive from the orange pack resulted in the second Dutch push over try.

Just before half time Curly, who seemed not affected by his nocturnal efforts, ducked and wriggled his way clear in a beautiful manoeuvre. He had only the full back to beat with Nipper in support. Curly drew the tackle and placed the ball in Nippers lap. With twenty yards to go Nipper must score as he was not opposed. Somehow he managed to tangle his feet together and fall over in a heap. He lay there giggling at his own stupidity, still grasping the ball tightly. The resulting penalty was kicked long by the Dutch stand off and chased by their left wing half. Red Rod would get their first and on arrival he made to hoof the ball into touch. He missed the ball by a country mile and his thankful opposite number scooped it up, running in a try under the posts. The conversion was made as the referee blew for half time. Panthers 21, Haven 0.

A sorry looking bunch of Brits crowded round Northern bloke at half time to eat the quarter oranges proffered by their hosts. Northern bloke made a rousing speech, which unfortunately roused no one. They were all astounded to suddenly find Evor had muscled his way into the middle of the group. "For my sake lads, I beg you, win this bloody game. That bastard Willem is getting on my bloody nerves, gloating about his Panthers. I know I'm asking a lot but please just win the fucking game. I don't care how." He then disappeared as quickly as he had appeared.

The players looked shocked. Thor most of all as he'd never seen his grandfather look so desperate. Pete Craddock had a plan. "It's not pretty boys but if we have to win, it will have to do." He outlined his idea and a happier Haven RUFC started the second half.

Harry punted the ball as far as he could. It was collected by the fullback who was immediately confronted by a newly confident Teflon who has sprinted his fastest to chase the ball down. The full back kicked and gained touch midway in his own half. Haven cut the line to four and when Paul Bennet rose high to capture the ball from the line out he immediately dropped it back into the lap of Pete Craddock who was storming in at pace. Pete crashed through the orange line and made ten yards before being brought to ground. Northern, Spoddy and Mike Bennet drove over him and Curly spun the ball back to Thor who was again crashing through at pace, making ten yards gain before hitting the deck and finding Chubby, Paul Bennet, and Simon Spencer driving the orange shirts away and leaving the ball for Curly to slip to Pete Craddock. This was repeated twice, until Pete crashed through the defensive line to score a try, a good way out to the right of the posts.

The conversion was missed and from Panthers' kick of the same process was repeated again and again. It took longer this time as the Dutch men were committing more men to the tackle area but eventually Haven scored again, via Thor. This time right under the posts and Harry duly picked up two points for the conversion.

Panthers were in disarray and replaced two of their lighter players with forwards to beef up their defence. From the kick Haven again used the same tactics to make ground. This time however Curly had spotted the Orangemen deploying in numbers to counter one of Thor's charges to the left of the ruck. There was a gap on the right which the cheeky scrum half exploited, wriggling through a couple of tackles to once again place the ball down under the posts. Harry duly converted.

Just two points behind now and only midway in the second half. Haven kept up this battering ram tactic and, as it's always more tiring to tackle than it is to be tackled, the Panthers pack began to fade. One more unconverted smash through by Pete put Haven in front. The Dutchmen just couldn't seem to get hold of the ball. Frustration set in and a couple of kickable penalties came Havens' way.

After a long driving maul by the Haven pack Curly slipped a pass to Harry who sold two of his signature, outrageous dummies before scoring Havens fourth try. Northern bloke could tell that the opposition were spent and asked Curly to switch tactics to bring the Haven back line into play. A try from Teflon and one from Posh Boy were both converted and with one more penalty from Harry and a spectacular drop goal from Curly, Haven ran out 55 – 21 winners.

The shell-shocked Dutch team sportingly lined up and applauded their victors off the field. They had hardly touched the ball in the second half, which for them seemed to last forever. The Haven players, conversely, thought that the second half had flown by.

The Dutch sports ground did not have a bath so in no time the players of both sides were showered and sat down ready for a meal in the big marquee. Most of the Dutch lads and their guests spoke English. Curly pointed out that many spoke more intelligible English that Jim Cameron. Evor asked if anyone had seen Jim. No one had but Mary Hynge informed the tourists that Jim was asleep on the back seat of the coach. The two nationalities were interspersed and mutual admiration flowed along with beer and spirits. Evor noted that Curly was sat down next to the younger, attractive wife of the local mayor and that he was telling her some story while gazing into her eyes. "Oh no! Here we go again!" Evor thought.

At the end of the meal the Mayor stood and gave a speech. He admitted to never having seen a game of rugby before but he and the lady Mayoress had thoroughly enjoyed the afternoon. He praised the skill of the Panthers and the power of the visitors. He reminded those present that it was his party, the PvdA, labour party that had funded the superb sports facility. He then asked the president of each club to say a few words and to choose the man of the match for their opponents.

Evor courteously responded with a swift, off the cuff speech thanking his hosts profusely and choosing their hard tackling full back as Panthers star man. Willem responded with a pre prepared speech, written on reams of paper produced from his pocket. At the end he shouted to wake up the audience and named Curly as the outstanding player. Thor had noted that Curly had disappeared from the marquee at the beginning of the speeches, as had the lady Mayoress. Fortunately Thor had been given the foresight to despatch Nipper to bring Curly back. As luck would have it, Curly strolled up to the front dais to collect his trophy just in time. It later transpired that he was just about to service the lady, on the coach, when Jim Cameron woke up and ruined the moment but saved Anglo Dutch diplomacy.

After a little singing. Some drinking and much joviality, many guests had departed and it was time for the tourists to do likewise. They stumbled drunkenly over to the coach. Mo Khan slipped and fell over into a pile of white stuff outside the rear of the bus. He was telling his son about his experience. "Don't be daft Dad" Teflon told him. "Why would anyone dump a pile of sugar on a rugby pitch? You're drunk."

There comes a point on every rugby tour when most sensible men vow, secretly, never to tour again. The alcohol intake, larking about and sleep deprivation take their toll on even the most hardened tourist. After a few days at home everyone will forget how bloody awful a tour can be and tell yarns of their prowess, on the field, in the bar and in bed. All will be greatly exaggerated and the next trip will be fully booked once again.

This low point had now been reached by most on return to the team hotel. The majority opted to slide quietly straight off to bed. The youngsters, in a show of bravado, decided to call into the bar across the road for one last drink as no one wanted to lose face. Thor however was perplexed. On the coach home, Curly had asked if they could have a private word about a problem that was worrying him. They made their way to another bar, a couple of streets away from the hotel. Curly obtained two large glasses of good brandy and sighed as he sat down next to his friend.

"Tom" Curly began "there's something that's been upsetting me for a while and I've been putting off telling you because I know you'll be hurt. I just don't know how to go about it."
"We've been friends since infant school John. We've shared joy and pain more than most. I'm not going to be that hurt am I?" Thor questioned with a very worried look on his face.

Curly stared at a light fitting for a few moments, took a gulp of the brandy and with tears in his eyes he told Thor that he had been asked to play for Malvil Park next season and that he was going to accept as they would pay him and guarantee county selection. He looked at Thor, sobbed and said "I'm really sorry Tom but I have to give it a go. It's not a decision I have taken lightly."

Thor breathed out and grinned "Thank god for that John. For a moment I thought you were going to tell me that you were going to run off with my wife." He paused, collected his thoughts and continued. "I'm pleased for you and I tell you what, whenever you turn out for Castrashire, you'll have me, Pam and your two biggest fans cheering you on." He paused again, looking grave. "I don't know how Evor will take it though."

When Curly told him that he had already asked Evor and had been given his blessing, Thor shouted for two more brandies and patted his friend on the shoulder. He noted that Curly still looked less than comfortable. "Is there something else worrying you buddy?" He asked.

Curly sucked air in through his teeth. He looked scared to death. "Tom, they want you too. Both Malvil Park and the county want you. They've talked to Evor about it and want to play us as a pairing. Please Tom. You know I'm useless without you there. I'll never ask another favour of you in my life I promise it."

Thor looked as though he's been hit. The waitress put the drinks down in front of him and he groped for the glass while staring at Curly. There was a silence that seemed to last for ever. Thor could not understand what his friend had just asked of him. He was furious, flattered and flummoxed all at once. "You know I can't do that John. I'm Haven. I haven't got time to train to play at that level. Pam won't like it and it could kill Evor. Pete Craddock'll look after you alright mate" He thought again. "What's more, you promised never to ask any more favours after I asked that ginger bird out for you at the Newport fair."

Curly looked upset. "That was fifteen years ago Tom. She said no anyway" he whined. "She married a trawlerman and has pushed out at least one kid a year for the past seven or eight years. Eloise and I see her some Saturdays with this huge brood in tow. Tom please just think about it will you? Have a word with Evor and Pam. It would be good for Haven."

Thor agreed and the pair left the bar and sauntered morosely back to their hotel.

Chapter 21 – Match Day Two

Thor hadn't slept well. He came down to the dining room in a grumpy mood. He met Evor in the reception area and they both noticed Jim Cameron shaking hands with a stranger just outside the hotel entrance. The stranger passed them and walked into the dining room. "What's that about?" Evor asked his grandson. "Don't know, don't care." Was Thor's glib response.

When they opened the door to the dining room, the Orres were amazed to see the place packed out. Evor made his way to his seat and when the waitress brought coffee he asked if there had been an influx of guests staying. "No sir" she replied "but many people have come for breakfast, to see your theatre. You know the judging."

Mo smiled at his chum, who growled "Bloody great. I was going to cut the court short today but seems we're expected to perform to an audience. Oh well. I'll do my best."

The tourists ate a hearty breakfast, mostly feeling refreshed after a relatively early night. At the end of the meal Evor left the room and his legal accomplices donned their formal attire. Mo Khan stood and banged the table with Evors Gavel. "Pray silence for Mr Justice Orre" he bellowed, enjoying his more prominent role. Evor entered, bewigged and stern faced. The room hushed and the packed breakfasters smiled and whispered among themselves.

Evor stood and looked around at his audience. He made his solemn request as for the previous day.

"I regret M'lud that I have a number of misdemeanours to report concerning my team members." This was Northern Bloke. "Firstly, one Jon Brown, a farmer of Castrashire, did sleep through the national anthem of both Her Majesty and our hosts the Netherlands."

The crowd, who had obviously taken to the spirit of the occasion, gave an outraged "Oooh!" Thor and Bill Mcclaren marched Spoddy before the judge. When offered an option of employing defence council Spoddy declined.
"John Brown" Evor thundered "How do you plead?"

"Your honour, I am guilty but on getting home I will bring you a dozen eggs a week for a month sir." Evor considered this and spoke to Red Rod before announcing his verdict. "John Brown, Attempting to bribe your way out of trouble is a very serious offence and I should banish you from Haven RUFC forthwith." Evor paused "However, taking into account the quality of your eggs and the fact that your new potatoes will soon be available, I shall let you off with a fine and you must remove your trousers and go and personally apologise to everyone in this room."

The crowd laughed and began to clap and Spoddy duly untrousered himself and began to walk around the room making his apologies.

Lee was called next, charged with playing in a pink tutu and acting like a girl on being tackled. Lee engaged Tommo to defend him again but asked for a better effort than the lawyer had given him on the previous day. Tommo's defence was thorough. He pointed out that he wore the tutu at the behest of this very court. He made the point that the Dutch full back who tackled him was a very rough boy and had been awarded man of the match for being so rough. He then brought in the mitigating circumstances that Lee was in fact a girl trapped in a man's body and asked that he not be fined as he was saving hard for a sex change operation.

The room laughed aloud at this and even Evor, when banging his gavel for silence could not restrain his laughter. When order had been restored Evor gave the judgement of guilty. A fine was extracted, a concoction was drank and Lee again had to don the hated pink tutu. "Bloody great." Lee called "I'll be in court again tomorrow for wearing this bloody tutu."

Father Devlin was up next for calling a mark outside his 22 metre line. Tommo jovially refused to defend him, claiming that he was part of a papist plot to bring down the monarchy and that Devlin had personally assisted Guy Fawkes in the gunpowder plot. The good father saw fit to admit all offences, including the gunpowder plot. He was relieved to be let off with a fine, a drink of the horrible stuff and having to wear a baseball cap with a large bright yellow cuddly dragon sewn on top.

Next Teflon received a fine, a drink and was made to drop his trousers and stand on a chair with his hands on his head for the duration of the court. Evor pointed out that this may seem a harsh punishment for downing the ball over the wrong line but what if he'd done it at Twickenham?
Evor whispered to Rod that they had run out of props as he couldn't find the second tutu. When the two Newport lads were dealt with for spewing in the scrum, they were fined and tied together, one right hand to the others left.

Last up was Nipper for falling over his own feet and laughing about it. He was asked to strip to his underpants and had a bath towel given to him to wear as a baby's nappy. He was fined, given the mixture and told to stay in the nappy all day.

Evor said that if there was no more business he would declare this session of the court closed. The audience were beginning to clap when a local man stood and shouted to Evor, "Please your honour. I have a most serious case to bring to your attention." A Hush fell over the room.

Evor consulted, worriedly with Red Rod before beckoning the man forward. The man spoke quietly to Evor. Evor's face turned into a big grin as he shook the man's hand. The room was quiet as Evor stood "Jens Willers, please come forward." A man rose from the rear of the room and approached the table. Thor and Bill pinned him firmly by the arms.

"Willers" Evor said theatrically, "this is the final case to be heard today. I understand that some six or seven months ago you borrowed a lawn mower from your brother in law and that you still have not returned it. Your brother in law's grass is now so high and you have an immaculate lawn. How do you plead?"

Without saying anything Jens laughed, put some notes into the tour bucket, swigged from the nasty jug, dropped his trousers and stood on a chair." When the tourists started to cheer, everyone joined in. Jens stepped down pulled up his pants and waved to the audience.

"Wait!" shouted Evor. He pointed at the brother in law. "Johan Van Linden. For bringing such a trivial matter before this court you will take the same punishment." A laughing Johan complied and then the two walked off, arms round each other laughing and enjoying their moment of fame.

"The court is now closed." Evor bellowed.

The rugby party had packed and placed their gear onto the coach. The hotel staff had been thanked, hands shaken, pretty waitresses pecked on the cheek and a healthy tip left for the staff. The sky looked ominously black as the, seemingly revitalised tourists set off to face their next challenge in Germany. At the appointed meeting place the two girls swayed in behind the coach on their powerful motorcycle and Sindy gave a few flashes of the bike's light to show her appreciation of the bare backsides that had appeared at the rear window of the bus.

An hour before kick off the coach was stopped at the barrier that barred access to the army base. A jovial military policeman climbed aboard, waving away a second MP with a collie dog. "I don't think I'll need to bring the drug dog aboard will I?" He questioned Evor. "You being sports superstars. Oh yes. We know all about you. Had a bloke watching your game yesterday." He sat at the front and instructed the driver through the barracks towards the sports pitches.

The coach stopped at a low prefabricated building adjacent to the football pitch. "This is your digs for tonight chaps" the MP informed them "and there's Major De'Laster to greet you. He's known as Major disaster behind his back but I'm sure you won't let that slip eh?" With a tap on the side of his nose, he alighted from the coach, saluted and had a brief chat with the Major before marching briskly off in the direction from which the coach had come.

The Major climbed aboard. He was a Monty Pythonesque caricature of an army officer. Removing his cap and placing his swagger stick under his arm he addressed the visitors. "Hello chaps. Welcome to BAOR Bielefeld. I'm Major Hugh De'Laster, you may addwess me as Major. There" he pointed with his swagger stick "is your bawwacks. Beds will be made and heating is on. There" he pointed to the right "are the changing wooms. Kick off 1500 hours on the pitch behind. We have a mix of squaddies, MPs and local fellows. Hope you enjoy. Oh by the way, I shall wefewee, when you may addwess me as sir. Questions? No. good." In a flash he was gone, leaving a stunned bus load of tourists behind in the coach.

It had started to rain, heavily. "OK chaps" shouted Curly "I suggest we decamp forthwith and go to our bawwacks. What say you my fellows?"

The coach burst into laughter as Curly grabbed his bag, climbed off the coach and marched swiftly across the shelter of the barracks doorway. He turned, saluted towards the coach and went in.

On entering the building Curly found a corporal Utterthwaite was there to "elp make you feel at ome." There were two wings to the block with about twenty beds in each. When the two girls arrived the corporal said that women weren't allowed in and was pleased when the girls explained that they had a hotel nearby and were here as medical support. There was hot tea and Parkin cake which the tourists tucked into with relish. The corporal had a chat with Norman Arkwright. "Listen mate. There's a big sergeant on t'other team, an MP called Eric Smith. Ees a bully, a southern git and calls me Utter-twat. If you get a chance, give him a bit of grief. You seem a good bloke despite being from over th'ill."

The lads had settled in and at 1450 hours they were kitted out in their change strip of all yellow with black collars and cuffs, going through a warm up routine on the pitch. The rain was steady enough to deter all but the hardiest of spectators and the Haven none playing tourists were gathered on the half way line under a number of umbrellas that had been procured by corporal Utterthwaite.

At 1455 hours the opposition walked calmly out of their changing room behind the referee. You could tell the squaddies by their short hair, the MPs by their shaved heads and the local lads by the fact that they looked normal, if somewhat Teutonic. At the rear of their line marched a being, that although resembling a human in many ways, was simply too large and automaton like to be considered as such. Its head was devoid of hair except for two jet black eyebrows that joined over the porcine nose. Two beady eyes darted about, judging the Haven team, looking for victims. They alighted on Curly and a menacing smile came over the beasts face. "Tom, keep that thing away from me." Curly whispered to Thor.

Major De'Laster marched to the centre spot, checked his watch. "Skippers" he bellowed. Northern bloke ambled across as did the beast. The major tossed a coin and looked to Northern Bloke who called heads. The major retrieved the coin from the grass and said "Oh bad luck old chap. Its tails. Your choice Ewic." He did not show the coin to the skipper as was usual but after Eric had chosen to kick off he said "Gentlemen, please impwess upon your team that I am stwict and will bwook no argument. Understand?"
"Sah!" was the response from the beast. "Yes sir" said a worried looking Northern Bloke.

Haven's skipper quickly called his lads in and told them not to expect much help from the ref and asked that they on no account argue or upset him. The teams then set up their formations to begin the match. Major De'Laster made them stand in the rain until precisely 1500 hours when he raised his hand and gave one long blast on the whistle.

The army stand-off kicked the ball high. It was aimed perfectly to land in field just past the ten metre line. It was coming down straight into Lee's arms. The world went into slow motion for Lee. Very slow motion. He had time to realise his predicament. If he caught the ball, the mob of white clad warriors charging at him would hit him before he had time to get rid of the bloody thing and probably dismantle him. If he stepped aside and let it bounce anything could happen and he would look a coward in front of his team mates. He could feign injury, drop on the floor and pretend to have a heart attack. No, he would be seen through and considered to be a soft footballer.

He had an idea. The ball was nearly here. The enemy were nearly on him. He kicked it, on the volley. Back it went, over the heads of the white clad men and he chased it, dodging under an arm that was meant to decapitate him. He could hear the blood pumping in his ears. The ball came down and bounced past the full back. He chased it. It seemed to jump into his arms and he was through, he dived under the posts, slid on the wet grass with the ball still in his arms. He'd scored. He had mixed emotions. Joy at his first try and knowledge that he had never been so scared in his life and never wanted to feel like that ever again. Nipper asked for the kick, which he duly slotted between the posts.

The rain had increased when the army side kicked off again. This time the ball went long and straight for Curly. He allowed it to bounce before trapping it with his foot and kicking it back. A blast on the whistle and raised arm signified knock on scrum white, just outside the Haven 22. "Sir, I trapped it with my feet," an unhappy Curly pointed out to the referee. Sir had no hesitation in moving the scrum a further ten yards nearer to the Haven line and calling Curly across. "Any further insubordination fwom you and you may vacate my field. Understand?" Curly was about to speak when Thor picked him up by the collar and apologised on his behalf.

The beast was wearing a number 8 shirt but he did not pack down in the scrum. Instead he swapped places with the inside centre, obviously looking to crash towards the line. The Haven pack had other ideas and pushed the military men back, assuring the ball for Curly to boot clear. The local lad, playing full back for the army, caught the spinning, wet ball perfectly and rushed forward, evading a couple of tackles. He punted the ball up chasing his kick and catching it despite opposition from Spoddy and Father Devlin. He quickly passed to the beast who stormed forward with the ball in his left paw. He shrugged off the attention of both Bennett brothers and stormed onwards with Thor hanging onto one leg. Pete Craddock rushed in but was handed off, clashing heads with Thor on the way as the beast roared and touched down under Haven's posts.

Northern Bloke rallied his troops as the opposition full back stepped up to pick up the conversion points. "What are we going to do about that monster?" Pete C asked. Northern bloke had a plan which he explained to his men. He noticed that Thor was not paying attention and waved the physio on to have a look at him. Janet declared him concussed and insisted on him leaving the field, despite his protests. "Right. I'm off too." Said Curly, making towards the touchline. He was checked by a big smiling, black face. "Trust me Curly. I'll look after you. I promise." Pete Craddock looked so absolutely genuine that Curly did trust him and agreed to stay on.

Janet had taken Thor onto the bus to examine him out of the rain which was increasing in volume yet again. She was shining a light into his eyes and began to doubt her earlier diagnosis when she found his pupils to be OK. "Do you feel dizzy at all Tom?" she asked. "Only when I'm around you

Janet." Was his reply as he gave her a roguish smile. He wrapped his arms around her and made to kiss her. A shocked Janet turned away and tried to free herself. "No Tom. No!" She shouted. "Come on. You know you want it. Let's play hide the sausage" Thor insisted trying to kiss her again. She slapped him hard across the face. "Tom, I'm sorry. I love only Sindy. I'm sorry to have teased you and lead you on but I'm really not interested." He released her with a smile and she rushed off the coach, passing Evor at the front.

"I had come to see if you were OK but I see that you're fine." Said Evor with a face like thunder. "How could you do that to Pam? You're not the man I thought you were." He turned to go. "Grandad, I can explain." Thor said this to an empty coach as Evor had left.

Meanwhile, back on the pitch the beast had the ball again and was forcing his way into the Haven half. Northern Bloke was desperately holding onto his left leg and being dragged along like a rag doll. Pete Craddock came in and got hold of the monsters other leg. Eric wasn't slowed in the slightest. Northern smiled at Pete, adjusted his grip on the leg and held out a hand. Pete grabbed his hand and the beast was brought crashing to the ground with a yelp. He did not release the ball so a few Haven boots were placed on the beast to remind him of the rules of the game. A brawl developed but Pete noticed that there were as many white armed fists aimed at the beast as there were yellow ones. A few old scores were being settled on the very rare occasion of Sergeant Smith being on the ground.

The rain had become a deluge. The pitch was fully waterlogged. Visibility was twenty yards, at best. Major De'Laster blew his whistle, which only bubbled. "Match abandoned," he shouted "extweme weather."

The half drowned players of both teams were grateful for the abandonment, all that is except for Lee. "I've come all this way, spent a fortune, probably damaged my liver and kidneys for life and only touched the bloody ball twice." He moaned. "Think yourself lucky" Jim Cameron responded, "that's
two times more than I've touched it."

After a steaming hot shower both teams loped, one by one, into a large sports hall that was set out with trestle tables. Young ladies, wearing the German national costume, were on hand to serve huge steins of lager to the players and guests who were happily interspersed and seated. Corporal Utterthwaite stood up and having got everyone's attention, apologised for Major disasters absence. The Major had taken Sergeant Smith to the medical centre with a broken nose and a serious cut above his left eye. The cheers of the Haven lads was only outdone by the roar of approval from every soldier in the room.

Outside the rain had eased but the pitches were totally under water. Inside the lads still had energy and adrenalin a plenty. One of the squaddies suggested a tug of war. The idea was welcomed by Haven, a long rope was produced and four teams of eight were picked, two from Haven, one from the army and one of local lads. The Haven B team were easily beaten by the Yorkshire regiment and Haven A despatched the local boys with ease. This set up a final, best of three pulls, between the army and a Haven team consisting of, the two Bennetts, Jim Cameron, Simon Spencer, Chubby, Northern Bloke, Pete Craddock and Thor.

On the first pull the army won fairly quickly. They were obviously well drilled at this sport as they moved in unison with a side to side motion that left Haven well beaten despite having plenty of power. Evor, who had observed the first pull intently, pulled the Haven lads together, gave them some sound advice and switched their order around on the rope. On Corporal Utterthwaite's command, Haven got in a fast arm pull, co-ordinated by Pete Craddock at the front of the line. This initial jerk caught the squaddies off guard, put them off balance and with a big heave Haven pulled them over, causing a few falls in the process. "All even, one apiece." Called Corporal Utterthwaite.

The teams set up again for the third and deciding pull. This time there would be no chance of pulling a trick. It would all be down to power and technique. The teams took the strain and pulled. The army seemed to take a slight advantage with their side to side pattern but after two minutes effort, the rag tied in the middle of the rope, hadn't moved more than a couple of inches from the chalk mark on the floor. All sixteen men on the rope had bright red faces with the effort. The tension mounted in the room as supporters cheered on their side, sweat poured from Thor, Pete Craddock's eyes were bulging out of his head and the younger Bennet had stopped talking. Something would have to give but it didn't.

The crowd went quiet. You could hear the breathing and grunts from both sides but the handkerchief didn't move. Each person was in pain but couldn't let their team down. It was perfect equilibrium. How long had it gone on? How long could it go on?

Haven's physio, Mary Hynge, was worried for her team. She put down her beer, smoothed her leather trousers and walked slowly towards the centre of the rope. She made eye contact with the squaddie at the front of the army team. She smiled at him. He tried to avoid her look. She put a finger to the corner of her mouth, licked her lips and breathed in and out, oh so slowly. He knew he mustn't look at her. He couldn't help it though. She moved her hand slowly away from her mouth and undid the top button of her blouse, then the second button, sighing as she did so.

"Don't look!" the squaddie told himself "Don't bloody look!" Private James Jones was a proud Yorkshireman. A disciplined fighting machine, as strong as an ox. However he was a man and despite some fourteen million years of evolution, or maybe because of it, he was automatically attracted by the female breast. She smiled at him. He felt his hands just give a little on the rope. He could feel his heart pounding. He could sense involuntary movement in the groin area. He let slip of the bloody rope. He tried to grab it but too late. The rope was moving. He felt the man behind him touch. He had to move forward to get space. He had the rope firmly again but that little move had done the damage. The Haven team slowly moved backwards. The handkerchief slowly moved forwards. The Corporals whistle blew. It was all over. "Haven win." Shouted Utterthwaite.

The two teams collapsed, exhausted. After a few moments they had recovered sufficiently to partake of one of life's necessities, beer. Much back slapping and joviality followed and even James Jones took his loss in good spirits. It seemed that his mates hadn't realised the cause of their defeat.

Food arrived. Various sausages, piping hot were served with butter smothered mashed potato and sauerkraut, all washed down by stein after stein of local lager. Genuine camaraderie and good feelings swamped the hall and after the food Evor offered the army lads the chance to take on Haven at the game of spoons. Dear reader, if ever you are asked to play spoons, I would advise that you decline.

The game goes thus. Haven put forward their champion. He sits facing the challenger with a desert spoon grasped between his teeth. The challenger bows his head and the champion hits him on the skull with the tooth gripped, spoon. The roles are reversed and the challenger gets a free hit on the champion. They take it in turns, hitting each other with the spoon until one of them has had enough and gives in.

Beware! Unknown to the challenger, he is not hit with the spoon but with a ladle from behind by another Haven player. The ladle strikes start as taps but increase steadily to full blows that really hurt. Why does the challenger not realise this? Two reasons, viz:- 1 Beer has flowed. 2 The champion is feigning great pain so the challenger thinks that he is winning.

Today the Champion was to be Paul Bennett, as he was a good actor. James Jones stepped up to the plate in order to redeem the pride of the Yorkshire Regiment. The two protagonists sat facing each other. The rules were explained and Jonah, as he was known to his mates, bowed his head. Thor stood behind him, placed his index finger to his lips and showed the ladle to the crowd. As always some giggled but no one spilt the beans. Pop! The first ladle tap caught Jonah unawares and he looked surprised at the weight of the blow he had received. Paul also looked surprised and rubbed his top gum. Paul bowed and took the first blow from Jonah's desert spoon, letting out an "oooh". After about the fifth or sixth turn the blows from the ladle had increased in strength but Jonah could see that Paul was distressed too and could sense victory coming his way. The crowd were now laughing out loud, particularly Jonah's mates. The game continued, the blows got harder, Jonah's teeth were starting to hurt but Paul wanted to stop and would have done so if not encouraged to continue by Evor, "for the pride and reputation of Haven RUFC."

A few bumps were appearing on Jonah's head and he was hurting now, both head and teeth but there was no way that he was going to let the regiment down. When Paul asked him to give in he refused and even Thor looked for advice when due to administer the next blow. No advice came so he plopped another ladle blow on Jonah's bonce, albeit weaker. Jonah noticed that the hit was less powerful and grinned at Paul. "This is Yorkshire grit lad. Give up!"

"Right. I'm stopping this now." Called Mary Hynge, storming forward from the back of the room. "You children have had your fun but there's a real danger of someone getting hurt. Thor show him the ladle. Now!" A very sheepish looking Thor pulled the ladle from behind his back and gave it to Jonah. Jonah's jaw dropped open, his eyes wide in disbelief as it slowly dawned on him that he had been set up. Everyone was laughing. Jonah looked at his mates. "You bunch of twats." He exclaimed.

Paul Bennett held his hand out. "Well done pal. No one has ever gone so far without giving up. You are a hero." Jonah's face fell into a big wide grin from ear to ear. He hugged Paul, shook Thor's hand and was hoisted onto the shoulders of some Yorkshire lads and carried around the room to cheers and applause from everyone, except Mary and Sindy. Sindy looked at her partner. "To think Janet. We spent years fighting to be considered intellectually equal. With this lot?" She shook her head in disbelief.

When the fuss had died down, one of the German lads said that they had a fun game. "It is called the mirror game," he explained and promised that no one will be harmed in any way. The Haven Physio asked for his assurance on this and when it was solemnly given, she agreed to allow the game to be played. Simon Spencer, the polite, mild mannered Dr

Jekyll asked if he could take part and his opponent was to be the scrum half, Gunter. "This is good you'll like this." Jonah nudged his new best friend, Paul Bennett.

This time the pair were to sit facing each other on opposite sides of a table. A warm plate was placed in front of each of them with a sausage on it. On one side a full stein of lager on the other side five glasses of schnapps. Gunter explained, "Simon, my friend, it's simple. Whatever I am doing you have to be doing also as you are my mirror. Do you see?" Dr Jekyll agreed and the game commenced.

Gunter stared at Simon who stared back. Gunter reached out for his stein with his right hand and took a big gulp. Simon simultaneously copied this with his left hand. Gunter Reached out for a schnapps with his left hand and downed it in one. Simon copied with his right. Gunter lifted his plate, put it back down, gulped more lager all copied exactly by Simon, the pair still staring at each other. Gunter bit his sausage, swigged his beer, downed a schnapps in one, all faithfully mirrored by Simon. Gunter grunted, bit the sausage again drank more beer, lifted the plate in his right hand and circled his left index finger around the plate underneath. All copied perfectly by Simon.

Gunter shifted in his chair leant further across to stare at Simon. He placed his left index finger on the bridge of his nose and moved to draw a pair of spectacles on his face. Obviously nothing had taken shape but the movements had become quicker. Simon kept pace, concentrating so hard that he didn't notice the giggles of the crowd.

Gunter supped beer, bit sausage, drank schnapps, fingered under plate and circled index finger round each cheek twice. Simon copied. The crowd laughed. This continued until all the sausage beer and schnapps had gone. Gunter stood up looked around at the crowd and lolled his tongue out in the style of a Maori warrior. As Simon copied this, feeling more than a little tipsy from the schnapps, he noticed that many were taking pictures of him and everyone was laughing. Only when Sindy produced a mirror did Simon realise that he had black lines all over his face.

Dr Jekyll suddenly became Mr Hyde. "I'll kill you, you Kraut bastard." He swung at Gunter who ducked. Thor and Mike Bennett grabbed him and tried to calm him down but he fought like a tiger, looking particularly fierce with the Maori war paint that had come from the soot from a candle held under his plate before the event. "Unhand me you bounders. Help! Help! I'm being abducted. I'll take all of you. You twats. Sorry ladies. More schnapps."

Thor, Mike and Evor eventually manhandled him out of the room, kicking and screaming. They took him to the barrack room, held him down and, once he'd calmed a little, tied him to his bed with sheets.

"I am thinking it is not we Germans who have no sense of humour." Said a visibly shaken Gunter. "I know let's have a drink." Suggested Northern bloke. "Can I have another go at the spoons game?" a confused Jonah asked. "Certainly not" replied Mary Hynge.

The rest of the evening went particularly well. Steins were gulped, songs were sung, yarns spun and everyone told everyone else what a damn fine bloke they were. Sindy and Janet left quietly after telling Evor that they would pick up their boxes on Monday evening. At one point Mr Hyde burst naked into the room, having freed himself from his bindings. "More Schnapps you tossers!" was met with one punch from

Spoddy Brown that laid him out. At last people started to leave, Evor, Tommo, Thor and Jim Cameron being the last to depart. There were a couple of squaddies asleep on the floor and Mr Hyde lay in a corner. "Shall I pick him up grandad?" Thor asked. "After today Tom you can do what the hell you like." Evor spat in reply.

Chapter 22 – Homeward Bound

After an excellent if somewhat hastily devoured breakfast the Haven tourists trooped onto the coach. Thor made to sit next to Evor to have a chat but Evor told him that Tommo would be sitting in that seat. Thor next moved to sit next to Curly. "Fuck off Tom," was Curly's response "I've heard about you trying it on with Janet. How could you do that? You have a lovely wife and two super kids. I have to say that I'm appalled at your behaviour." Thor was shocked at this stance from the man who had played away at every possible chance. He ambled down the coach and plonked himself down next to the window in an empty pair of seats. Pete Craddock came down the aisle. "Jump in here mate." Thor almost pleaded. "Later." Said Pete. "I need a word with Norman Arkwright first. The coach started up to loud cheers, conversation and laughter was the order of the day. Everyone was buoyant except for Thor. He sat alone. No one near him. A leper, an outcast. He felt very sorry for himself, sighed and settled down for a lonely trip home.

After the first half hour of travel many of the coach occupants were fast asleep. The tour, as always, had taken a toll. Evor had looked round towards his grandson on a number of occasions and a feeling of guilt had crept over him. He sighed heavily and with a weary tread, he ambled down the bus towards Thor. "Can we talk Tom?" Evor asked. Thor gave a weak smile and gestured to the empty seat.

"Tom, was your behaviour with that girl yesterday my fault?" Evor asked. As Thor shook his head, Evor continued. "I wondered if you had taken my advice to lighten up a bit too seriously. You know when you were unhappy with my antics in Amsterdam. I didn't mean for you to turn into Curly lad. I know my behaviour seemed wild for a man of my age but I had my reasons. I can't tell you now but maybe tomorrow Tom." Evor looked at his grandson with rheumy eyes.

Thor breathed in deeply. "Grandad, I don't want Mary bloody Hynge. How could you think that? There's only ever been Pam for me and that will never change. I made a promise when we got wed and I intend to keep it. I had my reasons too but I can't tell you yet either. You'll have to trust me for a few days then I'll explain." The two men looked at each other. Evor smiled, put his arm around Thor and said "Ok. Your words good enough for me. I'm sorry lad. Will you forgive me?" Tom smiled, hugged Evor "Grandad" was all he had to say.

After a while Evor padded back to his seat next to Tommo, a happier and younger looking man than the one who had boarded the bus.

There was a commotion at the back of the bus. "Thor." Shouted Nipper. "I think Mr Hyde has woken up. Shall we untie him?" Thor and Northern Bloke made their way to the rear where a bundle was fidgeting about and mumbling through a tea towel that had been used to roughly gag him.

"Good morning sir. How are we today" Northern bloke politely asked. More grunting through the tea towel followed. "If I undo the gag, will you behave politely my friend?" The bundle nodded, pleading with his eyes. "He seems Ok Norm. Undo his gag." Thor recommended and Northern bloke did as prompted.

"Can I have a drink of water please?" Asked a mild mannered Dr Jekyll. "Certainly." Norman replied, "as long as you're going to be good we'll let you free. No funny business mind or we'll tie you up again." Simon Spencer had returned to his normal self. "Sorry if there was a fracas chaps. I didn't like that Kraut fellow."

"No problem mate," said Northern bloke. Then as an aside to Thor "I don't think I'll tell him just yet that I've invited that Kraut and his team over for a pre-season game in Haven next August." Thor agreed that this was wise.

Thor returned to his seat and Northern bloke jumped in next to him. "I've got a bit of surprisingly good news for next season too Tom. Keep it hush hush for now though." The pair sat together, whispering conspiratorially for ten minutes. Thor was not too surprised but very pleased to hear what Norman had just told him.

Thor decided to make an attempt to rebuild his friendship with Curly. "Curly. Please." Thor said looking at his oldest friend. "Let's not fall out after everything we've gone through in life." Curly motioned him to sit down and gave him a lengthy lecture on why he should never again try it on with Mary hinge or anyone else. Thor sat and took it on the chin, despite the hypocrisy of the given advice.

Curly finished by offering Thor a deal. "Ok Tom, here's the deal. I'll not tell anyone and never mention it again if you agree to play at Malvil next season. You get on well with Pete Craddock. The three of us will have a good time."

"Ah, John" Thor patted the side of his nose with his index finger. "It seems that I am in receipt of some vital information concerning Malvils team for next season, that you aren't aware of. You and I won't be able to have a good time with Pete at Malvil because he won't be playing for them. We may have a good time at Haven as Pete intends to join us. He's just had a chat with northern Bloke who is only too glad to welcome Pete on board. So perhaps best if we stay put eh?"

Curly was flabbergasted. "Why would he want to leave a big club that gives him money, to come and piss around with us lot? Has he taken leave of his senses?" Thor said that Pete had his reasons and that maybe Curly should ask him directly. He also pointed out that the county selectors were unlikely to drop Pete as he was one of their best players. This may well lead to acceptance of Curly at county level despite him belonging to a junior club, particularly as Curly was a bloody good scrum half. Curly mused on this for a few moments. "The money would have been nice but I suppose what you've never had you never miss. Eloise does want me to play county though." He held out his hand to Thor. "Sorry about trying to get you to move." Then with a stern face, "never try to play away again Thor. It's not fair on Pam and I won't have it. Ok?"

"Deal." Thor replied smiling at his best mate.

The journey back to England was fairy eventless. The high spirits of the outward trip were replaced by sheer exhaustion. On the boat however, Evor gathered his troops together and a few words were spoken. Evor said that he had intended to hold court at this point but he just couldn't work up the energy. "Player of the tour," Evor announced "Pete Craddock, for unflagging work rate in both games." This greeted with general approval and applause by all present. Norman Arkwright in particular, clapped his arm round Pete and said "Well done." Those who had been present to witness Northern Blokes racism at the last committee meeting looked at each other bewildered but pleased at his change of stance. "Next trophy," Evor continued, "Try of the tour. There were a few contenders for this but it goes to Lee Washbrook for his unbelievable try yesterday." Lee went forward to collect his trophy to shouts of "fluke" and "lucky". Despite this his grin told the story of just how pleased he was. "This years award for plonker of the tour is shared by two men. Firstly Spoddy Brown for actions off the field, including the Dutch handkerchief and getting lost, twice. For actions on the field of play, I call forward, once again Lee Washbrook for not being able to accept a perfectly good tackle." Both lads received a cheap plastic toilet seat, placed over their head with the word "Plonker" painted on it. This was a decision that was cheered loudly by the tourists and the growing crowd of onlookers.

"Finally," Evor proclaimed, "The Tour gigolo award goes, as usual, to Curly Jones for , well I think we all know what for." A sheepish Curly was presented with a two foot long, inflatable penis that he was instructed to carry at all times until the coach passed the Haven border. "That concludes this years awards gentleman." Evor said grinning.

When the ferry docked, the Haven men trooped quietly down to the car deck and piled aboard the coach. One of the seamen recognised them and nudged Evor. "I heard you got away with it mate. I don't know how you did it but the word is that the French cops nearly arrested a mini bus full of nuns."

"I couldn't possibly comment," was Evors reply, with an accompanying cheeky wink.

As soon as the coach touched the tarmac on the quayside, Spoddy Brown stood up and with a big red faced grin, ran up and down the aisle shouting. "I've done it. I've done it." When asked what he'd done he exclaimed "I've explored abroad, eaten foreign food and come home to England, safe and sound."

Just before leaving the dock area the coach was signalled to pull over and a uniformed customs officer boarded. "Do we have a Mr Orre on board?" he asked. "Which one do you want?" Mo Khan enquired. "What. You have more than one?" said a startled customs man, who had never heard of this surname before. Mo Khan smiled at him. "There's either Evor Orre or Thor Orre," he clarified to a general cheer from the entire company.

"Hurray!" They all shouted. "What's the big joke?" asked the customs officer.

He was enlightened by Mo "The bloody author of this story has been trying to get that one in since chapter one."

Unsure of himself now the Customs man asked if both Orre's could accompany him for a few minutes, adding that there was nothing to worry about and that the party wouldn't be delayed for long. The Orres followed the smartly dressed officer into a drab grey building where they walked down a short corridor and into a room that both Orres recognised as the equivalent of a police interrogation suite. The Orres looked at each other with a mixture of angst and annoyance at their plight.

The room was spotlessly clean but nondescript, with grey and cream painted walls. The pair were offered chairs and sat as requested. Thor was just about to ask what the hell was all this about when the door opened again and in strolled Roger DeGroot, resplendent in his best uniform. He nodded and smiled at Evor and managed to almost hide his surprise on seeing Thor there too.

"Gentlemen," DeGroot began, "I apologise for impinging on your time but I have a serious matter that perhaps you could assist me with. You probably aren't aware, Tom, that there is a strong possibility that class A drugs have been brought into the UK aboard your coach. I had made your Grandfather aware of this and asked him to keep a subtle eye open." He paused and looked at Evor. "Have you noticed anything suspicious old friend? Oh, and by the way Tom, not a word spoken in this room goes outside it. Understand?" Thor nodded acceptance, putting on his professional persona.

"I have more than noticed something suspicious Rog. I've got your man." Evor proclaimed this with a puffed out chest and a wink to his Grandson. He held the suspense a few seconds longer before pronouncing that the drug smuggler was Nick Hayden-Smythe. A slightly flushed Deputy Chief Constable asked his reason for this assumption. "Not an assumption Rog. He's the man. Firstly he turns up in an expensive sports car. How's he paid for that when just a student. Oh he gave some Cock and bull yarn about money from his parents but I didn't buy that. Then he has been sliding off, shiftily and meeting the same chap. He did it on the boat going and in Amsterdam. I've been watching him."

The DCC said that he doubted if it was Hayden-Smythe and asked Evor if he had noticed anything else. "Rog. Trust me it's him. Get him off the bus and search his bag. If need be we can beat a confession out of him." The DCC looked acutely embarrassed and pointed out that beating suspects isn't the way that a modern police force should behave in a western democracy. Evor was about to argue but Thor butted in. "Grandad. It's not Posh Boy. He's a copper. "The chap he met is probably some European law man. He said this looking at the DCC for support. A visibly flustered Roger DeGroot said that he could not confirm that but said, "Evor, rest assured it's not him."

All three men sat, silent. The silence grew more awkward and the three sat looking at each other all feeling that they had said something stupid.

Eventually Evor cracked. "OK. It's Chubby then. He was expecting to come into money on his return and he's known to use cannabis. It's Chubby." Thor pointed out that Chubby's idea of coming into money was picking up fifty quid for doing a few odd jobs and in any case, a bit of wacky baccy is a far cry from class A.

"Bloody Hell Tom. It's Jim Cameron. He's also bragging about funds coming in soon and he went missing during the Dutch game. Well I'm shocked." Thor enlightened Evor. "Jim is expecting a down payment for renovating a yacht for Norman Arkwright and he is going to get help from Chubby. He was genuinely fast asleep on the coach when he went missing.

"My god. Are you saying it's Northern Bloke? That's a bit hard to stomach." Evor looked perplexed. "Mind you. He has come up with a mystery backer and put a thousand pounds into tour funds. Tom you've got him."

"No Grandad. Sorry." Tom explained that Northern Bloke would be coming into funds as his wife had sold their property up North and they would run one home from now on, not two."

"Tom Lad," Roger DeGroot interrupted, "before my oldest friend goes through the whole team, do you think there are drugs aboard and if so, do you know who is responsible?"

Thor delayed his response "Sir. I suspect there are drugs on our coach. I suppose we are all therefore drug smugglers but if that's the case, the person responsible for putting them aboard is not on the coach."

"Go on!" DeGroot urged.

Thor looked serious. "I'm sorry sir but I wouldn't like to say anything else until the Chief Constable himself is present and I must insist that we go to him immediately as the accusations that I intend to make could involve other police officers." He stared at the DCC, expecting to see him look worried or guilty but the expression he saw was one of genuine anger. This unnerved Thor somewhat.

"Acting Sergeant Orre. Are you accusing me of some involvement in drug smuggling?" The emphasis had been strongly on the word, acting. The DCC had a face that looked furious but Thor could see that he was also genuinely hurt. The room was shrinking. Had he got it wrong? Had he ruined his career? How would he explain to Pam? Thor's palms were sweating. What to do? What to say?

"Tom. Tom lad." It was almost a whisper from Evor. "I don't know what you're thinking and I know that I've just made a few wrong guesses but I can tell you, this man, this man here," he grabbed the DCC's arm "Roger, is the most honest copper you'll ever meet and he's brighter than he comes across. Trust him lad. Trust him with whatever you have got."

Roger DeGroot held his hand up. "Evor. Thank you for that, I think it was meant as a compliment. I believe that Tom has outlined something monumental and he's right. We do need to go to the Chief. Tom, I'll make one phone call, in your presence and we'll get taken straight to the Chief Constable. I have a squad car and driver out round the back." The DCC stood and walked over to a phone on a desk in the corner.

"Wait!" This was an order from Thor. He then realised that an acting sergeant should not order a DCC around. "I'm sorry sir. I was wrong. If we take that course of action then suspicions will be aroused. I'll tell you what I know but first, I would like to make a phone call." Thor paused. Tears were brimming in his eyes as he unfolded the first part of his story.

"You recall the journalist sir? The Ginger bird who made a pass at me?" DeGroot nodded and Thor continued. "She has given me information concerning the loss of the boat with my parents on board, all those years ago. Her father planted a bomb on that craft," he paused again, his eyes pleading with them both. "Her father planted this bomb on the instructions of a police officer. She has a signed confession from her father. It doesn't give the officers name but it does give his number. I'd like to call her and obtain that number?"

Roger DeGroot sighed and Evor whitened and looked as if he'd seen a ghost. Thor suddenly wished that he'd kept his mouth shut.

Evor sat and rocked with his head in his hands. Grandads rocking motion made Thor feel as though he was still at sea. He felt nauseous, seasick. No just sick. He didn't like the thought that was growing at the back of his mind. He decided to resign and let the whole thing drop but he couldn't. He wanted justice for his parents, Pam's parents and Curlys too.

"No need to make a call Tom." The DCC sounded almost kindly, concerned. When Thor looked at him, he was caught off balance by the moisture in the DCC's eyes. "I think I know that number." Roger DeGroot said with a heavy heart.

"Evor snatched his eyes upwards. "You know? You know and you've kept quiet Roger?" Evors eyes were in awe of his friend. "Thank you. Oh Rodger, thank you." Rodger said that he wasn't sure until today but he'd had his suspicions. He also said that he didn't know that Evor knew.

It was now Thor's turn to look amazed. "What? You mean it wasn't Grandad?"

"No Tom, not Evor" Roger was still being a human being, not the DCC. "The number Tom, it was 597. I'm sorry."

Tom hit the table so hard that the plywood cracked. "No Sir. No way. Emphatically no. You know that was my Dads collar number. Why would he have blown up a boat with his wife and best friends aboard? Why?"

No one spoke. Thor then continued. "How can you slur my father's name? How dare you? He was a good man, yet you're saying he was a bent copper. That's what your slanderous remark amounts to. DCC or not I've a good mind to kick your fucking head in." Thor stood and made to move towards Phil DeGroot. The DCC stood his ground facing Thor. Evor stepped between them. Light on his feet for his age. "Tom lad. He's right. I've suspected it for years but until you told us about the ginger bird's dad, well. I couldn't see how or why myself."

Thor sat down the fight gone from him. He looked into his grandfather's face and saw the truth of it. He burst into tears. His Dad, the man he tried to be, was not just a bent copper but a murderer too. The shock was too great to bear. "Why? Why Grandad?" the big man sobbed.

Evor was unable to speak. Phil DeGroot gave Thor the answer. "Your dad Tom, he was the best. The best copper and the best of men. He wasn't crooked but I think he may have become stressed out, unwell. At the time there was a drugs racket in Newport along with a bit of extortion. Your dad had found out who was behind it and was building a case against him. They found out and offered your dad a hefty bribe to lose his evidence. Of course he told them where to go. He came to me with the bribe story but wasn't ready to divulge the name of mister big. I think that he was then threatened. Not himself personally but your mother and you Tom. He should have come back to me. God knows I wish he had but, putting two and two together, I think that he decided to deal with the matter himself."

"What? Take out his closest people to kill this villain?" Tom screwed up his face in horror.

"No Tom." DeGroot continued. "I'm surmising that something went wrong with the timing device. The bomb maker, despite being ex-army, had a drink problem and cocked up. Your folks were due to be off the boat circa 9-30pm
And maybe the bomb should have gone off next morning but, sadly ...." He let his words trail off.

"Why didn't you bring this up at the inquest sir?" Thor was now showing great respect to his senior officer.

"And bring dishonour to the name of a bloody good Bobby. On a little more than a hunch? No Tom. Maybe I should have but I couldn't do it." The DCC replied.

There was another long pause before Thor thanked the DCC, apologised for his threat and asked if he was right in thinking that the owner of the boat was Sir Christian Penhale, local MP and potential benefactor of Haven RUFC. The DCC confirmed this and Evor informed Tom that Penhale had invited a few friends out for an evening meal on his luxury motor cruiser. Penhale and his wife were due to be aboard themselves but a track problem delayed their train from London. Penhale had telephoned his skipper with instructions to go ahead without him.

DeGroot filled in the gaps by informing Thor that the track problem was genuine and that after dropping his guests off back at Haven, the Penhales were planning to sail for a two week break in the Mediterranean.

Thor agreed that all assumptions made seemed plausible and the men sat quietly, then sat longer even more quietly before the DCC asked "So Tom, where do we go from here?"

Epilogue

Thomas Henry Orre told his Deputy Chief constable everything he knew.

The smugglers were Mary Hynge and her friend Sindy. The DCC had said "Come on Tom, I know you have nicknames for everyone in a rugby club but what's Mary Hynge's real name?" Thor certified that the girl really was called Mary Hynge. He then explained to Evor that this was the reason he had made a pass at her, to confirm his suspicion that she was not interested in men.

Thor informed them that at least one of the two boxes, brought on tour by the girls as medical equipment, contained illegal drugs, probably disguised as bags of sugar. He explained the chance meeting in the supermarket when the girls were buying up sugar. He then offered the pile of sugar left behind the coach in Breda as further evidence.

Thor and Evor needed an excuse for being taken off the coach by customs. Evor provided one and when the two Orre men returned to the coach, their fellow travellers accepted the story of a passport found on board ship. Evor waved his passport as proof.

The two girls turned up at Haven later that evening, as arranged and took the chequer plate boxes away in a van bearing the logo of the beauty salon where Sindy worked. They were unaware that DCC DeGroot had plain clothed officers watching them and taking pictures. When they arrived home they were arrested and taken to Castra Police

Headquarters. On arrival they were separated and confronted with their crime. Both admitted guilt, on tape and both agreed to assist the police in the case against Penhale.

While this was going on the touring party were being welcomed home, in the Bell, by their loved ones. One swift final beer, that many of them left, and home to peace.

Next morning the two girls drove up to Sir Christian Penhale's house. Penhale was not happy that they had turned up but when Sindy explained that they could not leave the stuff at the salon, as a woman police officer was in having treatment, he agreed to take the box in. He paid them a large sum in cash that they were asked to count and take away in a small leather suitcase. He then carried the box away and locked it up in an outbuilding. Most of this was captured on tape from the microphones concealed on the girls.

The girls left in the van and five minutes later, three police cars blasted up Sir Peter's drive with blue lights flashing and sirens wailing.

That evening Roger DeGroot had made national TV and bathed in the limelight of being the man behind the arrest of Sir Christian Penhale. The DCC had agreed to be interviewed on the strict understanding that Teresa Green would be the interviewer. Before the interview he had a private discussion with her and she agreed that there would be nothing to gain from sullying her father's name by opening up old wounds.

Some months later Penhale was jailed for a lengthy stretch, DeGroot was promoted on the retirement of the Chief Constable. Tom Orre had his acting Sergeant role confirmed as permanent and he along with Curly and Pete Craddock had received letters inviting them to the county training sessions.

What of Evor? He was a happy man with just one small concern. Who had got the bloody county cup?